MW00929131

THE WINKING MOON CRUSADERS

TIMOTHY J. ELLIOTT

Volume 1

DEDICATION

To you, Dad, with love. You witnessed some of *my* tomfoolery firsthand.

Table of Contents

INTRO:

BAD WINKING MOON ON THE RISE

17-year old Alex Carver stood in the kitchen, processing the information he had just received, as he slowly placed the phone back in the receiver. He got the job offer—again. So did his other three Crusader-buddies. He turned around slowly to face his mom, who had begun preparing dinner when he got the call. Her face was colorless and her expression filled with dread. "So… you going to take it?" she asked hesitantly.

"Why wouldn't I, Mom?" he answered. "I have to. It's for The Winking Moon, it's for the community. It's an honor-thing, you know?"

"It's an honor-thing to want to remain living, too," she said. She was only half joking and Alex knew it. Angela Carver was a youthful-looking woman in her forties, despite the long face and her current get-up of production attire.

He shook his head and looked at the floor. "Mom come on. Don't you think that's a bit extreme? It's just a drive-in movie theater job."

"A drive-in movie theater for the damned!"

Alex blew out a hot breath. He knew he was not going to win but decided to take one more swing. "Drive-in movie theaters are just family-friendly fun and the Winking Moon is an institution," he mentioned as he walked down the hall, rolling his eyes and heading into his bedroom.

Alex's mom followed. "'Family-friendly fun,' huh? Last summer one of the movies that played was called 'I Spit on Your Grave.'"

"Mom, come on," he said, "we have to play what sells. It's a cheap night out. Two-fifty for adults, fifty cents for kiddies under twelve. We got that hundred-foot screen, a four-hundred-and-eighty vehicle capacity, concession stand serving the most delicious food around. There's fresh air, movies under the stars, memories to last a lifetime…"

She had had enough. Turning to walk out of his bedroom, she said, "But in your case, that job means bruises to last a lifetime. I've heard enough for now; dinner will be ready in forty-five minutes." Shutting the door, she called from down the hallway of the house. "Having to work a summer job doesn't mean taking your life into your own hands, Alex! Remember that."

He could not help himself. His boyish smirk was now a full-on laugh. "A bit of an exaggeration, Mom!" he shouted. "The Winking Moon just has—I don't know—a type of *energy*."

He looked at the back of his bedroom door, on which hung a poster from his favorite movie: "George A. Romero's 'Dawn of the Dead." Looking at it now, he remembered some of his favorite scenes from when he saw it at the regular show, not the drive-in, taking him back to the fascination and chills of that experience, and wondered what might be in store for him from another gig at the Winking Moon. His thoughts raced with intrigue and excitement, but he could not help but feel a pang of guilt for giving his mother more unprecedented bad news.

Before Alex's mom made it back to the kitchen, she yelled over her shoulder, "And just so you know, mothers have their own memories that stick with them outside of the thrills and laughs their teenage sons might be having. And my memory of you working there last year is of racing to the hospital after you got a good bloody lip at the place."

Though touched by his mom's concern, Alex had to correct her. "'Joint,' Mom," he called out. "We call the drive-in 'the joint.'"

CHAPTER 1:

THE SEASON BEGINS

Rochester, New York. May 1979

The nonsense had already begun at the Winking Moon before the Crusaders had even started their summer gig. It was a warm May evening. Bill, a local, was beaming with pride to show off the drive-in to his family. He'd come here often as a kid and had been planning this outing for weeks, so much so that he was determined to be the first to arrive at the theater to get his family nestled into the best parking space.

He'd done everything right: set up the speaker in the window, had everyone take their restroom breaks and hit the concession stands before the show, and even set aside a few minutes to admire his brand-new station wagon, bragging to a nearby car about how he'd picked it up with his recent job promotion.

Bill's wife, young son and daughter were tucked comfortably inside the car with plenty of snacks and blankets, ready to enjoy the films. While the kiddie took in their surroundings, he leaned over to his wife and hinted about "a quick knobber" when the little ones dozed off later, reminiscent of their early dates at the drive-in.

"Behave, Bill," she giggled.

Rod Stewart's "Do Ya Think I'm Sexy" pre-show music boomed over the sound system. The vans, cars, hotrods and pick-up trucks all filed in, packing the asphalt and pebble theater rows tight.

"So whattya think kids?" Bill turned and asked his family. "Daddy did a good thing bringing you here, right?"

They all cheered in agreement, encouraging his walk down memory lane.

"Ah, just look at this place. The Winking Moon Drive-In. Been around since I was a teenager. Your mom and I used to come here together before you were even born. Some of the best times of my life were right here at this special venue. It feels like I'm visiting an old friend."

The kids were downright giddy seeing their dad so happy. They giggled, cheered, and tore into their candy.

"My folks took me here when I was a boy," Dad continued, "Saw 'Snow White and the Seven Dwarfs.' Not sure what our movies are going to be like, but I'm sure we'll have fun. It's a huge screen, isn't it? Yessiree, I don't think anything could spoil a night at the Winking Moon. What's not to love?"

BASH! Something red and juicy spattered across the station wagon's windshield, splitting into what looked like a thousand mushy pieces. The family let out a chorus of screams and practically jumped right out of their seats.

Bill blinked and took in the site of what he realized were rotten red apple bits sliding down his brand-new windshield into the wiper blades. There was a pause, then he lost all composure, letting loose a string of obscenities so foul they would have closed a massage parlor after midnight.

"Where in the hell did that come from?!" he yelled. The neighbors around him were chattering worriedly amongst themselves.

Suddenly, two rotten bananas sailed through the air, one hitting the Vega next to Bill: the other pounding into the pebbles and asphalt of the parking lot. A wild howling was heard somewhere in the distance and panic began to rise across the drive-in crowd as they nervously looked for the source.

"Over there!" a man shouted, pointing in the direction of the woods lining the north side of the theater. The crowd that had begun to gather ran towards the tall wooden fence—the only barrier between the dark woods and the theater-goers—and Bill was in the lead.

As they got closer, they saw a grungy, 40-something-year-old fellow, with an unkept beard and wild-looking hair, resembling something out of museum exhibit on Early Man. He was drinking from a flask in one hand and held a greasy paper bag in the other. He reached into the bag, pulled out a disgusting-smelling pear, and held it up as if he was presenting the first pitch in a ballgame. "Hee-hee-hee, ya-hooooo! I'm gonna throw another!" he howled. "Watch out below! Another season of fun at The Winking Moon begins! Suck a fat one, people!"

Positioned at the front of the mob, Bill stopped right under the tree. He shook his fist as he hollered up at the assailant, veins bulging from his forehead with the wrath of a viper. "Get down from there, whoever you are, you little son-of-a-bitch! I'm gonna rip your arms off and shove 'em down your throat! How dare you mess up my new station wagon! I paid six-thousand dollars for that!"

The Wild Man just lifted his head to the sky and laughed hysterically. Bill's wife and kids screamed at him from back at the car, begging him to come back. The children were crying, traumatized.

"Hee-hee-hee," said the Wild Man. "Mess on this!" He threw the pear, nearly hitting Bill who jumped out of the way to avoid being hit. It hit the asphalt, covering the ground in a jelly-like substance.

"Son-of-a-bitch!!" Bill yelled.

The mob was growing restless and wanted blood. Hordes of angry faces were shouting up at the man and grew angrier by the second.

"It hasn't even gotten dark yet," Bill thought to himself, a wave of worry chilling his body.

Members of the crowd picked up sticks, pebbles, and whatever else they could throw, ready to launch a full-on attack at the menace in the tree.

Suddenly, a disheveled, dumpy man in his late thirties came running across the lot from the concession stand, waving his hands. He had thin, whitish-blond hair, glasses barely hanging on to the tip of his nose, and his tie flapped up and over his buttoned-down shirt as he ran. "Hang on! Don't throw anything at him!" he yelled. "Let me handle this! I know him, I've handled this before. Please everyone, step back!"

But the crowd was not so keen on leaving. "No way! This bum is throwing rotten fruit at us!" Bill shouted.

"We know, we know! He's done this before. We call him 'The Wild Man of Borneo.'"

"'The Wild Man of Borneo?'" someone asked. "What the hell kind of a name is that?!"

"It's a nick-name for Christ's sake! We got some characters around here."

Bill was still frothing at the mouth, trying to get his attacker down from the tree. "Get down before I shoot ya down!" he screamed.

The dumpy man was one of the managers at the Winking Moon. He turned to face the crowd, stopping right in the middle of them. He was wheezing and trying to catch his breath after running across the drive-in lot. "My name is Lee-Willie Stuckerson. I'm the co-manager here. We know this guy. In fact, we've had problems with him in the past and are getting just as tired of this as you are." Looking up at the man in the tree, he yelled, "Get down! Stay on your side of the fence and leave us alone. We had enough of you last year, and we better never see you around here again!"

SPLAT! A piece of rotten fruit exploded at his feet and he threw his hands in the air.

"People, please, let us handle this. Go back to your cars and calm down. Violence will only make things worse. The sun's almost set, and the movie will be starting shortly."

It was not easy to disperse the crowd, but slowly, some of the more level-headed patrons turned and headed back to their cars. The Wild Man was loving the attention, laughing and howling even harder, he took a long pull from his flask, threw his head back and bayed even louder.

Lee-Willie Stuckerson wiped the sweat from his face, unable to hide his extreme frustration. "Mister get down this instant and get the hell outta here. We'll call the police if we have to. You're not watching movies for free that way."

"I ain't on Winkin' Moon's property," the Wild Man challenged. "You can't do anything 'bout me sittin' up here, watching."

"But you're physically bothering these people. You can't do that. Nobody can."

"You didn't get rid of me last year, and ya ain't getting' rid of me this year, chump."

Lee-Willie sizzled. Bill was right next to him, blowing out hot air like a leaking balloon. "Why're you doing this?!" he said.

"Because I can," said Wild Man.

The remaining crowd who had been less inclined to return to their cars began hurling threats and insults up at the man, taunting him to come down. Lee-Willie had panic in his eyes. Since opening a few weeks ago, this is how it had been. He clapped a hand to his face, and let it slide down. "I need the boys back," he said to himself. "I need The Winking Moon Crusaders…"

"The 'what'?" Bill said, snapping his head to the right to face manager.

"Nothing…" said Lee-Willie. "My boys, my staff, the patrolmen."

"Well you better get *something*."

Lee-Willie lifted the walkie-talkie to his mouth to call his wife, not realizing that she was right behind him after running over to join the crowd. Seeing her face inches from his startled the shit out of him. "Honey!" he said. "The Wild Man of Borneo is back again."

"I can see that Lee," she said. Gail-Lill Stuckerson was not much better-looking than her husband. She had more wrinkles on her clothes than a Shar-Pei at birth and her spectacles were overly thick and round.

"He's in his usual spot, throwing fruit at people," said Lee-Willie. "And he's drunk as a skunk. We're tryin' to get him down."

"Tear him down!" someone yelled.

"Want me to call the police?" Gail-Lill asked her husband.

"Not yet," he answered. "We don't want that spectacle if we can avoid it."

"Who're you?" asked the same patron.

"Gail-Lill Stuckerson," she answered. "Co-manager."

"Well you're not doing a better job of managing than this guy." He was pointing at Lee-Willie.

“Do something!” shouted another stranger.

The Wild Man extracted another bomb: a moldy orange. That exploded further out, almost hitting an airbrushed van. Bill practically had to be restrained from jumping up into the tree himself. “This place used to be a haven for decent people just wanting to enjoy a night out under the stars! You got idiots like this now?”

“Sir,” Lee-Willie said, “please stand ba—”

“We’re gettin’ this rat down, now!”

A battery of twigs and pebbles flew up at the Wild Man, but nothing seemed to faze him. He just kept laughing, taunting, sticking his tongue out, thumbing his nose. Wild Man tossed pears next, finished off his whiskey, and shouted to the lot, “Enjoy the show while ya can, chumps, the Winkin’ Moon’s days are numbered!”

The remark stuck. “What?” Lee-Willie reacted, shocked as he turned away from his attempt to stop the crowd from retaliating.

“What do you mean ‘the Winking Moon’s days are numbered’?” Gail-Lill asked.

“Never mind. You’ll see,” said Wild Man, finally shimmying down, able to avoid most of the crowd’s weapons given the protective tree branches and his array of baggy clothing.

Bill leapt at the fence. The fiend was going to disappear into the woods on the other side. Lee-Willie, despite just regaining his breath, pulled him back down. The mob pushed and shoved toward the fence while the Wild Man looked back, enjoying the row he had caused immensely. Lee-Willie managed to get his walkie-talkie to his face. "Jim! Jim! Can you get out here and help?"

"He's not in yet, he had some jumps this afternoon!" Gail-Lill responded in heightened alert.

Lee-Willie swore, then told his wife to get out of there. "You're gonna be hurt!"

"No, I'm not!"

"Yes, you are!"

Bill's wife and kids, along with the other patrons, watched the entire crowd argue and scream from back at the car, seeing the patriarch of the family lose all control.

Wild Man scuttled off like a crab, approaching a building out behind the screen. "Hee-hee-hee, your days are numbered, Stinking Moon! Enjoy 'em while you can!"

He disappeared into the twilight sky.

CHAPTER 2:

GALILEO HIGH SCHOOL

Friday, June 1, 1979

The Crusaders were anxiously counting down the days until they returned to the Winking Moon. They were ready for whatever the drive-in had to throw at them this summer, and their extracurricular activities the last few weeks of school were proof.

The patrolmen—Alex Carver, John Tambone, Steve Laneske and George Jocavelli, all seventeen-years-old and all juniors at Galileo High School—sat alone at one of the dozens of folded-up tables in the cafeteria during their last-period block, fantasizing about their upcoming adventures. They could not wait to get back into the action. Alex's mom's warnings echoed in the back of his mind, but he shoved them aside. Yes, he got banged up last year, but that was the gig. Crusaders took their chances.

They stared out the window onto the back parking of the school, seeing the dormant athletic fields beyond. Their baseball season had just ended, and football ended before that. The cycle carried on and now it was time to get to work.

John Tambone, the quietest of the Crusaders, spoke first. This was unusual and caught the group by surprise. "Think Mr. and Mrs. Stuckerson are hoping we're back yet?" he said.

George Jocavelli, the muscles of the group, answered first. "What do you think? The joint's probably already falling apart without us."

"I feel bad for 'em," John said. "They're total nerds."

"Don't," said Steve Laneske. His sandy blonde hair set him apart from the rest of the dark-haired Italian boys. "Mr. Stuckerson makes our lives a living hell. He's the worst boss."

"But Mrs. Stuckerson's not so bad," Alex said, still lost in thought as he stared out the window. Beyond the athletic fields was Lake Ontario, so close you could practically jump right in. "She at least pretends to like us."

A few peers drifted in and out of the cafeteria during their free period. The bell was going to ring at any moment, freeing them from the end of another long school day. On the old cafeteria jukebox, "Stayin' Alive" by The Bee Gees played. The disco-beat was infectious. George Jocavelli could not help but tap his toes.

The Crusaders were exhausted from another year of patrol at Galileo High School. Technically, no one asked for their services, but even the teachers silently agreed that they were required. The boys were good at what they did and kept the institution intact as a haven for students.

Gina Ciminetti walked into the cafeteria with three girlfriends and waved. George jumped up, grabbed her lightly by the wrist and started disco-dancing with her. He was good. She was good. The girls cut loose, laughing and clapping, just as ready for the school day to end as the rest of them were.

"Can't get enough of this," he regaled. "And you probably can't get enough of me, Gina, that's why you came in here."

Gina laughed, dismissed the comment. "Don't flatter yourself, George," she said. They kept right on dancing as they had done so often in the past.

The few seniors sitting over in the senior lounge—a designated spot against the far end of the cafeteria—looked over in judgement, pausing from their obnoxious foosball game. They shook their heads.

"So, you kids working at the Winking Moon again this summer?" asked one of Gina's friends.

"Yep," said Steve, still looking out the window.

"Gonna kick some asses again?" said another.

Alex looked at them. "We don't 'kick asses.'"

The girls smirked. *Sure, you don't.*

"You *do* kick asses, Alex," said Erin, another of Gina's friends. "That's why you're bouncers."

Alex looked even more intently at the one who had said that. "We're not 'bouncers,' Erin, we're patrol-men."

"Yeah right," said Erin. "Sounds good. Keeps the parents making their children stay at home, away from that wild place."

"'Joint,' Erin," said Steve. "We call it 'the joint.'"

George spoke up over the dancing. He and Gina were still going at it. "Only good, sane, civil stuff happens there, girls," he said. "You gotta behave or we're tossing ya."

"See?" said Erin. "You're bouncers."

The fourth girl spoke up. "Did you hear it's closing down?"

"What's closing down?" asked Alex.

"The drive-in. The Winking Moon."

George stopped dancing. Steve, John and Alex halted, too. They stared at the girls.

"What?" Steve asked, flatly.

She kept talking. "It's just the rumor. The place is getting too wild to keep open. Everybody keeps going there but it's just getting too risky."

"I didn't hear that," Alex said.

"Neither did I," said Steve.

This jolted the Crusaders.

"Yeah it's true, dudes," called out a senior shouting over the foosball table. "I heard it, too. A friend of my dad's at work says he knows people on the town board. They're talking of shutting it down. You macho-men might be shit outta luck."

Another senior chimed in, enjoying the opportunity to bust the

Crusaders' balls. "Yeah, you'll have to stick with just being idiots here. When you're seniors like us, you'll calm down, let administration handle the bad kids."

Steve poked a finger towards them. "Hey Davey, *we* stopped that indoor snowball-war this winter, not you. *We* caught the kids jamming jock straps up the vending machines. *We* saved a lot of asses around here."

"Dream on," Davy said, all in good fun. "You're not that cool, Laneske. None of you jamokes are. Sure, you're good athletes, but you're not superheroes for crying out loud."

"Bullshit," Alex said.

At that moment, a kid ran in—a dweeb of a kid. He was going on about some students on the bottom floor getting ready to blow up the boys' bathrooms by the library with firecrackers, flushing them right down the toilets, fuses lit. "It's the same knuckleheads who messed with the M-80s in the science lab in the fall!" he cried, waving at the Crusaders.

"Let's go!" Alex commanded, and they were off. Just as they stood up, the fire alarms went off and the hallways flooded with students and personnel.

It was a total logjam. Kids of every size, shape and demeanor poured out of the classrooms, flooding the halls, urgent to get to their lockers and get the hell out of the building.

"Stay calm! Stay calm!" one of the teachers yelled, hands flapping about the flood of students.

The Crusaders fought their way upstream. They had bolted from the cafeteria to make it down the stairs near the back-ramp to get to the bottom floor.

"Go get 'em, guys! Don't let 'em get away!" students cheered as they fought their way past. "Kick their asses! Destroy 'em!"

They pushed, fought, and vaulted the last few steps, landing on the hard floors and never missing a stride, running straight in the direction of the library, as the strident school bell continued to sound off. A science teacher held her ground in a hallway corner, avoiding the stampede.

"Gentlemen stop!" she yelled. "We know what's going on, let us deal with it! You're not playing heroes again!"

"Duty calls, Mr. Shecklee!" George fired back.

There was the sound of another explosion from the lavatory midway down, water pooling out from under the door. The odor of flash-powder permeated the hallway. Three very guilty-looking delinquents burst out from inside the latrine. Seeing the Crusaders fresh on their trails, they tore down the hall trying to escape.

"There they are!" Alex shouted. "Stop! We know who you are!"

"Run!" the one hollered. "It's the Crusaders!"

"Freshmen scum!" George barked. "We'll teach ya to mess with our toilets!"

One of the perpetrators tried ditching a fresh pack of their fireworks-of-choice and a lighter in the garbage receptacle. He missed and sent them clattering along the vinyl tile. They banked around the corner, making a dash toward the opposite end.

Another teacher popped his head out from a classroom— "Boys, stop! All of you: George, John, Steve, and Alex!"

But he was ignored. The teacher realized he was in the line of fire and dove back into his classroom to avoid the collision.

Galileo High School's esteemed Principal was next in their path, appearing at the end of the hallway. "Gentlemen, this is not the Winking Moon! What do you think you're all doing?!"

Steve bellowed, gesturing with a sweeping motion, trying to clear the path. "Principal Danner! Get outta the way!"

The disciplinarian backed up as the four caught up with the toilet perpetrators. They dove in the air with outstretched hands and landed on their targets. Clutching their shoulders, clothes, and necks, the Crusaders brought the pack down in one giant heap as they slid into the lockers at the end of the hall. Each Crusader purposefully allowed their heads to smack directly into the metal lockers, one after the other – "Bang! Bang! Bang!" George decided that it was only fitting to give his catch the worst wedgie known to mankind, tearing the underwear band in the process. His prey swore, yowled in pain, "Son-of-a-bitch! Fucking jocks."

The Crusaders continued to hold them in place. They were winded, but they were also satisfied with the justice they had served up. George emitted an evil laugh and Principal Danner, along with the rest of Galileo High School who had remained behind, ran in, instructing the Crusaders to pull the assailants to their feet and drag them to the principal's office.

The boys shoved them into Principal Danner's office, filing in behind them, as the school alarm continued to blare overhead.

Principal Danner slammed his door shut, glaring at the pranksters. He hiked up his belt and pointed a finger at them, "You three are going to have to pay for every last bit of damage you caused. Blowing up toilets with M-80s? Causing water to flood all over the place? Once we take care of the fire department—who should be here shortly, I might add—we're handing you right over to the authorities. And I'll be calling each one of your parents."

"And for you four…" he turned and said to the Crusaders. "You could have caused serious injury to these kids. I'm sick-and-tired of you macho-men thinking it's okay to run around this school treating it like your own personal hunting ground. You've helped us in the past, sure, but you can't keep doing this. You're a liability. Do you know what that is?"

"A key asset?" George answered, smugly.

Danner glared, clearly displeased. "Don't be smart, Jocavelli. You… you 'Crusaders'… are not at the Winking Moon. You're at a public school. Do you think you're the Justice League of America or something?"

"No sir," offered Steve. "We could be the Avengers, though. We prefer Marvel Comics."

"No," said John, correcting his friend. "Those are the chooches from The Smirking Star, the other drive-in."

"All right, all of you cool it," Principal Danner said, taking a moment to regain his composure. "We're going to sort this out. We're going to sort all of this out. Before I let you go, do you have anything to say for yourselves? A reason why I shouldn't call *your* parents, as well?"

Alex spoke up. "Just that we got these idiots in the end, sir, thank you very much. Get it, 'the end'? That's a butt-joke. They blew up the toilets."

Danner's face was flat. "Not funny, Carver. Now get out of my office. Go! I will talk with all of you later."

The Crusaders stood, saluted, then turned and grimaced at the troublemakers. They grimaced back, throwing them the finger. George pretended to start at them, making them jump. The Crusaders left the office, carefully closing the door behind them. They met the firemen coming in through the back entrance, and we're also met with a round of applause by a large group of their peers waiting for them in the school parking lot. Gina Ciminetti and her three girlfriends were right in the middle of the pack, grinning.

CHAPTER 3:

THE GODDESS OF GALILEO

A symphony of vehicle horns deafened the ears of Lee-Willie Stuckerson and "Big" Jim Barenta as they walked the lot of The Winking Moon. The two were taking a stroll around the perimeter, checking out the fence and surroundings. A good crowd was forming. Many of the patrons were honking boisterously, over-excited and already obnoxious.

"Start the show!" someone yelled.

"We want our movie!" shouted another. Folks were starting to grow impatient.

Lee-Willie, being Lee-Willie, could not help himself. He instantly fumed, shouting back at his antagonizers, "It's not dark yet! You'll have to wait!"

But, sure as hell, a reply came back. "We don't wanna wait! We didn't pay to stare at a blank screen!"

Lee-Willie choked down another bitter response and stared at the ground, kicking a few pebbles in the asphalt underfoot. There were a lot of cracks in the pavement now. Too many years of blistering heat and foot traffic.

Instead, it was Jim who spouted off this time, muttering insults under his breath. "They'll stare at a fist in a second," he said, smoking a cigarette.

Jim Barenta was a man of charisma. Thirty-one years old, solidly built with big, bushy hair, like an afro. Many had joked with him that he had "a bigger bush than most brothers." The pack of cigarettes stuck from his chest pocket of his frayed, blue-denim vest.

Continuing their walk, Lee-Willie said, "Jim, why didn't you help us with The Wild Man of Borneo last night?"

"He was here again?"

"Jim… c'mon… you knew."

"You didn't need my help, Lee, we'll get rid of him sooner or later."

"With ten more rogues to fill in the vacuum right behind him," Lee-Willie responded, being completely cynical.

Jim took another drag of his cigarette and blew out a huge smoke ring. "I'm a union projectionist, Lee, not a Crusader," he said. "You don't want me to get fired, do ya? They already caught me once, tossing those guys out the exit last year—literally."

"Nobody wants you to get fired," said Lee-Willie. "But your presence makes an impact to people, you have a certain sort of *influence*, especially over the Crusaders. They're starting next week, part-time until the school year ends."

"So, we got 'em again all summer? Poor saps."

"They look up to you. They like you a lot better than they like me. I just don't have the command like you do."

"You have a temper, like I don't," said Jim. "You're gonna have to hold it together more than you do, Lee. One of these days that trigger inside your head is gonna backfire on you. And it'll affect all of us. We gotta whole summer of operation, mister, pace yourself."

"Start the fucking movie!" came another cry from the peanut gallery.

"Shut the hell up!" Lee-Willie snapped, throwing it out there. "We just said it's too damn light to start!"

Jim encouraged Lee-Willie to walk faster. "What'd I just tell you?" he said to the manager. Lee-Willie was a worried man.

"We need the help. We're falling apart here," he said. "Did you hear the rumors that Bluestone will be shuttin' us down?"

"I don't pay attention to rumors," Jim answered. "I heard enough rumors in Vietnam. The only things that mattered in the end were the bullets blasting over our heads."

"This is our own battleground, isn't it, Jim?"

"In a certain way, it is. We ain't going' nowhere. At least let's pray on it. Long live the Winking Moon."

"I'm going into the concession stand," said Lee-Willie, heading over to the brightly lit building.

"Big" Jim saw him off with a slight wave. "See you at intermission."

Jim ground out his cigarette into the asphalt, craving another. There was already a crowd consisting of several Chevrolet pick-ups, getting drunk in the very back row. A girl had already taken off her tube top. She was running around, showing off her naked boobs.

Lee-Willie was right. The line of incoming traffic into the venue extended out the long entrance road into the country lane in both directions. Pick-up trucks, airbrushed vans, muscle cars, family sedans, coupes, and station wagons, of every size, shape and color, clogged the entrance, impatiently waiting to pull in. Late 70s rock, disco, and country from the cars' eight-tracks melded together with the endless honking to form one, giant roar. The movie inside had begun to play. The drive-in was now in full operation. Incoming patrons continued pouring in through the first twenty minutes of the second picture.

One car in particular—an AMC Gremlin—pulled up to the box office, four jamokes inside. They reeked of stale beer and weed. Kathy Berenger, eighteen, was the Winking Moon employee who landed the unfortunate task of processing their tickets, as she did all vehicles. She turned down Donna Summer's "Bad Girls" on her transistor radio beside the till on the counter and went to greet the car with a smile.

"Hey, can you hurry up? We wanna get in," the driver scolded, rudely.

Kathy kept her smile pinned on. She was in the middle of a painting (Lee was kind enough to let her bring side projects to work on as she waited for patrons to file in), but set down the paint brush she had in her right hand, moving attention from the canvas on a table-top easel beside her, also on the counter. "Welcome to The Winking Moon."

"Thanks, can ya hurry up?"

"I'm going as fast as I possibly can."

Kathy Berenger was a stunner. She was an introverted girl with raven-black hair down to the middle of her back, a perfectly sculpted athletic body, and bright green eyes. She was one of those girls that never quite knew just how beautiful she was.

The nineteen-year-old driver inside the Gremlin looked at her, calculatingly. "Hey, don't I know you?" he asked.

The other three passengers also seemed to recognize her.

"I don't think so," Kathy answered.

But the grin grew. The driver pointed a finger. "Yes, I do. You're the Goddess of Galileo. You graduated a couple of years ago. I was the class ahead of you."

Now Kathy was embarrassed. She hated this kind of attention. She said, "I don't remember you."

"You don't?" beamed the driver. His teeth were stained with nicotine. "I was pretty famous."

"For what?" Kathy asked.

"Skipping school," the chucklehead answered.

Unamused, Kathy put on her show-face. "Two-fifty, please, for each of you."

As the four fumbled and fussed with the money, each pulling out singles and change from their pockets and spilling it all over, the driver could not help but notice the oil painting next to Kathy. It was fantastic.

"Whattya doing in there?" he asked.

"Painting," she answered, collecting the crinkled bills, dirty coins.

"Your boss lets you paint?"

"Yeah, as long as I do my work."

"Let us see."

"Guys, you're holding up traffic." They were. The line behind them was restless. Kathy worked the register, placed the money in, pulled their tickets from the roll, and tore them each in half, handing them back for receipts.

"C'mon, show us," the driver insisted, handing each of his buddies a torn ticket.

Kathy relented. Quickly, she turned the easel around so they could fully see her work. It was beautiful—a scenery of woods, light from a setting sun coming through it.

"That's fantastic," the driver exclaimed. "You a professional artist or something?"

"I want to be. Going to college for it."

"Where?"

"Locally."

Finally, one of the passengers popped up from in the backseat, grabbing the headrest, pulling himself forward to be seen. "Why don't you go to some fancy European school? Some snotty art school in France?" he asked.

Kathy blushed. "Actually, I'm looking into it. Now guys…"

"C'mon, while we're young!" the yahoo behind them roared, sticking his head out the window. There were many more car horns.

"Wow, that really is a great painting." the driver said, then looked up to admire the back of the mammoth screen behind her. There was its giant, neon-lit Man-In-The-Moon caricature, way up, popping and fizzling with its hot gas inside: the Winking Moon's signature logo, the name of the drive-in sprawled in cursive letters under the silly face. "Same old Man in the Moon."

"Smiling and winking down on you," Kathy said, motioning them along with her hand.

"I'd be smiling and winking down on you, too," the driver said, redirecting his focus to her. Now he had a lascivious gaze on his face. "Looking down your smock."

She did not like that.

“Thanks. Have a good night, fellas,” she said, and they began creeping forward.

“Got any nudes of you?” the second chooch in the backseat shouted. “Most artist do self-portraits, ya know! I want yours to be a nude! I’ll pay any price!”

Then, there Lee-Willie was, stepping out of the dark. He chased after the Gremlin, shaking a thickly wrapped and reinforced power flashlight in his hand. “Get in there!” he warned. “I won’t have you talking a member of my staff like that.”

From inside the car, the kids were having a riot. “He said ‘member!’” one of them said. “Ha-haw, that’s hysterical!”

When the fiasco was over, and the Gremlin had rumbled around the bend, entering the theater, Lee-Willie came sauntering back, re-holstering his flashlight.

“Mr. Stuckerson, you didn’t have to do that,” said Kathy. “I can hold my own.”

The next car pulled up.

“I know you can, Miss Berenger,” Lee-Willie responded, calmly. “Get these cars through, please. Have you seen a little shit running through here?”

“A ‘little shit?’”

“You know, a punk, a hooligan? Isn’t that what the Crusaders call the ones already inside?"

"No, they're the rowdies and yahoos. The punks and hooligans sneak in from the outside."

"Whatever. He's about this big–" holding his hand at chest-level. "Ran through the concession stand squirting everybody with a water pistol. Soaked my wife to the bone."

Kathy went to speak, but before she could, a child, about eleven years of age, came darting out from the exit. He ran in front of them, inches away from being hit by a Ford Mustang, and stopped to taunt the manager— "Hey mister, bite this!" He grabbed his cock and balls in one hand, held the water pistol in aim-position with the other, and fired off a powerful stream in their direction, dousing the box office window. He immediately took off running and laughed in search of his next victim. Lee-Willie took off after him, full sprint. Kathy tried to yell after him to stop him, but it was too late. Her boss was already gone. Kathy greeted the next customer: a '78 Chevrolet Malibu Classic.

"Hey, baby, I'm a glass of milk…" said the driver, an obnoxious grin ruining his otherwise pleasant features. "Make me cream." His friends in the car cackled.

Kathy took her cup of Diet Tab and without hesitating, threw the contents into the car, dousing all of them.

CHAPTER 4:

ALEX'S DAD

After school, and one step closer to summer vacation, Steve and the Crusaders jumped into his banana-yellow Dodge Charger like they did every day. It was Steve's pride and joy. Getting ready to peel out the back-parking lot and fired up for the adventures that lay head, Steve opted for a mini-joyride before heading out of the parking lot. Stepping on the gas, he ran doughnut after doughnut and laid patches on the asphalt, raising smoke clouds. Van Halen's "Running With the Devil" blasted from the eight-track cassette tape machine.

Principal Danner watched from the cafeteria window, arms folded and head shaking in dismay. The boys laughed without a care in the world.

Later that afternoon when Alex got home, he retreated to his room to stare dreamingly at last year's yearbook, ignoring his mother ending an argument in the other room on the phone, taking in the pictures of the Goddess of Galileo: Kathy Berenger. The achievements of the graduated beauty when she had been in school were staggering. Class Valedictorian, Best-Looking, Class Artist, Most Talented, High Honors. The girl was just classic.

Suddenly, Alex's mom barged into his room, as she had become accustomed to doing (this was the third time in the past month).

Alex slammed the book closed. "Mom! Privacy?" he said, with

indignation. He quickly threw the yearbook under the bed and out of sight.

"You still taking that job at the Winking Moon?" Her hand was still on the doorknob.

He hid the book under the bed. "Yeah, of course. Why wouldn't I?"

"Even your father thinks it's a bad idea."

"Screw Dad," he said. Alex turned and faced the window. He could see the full moon from his open window. The night air felt good, blowing gently through the screen. "He hasn't been in the picture for over a year now. I heard everything you were saying, by the way. Every time you guys get on the phone; I hear everything. It's the most uncivilized thing I've ever heard."

"I told him you were taking the job again, among other things. He didn't like it."

"I don't care what he thinks. He's gone."

"It's the only thing I agree with him on. I've been worried sick about it ever since you told me."

"Mom, it's done. We'll be all right. More importantly—Dad. Is he ever coming back?"

She entered fully into his room, still standing and sighed. "Do you want him to?" she asked. She was already dressed in her work attire.

Alex made a face. "Are you kidding? After bailing on his family to be with some broad?"

"What about your brother? Does Randy?"

"Fuck no."

"Alex, language."

"Sorry, it slipped."

"Can I sit down?"

Alex made room, let her sit on the corner of his bed.

She sat and stared at him for a moment, making him uneasy. She was ready to smile, but instead raised an eyebrow. "Why'd you hide your yearbook?" she asked.

"I didn't."

She smiled knowingly. "I'm not sure why Kathy Berenger is working at that nuthouse again this year, either. Your business venture wouldn't have anything to do with trying to talk to Kathy… would it?"

He was totally thrown. How had she known?

"Kathy has nothing to do with it," he responded. "It's for the boys. The Crusaders."

"Yeah, right. And stop calling yourselves that: 'Crusaders.' It's so falsely grandiose."

"No, it isn't. We have a code."

"I'm sure you do. Is Vicki coming back, too?"

"Vicki and Emilio and Mr. and Mrs. Stuckerson, and Stanley Mason, I hope—always good for comic relief—and Jim Barenta, most of all."

"I'll wait to meet him."

"He's a legend."

Angela turned to look at the George A. Romero "Dawn of the Dead" movie poster on the back of the door and its ominous design: half a decomposed zombie's head creeping up from a horizon line. She cringed and turned back to him. "Your father called *me*, by the way. Not the other way around. I've never called him."

"I don't know why he bothers anymore," Alex said. "He's abandoned the three of us. Is he still with that girl?"

"Yes, and he's still in Seattle."

"Do you hate him?"

"Do you want me to hate him?"

"I dunno. Maybe. I'll have to think about it. I've got a lot on my plate."

"Like your room. Clean it up. Just because we move into a smaller house doesn't mean you have to trash it."

"I'm not trashing it."

"Do you like it here?"

"Mom, I do. You do your best for us. We love you for it. We know it's been tough. What kind of a father walks out on his family?"

She looked around again, as if expecting to find something additional. "By the way, where is your brother?"

"Probably with Becca, I have no idea," Alex said, then added, "I don't care."

"I wish you two would get along," Angela said, disappointed. "Ever since your father split, you've been at it like cats and dogs."

"He's turned into a bigger dick than he already was," Alex said. "Yelling and barking at me all the time, pushing me around. He's a bully."

"He's trying to be the man of the house now. He's older than you and he's trying to step into some big shoes."

"Well he's doing a pretty bad job of it. I'll smack him aside the head with those shoes if he doesn't lay off, trying to get me to work for him at his stupid towing service."

"It's a good idea," said his mother.

"Towing cars is not safer than working at The Winking Moon."

"I'd beg to differ."

Alex stared at her. "Ever seen an irate driver seeing his car getting' towed? It ain't pretty."

She stood. She kissed him on the forehead. "I have to go to work."

"Night shift again?"

"For two weeks. Best money. Kodak does us right, even though the hours suck."

"Thank God for Kodak," said Alex.

Angela paused again to disapprove of the decor. "And are you going to continue having this poster up in your room? You brought this from the move."

"It's my favorite horror movie, Mom," Alex said, feeling the need to lecture. "It's pure genius. George A. Romero came up with the entire living-dead thing. If we get more movies like 'Dawn of the Dead' at The Winking Moon, people would be mesmerized. They wouldn't be running around acting like idiots and pulling pranks. 'Dawn of the Dead' is a cinematic masterpiece."

"Whatever you say… you and your movies. Goodnight, baby, I love you. Turn your lights off and get some sleep."

"I will," said Alex. "And stay off the phone, Mom, it's not worth your aggravation."

"Sorry for my yelling. And if anybody's a dick, it's your father." She left and shut the door.

Alex pulled out the yearbook again.

CHAPTER 5:

THE LAST BASH BEFORE THE SEASON

The next morning, Randy Carver burst into Alex's room at sunrise. He overturned his bed, rolled Alex off the mattress in nothing but his underwear and pinned him clear to the wall, bracing his muscular shoulders and arms into the mattress to hold it in place. Alex was already screaming, trying to wriggle free. Randy *was* a dick as of late. A nineteen-year old dick. But he was trying to step into their AWOL father's shoes, like Mom had said.

"Heard you were talking to Mom last night about Dad," Randy said into the mattress, Alex thumping and bucking from the other side. "Heard you were saying he's coming back."

"What?! No! I didn't say that?" Alex yelled from beneath the weight of the mattress. His panicking voice was muffled. "I didn't say Dad was coming back! I swear!"

"Watcha doin' upsetting Mom like that? You know talking about him upsets her."

"That happens every time he calls! Let me the fuck up, you're suffocating me!"

Randy was taller than his brother by a few inches, donned in his mechanic's uniform: a jumpsuit with his employer's embroidered name on the back that read "TURK'S AUTO SERVICE & TOWING."

"You gotta stop doing that," he told his brother, enjoying the early-morning torture.

"I'm not doing shit!" Alex shrieked again. "He called *her* she didn't call him! We weren't even talking about him!"

"What were you talking about? We crossed each other in the driveway. I was coming back from Becca's. Good sex we had last night, me and Becca."

"Never mind what we were talking about! Let me the fuck go!"

"Starting at the Winking Moon again, huh?" Randy challenged.

"Yeah, next week!"

"Next week? Sooner than I thought. Bothering Mom talking about that then? Making her worry again about you getting your face cracked open like you did last year?"

"I didn't get my face cracked open! It was only a busted lip!"

"Making her worry about all the bullshit going on over there, too? It's gettin' worse every summer. Think the community ain't sick of the shit going on at that place?"

"'Joint'!" Alex stressed. "We call it 'a joint!'"

"Whatever you call it, it's trouble. It's comin' down, little brother, the talk is all over town."

"Randy, let me out!"

"I'm telling ya, little brother, I'm sick of bailing you out every time. One of these days you're gonna have a war on your hands there and you're gonna want me to come and save your ass. Save *all* your asses. The only good man at that place is Jim Barenta, and even he ain't indestructible."

"Randy, let me out, goddam it, let me out!"

Randy finally released the mattress. Alex came falling hard on it as it slapped back to the frame, almost breaking. Alex was dripping with sweat, panting from his near-death experience.

"There, little pussy, can ya breathe now? Bet you were gonna sleep all day, weren't ya?"

Alex was wheezing. "I… told you we're starting the drive-in soon. Part-time… full-time when school's out."

"You're gonna regret it."

Alex held his hand out. He wanted help up. Randy did not give it to him. Alex had to pull himself to his feet on his own. He wiped the brown hair away that was sticking to his face and wiped his mouth. "Help me fix this shit up," he said, looking around, disgusted. "Look at the mess you've made."

Instead of helping him with that—rumpled sheets, scattered pillows, clothes, pants all over the room—Randy sat down at Alex's desk, grabbed his gaming console and fired up a call of "Pong." Randy had gotten hooked on it weeks ago. He endlessly watched the little white ball bounce off the four sides of the screen towards the net.

Alex was pissed. "What the fuck are you doing in my room? This is *my* room. You've got yours, get out!"

"I'm leaving for work soon," Randy answered, not even turning around. "I work for a living."

"So do I."

"And I'm pissed you're still not taking my offer."

"I'm not towing cars," Alex said. "That's not what I want to do."

"It's a lot safer than the Winking Moon, I'll tell ya that much. And it's better money."

"Not everything's about money."

"The window's closing," said Randy. "You better think about it, the option's still on the table but closing fast."

"Finish your game and get out. I want a peaceful Saturday."

Randy finished up, scoring a quick ricochet off the bottom-right. He threw his arms up in the air in a yelp of triumph and tossed the console back on the table, nearly sending it off.

"Go back to sleep, chump," he said as he got up from his chair, jutting a finger at his brother.

"'Chump' this," Alex retorted as Randy left, grabbing his balls in his brother's direction.

Later that morning, Alex was engrossed in a program on TV about the latest scientific space mission from NASA. Unprecedented jaw-dropping photographs were coming in of the solar system's largest planet. He was enthralled and watched happily from the living room recliner, a bowl of Cap'n Crunch in his lap.

The phone in the kitchen rang and he quickly put his bowl down and ran across the room to answer it. The ring was loud, and he did not want to wake his mother. She had not been asleep that long after returning from her night shift. He tripped over a kitchen table chair in the process and knocked it clean over. Picking it back up, he snatched the phone from its wall cradle, the curled cord stretching all the way to the family room as he retreated to the TV.

"Hey. Whattya doing?" Steve asked.

"Watching a program on this new NASA mission," Alex answered, getting comfortable in the recliner again. "It's called The Voyager Spacecraft. It's taking pictures of Jupiter that no human has ever seen before. It's fascinating."

"More fascinating is the Mastersons having a party tonight."

"The Mastersons? A party?"

"That's right," said Steve. "I guess they recovered from last time. Their parents are out at their cottage in the Thousand Islands again and they decided to have a few people over."

Alex did not take his eyes from the screen. "A few people, huh?

And we're the first to know?"

"They said they're only havin' a handful or so over. Drink some beer, eat some pizza. We gotta get this in before we can't go to any more parties. We'll be busting our asses at The Moon soon enough. They say they have this new thing called BetaMax. It's a videotape player in their basement. Got it all set up as a home entertainment system. Scott and Terry say they can watch first-run movies on it, movies that just came out of the theaters."

"What?" said Alex. "That's impossible."

"It's worth checking out. I can pick you up at seven. I'll get George and John first."

"That's hours away yet."

"I'm giving you time to beat off," said Steve.

"The last time the twins threw one of these things it turned into a disaster and we had to break up bullshit just like we do at the Moon so their house didn't get trashed."

"That's not gonna happen tonight. Tonight's mellow. We're just going for fun."

"Vicki gonna be there?" Alex asked.

"I told her, but again, the Mastersons don't want a ton of people. They got enough balls just sneaking-in these few."

"I'm not going into Crusader-mode," Alex reiterated.

"Al, relax, we won't have to. We're just doing this to bust balls."

Alex eyes were on what they called The Great Red Spot, one of Jupiter's signature features. It was true: no one had ever seen detail like this before. "Sounds like famous last words," he muttered, thinking of the splendor.

"No," said Steve, "the last words will be 'Why-did-you-tell-Stanley Mason-about-that-show?' from Mr. Stuckerson, if you mention the subject to the old goat. Don't get him started again this year on his UFOs and all that space-stuff. The man will never get back to work."

Alex was just as skeptical. "We'll be dealing with that soon enough, whether or not I bring the subject up."

"You know it," said Steve. "See you at seven."

"See you at seven."

The phone slipped out of Alex hand as he tried to punch the button with one hand to hang up, balancing the bowl of cereal in the other. It dropped to the floor with a bash and snapped all the way back to the kitchen from the cord, making a cracking sound hitting off the wall by the pantry door. As he got up to get it, he saw his mother standing in her pajamas—half-in and half-out of her bedroom down the hall. Her face was bleary, make-up smudged.

"You through making noise?" she asked groggily.

"Yeah, Mom, sorry."

"I'm going back to sleep." And she went back in, closed the door.

The entire neighborhood was packed with vehicles, parked all up and down the residential street. There must have been two hundred high school kids at the house. Terry and Scott Masterson, identical twins, were already tearing their hair out, going nuts trying to contain the amount of moronic behavior their peers were participating in all over the house: running around, drinking beer, smoking cigarettes, horse playing, climbing trees in the front yard, getting up on the roof, raiding the refrigerator and pantry for whatever they could put in their mouths, microwaving cheese sandwiches, getting cheese stuck all over the glass. One album after the next was being blasted on the hi-fi stereo in the living room, shaking the walls with its energy.

Steve saw it as he pulled up—a perfect parking spot almost right in front of the house. He took it, carefully parallel parking his Charger. As he was concentrating on that, George, John and Alex, all stared in awe from the passenger seats at the scene before them. Sure, it was not their first party, but the wildness never ceased to amaze them.

Alex was the one who spoke up first, as Steve was shutting off the engine. "Just a dozen kids, huh?"

Steve nonchalantly answered, as he stepped out of the car with the others following, "What can I say? I don't have a crystal ball."

"Their parents are gonna kill him," said George. They were all now standing on the sidewalk. "No way a bunch of things aren't getting busted in that house."

John said, "Are we gonna have to save the day?"

"Hell no," said Steve. "We're gonna party."

Jamokes had a beer keg on the roof that had just been emptied. The goofballs who were holding it lost their grip and it rolled off, making one hell of a clang on the driveway. Another guy was being dared to hang by his hands from the gutter, hanging over one side of the basketball net.

"Do we know him?" Alex asked.

"I think he's a freshman," said John.

"Freshmen are at this party? We weren't at parties when we were freshmen."

Steve clapped Alex on the back to get them all moving towards the front door. "Let's go in."

As they got to the stoop, they pulled two kids from the bushes who were stuck head-first, legs kicking, shoes falling off. They set them down on the walkway and told them to behave. As soon as they opened the door, the party encapsulated them. Music, lights, activity, movement. There were welcoming shouts of recognition from all around: "Hey! Look who it is! It's the Winking Moon Crusaders!" "All hail, Winking Moon!" "Let 'em in!"

Big George already had his arms up, tamping down the excitement. "Calm down, calm down. We'll be giving out autographs later."

"Steve, John, George, Alex!" someone yelled. "Ya made it! You gonna chaperone the party?"

"No," answered Steve, "We're going to *enjoy* the party!"

Suddenly, the Masterson twins came running up from the crowd.

"Guys! Guys! You have to help us! We had no idea how many kids were gonna show up! They're all over the house, acting wild!"

"Terry… Scott…" Steve said to them, coolly, "this is your doing."

"This is nuts," said Terry. "There's couples in our parents' bedroom right now having sex! We threw 'em out and they went right back in."

"Did they finish?" George joked.

"George!" Scott pleaded.

Before they got a chance to respond, they were greeted by more of their peers, eager to get the Crusaders' attention. "Hey kids, how are ya?" slurred a sloppy friend. "Heard about what you did with those dumb-asses with the M-80s. Blowing up toilets? Good thing you got to 'em before they went up to the second floor."

"If they go up to the second floor," said George, "we woulda flushed 'em down a toilet."

"Ha-ha-ha, you guys are hysterical," gurgled another, pushing them forward. "Go into the kitchen, there's tons of beer."

"Who brought it?" Alex asked, moving right along.

"Who knows? But they got a keg tapped."

The four went into the kitchen. Indeed, there was another keg, tapped, right atop the kitchen table. There was a kid lying directly under it, his friend with a hand on the spigot, freely flowing a steady stream of the frothy stuff directly into his mouth. The laughing in the room was deafening. Someone finally dragged him away and beer sloshed all over the linoleum tiling.

"Hey, it's the Crusaders!" Recognized, once again. "You gonna get us into the drive-in for free this year?"

"Bailey, we can't do that," said Alex. "We'd get fired."

"We run an honest joint," John asserted.

"Speaking of joints," came another classmate, gesturing toward the kitchen toward, "They're smoking 'em in the backyard. Go for it."

Steve was up with his hand, waving it away. "No, thanks."

"Goody-two-shoes."

"Bullshit," said George. "We're hardly goody-two-shoes."

"Prove it."

"We don't have anything to prove," said Alex. "We're just here to have a good time before we start back at the drive-in next week."

More high schoolers surged into the kitchen. "You kids working there again?" said a chirpy chick with a glass bottle of beer in her hand.

"How brave."

"We heard it's shutting down," said another.

Alex turned to his friends in frustration. "Why is everybody saying this? What do they know that we don't?"

"Nothing," said George, puffing his chest out. "They don't know anything we don't know. We know everything."

A kid poked his head in, hearing him. "Hey George, you love 'Saturday Night Fever,' right?"

"Best movie ever," George answered. "Best music ever."

Soon after, "Staying Alive" by The Bee Gees, exploded from the stereo in the living room. "C'mon, Georgie-boy," shouted a girl, waving him over, "we know you can't resist this."

"Yeah, do here what you do in the cafeteria," said another.

George smirked at his buddies, slicked his hair back with his hand. "Excuse me while I address my fans."

He boogied down like a king. It was an even better display of his choreographic talent than in the cafeteria. His female classmates flocked to dance around him. He obliged all through the song, one after the other. After a few disco songs, the stereo switched to "How Deep Is Your Love," by Yvonne Elliman, and slowed things way down. Wiping the sweat from his brow, he strutted off the makeshift dancefloor and made his way back toward the kitchen. On his way, a geeky classmate jumped on his back with full plastic cup of beer in his hands, spilling it all over George's back.

"Sorry, George," he said, "That was an accident. It's just so good to have the Crusaders here. I'm freakin' drunk! Isn't it, great? I'm freakin' wasted."

George said, "Ronnie, I'll show you what an accident looks like."

He picked the skinny kid up over his head, held him there like a championship wrestler on TV, and power-slammed him onto the sofa nearest them, knocking every Masterson family portrait off of the wall. The frames crashed to the floor. Everyone screamed with laughter, except from Terry Masterson, who'd witnessed the encounter from the next room.

"George! What the fuck?" he bellowed.

"Sorry, Terry," said George, "had to teach Ronnie here not to jump on people's backs with beer in their hands. Look at my shirt, it's soaked. Don't mess with a man comin' off the floor."

Another kid was in hysterics, pointing around the room as he had just become aware of something. "Look at all the pictures that didn't come down! They're upside down!"

And they were. Every single painting and photograph in the room had been re-hung topside-down. The illusion threw off many.

"Who did that?" shouted the twin. "Who the fuck did that? Who's the chucklehead that turned every single picture in our house upside-down? I'll murder ya!"

Everyone broke into hysterics at the scene.

At that moment Vicki Richards came crashing into the party, holding her hands up, earrings bouncing from her lobes. "Hey-hey everyone, I'm here, the party can start now. Jasper: pick up that cup. Heath: you're spilling your chips. Erin: you really came with David? Thought you two Melvins were gonna stay away from each other. Isabella: orange with purple? How many fashion faux pas can you make, chick? Where's my beer? I'm already ten feet in the door."

"Vicki!" From the left and the right, she was swarmed with attention, too.

Vicki Richards was the Crusaders' redheaded, dynamo team member. She had personality to last for miles, a true mother-hen like no one's business. She was seventeen, too. The crowd met her with open arms.

"Vick," a friend beamed, "we hear you're gonna work at The Moon, too, this year. Back for more? Did you take karate lessons?"

"Whatcha gonna do when the shit hits the fan?" asked another.

"Shit back," she answered.

"You're one brave girl even though you work in the concession stand," said a girlfriend, laughing too close to her face.

"Working in the concession stand is just as dangerous," Vicki responded, dismissing the comment. "I know how to keep my head down."

Yet another came up behind her. "Well ya got Steve, John, Alex and George to back ya up."

Jokingly, Vicki replied, "I don't need back-up." She laughed and waved "hello" to the rest of the Crusaders in the kitchen. Somebody handed her a beer.

Scott and Terry Masterson continued to chase people around the house, one wearing their mother's bathrobe with nothing but underwear on underneath, running around with a shower cap on his head.

Vicki merged with the Crusaders as they hugged, saluted with beers, and talked about this being the last party before the "season" started. "Where's your girlfriend, Steve?" she asked.

"Jody had to babysit," he answered. "It's amazing I get to see her at all with her parents being so paranoid about her hanging around us."

"Do you blame them?" she said. "If I was Jody's parents, I wouldn't let them hang around you scoundrels, either."

"Speaking of starting," said Alex, "Mr. Stuckerson called my mom and said we're getting our new uniforms mid-week."

"Has to be before next Friday," Vicki said. "That's when our fun begins."

"I wonder who paid for 'em," said John. "Remember Mrs.

Stuckerson going nuts last year with Mr. Stuckerson using all their own money to pay for shit around the drive-in?"

"He'll do it again this year," said George.

"That man is hardcore," said Alex.

"And a ball-buster," said Vicki, prompting them all to look at her. "What? He is. He rides us like a two-bit camel."

Another schoolmate came flying in, half a piece of pizza sticking out of his mouth. "Speaking of camels, would you like to see my humps, Vicki?"

She slapped him clear across the face.

"Hey, let's check out this new BetaMax thing everyone's talking about," he said.

"Where is it?" asked Steve.

"The basement!" someone yelled from the stairs. "C'mon down, they're playing 'Superman.'"

Vicki and the Crusaders turned to each other. Really? "'Superman?'" Alex asked. "With Christopher Reeve? That just came out last year."

"Get down here!" came the voice.

And so, they did. The furnished basement was a fancy, wood-paneled chamber, decked-out with the latest of "what-was" to create a family living center. A front projection TV with sofas around it played with surround sound for optimal effect. Indeed, Christopher Reeve, the Man of Steel, was there on the big screen, flying around the sky with Margot Kidder as Lois Lane.

"Holy shit…" Alex exclaimed.

The room smelled of beer and popcorn. Almost all were rapt, watching the movie. A few were making out in the corners by the billiards table and washing machine. Vicki continued her supervision, telling people to clean up their mess, get their feet off the coffee table, stop blocking the screen, no talking. John, Steve, Alex and George discussed in low tones the future of drive-in theaters. Was this an omen? Does this legitimize the rumors if everybody someday wanted a BetaMax in their home?

Alex tried to reassure himself. "It'll never take off," he said. "Who'd rather sit at home and watch movies when you can come out to the drive-in, under the stars and meet cool kids like us, catering to your every need?"

"You're not catering to my needs, Carver," an anonymous male said, "so shut-up."

A crash behind them sounded. The perpetrator with the bathrobe and shower cap had fallen, ripping the stairwell railing right off the wall. He tumbled down the staircase, too hammered to feel any pain.

As Terry Masterson ripped him a new asshole for his stupidity, screaming at him at the top of his lungs, kids sent an alarming message from upstairs. "Uh, guys, the police are here…" calling down to the

Mastersons. The entire room began emptying out, teenagers running up the stairs, knocking their cohorts aside, scrambling to get out of the house first so they would not get busted. Upstairs and in all the rooms, the same migration was going on. Kids were running amok, squeezing out back doors, tripping, jumping over fences and running into the neighbor's lawns.

Scott had now joined his brother, running down the stairs, begging the Crusaders and Vicki to help. Those five had remained calm and collected.

"You gotta help us!" Scott was begging. "Wilfred Barton—that Melvin—made off with our blender upstairs! That's not why the police are here but the kid ran off with the fucking thing, says he's going door-to-door trying to sell it! Says he's a late-night appliance salesman or something!"

So, duty called again. They all took a breath. Alex said, "Where's Wilfred now? We know that dweeb."

"He's down the street!" said Scott. "I was just watching him when the cops got here!"

"Omigod, we want that fucking thing back!" said Terry. "Dad just bought that for Mom for their anniversary! They'll kill us!"

Alex turned to his team. "Well, Crusaders, Vicki… we said we weren't gonna do this but looks we're needed. A short celebration for us. Let's go get 'em."

"Let's…" said Vicki, John, George and Steven in unison.

They burst out of the house as the twins dealt with the police, taking out a couple of drunken morons in their path. There were, in fact, two cruisers out front. That did not deter them. They split up, Alex directing. They looked high and low for the idiot who had fled the coop with their friends' stolen blender. One of the kids who had tried escaping up a tree was pointing. "Alex, Steve, John, George! He's down there at the corner house!"

They saw him. A porch light was on. A few houses down, Wilfred Barton was soliciting at the door, making the pitch to a furious neighbor. They were silhouettes against the dark and quiet night. Loose clothes flapping in the breeze, the outline of a blender, held high. "It's one in the morning!" Vicki was saying in disbelief.

"Crusaders unite!" said Alex. "Charge!"

They went running. Wilfred caught on that someone was chasing him down and took off from the porch. As usual, John was the fastest, followed by Steve and Alex, George last (but not by much). They tackled the thief into the bushes, disappearing inside the shrubbery, shoes, socks and feet sticking out. Miraculously, the blender remained intact. When they were finished roughing up Wilfred, the Crusaders dragged him back to the house, turning him over to the police.

"Say, aren't you the kids who work at the Winking Moon?" they asked the four.

"Yes, we are, Officer," said Alex. "The very ones."

The officer glanced at his partner, then pretended to reach for his holster of weapons and batons. "Maybe we should give you these for the season," he said.

"Cool," said John, unclear if the lawmen were kidding.

Terry and Scott were thrilled to have the blender returned but were read The Riot Act for having the bash to begin with. The police gave Wilfred an earful and put him into the back of one of the cruisers.

The kid who had threatened to hang onto the gutter when the Crusaders first pulled in was now doing it, hanging by his fingertips, laughing and giggling. The corrugated metal gave way, slowly peeling from the roof until the fool lowered all the way to the asphalt, sideways, still holding on.

"I… love these parties…" he mumbled, then passed out.

Scott and Terry were reduced to their wit's end.

CHAPTER 6:

NEW UNIFORMS

June 7, 1979

It was the Thursday before they started back at the Winking Moon. The Crusaders and Vicki motored down to the drive-in in Steve's Charger after school to pick up those new uniforms they had been promised. Completely missing Mr. and Mrs. Stuckerson and their cars when they first pulled into the theater, the group took the liberty of going for a joyride inside the empty drive-in. They did doughnut after doughnut, screaming at the top of their lungs, having loads of fun. The Cars *Candy-O* album cranked at top volume as they carried on, speeding down the open side lanes, sending the pebbles from the asphalt spitting in all directions, smacking the fences.

They had temporarily lost their minds, the exuberance of youth coursing their veins until only they decided enough was enough. They drove back to the exit, where the manager's office was located, stunned to see Mr. and Mrs. Stuckerson there, having just pulled up in their beat-up, '74 brown and gold Lincoln Versailles, staring at them with the box of uniforms in hand. Clearly, they were not happy.

Steve pulled up alongside them, turned the music off. "Oops," he said.

The managers' flat expressions said it all. "Steve Laneske… Vicki Richards… John Tambone… George Jocavelli and Alex Carver," Lee-

Willie started, voice choking back anger. "Welcome back. I see you haven't matured one iota since last year."

"Nice to finally see you again, Mr. and Mrs. Stuckerson," chirped Vicki. "How was your winter?"

"Long…" answered Lee-Willie before his wife could. "Like my face. Park there and let us give you these things, we have to get ready for opening night."

Steve coasted his car to the shoulder and turned off the ignition. Everybody hopped out. Gail-Lill was making an effort to be friendlier than her husband out of sheer politeness. "How's it going, everyone?" she asked as all five approached. "Having a good school year so far?"

Vicki continued speaking. "Yes, Mrs. Stuckerson, we are. We've stopped a lot of issues in the school this year. We're world-famous there."

"Well… good," she responded. "Education has a way of evolving."

"We hired you fools back because we need the help," Lee-Willie said next, ending the chit-chat. "Things have been wild already. You worked here last year; you know how crazy it gets." He set the box down, reached in, and pulled out a handful of black-colored smocks, throwing them one-by-one at the kids. "Seems we haven't stopped at all since we closed up last fall. Take these, as promised. Hope I got your sizes right."

They each held them up, taking in their new uniforms. They were quite fancy. Like the logo on the screen, a neon-green Man-In-The-

Moon was caught—mid-wink—standing out from a jet-black background. The zipper ran from waist to collar, and the lapels as wide as airplane wings, right at the neckline. "Wow, they're mint!" exclaimed Alex. "Look at these! And you got The Winking Moon logo on the back *and* on the front. Very chic. Very cool." The others were just as enthusiastic.

"And they're stain-resistant," Lee-Willie stressed. "As best as possible. God knows what kind of shit you kids get yourselves into on the job. Figured you slobs need all the protection you can get. Try 'em on, see if they fit."

The kids tried them on. They were perfect. George was fascinated by his zipper and demonstrated as he repeatedly zipped it up and down.

"You can stop that anytime, George," said Lee-Willie, "I think it works."

Steve came right out and asked them, "These are the best, Mr. and Mrs. Stuckerson. Did you pay for them outta your own pocket?"

That stopped the conversation dead. Gail-Lill stared at her husband. *See, honey? They know.* Lee-Willie side-stepped the issue. "We got 'em from somewhere," he said. "Glad they fit. Now each of you only got two, take care of 'em as best you can."

"Got the same weapons this year?" asked George. "I still got my holster."

Lee-Willie was peeved at the insinuation. "If you mean 'flashlights,' then yes," he answered. "*And* the walkie-talkies. You'll all get them."

"Still got that huge one, Mr. Stuckerson?" Alex asked. "The flashlight?"

The boys giggled. Vicki was embarrassed.

"Yes, I still have my *big* flashlight, Mr. Carver," he replied. "Now you're all set to start tomorrow night, right? It's gonna be a big crowd so I want you here early."

"Sure thing," said John. "Everybody already working? Same crew? Stanley? Emilio? Big Jim? Kathy?"

"Yes, they're all back," said Lee-Willie. "They're all as nutty as we are."

"How is everyone?" Vicki asked. "Kathy still painting?"

"Yes, she's still painting," Lee-Willie said.

George nudged Alex, next to him. "Alex is gonna be her art critic this year, aren't ya, Alex? Gonna watch her do those master strokes?"

"Shut-up, George," Alex said, ignoring him.

"Big Jim's back? The main man?" John was insistent.

"Of course, he's back," said Lee-Willie. "He's our projectionist."

"And Emilio?" said Steve. "That chooch we all love?"

"Who else would cook?" said Lee-Willie.

"And Stanley?" said Alex. "What about our old fart? Still waitin' for a flying saucer to come whisk him away?"

"Still waiting," answered Lee-Willie. "Don't imagine that's gonna happen this year, either, but hey—ya never know. Well, if that's it for questions…"

"It's not, sir." Vicki was raising her hand.

"Oh?"

"Uh, um… the rumors," she said.

"About the drive-in closing down…" Lee-Willie responded, shutting his eyes. *Yes, of course I would have to deal with this*, he thought.

Gail-Lill picked up on his frustration and stepped in front. "We don't know anything about the Winking Moon closing down. Or the Smirking Star. Bluestone hasn't responded back to us after we've made several calls. Lee and I have heard about the rumors, to be sure."

"They suck," John grumbled. "If any drive-in should close down it should be The Star. Those guys are knobs."

"They're our sister drive-in," said Gail-Lill. "If they go down, we go down. We don't wish for that to happen, do we, John?"

"No, ma'am," he answered. "But the Avengers are still knobs."

Lee-Willie turned to his wife. "Why does The Smirking Star have to have patrolmen again? They don't need it."

Gail-Lill raised her eyebrows at him. "That's Bluestone's call, dear. Things are getting wild all over. The 80's are coming, and people are getting weird."

"Well, if those guys set foot on our drive-in, we're kicking their asses," said Steve.

"You're not kicking their asses, Steve, and you're all going to behave this year." Lee-Willie was getting peeved at all the macho-talk. "No taking matters into your own hands. No violence, no mayhem. You stop that shit, got it? You don't go off half-cocked like you did last summer."

The boys snickered again, John nudging George. "He said 'half-cocked.'"

Lee-Willie slapped the empty box shut, picked it up, hurled it toward the manager's door. "Alright, now if you morons are through, Gail and I have to get ready for tonight's operation."

"Still living in those apartments, sir and ma'am?" Vicki asked.

"We are," said Lee-Willie.

"Still wanting to settle down in Rochester, sir and ma'am?" said John.

"We are," said Gail-Lill.

"Still think we're the best damn drive-in bouncers in the world, sir and ma'am?" said Alex.

Lee-Willie once again made the aggravated-face. "You're not

bouncers," he said. "You're *patrol*-men. Now get going, play in traffic or something. See you tomorrow night. And be well-rested, we're playing the first film over as we always did on weekends."

Heading to his car, Steve said, "Great. We'll be ready for it, sir and ma'am."

"We're looking forward to it, Mr. and Mrs. Stuckerson," said Vicki.

"We'll do the best damn job possible. We won't disappoint you," said Alex.

"We'll watch all that sex taking place in the vehicles, sir and ma'am," said George.

Lee-Willie shooed them away as he and his wife headed into the office.

The five climbed back into Steve's Charger, turned the ignition back on, and resumed blowing out the speakers with "The Cars." Lee-Willie was looking out his office blinds at them. "It's amazing they let those idiots advance another year in school," he said. "God bless the failing United States education system."

"Lee," said Gail-Lill. "Be nice."

“THE BROOD” & “THE TOOLBOX MURDERS”

CHAPTER 7:
AND SO, IT BEGINS

Friday, June 8, 1979

At 1:49 p.m., all of Galileo High's students were staring at the clock, waiting for the bell to ring. When it finally did, the whole school ran out of the building like a wild stampede. Some went out wrong doors and exits on purpose: more or less a rite-of-passage. They poured into the front and back parking lots, jumping on school buses, family cars, and whatever else they could find, screaming their way into summer vacation. A mixture of rock, pop, disco, country and soul all blended into one giant concert of noise. The Crusaders took in the excitement around them but had to keep their cool. It was time to focus and rest up for their first night back on the job. They all went home to their separate houses to take naps, regroup, and prepare themselves for their shift.

George, John, Vicki, Steve and Alex all attempted to nap, drawing the shades closed, pulling a thin sheet over themselves in bed. But it did not do much good. The excitement and anticipation were pure agony.

Alex had already been dressed in his new uniform for a half-hour as he waited in the kitchen for Steve to pull up. He anxiously jammed a bologna sandwich down his throat as fast as physically possible. As he heard the honk of Steve's Charger, he ran out the front door to meet his buddies, but Randy was on the porch reading a newspaper, legs propped up on the porch railing, ready for battle. "Well, don't you look sharp," he said in a mocking tone. "Those new uniforms? Think you look bad-ass in those things?"

Alex halted, looked at his proud apparel, smoothed it out. "Actually, yes. I think I look very cool in them. I think we all do."

Steve, George and John had kept their distance, waiting curbside in the street and watching from the car, Led Zeppelin's "In Through the Out Door" playing from the eight-track.

Randy shook his head. "That's only gonna start more trouble than it solves."

"What do you mean?" asked Alex.

Randy answered without looking up from the paper. "Trying to be cooler than you actually are. People are gonna see you idiots struttin' around in 'em—like you're an actual strike force or something — they're gonna want a piece of you."

"Bullshit, you don't know everything, Randy."

"I do know you're making a mistake."

"Thanks for the warning, I gotta go." Raising his voice— "I'll be right there, guys!"

George lifted a hand. *Okay.* Then called out from the passenger seat— "Hey, Randy."

John and Steve echoing the greeting, too.

"Steve, John, George," Randy answered back, monotone. "Starting this crap all over again, huh?"

"Yep," said George.

"Hope it works out for ya," he said to the three, then, to Alex, "Were you just eating again in there?"

"Yeah, so what?" said Alex. "It was a sandwich."

"You're gonna be eating unhealthy concession food all night."

"It's not 'unhealthy,' it's delicious food. Emilio is an awesome cook."

"When are you gonna start contributing to the groceries around here? Mom is strapped."

"I will. Whattya think I'm going to work for?"

"Towing makes a lot more money."

"Have a good night, Randy, I'm booking."

Alex jogged down the driveway. George opened the front door for him, revealing the packed car all decked out in their new uniforms. Alex leaned forward to let him crawl in the back with John.

"Hope your parents like you guys coming home in body bags," Randy called out.

Alex had his head popped out, let loose an angry one— "Up yours, Randy."

Randy got up, set the newspaper down, took steps like he was going to saunter down the driveway.

"Gun it!" Alex instructed Steve.

Steve hit the gas, remembering that he needed to pull a U-ey to escape Alex's dead-end street, and accidentally went up-and-over the boulevard on the lawn of the elderly couple who lived across the street.

"And turn down the music!" Randy yelled after them. "Idiots," he muttered once they were out of his line of vision. In the clearing, the elderly neighbor swept off his front porch and stared.

"Sorry," Randy said. "They're going to work at The Winking Moon. First night back."

"They have my sympathies," the old man retorted.

Before heading down rural Sing Road, they stopped first at the infamous intersection a mile from the drive-in. They stepped out to pose in front of the massive, electronic Winking Moon marquee with the Man-in-the-Moon emblem smiling down on traffic. The two current movies, "The Brood" and "Toolbox Murders"—both rated "R"—were sure to be hits.

The goofballs pulled along the shoulder and began taking snapshots with a Kodamatic Camera. They bared their huge grins and flexed their muscles for posterity. Passing vehicles honked at the attention, while Alex described the details of the first film. "'The Brood,'" he said, "is

Canadian filmmaker's follow-up to his horror hit, 'Rabid,' starring Marilyn Chambers."

Steve, John and George were remotely interested.

"The porn chick?" Steve asked.

"It wasn't porn," Alex corrected. "But yeah—her."

"Was it any good?" asked John.

"It was sick, it was twisted, it was disturbing. I loved it." Alex said with excitement.

"You and your horror films," George said as they filed back toward the car

Alex said, "Can't wait to see the ones playing this summer. All for free. Maybe we'll get 'Dawn of the Dead' again."

"I hope not," Steve said, pausing before getting behind the wheel. "How many fucking times have you seen that?"

"Just twice," Alex answered. "At the regular show. Maybe we'll get it at The Moon."

"God help us if we do."

"Steve!" A girl's voice shouted from across the street. The Crusaders looked over.

"Jody!" Steve had looked up, saw his girlfriend racing towards him, happily.

Jody McBrennan had come bounding from her part-time job as store clerk at The Lapping Waves convenience mart, across the road at the strip mall, her work apron flapping with her chaotic arm movements. Jody was 16 years old, a pretty girl with long, curly blonde hair and long eyelashes jutting from her face like a doll.

A car honked its horn and came to an abrupt, screeching stop as Jody jutted out in front of it. Jody threw it the finger, half-jesting, and kept right on going, straight into Steve Laneske's arms. She locked him up in an embrace, kissing him passionately. When they separated, he was half-exasperated. "Honey, what are you doing? You almost got hit."

"Screw them," she responded with complete disregard. "I wanted to see you before you headed to the Winking Moon. How you boys doing tonight?"

Alex, John and George were all amazed. Jody and Steve had such passion. They waved. "Good, Jody," said Alex. "What's new?"

"Another summer," she replied, throwing her arms out. She still had that big smile on her face. "You dickwads better make the most of it. Unlike you, I worked here all winter. You're just starting now when the weather got nice."

"The weather's not that nice," said Steve.

She pointed animatedly at each of them — "And you're back for more fights and chaos."

"Hopefully not that," said John.

"Oh, there'll be a lot of that, John, just you wait," she said. "Fuckin'-A there'll be a lot of that, and I for one am looking forward to it. I hope you kids kick major asses this year. *I* hope to kick major asses." She began shadowboxing. Steve tried to stop her.

"That's not what our boxing lessons have been for," he said, trying to get her hands down.

"Oh yeah, that's right, I forgot," she said, stopping. "This is what the boxing lessons have been for—" Boom! She sucker-punched him right in the gut, doubling him over. Steve made a loud and funny "Oof!," and John, Alex and George continued to be in shock.

"Jody!" George said.

She apologized. She did not mean any harm, though was proud of her fighting prowess. She backed off, snorting. "That's for not picking me up yesterday when you went to get your uniforms after school, Steve."

Steve was wheezing. "We were in a hurry."

"Well you better be in a hurry to show your girlfriend a little more appreciation."

"Jody, want to get a picture with us?" John asked, holding up the camera.

"Sure!" They did. Jody posed with both biceps flexed in front of the sign.

"What do you think of our new smocks?" Alex said, spreading arms wide so she could get a good look.

"I'd say you look gay but you already know that," she said. "Just kidding, Alex. They're cool. Outta the Stuckersons own pocket again?"

"We don't talk about that."

"What we will talk about is you guys being right down the street from me again. You can pick me every night after work. We can go out partying."

"Yeah," said Steve, finally getting his breath back. "Every night."

That made her exuberant. She launched at him again. They made out again, fiercely, tongues going right down each other's throats, cars beeping at the site of them. Alex, John and George laughed. At the strip mall, customers were pulling in the lot to get their fill of snacks and alcohol. Jody's boss, Mr. Smith—a portly, mean, short, pester of a man—came stomping out of the store, glaring at Jody from his fixed vantage point. "Jody!" he shouted. "Get back in here! You can't just run off leaving the register un-manned."

"Un-*womaned*,' Mr. Smith!" she shouted back. "I'm a *woman*, not a man."

"Get back here!" he demanded. This time he addressed the Crusaders, sarcastically. "Steve, John, Alex, George. How wonderful to see you four again, I see the peanut gallery's back. You starting tonight?"

"We are starting tonight, Mr. Smith. We'll be here all summer,"

Steve spat back in response.

The shop owner looked peeved. "Great, I can't… wait. Just don't you be bugging my Jody like you did last year."

"Correction!" said Steve. "I think she's 'my' Jody, sir."

"Whatever! Get back to work, all of yas. And Jody—get back in here."

Steve looked her in the eyes. "Go."

"For you," she said, starting to break away. "Remember: kick lots of asses this summer. No mercy. Kick 'em in the nuts if ya have to. Love you!"

"Love you, too," Steve said back.

Jody said goodbye to the Crusaders and darted-off back across the street, causing another truck to lock up its brakes. "Sorry!" she said after it laid on the horn, then thought again. "On second thought, no—I'm not sorry. Here." She flipped the driver off, then ran all the way in. When she got there, Mr. Smith continued to glare at the Crusaders for a moment more before going in.

When he was gone, Steve had to express his disdain "I never like that guy," he muttered. "I don't trust him. I think he has a thing for Jody."

"That's sick," said George. "He must be Stuckerson's age."

"Still," said Steve. "Measly-mouthed Melvin. I'll kick his ass. He ain't nothing like Mr. Stuckerson."

"He does look like a Melvin," said John.

"He does," said Alex. "Textbook."

"Let's go," said Steve, and they all hopped in and took off eastward.

"Hey Steve, you changing the marquee every Friday night again?" Alex asked.

"Yup," he answered. "Worked it out when Mr. and Mrs. Stuckerson called a few weeks ago. I'm good at it. It's a nice little breakaway from all the craziness. And I get to see Jody. I'll be doing it tonight, as a matter-of-fact."

Alex asked, "How come you're the only one who gets to change the titles?"

"I'm the only one who can spell, dummies," Steve joked.

The Crusaders pulled into the entrance where an already-packed line of vehicles was tooting their horns, cranking music, and yelling for the box office to open—the joint was as rowdy as ever.

"Some things never change," Steve gleamed.

"Go past everyone," George instructed, pointing to the side. "Go along the shoulder, park up there near where Kathy's car is." Way up, they could see the raven-haired beauty in the box office window. "There she is fellas: The Goddess of Galileo. In person and in the flesh."

"George," Alex said, "I don't know if she wants to be called that."

The big kid turned around. "Listen to you, defending her honor already. Nothing's even happened yet. Relax, killer, you'll get your chance."

Steve motored past the customers, met with curiosity and ridicule from the rest of the anxious patrons. "Hey, whattya think you're doing?" said one Chevelle.

"You better not be cuttin' in line!" came a line from a hearse. Yes, a hearse.

George pulled himself out the window, holding on to the roof of the car, and put his smock on full display. "We work here! See our uniforms?"

"Big deal!" somebody else shouted.

Kathy Berenger was prepping for the night in the tiny ticket booth. When Steve pulled up next to the booth, Kathy's black Malibu Classic in the grass next to them, she looked up, hesitating a moment, then exploded with recognition and happiness. "Oh my God, it's the Winking Moon Crusaders! Get out of that car and give me hugs!"

She scrambled out of the booth as Steve, George and John smiled. Alex just stared, pining away in the backseat. She was so tremendous to look at in-person, decked in her new Moon-smock, curves showing through and under it, that he was speechless. Steve put the ignition in park and all four Crusaders jumped out. Kathy was as ebullient as ever, squealing in joy, hugging and cheek-kissing every one of them with delight. Alex remained in the background, left breathless when she let go of him.

"How have you been?!" She asked.

"We've been great. Did ya know we're officially seniors now?" remarked George, proudly.

"Been there, done that, I know the feeling," Kathy said. "It's great, isn't it? Congratulations! Oh, I'm so glad you boys are back this summer. I wasn't sure you'd get the chance to return. Mrs. Stuckerson said your mothers weren't exactly thrilled with the idea when she spoke to them a month ago."

"Well, here we are," said Steve. "And ready for round two."

She gave them the once-over. "Oh my God and look at those uniforms. So handsome. All of you."

Steve laughed. "You, too. *Beautiful*, that is, not handsome. You look great. How long you been wearing that now?"

"Since the start of the season," Kathy answered. "I've been here since day one. Gosh, where do we start with all the catching up?"

"We got all summer, Berenger," George. "But we see the bosses still have ya painting."

Inside the booth, there was a relatively small, tabletop easel, canvas on top of that, rags, linseed oil and turpentine, a palette with oil paints on it, brushes, and a transistor radio, "K.C. and The Sunshine Band" playing softly from the speakers.

"Yeah, they're letting me do it again," she said. "Just as long as I get my work done. I'm working on my portfolio for a major art school. Don't know which one yet but I've been looking. Might be trying to get into a fancy one. Community college is great, but I got my sights set on bigger things.'"

"Wow let's see what you're doing, Kathy," said John, stepping closer.

She showed them. Turned the easel, got out of their way so they could see. It was an open field, at sunset. Photographs she had taken as reference were taped up along the far window. They all agreed: the painting was grand. "Marvelous," said John. "Should be hanging in the Memorial Art Gallery."

"Thank you, you're too kind," she said.

"You've improved since last year," said George.

"Yeah, and you were great last year," said Steve.

"Makes me think of the beauty of a soul. You have the soul of Picasso… or Michelangelo," Alex said, breaking the silence.

Kathy looked at him with admiration and surprise. She smiled and thanked him, then got distracted by another angry customer— "It's fucking seven o'clock already! Open the goddam box office."

"Hey! Who the hell said that? Who's the foul-mouthed nincompoop who's disrespecting my workers?" Here came Lee-Willie, out of the manager's office door, flushed in the face, glasses bouncing off the bridge of his nose, ready to kick some ass. "Who said it? Who's swearing out here?"

The patron who said it clammed up, but the next car behind him spoke up instead. "Mister, it's seven o'clock, time to open. We wanna get in so we can get a good spot."

Lee-Willie checked his watch, confirmed it was time, turned to Kathy and the Crusaders. "He's right, it's seven o'clock. Why the hell you kids standing around doing nothing when you should be opening? Kathy, get in the booth. John, George, Steve, Alex, get your asses in gear. I don't pay you to stand around and chit-chat. You've said your 'helloes,' now get in the concession stand, clock-in and get out in the field and patrol. You are *patrol*-men, right? Get moving!"

"Yes, sir!" They all said and jumped back in the Charger.

"See you later, Kathy," said Steve, turning the engine back on, making sure he could get around her Malibu.

"See you," she said. "Glad you're back."

"Yee-haw!" Steve stepped on it, kicking up dust and turning up the music (Van Halen's *11* album). He went around the bend of the south end of the drive-in, entering the lot, blowing dust and gravel all over the place. There was no one inside yet, save their coworkers, whose rides were stationed on both the north and the south sides of the concession stand, smack dab in the middle.

The noise and mayhem drew the players out. Emilio Varentez, the Winking Moon cook, a thin twenty-four-year old man, though looking more like a teenager himself, came out of the double-doors first. His black ponytail was tied behind his head, one of the newfangled hairnets holding it in place. Next came big Jim Barenta, out of his projection booth, located in the front section of the stand, and saddled up to Emilio. They both watched with amusement. Jim raised his mug of carbonated water to his lips, remembering his days of clowning around with friends, afros gently blowing in the light breeze. Vicki Richards, who had already arrived earlier, shook her head and wiped her hands as she walked out of the concession stand. And finally, seventy-something year-old Stanley Mason, oddball extraordinaire, followed last, fishing cap and new smock marred by just about every UFO and science fiction button around. "Just park, ya good-for-nothing dumb-asses," he shouted. "Stop screwing around and get in here. I see you, you teenage prickheads."

"Stanley!" Vicki was always amazed at the man's language.

Steve sped toward the stand, slammed on the brakes and skidded to a halt not far from them, expertly sliding into his parking space behind Jim's 1970 4x4 Chevy Fleetside light-blue pickup, Emilio's 1976 Volkswagen Kombi and Stanley's 1972 Nissan Skyline, sending a wave of pebbles all over the side of the building, peppering off like gunpowder caps. When the Crusaders hopped out, they all high-fived each other and did a round of chest bumps, Jim took another sip of from his mug, lowering it with purpose. "Good thing nothing hit my truck. I'd be burying all of you six-feet under before the season even started."

"Jim!" they shouted, mobbing him with handshakes and hugs, slapping him on the shoulder, unable to contain their excitement. Jim was equally heartened to see them but kept that a secret to prevent their egos from ballooning.

Emilio stepped up and greeted everybody with smiles and well-wishes. "So glad you guys are back, we need you, like yesterday," he said.

"Hey, Emilio, how ya doing?" Steve said. "How's your massive family?"

"They're doing good, they're doing good," he replied.

George was all over him. "Gonna give us some of that world-famous Emilio Varentez pizza this year?"

"You're going to have to buy it like everyone else," was the answer. "There's a cost for gold."

George laughed. "Same old cocky Emilio."

John nudged him. "You said 'cocky.'"

Alex saw their female counterpart standing in the doorway, judging. "Hey, Vick, got here before us, huh?"

"I wouldn't wait for you guys," she said. "You're boofing the pooch all the time. You're not making me look bad."

Alex turned to his friends, laughing. "She said 'boofing the pooch.' Ha! Love it. You know what that means, don't ya, Vick?"

"Yeah," she said. "It means 'wasting time' but it sounds a whole lot worse."

"You got it, Vicki. Look at you in that smock."

They went to start at her. She held them back. "Mess it up and I'm hurting ya."

"And look at this—" continued George. By this point, the boys had all noticed the crotchety little man with the attitude glowering at them from the edge. "Stanley Mason: the one and only. Same old, miserable curmudgeon. How's it going, old man? Still miserable as always?"

Stanley gave the salty retort they all expected. "Still stupid as ever, Jocavelli? I see you kids have grown, physically, but you're all still dumb as shit in the head."

"Ha-ha-ha!" The boys erupted in laughter. They loved the son-of-a-bitch. They swarmed him, too, embracing him, knocking his fishing cap off, playing with the UFO buttons. He grabbed his cap back, warned them not to fuck with him for fear he'd gut them. "Just like we did fish in the Navy," Stanley said. "We were out at sea a long time. We learned how to do terrible things to watery organisms."

He put everything back on. The four could not resist giving him a few shots for old times' sake.

"Still thinking your flying saucer is gonna come and invite you aboard this summer, Stanley?" George howled. "Take you on that joyride through the universe?"

Steve said, "Yeah, we waited all summer last year for that to happen and it never did. You bummed us out, Stanley, we wanted to see you go."

More laughter. Stanley just grumbled, dismissed the whole lot. "Just you see," he said. "They're better than all of us, better than anybody here on this stinking planet, I'll tell ya that much. They're more evolved. Being out here at night gives me a better chance of gettin' noticed. And when I do, I'll be gone, ya shit-for-brains. I'll leave all my troubles and strife behind. None of ya will be laughing then."

"We won't hold our breath, Stanley," said John. "We won't hold our breath."

During all this, Mr. and Mrs. Stuckerson had been drawing nearer across the open lot and humps. "What the hell is this, a family reunion?" Lee-Willie growled before even getting here, his wife in tow, being subservient, jowls bouncing.

"Kind of," said George as they pulled up to a halt.

"I told you idiots to get moving," he told the patrolmen. "Clock-in and get to work, I don't wanna have to tell you again. The first cars are coming in."

And they were. There started the steady flow of customer-traffic, spreading out to reserve their coveted parking spaces.

When George was the last one to move, hesitating to try snatching Stanley's fishing cap off again, Lee-Willie tried kicking him in the seat of the pants. He missed, and his wife reached over, stopping him. *Do not do that.* The Crusaders pretended to all get shmushed-up, caught, in the double-doors, like the Three Stooges.

"Remind me again why I re-hired them?" Lee-Willie asked his wife.

"Because you couldn't find any other hapless chumps to take the job," Jim interjected over his shoulder as he walked back to the projection booth.

Alex didn't get to see much of "The Brood." The first movie had the Crusaders busy from the jump, watching for jamokes sneaking friends into the drive-in in the backs of cars or in their trunks. This happened all the time. The crowd was still rolling in strong, all through the first feature. Plenty of spots remained. Alex and Steve took the back of the lot while George and John took the front. They'd ventured out to kick off the gig, meeting-and-greeting people, asking how they were doing, if they needed anything from the concession stand, assuring folks that anything they could do to make their evening better, they shouldn't hesitate to ask.

"Good," said one long-bearded man in a '57 Nash Cosmopolitan, "you could start by not bugging us like you are now during the movies."

"Man, that guy was rude," John said to George after they had walked away.

George said, "People are getting coarser. They just wanna do what they wanna do."

Alex and Steve came across their first target in the back of the lot—right side, facing the screen. A lone driver had entered in an AMC Matador Barcelona—a lone driver at the theater always looked suspicious. "Remember how to do this?" Alex whispered to Steve as they stayed twenty yards back, in the dark.

"How could I forget?" Steve answered. "Stand back, let 'em settle so they think they're safe. Let 'em get out to open the trunk. We'll bust 'em in the act and show no mercy. I think we got one already."

And they did. The two waited. The man in his twenties got out, looked about again, swung around to the back of the car, keys still in his hands. Steve and Alex could hear the giggling in the trunk. A few thumps, signaling that whoever was in there wanted to be let out.

Adrenaline began to flow. "Get ready," Alex said.

When the man opened the trunk, three 20-something-year-olds got out, laughing and snorting, trying to be quiet. All four shook hands then a contraband cooler came out filled with illegal alcohol. The stowaways began distributing them to one another, popping them open and settling in. Alex and Steve pounced, Alex with an— "Excuse me, can we see all of your ticket stubs?"— shining his flashlight directly into the vehicle.

"Jesus!" the one exclaimed.

"What the hell?" gasped another.

"Who *are* you guys?" the driver demanded.

"We work here," said Steve, still holding the light to their eyes. "We make sure no one sneaks in."

The driver scoffed. "What are you, the drive-in police?"

"Something like it," said Alex. "Now show us your ticket receipts. We need proof that all of you paid to get in."

"Man…" They were busted and they knew it.

"We saw the whole thing," Steve said, coolly. "Think we haven't seen this a thousand times? Hiding in a trunk? We're professionals. Now were gonna march you right out to the box office, where you'll either pay the nice lady for the three of you who didn't come in legally, or we'll throw you out. Those are the terms."

"What'll it be?" said Alex.

The four thought for a moment. "Holy fuck," said the driver. "This place is hardcore. We'll pay, let's go. Shit."

Alex and Steve escorted the young men all the way to the box office, where they introduced the "crooks" to Kathy and made them fork over the dough for legitimate tickets. "You should know better than to try to sneak into The Winking Moon," she said to them, putting the bills in the till and ripping off the tickers. "Good job, boys."

The beauty had been taking a break from her painting. She had been reading People magazine with a story about Charlie's Angels. She wanted hair tips. The boys marched the four straight back to their car, where they made them get in and sit quietly. "Make another disturbance," Alex warned, "and we'll kick you out for good. We take no prisoners here."

"Holy shit, this place is serious," moaned one of them. "And this is a drive-in?"

"Not just a drive-in," said Steve. "The Winking *Moon* drive-in. Don't you forget it."

"We're back," said Alex.

"Who's back?" the driver asked, confused.

Steve and Alex did not answer. They haughtily walked away.

John and George were next. They had been watching a suspicious character in a Plymouth Barracuda, up by the front row, direct center. He had come in and parked but wasn't moving. They got a good perspective, used the light from the movie to see the solo silhouette inside, watched the guy looking around, acting peculiar. They crept closer, heard muffled voices snickering in the trunk. "Let us out, Larry, we can't breathe in here."

The driver finally ventured out, unlocked the trunk. George and John moved closer, ready to go to town, their adrenaline drumming. They were set to move in when a voice called out from the left of them, blowing their cover— "What the hell are you two doing?"

The Barracuda owner turned and saw the patrolmen.

"Shit!" and both stowaways were out of the trunk, the three men running in separate directions.

"Damn it," George said, not even running after them. George got on the walkie-talkie— "Alex, Steve, if you see three idiots running your way, two of them escaped from a trunk. We'd been made."

"There's a lot of people out and about," argued Alex.

"I'm just saying. We lost 'em, it's too dark. We can always wait here and wait for 'em to return."

"Do that then," said Alex. "We gotta make our presence known right away."

And so, George and John waited. A half hour went by. It was getting close to intermission. Steve and Alex came around, found them, asked if anybody from the vehicle had come back yet.

"Not yet, but when they do, we'll be ready for 'em," said John.

"It's almost intermission already," said Alex. "we gotta go in and serve food."

"I know," said George.

"Hey you guys." Steve, Alex, John and George jumped. A patron walked up from out of the dark. The boys eyed him. He was an older man and he was standing so close that you could see the movie reflecting off his glasses.

"Yes, sir?" asked George.

"You're bouncers, right?" the guy asked. "I saw you in the daylight."

"Technically, we're 'patrol-men,'" said John. "How can we help you?"

"There's a couple having loud sex in the car in front of us. They're so loud we can't concentrate on the movie. It's really distracting. I'm betting that we're the only ones who have the balls to say something about it."

This perked the Crusaders up. They forgot about everything else. "Loud sex?" George cried out. "Where is it?"

All four followed the man, eager to investigate. He pointed to a few rows back, a Mercury Comet parked in a side lane. The Crusaders could both see and hear them as they approached the car. A naked man and woman, entangled in the backseat were going at it heavily, moaning, and groaning, having a grand old time, not giving a fanny's hoot who could see or who was listening. The Crusaders could see buttocks going up and down. The man who had alerted them shrugged his shoulders. "See?" he said. "You try watching a movie with that."

"We'll take care of it," said Alex.

The Crusaders busted out in quiet hysterics. *They would take care of it, all right.* They first wanted to catch a little sneak preview. Keeping a car-length away, they observed, covering their mouths, trying not to make too much noise. Patrons around them were getting pissed. They had to draw straws. Who was going to do the knocking? They used blades of grass as makeshift straws and John drew the unlucky winner.

With the gruesome horrors going on on-screen, the reserved buddy crept up to the car and tapped on the window with his flashlight. The young man, on top, paused and whipped his head around— "Who are you? What're you doing, man?"

"Some people complained," John responded calmly and professionally. "I have to ask you to calm down a little and not make so much noise."

"Are you fucking serious?"
"Yes."

"Who are you?"

"I work here. This is what we do."

"Interrupt people bouncing the Brillo? Who complained?"

"Never mind. Can you just do it? I'm being polite."

"We're having a good time here, man, I don't like being interrupted."

"We're trying to be respectful. If I have to call people, I'll call people."

"What the hell?" The man rolled up the windows, threw the finger, got a little quieter but went right back to business.

John walked away, the guys rolling, holding their sides. "He's quieter, at least."

"Not as quiet as you," George giggled. "Did that make you think of Vicki? When you gonna ask her out?"

"Don't start that shit again, George."

"She's only had a crush on you since third grade."

"Can we just do our jobs? Where's that guy?" John spotted the man awaiting the information. He threw him the thumbs-up. "Mister, we solved your problem."

The guy poked his head out the driver's side window. "Thank God. My wife said she was getting a boner. And she's a woman."

The Crusaders snickered even harder. Time to move on. "Let's visit Jim before intermission. We got about five minutes; I think."

The four moseyed-up to the projection booth, located at the front section of the stand. The whole building resembled one big flat bunker, about eight feet in height on all four sides. Jim's door was open. He did this on nice nights. They could see him working in there on something. He looked peaceful and calm, had precision tools in his fingers. Smoking a cigarette, sitting on a decrepit sofa in the middle of the cave-dark room, editing bench and splicer, cabinet of lenses and other projection-gear behind him, last reel in the current projector chugging away behind him, throwing the film out the projection-window onto the screen. The room was extremely dark, save the lamp that hung over his head. They had to knock loudly as the sound of the projector kept him distracted. When he waved them in, they asked if it was okay enter.

"Like last year, it's okay when you're invited," he replied. "And you're invited. For now. Don't touch anything, union rules."

"Intermission's about to start and we have to go in," said Steve. "We just decided to swing past, say 'hi' again, let you know we're totally psyched to be working here another summer."

"As you should be," Jim said. "You'll remember these days for the rest of your lives."

"What are you working on?" asked Alex.

"Model airplane. Revell. Second World War Spitfire."

"Wow," said John.

"You know we're gonna be busy as fuck this year. We've already had a few from the Rogue Gallery turn up. The Wild Man of Borneo made his appearance the other week."

"Really?" said Steve. "Did you take care of it?"

"Nope, he went away by himself. He'll be back though. Maybe you guys will handle it."

"We expect the full roster of rogues and rapscallions again this year," said George.

"How did you guys define it? Who's inside, and who's outside?"

Alex explained for Jim. "Punks and hooligans are the kids that sneak in from the outside. The yahoos and the rowdies are the ones already in, paying patrons, the ones deciding to act up once they're here."

"And how do you decide which ones to toss?"

"When we feel like it," said Steve.

"When they're rude," said Alex.

"Shit!" said John, abruptly. "That Barracuda with the kids who ran away. We gotta check on 'em before intermission. Jim, we gotta go."

"Go do your thing."

As the four prepared to leave, George asked, "Still hosting Sunday night after-hours parties this year?"

"Yes, and you'll get an invite if you behave," answered Jim, never breaking from his model.

"How's Jeannie?" Steve asked. "You still together? You're a lot older, right?"

"Don't you know better than to ask? Or would you like your teeth knocked out?"

They all laughed. Steve said, "You're the best, man, tell her we said 'hello.'"

When they got there, the Barracuda was gone. It was an empty spot. The fiends had either relocated or left. They ran to Kathy as the closing titles were rolling, asking if she saw them.

"They left," she said. "They drove out. Threw us the finger as they did."

The Moon Tower in the very back of the lot came on it was. It was a massive light-tower on the grounds that stood a hundred-feet high and illuminated the entire area like a baseball stadium. Patrons began getting out of their vehicles, stretching arms, legs, lighting up cigarettes, finishing their beers, slapping girlfriends' butts, and hitting the concessions.

By the time the Crusaders made it inside the concession stand, adjusting to the bright lights from their night vision, things were hopping. Both sets of double-doors—north and south side of the building—were crammed with people coming in and out. Lines were forming outside the ladies and men's rooms, also on opposite sides of the building. An automated announcement was playing over the P.A. system, a scratchy voice-over encouraged guests to snack-up, drink-up, relax and stretch. Lee-Willie hollered at the boys for being late, glaring at them over the counter while performing food service duties.

"We were keeping the peace, sir," answered Alex. "You'd be damn proud of us."

Gail-Lill, beside her husband, digging in the candy counter for sweet tooth treats, told her husband to calm down and concentrate on the tasks at hand. "You can't be hounding them, already, dear," she said. "Not on their first night back. Let them get broken in first."

"I'll break 'em in," he muttered. "I'll break 'em in like the mindless puppies they are."

"Lee…"

Patrons were filing up and back along the safety railings under the menu, forming the lines for hot food. There was quite a selection to choose from: hamburgers, hotdogs, pizza, you name it. Alex, John, George and Steve were set to work those stations and were instructed to grab their hairnets. Alex grabbed a handful, handed them out. A couple of friends from high school saw them, laughed, told the Crusaders they looked gay. George jokingly asked, "How gay will my fists look upside your jaws?"

They looked over at Emilio who wore a nice crocheted hairnet.

"How'd you pull that off, Emilio?" Steve asked. "We'd like ones like that."

"Sorry, amigo," Emilio replied. "My wife knitted it for me. I knew this trend was coming."

"Kiss ass," Steve grumbled.

One side of the stand had a pinball and video-kiosk arcade. *Star Trek* was the pinball, *Asteroids* and *Galaxian* were the video games. Not much, but enough to cause a racket. One moron was already pretending to hump the pinball machine. Stanley, manning the only register open, yelled at him to cut it out. The kid backtalked, saying, "Hey, ya got Lieutenant Uhuru on the back glass in a skirt, how could I *not* bang this thing?"

"Do it again and you're out," said the old man.

Business was booming. Emilio was trying to keep up the orders on his handmade pizza, throwing one pie into the double-ovens as fast as he could, tossing dough into the air the next, John fetch ingredients and supplies from the freezer as needed. Vicki was at the front, greeting customers and taking orders. Alex, Steve and George cooked and heated everything else on the grills. There was a deep fryer for the fries and an old-fashioned popcorn maker that very well may have dated back to the early 1900s, popping the popcorn. This machine was Lee-Willie Stuckerson's pride-and-joy. "You like it?" he asked a customer, querying about it. "I bought it at a flea market in Pennsylvania over the winter. Thought it looked nicer than the standard one that I still got in the back."

"Just as long as it pops quickly and gets me back out to my movie," the man said. "'The Toolbox Murders' sounds like my cup of tea."

"Oh, you kill people with power tools?" Vicki remarked.

"Just stick to your business, Miss Richards," said Lee-Willie.

The soundtracks from the trailers pounded on the four sides of the room, intercut with more commercials. The amiable voice-over continued to encourage patrons. "Only ten minutes before showtime, still plenty of time to visit our concession stand."

The speakers attracted the attention of one drunkard. He asked Steve, "That thing play the whole time in here?"

"Yep," said Steve.

"Like when there's a horror film, can you hear the screaming and killing the entire time you're working in here?"

"That's right. Although they turn it down during showtime. It's all controlled in the projection booth."

The guy belched, then laughed. "Shit, I'd be messing with people. I'd wait 'till they had drinks in their hands, then I'd scare the shit outta them, turning it up. Whoever's working it must be having the time of their lives."

"But I'm respectful," said Jim, walking in behind the customer, surprising everyone again with his stealth. "You wouldn't do something like that, would you?"

"Who are *you*?"

"I'm the projectionist.

Just looking at Jim's face said it all. "No, man, I wouldn't do that. I was only kidding."

"Of course, you were."

Since John was just returning from the back room, Steve asked, "Hey John, there still those cans of "of *Off* mosquito repellent back there?"

Before the kid could answer, Lee-Willie did it for him. "Don't any of you start spraying that stuff. There's no mosquitoes out yet."

George found this amusing. "I wanna blast a cloud of it. You used to love when we did that last year, didn't ya, Mr. Stuckerson?"

"Oh yeah, loved it, Jocavelli," the manager answered. "Do it around here and you die."

Alex said, "Anybody check on Kathy yet, see if she needs a break? If she's hungry or she's thirsty? Do we need to bring her anything?"

"No, she's alright through the first intermission," Lee-Willie responded, then brought the walkie to his lips, pressed the button. "Kathy? You okay? You need anything?"

"No, I'm okay, Mr. Stuckerson," returned her voice. "I'll last a little longer but then I'll need to go to the ladies' room."

"I'll escort her," volunteered Alex.

The Stuckersons looked at Alex. *Really?* Crusaders looked at him. *You sly dog.* Vicki eyeballed him, smirking and winking. "Way to step up, Alex," she said. "You get an A-plus."

But Lee-Willie once more stepped in. "You'll do nothing of the sort. In a couple minutes, you dunderheads get back out there. We'll take care of Kathy."

"Yes, sir," the Crusaders all said in unison.

Stanley had to end a thirteen-year old's fun by the plastic utensil island. He'd stuffed his nose and ears with disposal paper napkins as a gag for his friend. "Waste any more napkins, kid," he cautioned, "and I'll shove 'em in areas on you ya can't even pronounce."

Alex could not believe what he was seeing on the screen. He had loved plenty of horror films in the past, but the "Toolbox Murders" was taking the cake. As he stood alone in the back of the lot, the massive Moon Tower looming over his head, eyes fully adjusted back to night vision again, keeping a sharp ear out for any noises around him, he watched the movie in fascination. The superintendent in the film was actually a sadistic killer. He had just broken into a beautiful woman's apartment—she was in the bathtub, naked, of course—and slayed her with a long power drill. Put it right through her, so far, in fact, the drill bit went straight through the floor below and out from the downstairs' neighbor's ceiling, blood flowing down that hole. Thank goodness most of the gore was not actually shown. Alex could not believe it, wondered how the studios got away with these things. He checked-in with his mates over the walkie, asking how they were doing.

"Nothing's going on over here," George replied. "I'm at the southeast corner, by the apple orchard. So far all's quiet."

"I'm by the brush," Steve said. "Nothing here either. I can hear the music coming from the Roller Rink, but no signs of trouble yet. Hope it stays that way."

"I'm in the playground," answered John. "Some jamokes decided to play on the equipment during the movie. Had to kick 'em out."

Alex said, "Do ya think they'll turn into yahoos or rowdies?"

"I don't think so," John reported. "They were pretty cooperative, I just had to tell 'em about the rules."

"Good," said Alex. "We'll stay apart for a while, meet in fifteen minutes, behind the concession stand." They all agreed. "In the meantime," he said aloud, to himself, "Better go and visit Kathy, ya rummy."

Alex made his way through the hefty audience, cutting through the vehicles, hearing the murmuring of all the speakers attached to the windows, playing the soundtrack. In some cars, he could hear laughing. In others, kissing. Some had aluminum cans being popped open. He rounded the bend of the exit and came upon the sight of Kathy again, looking incredible. He took a mental photograph for posterity, then took a moment and built up his courage.

"Hey Kathy," he said as he approached, careful not to startle her.

She turned and looked. "Hi Alex," she said, and put her brush down.

There was a tiny smear of paint against her cheek. Green. He wanted to wipe it off. Kiss it off. "Did you get your break?" he asked.

She turned her music down from the transistor. *How Long*, by Ace. "Yep, Mrs. Stuckerson came up and relieved me. I'll be good for the rest of this film. We're playing the first one over, you know."

Alex felt his heart pounding through his chest. "I remember how we did things."

"Can't pull one over on you," she said. "So, how are you?"

He walked around so he had a better angle on her. "I'm doing, okay," he said. "How are you?"

"Great. Still living at home with Mom and Dad, made it through my first year of community college. Like I said, I'm trying to get a scholarship." Her voice was like music to his ears.

"Thinking of going away for art school?" he asked.

"Maybe, if something pans out. I'm going to double-major art with psychology."

"You can't… find anything around here?"

"I could," she answered. "But… maybe I should go somewhere else."

"Oh." He was thrown. Had no right to be surprised, but he was. "I'm going to be sticking around here for a while."

"I know," Kathy said. "You still have another year of high school."

"Can I see what you're working on?"

"Sure."

It was that open field landscape again. It really was spectacular. The odors of her paints mixed in with the light perfume she was wearing nearly intoxicated him right there on the spot. He was completely smitten. "Still using oils?" he said, looking around at her set-up. "I can smell the linseed oil."

She smiled. "You remember. You get an A-plus."

"I don't forget you… Kathy." Then, quickly, "Er—I mean your

artwork. I don't forget your artwork." He scrambled. "Wanna hear about the movie? This 'Toolbox Murders' is really gruesome."

"No, I don't want to hear about it," she scowled. "Are you kidding? I'm out here, on the other side of the screen—alone. Do you think I want to hear about somebody getting murdered in all sorts of awful ways?"

"Do you want to hear about 'The Brood'? It's David Cronenberg's follow-up to 'Rabid,' about a virus that turns people into psychopaths. 'The Brood' is about killer children who get born out of an evil woman with an egg sac on the outside of her body."

Her face was contorted. "Alex! You're joking, right? I don't want to hear about that, I have a hard enough time just hearing the soundtrack sometimes."

"Why do you keep coming back here then?"

She drew in a breath and blew it out, brushing the long hair out of her eyes and mixing the paints with a palette knife. "The peace of the night. It's spiritual. Plus, it's fun working with you guys. I was looking forward to seeing you jokesters again. Especially you, Alex."

He felt his heart stop. "Uh…" was all he managed as she stared at him. His walkie-talkie squeaked, saving him from complete embarrassment.

"Alex, you better come back here." It was Steve. "I think we got something."

Alex met John, George and Steve along the back fence in the northeast corner. It was quiet, cool, and very dark here. The grass was tall and moist, in need of a mowing. Densely packed woods were beyond them, leading about a hundred yards to something that looked like a large medical facility, a five-story high-rise jutting over the trees. Alex kept his voice low. There were cars that had parked all the way back here. "What's up?" he asked.

Steve pointed to the top portion of the fence. "We saw one, two minutes ago. A hooligan, a punk, right here. Popped his head up, disappeared. Think he was gettin' ready to hop over when he saw us coming."

John had more to add. "And where there's one hooligan or punk, there're more."

Alex agreed, considering the situation. He jumped up looking at the facility through the trees and jumped back down. "In Edgewater's property, huh? Little bastards just can't stick to the brush? Gotta invade the old folks' territory, use their land to sneak into our drive-in? Not on our watch. This is what we gotta get ahead of this year, gents, we had too many last year. You sure they're not still there now?"

"We hopped up like you just did," said George. "Shined our flashlights. Didn't see anybody."

"Well, we know Roller Rink is loaded with 'em right now," Alex said. "That joint's in full-operation for about another half hour.

Somebody camp-out here, make sure they don't return. If they do, scare the hell out of 'em. How old was the little shit?"

"From what we could see—" said Steve, "same as all the hooligans and punks: about eleven, twelve. Perfect age for shenanigans."

Alex snarled. "Little bastards."

"I'll go back to the orchard," said George. "I think I heard something there, too."

"I'll take the brush," said Alex. "Someone's bound to try sneaking through soon. It's late."

They split up again, the Crusaders going off in separate directions, keenly the outside perimeter and what lay beyond.

Alex was still thinking about Kathy and how good it felt to talk to her. She had said she was especially glad to see him. He hid right under the fence in the center section of the north wall, quiet as a mouse, listening for somebody coming up behind him, watching more of the gruesome acts being carried out up on the big screen. About five minutes into keeping watch, his mind began to wander. He thought about his Dad, and how the crumb had abandoned the family, flown the coop to take up with a younger broad in Seattle. Hell, that was a long way from Rochester. "Well Dad…" he whispered, "I'm back at it, back at the Winking Moon. Why don't ya try sneaking in here so I can throw you out on your ass."

Crack. There were noises behind him. Someone was drawing closer to the fence on the other side. Punks? Hooligans? He got ready, took his flashlight off his holster, held it tight, thumb on the switch, ready to flip it on. He could have called his friends for back-up, but he wanted to be the guy to nail the first prey of the season. The crunching and rustling steadily came closer–it sounded like more than one perpetrator, for sure. The clumsy fools were stepping on everything. There appeared multiple encroachers. Alex's adrenaline began to soar. "You're not sneaking into my Winking Moon this year," he thought to himself. "Not tonight or any night."

They were right behind him, the wooden fence being the only thing separating them. Alex stood, still crouched, ready to use the muscles in his legs to spring. "One-two-three—" He leapt up, grabbing the top of the high fence with one hand, feet on the two-by-four support beams midway up—"A-ha, gotcha!" he barked, shining the light down, expecting to see scared shitless little faces of pre-teeners.

Instead he saw raccoons. A family of them. They nonchalantly stopped what they were doing, waddling along the fence, looked up, gave Alex a look as if to say *Yeah, what do you want?* and continued. Alex felt like a horse's behind as he hopped back down, blowing out a lungful of held air. Just then, his walkie-talkie squeaked. "Alex, come in." Mr. Stuckerson.

"Go ahead, Mr. Stuckerson," he responded.

"What was that? Was that you yelling?"

"It was nothing, sir, I thought I had something."

Annoyed, Lee-Willie kept on the radio. "Steve, time for the marquee already. Get in here, I'll give ya the list."

"Already?" squawked George's voice.

"Already, Mr. Jocavelli, it's Friday night."

"On my way, sir," said Steve.

"The rest of you keep doing what you're doing."

Being an idiot? Alex thought to himself.

Alex was still high on adrenaline and went to see Jim Barenta, who invited him in with one stipulation, "Keep your hands off my fucking equipment."

Alex agreed, stepping into the murkier-than-thou projection-cave once more. Even though his eyes had adjusted back to darkness, he still tripped on the coffee table. "Watch it," Jim warned. The big guy had put aside the Spitfire model and was now flipping through an old Vietnam photo album. Alex had seen the album last year but did not want to pry about Jim's stay when he'd been stationed there in the Army. The big guy was studying the pictures the same way he'd been at the model: quiet, serious, glasses-on.

Alex sat on the dilapidated sofa in front of, almost went to the floor through it.

"Gotta put one butt-cheek on the edge. The middle'll kill ya."

Alex worked his way to a humane position.

"So, what's up?" asked Jim. "Two visits in one night? To what do I owe this pleasure?

"Stanley's asking you not to play the volume so loud in the stand during intermission."

"Why didn't he tell me himself?"

"I dunno, I just thought I'd tell ya."

Jim was in his wooden swivel-chair, the same lone light shone from a lamp overhead. "How's your family? Still haven't seen Dad?"

"You remembered."

"I remember a lot."

"Nope, he's still gone. No sign of him through the fall and winter. He and Mom talk occasionally on the phone. They just yell."

"Sorry about that. How's it out there? I heard you yell."

"I thought I had a punk or a hooligan. It was nothing, though."

"What was it, an animal?"

Alex felt his face flush. "Maybe." He had to reacclimate himself to the honor of being in here, a sanctuary he thought often of in the off-season.

Alex could see that Jim was immersed in his own thoughts. Still, the big guy could do more than one thing at a time. "How's your mom holding up?"

"Pretty good."

"How about your older brother? Randy, right?"

"He's grown into a bigger asshole."

"I'm sure he feels he's the man of the family now, has to protect you guys."

"That's what Mom says. I don't want to burden you with talk of my family. How's yours? You said you and Jeannie are still together? You guys gonna get married?"

Jim paused, first time not flipping through the album. Alex could feel his intense eyes cutting right through him. "That's one question too many, boy."

"Sorry. I've never seen you open that photo album, Jim. I see it's you in the Army. I never saw it."

"That's 'cause I didn't show it to you."

"Oh."

"Wanna see it?" Jim stopped the page-flipping, turned it around and handed it to Alex so he could examine it. There was a lot of cellophane tape involved, so Alex had to be extra careful. He worked himself to a better angle, stepping closer. Jim adjusted the lamp to make it easier to see. The big guy with his war-buddies, posing in innumerous situations. Miserable faces, serious faces, worn faces. "101st Airborne, Special

Forces," he recounted. "I don't usually show people."

Alex pointed. "Who's this?"

"A friend."

"And him?"

"Another friend."

"You were a real hero, over there. It wasn't that long ago."

"Just four years," Jim said. "And I'm not a hero, these jamokes are the heroes. And I'm not telling ya which of 'em came back and which didn't. I'm in too peaceful of a place tonight."

"What was it like over there?"

"Like something you'd never want to imagine."

"Worse than The Moon on a bad night?"

"Don't even fuckin' compare."

"Thanks for your service."

Jim turned to Alex, nodded, then said, "I need a little picker-upper." He got up and moved to the paneled wall behind the projector, slid aside a fake rubber tree plant and removed a section hiding a secret crop of thriving marijuana plants—thanks to a UV-lightbulb kit, a watering can and tin foil encasements around each growth. Alex had not forgotten this trick, either. Jim had a few pre-rolled joints in a nice little coffee can. He plucked one out, returned the section of paneling, sat down and lit up. He let the curl of smoke out with an "Aaaah," then eyeballed his young friend. "Don't look at me that way, Carver, I ain't gonna ask ya if you want some."

Alex feigned innocence. "I didn't say anything."

"Jeannie's trying to get me to quit. Cigarettes."

"But not those."

"How could I? Makes me make sense."

Knock-knock-knock. It was Gail-Lill at the door, wanting to come in. Jim was right in the middle of another deep one. Alex grabbed a nearby can of air freshener, sprayed the shit out of the projection room, blasting Jim in the face, accidentally ruining his smoke. Jim told him to relax, did not do squat to cover his recreation. "C'mon in, Gail," he hailed over the projector noise. "I'm an open book tonight."

As she walked in, a mere silhouette for the moment, Alex was up on his feet— "I was just leaving, Mrs. Stuckerson."

"Relax, Alex," she said. "It's your first night back, I know you and Jimmy are friends."

'Jimmy' saw the notebook tucked under her arm and the flicker in her eye that read *I have something important on my mind* as she approached the lamplight. "Go to work," he told Alex.

And Alex did, skedaddling out with a, "Yes, sir. Talk to you later."

"We got the whole summer," Jim said as he left, shutting the door.

Gail-Lill turned to the projectionist, had a big smile on her face. The usual wallflower was up to something, and the big guy knew what it was. Jim solemnly closed the photo album, tucked it back on the only bookshelf in the room, and said, "What's that under your arm, darlin'?"

"I've been writing all winter, Jimmy. May I?"

"No, you may not. You wanna get me fired?"

"You're not going to get fired, just let me dip into the trailers at intermission, read one or two."

He put the doobie down in an ashtray. "Gail, I love ya, darlin', but reading your hand-crafted poetry over the airwaves just puts me in a shit light. It nearly starts riots."

"C'mon, Jimmy, I'm an artist just like Kathy, but I paint with words. Lee won't let me do it, even for pre-show."

"And I won't let you do it here anytime. Remember what happened last year when I let ya? It was only one poem but by the end the entire audience was ready to kick down my door and set fire to the booth."

"Don't be so dramatic, Jimmy, my poetry's not that bad."

"Not sayin' it is—it's kinda good—but this isn't the venue for it. A drive-in movie theater? It's inappropriate, it's jarring, and it gets people mad. And we definitely don't need 'mad' here."

"I just want an audience."

"Try your husband."

"He hates my poetry. He walks out of the room when I try to read to him."

"That's not very supportive."

"He has no patience. You see how he is around here. He doesn't believe I'm good at anything other than co-managing this place and being his wife."

"Can't do it, darling, sorry."

She showed him the notebook. Flipped through page-after-page of verses, sonnets. She was really passionate, everything written in pen. There were few cross-outs. "Sometime this summer?"

He softened, just a smidge. "Can't promise ya."

"And I can't promise your union won't do a system-check on your operation here. They just might smell a certain fragrance wafting from that secret supply behind your wall."

"What? You *know*?"

"Jimmy, this is *our* drive-in," Gail-Lill said. "We know everything."

"But this is *my* projection booth. You're not supposed to be in here when I'm not."

"We love our drive-in, Jimmy. We *love* our projectionist and we *love* our drive-in."

"Sweetheart, never figured you for a black-mailer. We'll see about that 'sometime.'"

She jumped for joy— "Wee-hee!"—clapping her hands together, the notebook tucked back under her arm. She leaned down, kissed him on the cheek, said, "Thanks, Jimmy," and left.

"Shit…" he mused out loud. "Well I'll be a tinker's dinkle, she's got balls."

As Gail-Lill was trying to slip the notebook back in their rusty '74 Lincoln Versailles parked just outside the concession stand, she spotted her husband, skulking the lot. "Lee—" she hissed, trying to keep her voice down. "What're you doing?"

"Looking for the Crusaders, making sure they're not screwin' around on their first night back."

"They're not screwing around, Lee, leave them alone. They can be trusted."

"Bullshit. Hormone-filled jokesters, always making light of their work."

"Yeah, God forbid anyone tries to have fun at their jobs. Especially at the Winking Moon."

Retracting her arm from the car and shutting the door, he became suspicious. "What's that?" he snapped. "What were you doing? What'd you just put in the car? Was that your poetry notebook? Please tell me you're not doing that again this year. You didn't just try to get Jim to let you read one over the P.A., did you?" Her hesitation was all Lee needed. She had. "Gail, I thought you said you weren't going to try that this year. That was a pact. We agreed it causes too much disruption and we can't be stirring things up like that again."

"Sometimes… at second intermission… the people need something different to entertain them."

"Gail!"

"Shh!" hushed a patron in his car.

Lee-Willie was mad, barely containing himself. At that moment, a boy, just about eleven years old, came barreling out of the concession stand with Stanley's fishing cap in his hands and ran off into the darkness. Stanley was right behind, halting at the threshold of the double-doors— "Hey, he's got my hat! Get that kid!"

"Why'd he take your hat, Stanley?" said Lee-Willie, confused.

"I dunno, he just grabbed it off my head and took off with it! Get him!"

"What's going on?" another annoyed audience member fumed.

The Stuckersons were all set to pursue him when they heard a sharp scuffle and swearing. George's voice informed confidently from out of the dark— "We got 'em, Mr. and Mrs. Stuckerson, we saw the whole thing."

Back into the light walked the four patrolmen, carrying the child by all four limbs, suspended above the ground, struggling and swearing, pissed off to the heavens. John had Stanley's cap in his free hand. "Lemme go!" the kid was braying. "Get your filthy paws off me, ya damn dirty apes!"

They did not. Arriving at their bosses, they set the boy down, but continued holding him tight. John gave the hat back to the enraged Stanley— "Here, Stanley. He never got further than a few rows."

"Mr. and Mrs. Stuckerson," Alex stated, making an example, "here is a true, bonafide yahoo. Or rowdie. Whatever ya wanna call him."

"What's your name, kid?" said Lee-Willie, getting in the youngster's face.

"Not tellin.'"

"Why'd you take this man's hat?"

"'Cause it was on his head. A friend dared me."

"Where're your parents?" said Gail-Lill.

"In the car."

"Where are they?" said Lee-Willie.

"Not tellin.'"

Steve twisted the kid's ear, made him yelp. "Okay, okay, they're out by the side, in the middle. They thought we were getting popcorn; my friend was watching from the outside."

"It's not nice to take hats off of old men," said Lee-Willie.

"I'm not old," Stanley corrected.

The manager straightened. "Crusaders take this boy back to his parents the same way you brought him here. Tell 'em if he gets out again, we'll bury him in the ice cream freezer."

"Your parents take you to these movies?" asked Gail-Lill.

"They don't care," said the boy.

"That's part of the problem," said Lee-Willie. "Take him away."

The Crusaders picked the kid up again—squealing and protesting aggressively—and carried him off into the night. When they were gone, Gail-Lill turned to her husband. "Still think you need to supervise them, Lee?"

Lee-Willie ignored the question and, instead, doled out the orders. "Stanley, get back in there."

He'd been putting his cap back on, making sure nothing was ruined, all the buttons were there. "Don't tell me what to do, Lee, I was doin' this job while you were still dangling in your daddy's balls."

Lee-Willie drew in a breath and let it out slowly. "Stanley? Please?"

Stanley did go in, but not before setting a precedent to the missus. "Gail, better get your spouse here to address me with a little more respect. I never appreciated his tone of voice."

After he was gone, the two looked at each other. "Carry on," said Lee-Willie.

Steve blazed up Sing Road to the intersection where the grand marquee was, seeing how fast he could get the Charger's speedometer up to before having to de-accelerate. 80-miles per hour! It always amazed him how free he felt with just miles of rural lane ahead. He had been cranking *New York Groove*, by Kiss, feeling the adrenaline in his veins. *Damn, it's good to be back!* he thought.

Pulling off to the shoulder of the road, he cut the music and shut off the engine, getting out and waiting for the dust to clear in order to see Jody across the street ringing up customers at the Lapping Waves. There he saw her, lit up and as obvious as a fish in a goldfish bowl. He waited for the customer to leave, took out his flashlight, and began sending her a signal in Morse-coding to get her attention.

"I-LOVE-YOU" he spelled out as he said it aloud, and she knew how to read it. They'd done this a countless number of times last year. It had become their "thing."

Unfortunately, Mr. Smith saw it, too and came bolting out of the store onto the sidewalk, blocking the love-beam from Jody. He set his hands on his hips, scolding Steve. "I told you, Mr. Laneske, we're not doing that again this year." He had lifted his voice so it could be heard from across the street. "Just change the titles and get back down the street."

Steve wanted a laugh. He responded to Mr. Smith in Morse code and spoke aloud as he did it— "HI-MISTER-SMITH-HOW-YOU-DOING-NICE-TO-SEE-YOU-AGAIN-TOO"

Smith did not appreciate the cleverness. "Funny, Steve. I mean it. Don't bother her."

"Yes, sir."

The manager huffed back in, Jody managing a wave and a self boob-grab for her boyfriend, then was snapped at by Smith seeing her do so, ordering her back to work.

Steve shook off the exasperation, got out the padlock key from his smock pocket, trudged across the lawn to the metal shed under the massive structure, unlocked the rusty lock and opened the shed door. He ducked immediately, as what looked like a Pterodactyl-sized creature flew out at his head. He looked back to see that it was just a moth. And not a very big one.

He stepped inside, tugging on the chain suspended to a rafter over his head that controlled the 75-watt lightbulb, illuminating the musty interior. The cramped space was just as he'd remembered it: motor oil and garden tools, an assortment of rakes, the lawn mower and shovel, and the shelves of red plastic Snap-on letters (all upper case) used to form the titles.

He pulled out his note, hand-written by none-other than Lee-Willie, memorized what he needed to display, and selected the appropriate letters. Putting those into a spare crate and setting that outside, he then pulled out the ladder, set that up, and began to climb—getting the letters onto the catwalk so that he could crab-walk back-and-forth to spell out the titles. One-by-one he inched along, unhooking the present letters, replacing them with the new ones, trying to center everything, careful not to back into one of the hot spotlights attached to the bottom of the catwalk. He had burned his calf on one last year. The width of the plank he was walking on was so narrow—he had to be careful. He was suspended eight feet above the ground, and it was easy to lose one's balance with the brightness of the animated lightbulbs and arrows all around him.

And there were always the foolhardy hecklers who drove by and could not leave him alone. As usual, tonight was no different. "Get a grip! Don't fall!" shouted one, motoring by in a Chevy van. A plain old nasty scream, at the top of their lungs for maximum efficiency. Steve threw the finger but mostly just ho-hummed it.

Finishing his work, he climbed down, stood back to admire his handiwork: UP IN SMOKE, H.O.T.S, RATED R. He put everything back where it belonged in the shed, locked the padlock, turned around to check on Jody one more time and got back in the Charger. On his way back he beat his previous acceleration by four more miles-per-hour.

Steve returned to pure craziness at the concession stand. It was second intermission and they would be closing up twenty minutes after this next film started. Same went for the box office. Some would still drive in at the last minute, paying full fare to see three-quarters of one film. It was a given: those were the ones they usually had to kick out at the end of the night.

"Because they sure ain't coming in to watch the movie," George proclaimed when they were talking about it. "That's for sure."

Jim made the last call announcement over the P.A. This only intensified the mad rush on the stand. Popcorn was being popped, soda drawn from the dispenser in gallons. Hotdogs, hamburgers and French fries were flying off the grill. Emilio was busy churning out his famous pizzas, sliding the uncooked ones in the oven, spinning the dough for the new ones in the air like a pro.

Stanley had been daydreaming. As there was a slight lull at the register—people waiting to place their orders or pick them up—he zoned-out, staring at the spinning dough in a near trance, mentally turning the disc-shaped pies into flying saucers, imagining them the heralded fleet, arriving to get him. He smiled in bliss thinking of the moment. The one tossed especially high in the air, almost hitting the ceiling, became the mother ship, tiny portholes all around it with the inhabitants clearly visible through them: three-fingered Martians with eyes on stalks, smiling at the goat, waving him over, beckoning him onboard. The excitement was too much.

"Stanley!" yelled Lee-Willie, snapping the senior cashier out of his trance. A dozen people stood at the till, waiting to be cashed out.

Emilio was arguing with several new customers who wanted to know what he put in his sauce. "What makes it taste so fuckin' good?!" they pleaded. Emilio's sauce was the young cook's pride and joy, and he was not about to give it up. Never had, never would.

"I told everybody last year I'm not telling a soul," he stressed. "What I put in my sauce is my business. That's what keeps you coming back for more. You know Colonel Sanders with his finger-licking-good chicken recipe? This is mine."

"C'mon, man," insisted one of the dues, "don't do us like that. We're only trying to compliment you, it's fuckin' delicious. Whattya put in it?"

"Not telling. Next!"

"Man, you're a ball-sack," said the second.

"Better to be one than to look like one."

"What does that mean?"

"Gentlemen, gentlemen," said Lee-Willie, breaking away from his wife and stepping in. "Let's everyone be level-headed. Can you stand over there and wait for your order, sirs? We're trying to clear everyone so they can get out for the encore feature."

Reluctantly, the two men moved away, but unhappily. "That guy's a knob," the first one pointed.

Vicki waited until the coast was clear, then neared her friend.

"Emilio, one of these days you're gonna get us in trouble with your arrogance over that. You can't *not* tell people what's in your sauce, you did this last year."

"I can do whatever I want, Vicki, it's the American way."

"You're not even American, Emilio," Stanley said, butting in, making his current crop of customers in line laugh.

Emilio was insulted. "Yes, I am, Stanley. Why do you say that?"

"'Cause you're Mexican," Stanley answered.

"I was born here, you idiot old man. Mind your business."

"Hey," Stanley argued, "then recite the Pledge of Allegiance right now. Prove it."

Again, Lee-Willie had to step in. "Gentlemen, stop the nonsense and get back to work." To Steve, "Mr. Laneske, how'd everything go out there? Did you get the spelling right? Forget how to do everything?"

"Everything went fine, Mr. Stuckerson." To his buddies, "But I know someone who really *is* a knob—Mr. Smith, the douche bag."

Lee-Willie got John's attention, fetching frozen fries from the back freezer. "John, could tell Jim to turn the speakers down? We asked him already." The soundtrack of the trailers was extra-loud. John split.

Alex, George and Steve were hustling as they did, serving ice cream, candy, hot food and cold. They were extremely efficient.

Their high school pals came back in and called them "gay" again with their hairnets.

Jim appeared in the doorway. "Who said they wanted the volume down in here?"

"I did, Jim," said Lee-Willie. Patrons were observing.

"Poll the people." Jim raised his voice. "People: who wants it quieter in here?"

"No way!" "Hell no!" "Make it louder!" The litany of negative responses made things crystal clear. Jim tipped his mug to Lee-Willie, turned around, disappeared. Lee-Willie murmured to his wife. "I really hate when he shows me up like that in front of the crew."

She murmured back, "He's not showing you up, Lee, he just wants a lively drive-in. It's better for commerce."

As soon as she said that, a drunken dodo came roaring in, chasing his screaming girlfriend—also hammered and sloppy—pretending he was the psycho from "Toolbox Murders," making power drill noises with his mouth, knocking into people, bumping into the pinball machine, tilting it.

During the second run of "The Brood," Lee-Willie set out to visit the back fence in the northeast corner. He radioed the Crusaders and told them to meet him there. He was shoving one candy bar after the next into his nervous mouth. His mega-flashlight thumped off his thigh as he walked.

"Edgewater's been leaving messages again," he said quietly to the four as they met up three-quarters of the way there. "They're really getting to be a pain-in-the-ass. Says there's kids in their backyard, fucking around. They're probably going to sneak-in. Can you dopes keep an eye on that area?"

"Mr. Stuckerson, we're on it," said Steve as they tried to keep up with him. "We already chased away one hooligan, probably. We think it was one of 'em who stuck his head up, surveyed the area and he took off when we approached."

Lee-Willie was frustrated, nervous. "Why did they put an old folk's home like Edgewater behind a drive-in movie theater?" he said, rhetorically.

"We've asked ourselves the same question," George said.

"Let's check this out, I'm sick of catering to these old goats."

When they got there, all appeared quiet, though this was a notoriously busy corner. They had to jump up on the fence to take a look around. "Let's take a look," Lee-Willie said, preparing to do so.

Alex intervened. "Mr. Stuckerson, you stay here, we'll jump up."

"Think I can't do it, Carver? Watch me. I may not be the athlete you chipmunks are, but I can hold my own. I played basketball in junior high, for the love of all the saints."

He went to leap up onto the high barricade, using the same strategy Alex used—go for the top and pull, placing his feet on the horizontal support beams, midway-up. He missed, cracked his knee and fell back onto the boulevard with a "thud." Thank God it was grass. The Crusaders went to help him up, but he batted away their hands. Getting to his feet, holding his knee in pain, they put their hands on him and gave him a hoist. He finally got himself poised in position, standing above the teenagers now who remained below, looked around at the sight before him.

Through the woods he could somewhat make out the back of the Edgewater Retirement Home: a multi-storied building with sprawling wings on both ends. There were enough lights on from the complex that the interior was visible, even this late at night. A long, luxurious deck stretched from side-to-side, coupling as an entrance into the first floor. Most likely a dining hall. There was furniture aplenty. The residents could sit for hours out here on a good day. Fancy lounges graced the area behind the round tables with umbrellas. Chairs were tucked around each one and well-nourished plants bloomed from planters.

"Shit…" Lee-Willie said. "They live in paradise." He turned on his power light, swept around the woods.

"Whattya see?" asked George.

"Nothing," Lee-Willie responded. "All's quiet." Then he angled the flashlight down. There was a group of five old men, standing there with their arms folded, staring up at him, waiting to be seen. "Agh!" Lee-Willie cried out, losing his grip, falling backwards. Without helping him and leaving their boss there, the Crusaders all jumped on, shined their flashlights down.

"Who are you people?" exclaimed Steve.

"No, who are *you*?" one of the old men retorted, voice crackling with disdain.

"We're the Crusaders," said Alex. "The Winking Moon Crusaders. We're patrolmen here."

"Well you sure as shit ain't doing a good job of patrolling. We have kids hangin' around here all night."

"We came out to take care of it ourselves," snarled another.

"You live here?" asked John.

"We're residents," said a third. "This is our home, our property. These woods here, that facility—it's all ours, right up to this fence."

"Are you the people who called?" Lee-Willie said from the ground.

"Yeah, we are," said the fourth. "We're sick of this crap. Night-after-night there's bullshit 'cause you people are here. We just had a kid soaping our windows. When you gonna finally do something about it?"

"Men help me up," Lee-Willie said to his crew.

The Crusaders got him back into position with them. Lee-Willie hung on tight. "I'm the manager at the Winking Moon," he wheezed, still wincing from the pain. "Co-manager. We're doing everything in our power to eliminate your problems. The authorities are completely aware of the issues."

"We know," said the fifth. "We call 'em all the time."

"In addition to the filth and violence you show," started the first one over, "we have oodles of little maniacs wanting to see it, sneaking into our property, causing us grief, pulling pranks, acting like animals. Our whole community here at Edgewater is furious."

The first man who spoke—the most formidable-looking one—nudged the others. *Let's go.* "Take care of it, Winking Moon," he said, as he led the others away, back through the woods toward the facility, "or we'll do it for ya."

Their silhouettes melded into the woods, the darkness, disappearing into the denseness of the trees. The Crusaders helped Lee-Willie down, shoving a new candy bar into his face. They walked away, too, Lee-Willie limping "What did *that* mean?" he said. They were all confused.

"I dunno," replied Alex. "But it sure sounded like a threat."

At the end of the encore movie, when everybody—including the remaining audience members—really did have enough of the dismembering and screaming, the Crusaders plodded into the stand to clean it out—another glamorous part of the job description. The doors had been locked for over an hour, and Stanley had to let them in to do their share.

"You clods enjoy your first night back?" he asked.

"Yeah, the best part was the look on your face when the kid took off with your cap," said George. "We shoulda let you run after him."

"And I should slap your smart-ass face, Jocavelli. Get in here, all ya chooches."

Time to do what needed to be done to get the joint sparkling clean. Emilio took care of the oven: a terrible, screeching sound as he scraped the bottom of all four tiers with the metal rasp, used to get the charred pizza-leftovers out. Stanley got the floor. He was used to swabbing from all his years in the Navy. "Stanley, next week you wanna come through the school and swab the floors?" Vicki joked. "You do such a good job at it. We're almost out for the year and it needs to be cleaned."

"Vicki, if I did, I'd use your red mop of a head to do it," Stanley said.

Kathy had long-since closed the box office and gave the money over to the Stuckersons, tallied and bagged and ready for "the drop." Right now, she was bent over the pinball machine, getting the smears and greasy fingerprints off with paper toweling and her own cleaner. It was all Alex could do to keep his eyes off her. They found themselves nearly face-to-face. She smiled, brushed her hair behind her ears and said, "You're going to have to give me some room here."

He stepped back. "Sorry."

Stanley was on to them. "The deep fryer, Carver, the deep fryer. That's your detail tonight."

Shit. Worst duty of the job. Alex emptied the bins of used oil into garbage bags, tied those up, threw them out in the dumpsters and had to scoop out the thick glops that had settled at the bottom like coalesced Crisco. Steve, John and George put the unused food away in the back freezer, tidied up the condiment and napkin island, wiped down the soda dispenser machine and made sure the windows were squeaky-clean. Nothing went unchecked.

When the last frame rolled through the gate, and Jim shut off the projector, making sure all of the reels were re-wound, ready to go in the metal film canisters they were delivered in for pick-up, he radioed Lee-Willie and asked if he was good to go for the drop. Lee-Willie confirmed after a few minutes. Jim got out his keys, shut and locked the projection booth door with a padlock, and stepped outside—just in time to get blinded by The Moon Tower coming on, courtesy of Stanley Mason, who enjoyed turning on the electric monstrosity from the utility room in the back of the stand. "Stanley… my friend…" he griped into the radio. "Ya gotta learn to warn us when you're turning that thing on. You wanna fry our eyeballs?"

"Sorry, Jim," he replied, grabbing Vicki's radio from her. "It's my favorite time of night, I can go home and do some deep-space observation in my telescope. The Moon Tower's just a good calling-card to attract the aliens."

"I bet it is, Stanley. I bet it is." Jim climbed into his Chevy pickup and waited for the boss-man to arrive with the money bags. "Where is this guy?" he said aloud out the window, the girls hanging outside, drinking sodas to quench their thirsts.

Kathy answered, "They've been in the office a lot tonight. I don't know what they're doing."

Into the radio Jim spoke again, "Lee, let's go, I like this place, but I don't wanna be buried here."

"On my way, Jim," came the response.

Lee-Willie and Gail-Lill eventually made their way through the lot, up and over the humps at their usual diagonal, a steady stream of traffic flowing out behind them and to the sides—some with their parking lights on, others with the full headlights blazing. He stopped at Jim, who immediately made note of their turned-up collars, the messed-up hair (what was left of it on Lee-Willie), and the smeary lipstick on Gail-Lill's face. "What've you guys been doing in there?"

"Uh… re-counting the money," said Lee-Willie. "Some nights we're missing a few pennies."

"I'm sure you are," said Jim, not believing the Stuckerson's cover story. "Get in." Jim brushed it off, telling the gang—now all of them in the doorway—that they would be right back after they swung by the bank.

"Still got your piece, Jim?" Steve asked, eagerly hoping to see it.

Jim held up his gun, had it pointed straight in the sky. "Never leave home without it," he said, drawing a round of applause from the heartened Crusaders. Vicki and Kathy just rolled their eyes. Gail-Lill told them to be careful.

"In the meantime, clear whoever's left outta the lot," ordered Lee-Willie. "You kids remember we have to get stragglers out? We don't want people hangin' out all night. We wanna go home."

A resounding "Yes sir!" followed. As Jim and Lee-Willie joined the flow of vehicles, the Crusaders watched the steady line of traffic choking the exit to get out, slowly draining the lot, like fish escaping back into the river.

There were some stragglers left over. Six, to be exact. This was a pain-in-the-ass, too, but it had its hilarious moments from time to time. The solitary vehicles were spread out all around the grounds. Some could be heard with music playing, two trucks could be seen with sleeping passengers in them, the others with questionable activity taking place inside.

"Too much sex or not enough?" John said, a bold question for such a quiet kid.

"You can never get enough sex," said George.

"Shall we do it?" asked Steve.

"We have to," said Alex.

The Crusaders took to each, knocking on the windows, telling patrons they had to leave. Gail-Lill, Vicki, Emilio and Kathy all watched from the sidelines, having a good laugh. Stanley had gone back into the utility room, flicked The Moon Tower off and on a few times, hoping to attract aliens. He was told to stop and then he sulked the rest of the time, sitting in his '72 Nissan Skyline, waiting to be told he could go home.

The Crusaders discovered a mysterious Ford Fairmont parked alongside the brush, smack-dab in the middle of the north side, all four windows down with Barry Manilow lilting from its eight-track. Love music.

"At least the mood's right," said John. "Where are these guys?"

They looked all around. They could see virtually everything with the tower shining bright. But there are some dark spots along the fences, courtesy of the elms, birches and oaks, hanging over with their huge branches. Alex deemed it necessary to call out into the night. "Owners and occupants of the Ford Fairmont, show yourself and return to your vehicle. We have to close up and we need you all out. Thank you for your patronage and please visit the Winking Moon again."

There was a shuffle by the fence, straight across from them. A young man and woman emerged from the shadows, the man zipping up his fly, the woman lagging, adjusting her bra. Her blouse was still unbuttoned, and it was quite obvious what the two had been doing. Nobody said a word as they watched the couple slow-poke their way back to the automobile, getting in, lighting two cigarettes. They looked like death warmed over. Smelled like it, too. Strong whiskey and plenty of pot.

"Really?" said Alex, finally breaking the silence. "Against the fence?"

"We like standing," the man replied, indifferently. "Gives me better thrust."

The woman giggled and took a long drag. Made eye contact with the patrolmen, wiggled her eyebrows up-and-down and smiled. She took another long drag, went to blow it out, and the man put the car in gear and took off like a jackrabbit, jolting his passenger's head backwards and heading for the exit, the trail of cigarette smoke forming a long, thin line behind them.

George turned to the girls, beamed a cynical grin and pointed to where the car used to be. "Tips from the ones in the know. I should have a notebook like you do, Mrs. Stuckerson."

Gail-Lill held her hands up to her mouth, shocked. There was nothing she could say.

Everybody was back now, huddling by the white picket fence outside of the manager's office. All the Winking Moon patrons had gone home for the night. All was quiet and peaceful, save the employee's chattering and swapping stories from the night. The Stuckersons just looked on, Gail-Lill rubbing her tired face, Lee-Willie cramming more candy bars in his mouth, looking like he was afraid to die of hunger if he did not consume them. The youngsters had purposefully parked their cars to block Stanley Mason at the exit. The coot was threatening to drive out the other way and laid on the horn a couple of times to get them moving. Nothing worked. He continued pouting and long faced in his Nissan Skyline, asking the galactic brotherhood to take him away from his misery. When they finally let him out, he tore away down the entrance road, throwing them the finger—which seemed to be a very common occurrence on the Crusaders' first nights back at work.

Lee-Willie got tired of the camaraderie, pushed his butt off the fence, came at the young people with his arms flapping—"Get outta here, ya meatheads, I'm not gonna stand around here all night reminiscing, we wanna lock up and go home. This is the tip of the iceberg only, puppies, gotta a long way to go."

George snickered. "He said 'tip,'" gesturing to his crotch, making John, Steve and Alex snort. Mrs. Stuckerson heard, and did not approve.

"See everybody tomorrow night," said Jim, and drove off. "Ya better not all be T-A-F, Saturday nights are even crazier."

"What's 'T-A-F'?" Emilio asked.

Jim was answering, "Tired-As-Fu—" as Gail-Lill shouted over him, blocking out the word. "Jimmy! Language!" They heard him say "I'm sorry" as he turned west on Sing.

They all parted ways, Steve getting airborne over the lesser-used railroad tracks south of the drive-in and apple orchard, George, Alex and John non-stop guffawing the whole time. The Who's "Won't Get Fooled Again" screamed from the eight-track.

The neon lights went out on The Man-in-the-Moon on the back of the huge screen. The face seemed to still be winking, even in the dark.

"UP IN SMOKE" &
"H.O.T.S."

CHAPTER 8:

AT HOME

The Stuckersons awoke at noon in their one-bedroom, tattered-and-cluttered, bare bones apartment. Managing drive-ins across the country never made them rich or provided them with a stable enough base to feel comfortable purchasing a modest house. The complex they lived in was located only a mile from The Winking Moon, near the shores of Lake Ontario. They were constantly spending their own dough on the places they managed, which didn't help matters, either. Lee-Willie had spent fortunes on advertising, cosmetic enhancements, and impulse buys like the old-fashioned popcorn-maker.

It took Gail-Lill a few moments to realize something was wrong as she shook the cobwebs from her mind from the restless night's sleep she'd had. She snapped up in bed—nothing more than a queen-size mattress on the floor of their apartment—and pried a loose sock from her hair that'd gotten lodged in there during the night from the overload of hairspray she'd applied the night before. "Ohmigod, the rent!"

Lee-Willie tumbled off the mattress next to her, kerplunking on the floor. "Gail? Wha—? Huh?"

"Lee, I forgot to pay the rent!"

Regaining his senses, he said, "You forgot to pay the rent? What? Gail!" He worked himself to a standing position, the fly in his Popeye the Sailor Man pajama-bottoms being open, his donager hanging out through it for all the world to see.

"Mr. Winnechum!" she replied, motioning for him to tuck it back in. "Our landlord! I haven't gotten him the rent yet, I just remembered. It was due four days ago—we've been so busy."

The wispy hair that Lee-Willie had left looked as bad as his wife's did, sticking in eight different directions at once. "How could you forget to pay the rent again? That's your job."

She rubbed her face like a mad chipmunk, jowls reverberating like strawberries in a blender. "I wrote myself a note, where is it? I put it right where it could remind me. Lee, we've got to get more organized."

"'We've' gotta get more organized? You mean 'you.' You're the bill-payer."

"Oh Lee, show some understanding. And remember you're spending all our money. Don't you think that sidetracks me?"

"I dunno what 'sidetracks' you. Maybe it's the poetry you're trying to get read over the P.A. system."

"Gotta think. It's June 9th. Rent was due on the 5th. Mr. Winnechum usually comes 'round on Saturdays, he might be knocking at our door any minute now, look at the time. Oh, Lee, he could evict us."

"Winne-schmuck's not gonna evict us. Don't bring up that jerk's name, I don't wanna hear it right now."

"Lee, I have to write it out and get it to his office before he comes looking for it."

As she got out of bed and stumbled out of the room in her own ridiculous pajamas to the dining area, rifling around in her rickety writing desk for the ledger, Lee-Willie followed her out.

"Jack-ass blowhard, who does he think he is anyway? Always money-grubbing for rent, hassling people. Can't enjoy a Saturday morning without his wise-ass name being brought up."

As she was tearing through the stationary, notes and batteries, looking for the checkbook and a pen, she reminded him, "He's our landlord, Lee, it's his business, we're his tenants. He's not letting us live here just out of the goodness of his heart."

She was encumbered by the disarray around her. There were still unpacked boxes from their move blocking their every step. Stacks of office work teetered on the coffee table; clothes thrown everywhere that hadn't been put away yet. When she finally found what she was looking for, she cleared a space at the kitchen table, clicked the pen and sat down.

Lee-Willie was right behind her. "How could you be so careless?"

"Lee, stop! I don't need that right now. We've been late the past three months."

"*You've* been late."

She was in a panic, blowing her thinning, shoulder-length hair from her eyes. "We get so busy we don't even have time to catch our breath. You and your spending-sprees. The stress you give me from all those purchases. Those new uniforms…"

"Hey, everybody likes 'em. You, too."

"We're going to be homeless one of these days because of it. And now we're going to have to pay yet another late fee."

"For crying out loud, just get the check off to him."

"He's probably already driving out front."

"Better not be, the dork."

After flipping through the checkbook, finding a blank one, she had to look at the balance, also had to find the number to the landlord's office. Lee-Willie would not leave her alone, determined to find out what she thought of his performance the night before. "So… think I set the boys straight last night, their first night back? Told 'em what's-what and who's-who? Have to get 'em off on the right foot."

"Lee, now's not a good time."

"Surely you have some feedback. You do for everything else."

"Lee, I told you not to start riding them. Make yourself useful now, help me find Winnechum's office number so I can head this off at the pass."

"A piss, first."

He went to the bathroom, closed the off-kilter door, clanked the toilet-lid up, peed like a racehorse. Came out without washing his hands.

She made him go back in and do it. He threw the hand towel on the floor with several of the others, wanted to know if she had washed any.

"Not yet, Lee, I can't do a million things at once. You can always run laundry."

She suddenly stopped. "Oh, damn… we don't have enough. Lee, there's not enough funds to cover the rent. We had it five days ago, you spent it on that paint for the fence outside our office. We'll have to wait till next week now when we get paid."

"Blaming me, huh?"

"Yeah well, you keep mishandling our finances, this is going to keep happening. There's more of our own, personal blood in that theater than the gore we show on the screen."

Lee-Willie was looking around. "This place is a dump. Why haven't you cleaned?"

"Lee!"

"You should interface better with Winnechum."

"What the hell do you think I'm trying here?"

"Maybe we should go somewhere today."

"Where, The Ritz? Are you talking about slipping out and disappearing so he can't find us?"

"I promise, someday, sweetheart, I'll put you in the lap of luxury."

"Don't make promises, Lee, right now you're putting us in the poor house."

"I'm a man of my convictions."

"Don't hover over me, start making breakfast."

And so he did. Not eggs, bacon and toast, like she asked, but Cornflakes. Two bowls, two spoons, gallon of milk from the fridge. He even made instant coffee. "Crystal crap," as she called it. Gail-Lill chased it with orange juice, Lee-Willie adding a mining colony of sugar to his. They ate while continuing the hunt. Lee-Willie eyeballed the pathetic means they were living in, including the unreliable TV, set atop the permanently scratched coffee table. "Gail," he said, "you deserve nicer furniture. I'm gonna get that for you someday."

"What did I just say about promises?"

"But, Gail, you're right, our money shouldn't all go toward Winking Moon stuff. You deserve better."

"We both do, dear, but let's be realistic."

"I am realistic."

"Well you did breakfast, I'll clean up. We'll work this out with Mr. Winnechum."

"I'll work it out with his head if he comes round, pestering for it." And with that, his rickety chair collapsed, sending him *and* his cornflakes to the floor.

CHAPTER 9:

THE FIRST SATURDAY OF THE SEASON

The first Saturday night back was even crazier than the night before. Nearly every American-made van, truck and muscle car known to creation was represented, along with station wagons, compacts, ponies, and convertibles. They all funneled in, paying their share, moving around the screen into the lot. Kathy's transistor played the latest Top 40 hits. Currently, Peter Frampton's "Baby I Love Your Way" competed with Jim's omnipresent pre-show music over the P.A.

Steve was aimed at the exit. He wanted to make yet another obnoxious entrance into work to make his mark. When he started roaring toward the illegal entrance point, Kathy shouted at them to stop. They heard her. She had quite a voice. Steve locked up the brakes and came to a skidding halt in front of the white picket fence, damaging the paint job further. "Did you kids end up doing anything last night after everybody split?"

"Like what, Kathy?" George shouted out the window. He was riding shotgun.

"Like an after-hours party," she said, never missing a beat with the customers. "Something fun?"

"No, we were too beat," George answered. "Are you kidding?"

"No, I'm not kidding. If you do, don't forget me."

The boys looked at each other. Kathy's asking to be invited to an after-hours party?

Steve hollered, "Kathy, we would never forget you. If you wanna be invited, we'll invite ya!"

"I want in. Thought you clucks were talking about something last night."

"Nope, we were just busting balls. Fun is yet to come."

"We would never forget you," John assured, Alex just staring from the backseat.

The next in line—a dude with his friends in a Mercury Cougar—could not help but overhear. "I couldn't forget you either, girl. Can I come in and paint with you?"

"No," Kathy said instantly, getting the money, giving them their tickets. "Go on through." When he passed, she turned back to the Crusaders, shaking her head— "Melvin."

They all laughed. "Ha!" said George. "You learned one of our words. See ya, Kathy!"

"See ya—" she returned, then emphasized, 'Melvins'!"

They tore into the exit.

Concessions were swamped early. Pre-show madness. There was the usual assortment of clods and dopes, shoving and pushing each other in jest. Others were drunk or stoned already, reeking of substances. One schmo and his sidekick were performing wheelbarrow races across the floor—holding each other's legs while the man on the floor flapped his hands mightily, propelling forward. They crashed and laughed, crashed and laughed. Stanley executed his first holler of the night. "Keep doing that and I'll reverse-Pilgrim your asses back to wherever your ancestors came from."

Food and drink were leaping off the grill and fountains, warming trays stocked, pizzas baking, popcorn popping. Patrons balanced trays of refreshments out the doors, setting up camps around their vehicles. Condiments were slathered on hotdogs and burgers, napkins ripped from the dispensers like butterflies fleeing in mass migration. Laughter was everywhere. So was the smell of cigarettes, pot and alcohol.

The Stuckersons weren't around yet so the Crusaders were busting balls with girls they knew from school, showing off their smocks, modeling, zipping-and-unzipping their zippers as fast as they could. Vicki snapped them back into place, reminding them where they were and what they were getting paid for.

Alex, John, George and Steve asked Stanley why the back-storage room had gotten more congested and unorganized since last season.

"First of all: it's none of your business," he answered. "Second: your bosses just kept storin' stuff there over the winter. They're screwin' up Franco's old space. That was his domain and always will be."

"Ah, 'Franco,' that name came up awful quick," said George.

"And don't you disrespect it. He was my buddy and best-damn

manager this joint ever saw. You mudhens never met him, but I worked with him for twenty years. Keep your comments to yourself."

George threw his hands up. "I didn't say anything, I didn't say anything."

"Franco" was someone the Crusaders had heard much about but had never met. And they would *continue* hearing about him as long as Stanley worked at the Winking Moon.

Vicki was on ice cream duty, bowed over the trunk accessible to the public from their side of the counter, re-stocking Nutty Buddy's, Popsicles and ice cream sandwiches. Stanley told her to work faster. "Stanley," she said. "You got me bending over this thing like a Hebrew slave. How long you want me here?"

Before Stanley could answer, a male patron answered, "All night, baby."

The Crusaders chased him out with raised fists.

It was a night of mayhem. The first firecracker exploded just before twilight. Instantly, Lee-Willie and Gail-Lill dispatched the patrolmen to squelch the nonsense. "There'll be a thousand more if you boys don't end that right away," said Mr. Stuckerson. The Crusaders had no problem showing their muscle. They found the kids responsible, took their remaining packs, walked them over to the bucket of soap-water they'd been using to clean the windows and dumped them right in it.

"There. Anymore and next time it'll be your heads," said Steve.

A Frisbee war broke out—an occasional occurrence at the Winking Moon while it was still light out. Three or four dozen of the play discs went sailing over people's heads and cars, narrowly missing some, hitting others. One AMC Pacer got clipped in the quarter-panel. The owner, a burly-looking guy with a full beard and mustache came out wanting to fight. The Crusaders ran over to get in the middle to smooth things over.

"Who are you guys?" the man asked, catching notice of their uniforms.

"We're the patrolmen here," said Alex, the voluntary spokesmen. "We make sure stuff like this doesn't happen."

"Well you're not doing a very good job of it. Look at my car."

There was a scuff in the shining metal. It could probably be rubbed out, but the paint job was slightly marred. Alex stood as tall as he could and turned to face the majority of the audience, Steve, John and George getting out of his way. Alex wound his lungs up, and blared-out to the crowd, in competition with the music and laughing, "Stop with the Frisbees already, people, or there's gonna be trouble! Someone's gonna get hurt!"

This was met with a volley of horns from every direction. The whole lot had pockets of the blasts breaking out, rebels eager to defy authority. The patrolmen had become reacquainted with this response, enduring the dissonance until it was over.

Next, they stopped some eighteen-year olds from deflating the tires of a friend who had unexpectedly pulled up behind them and parked for the show. The sap had gone to the bathroom and the jamokes were going to let the air out while he was gone. They had the cap off and the primary goon was using his thumbnail to let the air escape. The Crusaders stood looming behind them until the teens noticed. "If that thing deflates," Steve asked assuredly, "who's gonna pump it back up again?"

The pack leader was startled, letting go of the valve-stem. "We dunno but this'll be funny."

"And he'll be stuck here all night waiting for a tow truck to come and blow his tires back up," said Alex. "We're gonna be tired by that point, we're gonna wanna go home, *we're* not letting you do this."

"C'mon man, it's a joke, it'll be funny."

"What will be funny is seeing how far up your buttocks we can stick the air hose when it arrives," said George, puffing out his chest. "You're not goin' anywhere if those tires are down."

The three mischief-makers looked at The Crusaders: their embroidered insignia, the walkie-talkies, flashlights. They gave up, stopped the prank. "Man…" the guys resigned, standing.

An older man of about forty came striding up, having watched the exchange from a distance. "Why do you kids talk so tough?" he asked the patrolmen.

"We're just trying to keep the peace, sir," John answered.

"That's your job?"

"Yes, sir," John continued. "Keeps the police and authorities at bay. And we call 'em."

The man scratched his head. "I heard this place was wild, but I didn't know they needed bouncers around, threatening to beat people up."

Alex was quick to the point— "We're not threatening to 'beat people up,' sir."

"That's how you got your busted lip last year, Al."

"John, shh. Don't bring that up. Lucky shot."

Squawk. Lee Willie on the radios got their attention. "Crusaders, did you find the knuckleheads with the firecrackers?"

"We did, sir," George answered. "We took care of it. Where are you, sir?"

"In the office," Lee-Willie responded. "We're taking care of a few things; we'll be out before the first film. Everybody clock-in?

"Yes, sir, as soon as we got here," said George.

"Good, ya did something right tonight."

Lee-Willie's stressed face resembled a pinched whiffle ball as he and his wife were indeed in the office, sweating away with a barely-functioning electric fan atop a teetering filing cabinet, sifting through the muckety-muck of urgent paperwork and piles of company books and manuals. They each grabbed a cool drink from the small refrigerator in the corner—little else in it but a bottle of mustard, soy sauce packets and half-eaten Ramen noodles—parked their butts on rickety chairs, stared at the playing answering-service machine spinning its capstans, answering the public, calling about the movies. "So, we can't write out our current rent-check yet because of insufficient funds, do you think we can get on the phone with Bannabock and ask if Bluestone would give us an advance?"

"That's a risky play, Lee," said Gail-Lill. "We survived the day without Mr. Winnechum coming looking for it."

"Bannabock will do something, he's regional director."

"Maybe he will, maybe he won't. I'm sorry about all this, Lee."

"It's okay, honey. Bluestone has to get on the ball. They have to pay us better."

"You think they will with things looking bleak?" she asked.

"They're not looking bleak," said Lee-Willie. "If you're talkin' about the rumors, we've never been busier. I mean just look at the parking lot, it's fucking Mardi Gras."

"Well, we have to be more careful with our spending."

"Bluestone gonna do some of the repairs around here? Maybe we wouldn't have to be spending our own money if they ran this place like they're supposed to and did the fucking repairs themselves. They're corporate, they own the drive-in."

"You know how Kurt is, Lee, he hasn't exactly been Johnny-On-The-Spot returning calls. This could go unanswered."

"Everybody wants something from us but nobody's giving back. One of these days I'll march right over to headquarters myself, ask what the hell's going on. That's what it takes: balls. Maybe I'll even ask what's up with the rumors. Is Bluestone really thinkin' of closing us up? We have a right to know."

"Lee, just relax, I'm sure Mr. Bannabock will explain everything in due time. This is all just a big misunderstanding, probably."

"Winnechum, Bannabock. These names. Jocavelli, Tambone, Laneske, Barenta. Why can't anybody have normal names anymore? Why do they have to be so messed-up?"

Gail-Lill wryly lifted an eyebrow. "'Stuckerson'?"

Bam-bam-bam! Something pelted the doors. The Stuckersons raced to it, opening it up. There was gooey egg-yolk and slime running all down the side of it. God knew how many had hit. Looked like a freakin' dozen. Lee-Willie locked eyes at Kathy, called to her from across the mini lawn dividing them— "Ms. Berenger? Who threw eggs at our door?"

Looking over, she said, "Who threw 'what' at your door, Mr. Stuckerson?"

Lee-Willie took a step aside, gesturing at the door so Kathy could get a better look. "Look at this: eggs! All over our door. Somebody just threw a bunch at it and now there's shells and guck all over down here and they took off running. Did you see anybody?"

The current patron she was exchanging money with was telling Kathy to hurry. "Mr. Stuckerson, do you see the traffic I'm dealing with?" And there was a line, still. "Sorry, I didn't."

"Well, grow eyes in the back of your head!" Lee-Willie snapped. "Or take longer breaks between brush strokes." He shut the door, swore. "Get some paper toweling," he said to his wife. "We gotta clean this off, it's almost dark."

Gail-Lill dutifully went for the bathroom to retrieve paper towels. The speaker with the pre-show music playing halted, Jim's voice cutting in. "Ready, Winking Moon? It's showtime!" Jim did this on occasion, especially on Saturdays. The crowd honked loud as shit and cheered, the Stuckersons feeling the power all the way from the inside of the office.

The first real trouble of the night occurred early as Cheech Marin lit up his sixth doobie in the film "Up In Smoke," currently playing. A couple was going at it in a Ford Mustang, windows down and grunts and groans mixing with the sounds from the film. The guy had his pants all the way down to his ankles, bouncing up-and-down on the chick like an amusement park ride. Some of his neighbors were not appreciating the goings-on. A group of kids had been walking by, flying paper airplanes made of heavy newspaper. One particularly clever entrepreneur paid the kids off to throw a few into the open window of the Mustang, curtailing the intolerable activity.

The second stuck right in the butt-crack of the stud in the compromised position, infuriating him and shocking the hell out of his girlfriend. He stopped and got out, pulling his pants up, un-sticking the paper 747 from between his glutes, holding it in his hands, shaking with anger as he shouted around, trying to draw out the audacious bastard who had the nerve to interrupt him. Patrons were cackling at him. The Crusaders heard the squabbling, rushed to the scene. They tried hard to maintain their composure after hearing of the incident, but the offended pointed an angry finger at the teenagers, saying they were partially responsible for "creating an atmosphere where something like this could happen."

"No, sir," said Alex, pushing back verbally. "We had nothing to do with this. We prevent this stuff. Whoever did it ran off. There's no point in getting mad, sir."

"In fact, there're a lot of empty spaces in the back, still," said Steve, siding with his buddy. "Maybe you wanna relocate to back there where you and your date can have some privacy? We promise we won't bother you. Ya just have to leave at night's end, okay?"

"I just might do that. Here," he said, realizing this was a losing battle, holding the paper airplane extracted from the personal area to the security force. "Take this, throw it away somewhere. I oughtta sue."

The Crusaders backed up, hands up. They were not touching the thing. "Sir," said George, "there's plenty of garbage receptacles in the concession stand. Throw it out yourself on the way. Better yet, there's dumpsters. With *incinerators* in 'em."

The howling from the patrons around them was not generated from Cheech & Chong up on screen. This had been better than the entire movie thus far.

"He's back," said Lee-Willie to the Crusaders, catching them just as they were getting set to split apart to patrol different quadrants.

"Who's back?" asked Steve.

"The Wild Man of Borneo."

"You're kidding," said Alex. "Where?"

"Over there." Lee-Willie pointed to the north side of the lot, where the character had appeared earlier. "Where he always is: the birches, the stretch of them there between the oaks and elms. He's in a particularly thin one tonight."

"Holy shit, he's back, already?" queried George. "Thought he'd wait another month or so. He's got balls."

"And we gotta do something about it. He's already thrown a couple of rotten apples at customers. Luckily, he didn't hit anyone. My wife is back in the office crying, she's so sick of dealing with him." There was already a crowd of patrons there. The five could hear the disturbance. Additional onlookers were getting out of their vehicles. "I'm gonna kill the guy if I go over there, you Crusaders handle it. But remember: be diplomatic. No violence."

"Oh we'll 'be diplomatic' all over his ass," said Alex, leading his team away.

Alex, John, George and Steve had to clear the throng away on the boulevard. Some patrons had flashlights already aimed up at the bum, taunting the man, begging him to come down so they could murder him. He was perched way up high, camped out on a long, thin limb, arrogantly drinking from his flask and belching, being disgusting, watching the movie and laughing.

"He must've gotten bolder from last year," George said, as the four reached the scene.

Alex turned up to face the Wild Man. "Mister get down."

Wild Man said, "Ah, you're the children whom they were talking about last time I was here. Up yours." He chucked an apple down—*splat!*—and cleared everybody away. The crowd began picking up loose sticks and stones, ready to pelt him down.

"No-no-no-no!" warned Alex. "We're not doin' that! Everybody back off! Please!"

"We can't enjoy the movie with him up there," seared another. "It's fucking creepy and unsafe with that asshole looming up there. He's going to hit somebody!"

"Mister get down," said Alex again. "We heard you've been here already, time to get down and go away. You can't watch the movies for free."

"I'm not in your drive-in, I'm on this side of the fence. It's not your property. I can do whatever I want."

"Wild Man," he said, "we don't wanna have to call the police."

"There's that name again: 'Wild Man.' Told ya I ain't never been to Borneo. Go away, make popcorn, do some-fucking-thing, call the police if ya want. You have crappy movies anyway."

Alex lowered his voice, said to his buddies, "Now he's really insulting us."

"Mister, you're bothering these nice people," tried Steve, calling up to him. "They paid to get in here. You're ruining their movie and it's not fair to them. Now we're asking ya nicely."

"Fuck you," Wild Man repeated, followed by an even-louder—"Wa-hoooo!"

Alex said to the three, "Get on the radio, call Jim. Ask him to come out here."

John removed his walkie from his holster, lifted it to his mouth. "Jim, can you—?"

Squawk. "You guys handle it," came Jim's voice over all four radios. "I've mentored you well. Been hearing the whole thing from the booth."

"How do you want us to handle it?" John asked.

"Didn't you tell me about a certain technique you chooches were looking to utilize last year? The 'old Shake-n-Bake'? Just like in the commercials?"

They looked at each other, grinning from ear to ear. "He's right," said John.

"Now's the time to use it," said George.

Alex once again turned upward to face the Wild Man. "Mister, we're giving ya one more opportunity. Please come down and walk away. Nicely."

Thwap! Splush! All his residual fruit came down, smashing around everyone's feet. The Wild Man then made a point to finish off his whiskey, holding the flask upside-down. "Oh damn, I'm out," he boasted. "Maybe I'll come back later with a refill."

That is when Alex engaged. "He's out," he whispered to his men. "Now's the time."

"Let's go!" said George, and they all went up-and-over the fence. George, Steve, John and Alex came down into the brush, on the other side. Now they were at the base of the birch tree. Wild Man was directly above them. The crowd came alive with anticipation.

This made the Wild Man nervous. "Wh-what are you doing? What's g-going on?" he said.

"We gave you enough chances," said Alex. "Now it's time to take matters into our own hands."

"You can't come over here," said Wild Man, sounding more distressed. "This is *not* your property; this is *not* your jurisdiction."

"You can take your 'jurisdiction'," said John, "and shove it up your ass."

"The old Shake-n-Bake!" said Steve, and they grew giddy.

Slowly but surely, they got the birch tree rocking, surrounding the base—each of the Crusaders taking a side—moving in harmony, coordinated synchronization, pushing and pulling back-and-forth. Before long, the whole tree was shaking madly, crashing into the ones next to it. Leaves and twigs were starting to fall from this tree and the ones next to it. The Wild Man was holding on tight but starting to lose his grip. The crowd was no longer watching the movie. They were loving this. Tink! Thud! The flask and greasy bag came loose, bounced off all the branches on the way down. There was no more ammo. No more whiskey. John, Steve, George and Alex were working up a sweat, careening the high, lean tree against the night sky, Wild Man desperately trying to cling to it but was losing the battle. "I'm losing my grip!" he was braying. "I'm losing my grip!"

"Good!" shouted Alex.

"Aaaaggghhh!" Wild Man screamed, tumbling earthward, all the way from the top, terrified for his life, hitting and bouncing off each branch on the way down, breaking many of them in the process.

"Watch out!" Alex cried, and all four jumped out of the way.

Thud! Wild Man landed in the underbrush, face-down, spread-eagled, at the base of the trunk—seemingly lifeless, if not for the rise and fall of his breath. The audience erupted in applause, leaping up and hoisting themselves onto the fence, lauding the heroic patrolmen who just made their night, thanking them for an excellent job. Alex extracted rubber gloves from his smock, calmly put them on. "Borrowed a few from the stand," he said. "Thought they might come in handy."

He lifted Wild Man's scraggly face out of the mud by his matted hair like a hunter's prize— just enough for the light-beams to show off the pattern of dirt and leaves stuck between his teeth. "I… hate… you… guys…." the Wild Man managed, wheezing it out as he spit some of the grime and dirt from his tongue. Alex dropped his face back to the soil.

"But we love this…" he said, proudly.

The Crusaders felt like conquerors. Amidst the clapping and cheering, Alex took out the extra gloves for his pals, threw them to Steve, George and John, said "Put em on, we haven't been through the brush in a while," and motioned to the lump of human lying on the ground. "They got bigger dumpsters there than we do."

Each of the teenagers picked up the near-comatose Wild Man by his limp arms and legs, carried him cracking and crunching through the fifty yards of harrowing woods there, guided by the spotlights hanging in the back parking lot of Roller Town—pumping away with disco-music inside—and heave-hoed the grubby rogue into one of the two open dumpsters there, among the trash and debris.

"There," said Alex with a sense of accomplishment. They peeled off the rubber gloves, threw them in over Wild Man's face. "Now we can call Sergeant Leo. Jim will at least do that for us."

"What about the no-violence thing Stuckerson just told us?" asked

John.

"I think we'll get a pass on this one."

They could hear the applause still raging at the drive-in, the light-beams from the flashlights sweeping through the trees. The radio squawked and it was the Stuckersons, demanding to know what had just happened.

Sergeant Leo had Wild Man hand-cuffed in the back of his '78 Plymouth Volare police cruiser. He was fairly beaten and bruised from the encounter with the Crusaders, eyes glazing open and closed. The lawman read the Riot Act to the Crusaders for ten minutes, reminding them of the need to keep a more tolerable drive-in this year. He, the boys, big Jim and the Stuckersons were keeping their voices low. The boys had doubted the severity of the some of the offenses.

"No—George, Steve, John, Alex—this place *isn't* getting out-of-control, it *is* out-of-control. One of these days you're going to have a war on your hands. Now I don't need to know exactly how the perpetrator ended up in the dumpster at Roller Town, or how you kids found out about it—but I'm just telling all of you to watch it. I have too much going on this evening to stand around here and lecture you all night. I know this won't be the last time I'll be called here but it better be the last *tonight*. Don't make this any more of an embarrassment to the community than it already is. Jim, buddy: keep a leash on your boys. Now I gotta go."

Jim was leaning against his truck, enjoying a good cigarette. He seemed as cool as a glass of iced tea. "'My boys'?" he said. "Why all of a sudden are they 'my boys'?"

"Because they are." Lee-Willie bristled. Leo saw the reaction. "No disrespect, Mr. Stuckerson. How you two doing through all this? Mrs. Stuckerson? You look a little wiped-out."

"Off to a rough start, Sergeant Leo," Gail-Lill said.

"Mr. Stuckerson—" said the sergeant, "you wouldn't be telling your staff to shake people out of trees, would you?"

"Now come on, Sergeant," said Lee-Willie, "why on Earth would I do something so foolish? I'm running a respectable drive-in." Then, glaring at the projectionist, "Jim wouldn't do that, either."

Jim smiled, took a long drag of his cigarette. Showed all his teeth.

Leo prepared to leave. "Just keep my life simple, okay? Please." Then he glanced up at the screen. "What the hell is this movie?"

"'Cheech & Chong's Up In Smoke,'" said Alex.

Leo made a face. "Nice role models. I can smell the weed coming off the screen. Or is that from the lot? That certainly wouldn't be coming from the cars, would it?"

"Thanks for coming over, Sergeant Leo," said Mr. Stuckerson, extending his hand. They shook.

"Goodnight, gentlemen," said Sergeant Leo.

The Crusaders all waved to him. They liked the man very much. "See ya, Sergeant Leo," said Steve. "You're the best."

Leo looked doubtfully at the teenagers. "Sure I am. Jim—when we doing that barbecue? Maggie and me got all the fixings. You and Jeannie just have to show up with the appetites."

"I'll tell her," said Jim. "We're excited."

"Marry that girl."

"You, too?"

Leo got in the cruiser. "Hooah."

"Hooah, buddy," Jim said in return. "We'll go skydiving."

Hearing the military cry but not knowing what it was, Wild Man impulsively loose a shrill and discordant howl as Sergeant Leo drove out of the lot, a chunk of patrons applauding the departure as they went. "And keep him out!" someone yelled.

When it was just the seven of the Mooners left, Lee-Willie turned his silent rage toward the patrolmen. "'The Old Shake-n-Bake'? Where'd ya learn that?"

Alex, again, played the spokesman. "Just something we chooches ran by each other over the winter, sir. Effective, wasn't it?"

John added, "He won't be back this year, Mr. and Mrs. Stuckerson."

Lee-Willie choked down a snappy comeback. Turned and led his wife away, saying to the

boys, "Clean up for intermission."

Jim waved the couple off with the cigarette burning in his fingers. "See ya, Lee. Gail."

"See ya, Jimmy," said Gail-Lill.

Lee-Willie said, "I don't like that smile."

When the bosses were gone, Jim pushed off his Chevy Fleetside, informed the Crusaders

that he was going back in the booth. "Keep your heads low, gentlemen, keep your heads low."

The Crusaders were set to go in for intermission, still feeling superior about their conquest, when they heard hooligans and punks sneaking through the brush on the other side of the fence on the north side—not far from their latest scuffle.

They got up close, all four of them, listened carefully, keeping their mouths shut. They knew just what to do from last year. Figured there was about five of the little bastards over there, making their way from Roller Town to the drive-in. "This is a lot better than skatin' around all night," said one of the underage squeakers. "My older brother says he sneaks-in all the time."

Steve, George, John and Alex got up to practically right under the hot spot, just to the side, exactly where they knew the kids were going to leap onto the fence. They had done this multitudes of times last year, this is what they signed up for. They were giddy, practically unable to contain their excitement. said he even felt his balls tingling with excitement: a joke that had carried over from last year.

One… two… three… four… five… six! Six young boys stuck their heads up, peeking around. The Crusaders were looking at their semi-lit faces from below. The movie screen accentuated their dopey, innocent faces. The end titles were set to scroll, the final shot of "Up In Smoke" projected, as people stepped out of their vehicles, heading for a bathroom break and the concession stand.

"Let's go," their leader said. "No one's looking."

There was a mad scramble. Feet and hands against wood. All six came up and over at once, landing in the boulevard on The Moon's side with various coordination. One fell, two stumbled. Floom! Right on cue, The Moon Tower lit the lot, Crusaders springing in like a pack of cheetahs, blasting the pre-teener's faces with even more light.

"Hold it right there!" Alex bellowed with a distinctively low voice, surrounding the scofflaws.

The six screamed, scrambled back over the fence, fighting and stepping on one another.

"Yeah, that's right, you get back over!" Steve said. "Don't even think twice about doing this again!" said George "Next time we'll bury ya!" John added. As they heard the punks and hooligans falling to the underbrush below, hurting themselves, stumbling to get up and swearing as they ran away, the patrolmen burst into hysterics.

After catching their breath and wiping the sweat from their brows, the Crusaders high-fived each other and slapped one another on the back in celebration. "*Now* we can go in, thank you very much," said Steve. "I'm ready for intermission."

Alex was sent to the rooftop of the concession stand for rinsing-and-cleaning detail. Each of the Crusaders had to take a turn at this at least once last summer. Whoever was assigned had to take the power-hose from the back-storage room, coiled up haphazardly under tons of boxes, and hook it up to the slop sink in the utility closet adjacent to the freezer. Then, they had set the eight-foot ladder up under the trapdoor in the center of the ceiling, and hoist that up—water on—along with a broom, dust pan, and a plastic contractor's bag, finally climbing and crawling up onto the flat pitch-and-tar roof that stretched the length of the concession stand. There were always tons of shit up here, and tonight was no exception. Once last year, Alex found a prosthetic leg. A *prosthetic leg!*

This particular night, there were the usual assortment of empty pizza boxes, popcorn tubs, candy wrappers, soda cups, loose clothing items (a pair of panties and a bra top), coins, puddles of God-knew-what, and a few condoms. He did not check to see if they'd been used.

But the view from up there was magical, always bringing him a sense of peace. He could see everything from every direction—the entire spread of the drive-in and beyond. He was star struck. Literally, an eight-year old kid called up from below— "Hey mister, whatcha doin'?"

"Cleaning off this rooftop," Alex answered.

"Why?"

"'Cause it gets kinda dirty up here."

"Ever find people up there?"

"What do you mean?"

"Having sex!" the boy stated. "My Dad had to re-locate three times from where we first parked 'cause of all the people gettin' it on."

Before Alex could think of a good way to address that, "Dad" walked into the scene from a pack of vans and collected his boy on the way in the stand, telling him not to bother Alex. "He's busy, son, leave him alone."

"Alex, get to work!" said Lee-Willie, stepping out from the opposite side, catching him lollygagging. "I don't want you up there all night boofing the pooch. You got things to do down here in concessions."

"Yes, sir."

Alex put on more plastic gloves, took to sweeping up and bagging what he could, waiting until it was safe below before turning the power-hose on. When he did, he was careful not to get anybody wet down there. Many asked questions. Several times he had to turn the freakin' thing off just to answer.

He watched as George came waltzing out of the stand, still wearing his hairnet and making a path in the direction of the ticket box, where Kathy sat. He was carrying a box of goodies and drinks, angling up-and-over the humps, through the parked vehicles. "Where're ya going?" Alex shouted at him.

George halted, turned around. "Giving Kathy a snack. Stuckersons wanted me to do it. She's stuck in the box office all night, customers are still comin' in."

"Wanna switch?" Alex pleaded.

George laughed. "You wish. I'm the lucky one tonight, buddy."

Alex turned back to the roof, turning on the powerful water-flow.

George greeted Kathy in her solitary workspace, as she managed the semi-steady flow of incoming traffic, painting, still listening to her Top 40 hits on the transistor. One of George's favorites, "I'm Not In Love," by 10cc, was playing. He sang a few bars, making her laugh. She took her refreshments graciously, thanked him and told him to thank the Stuckersons for treating her.

"It's tough being out here all the time," she said. "I get hungry. Look at these people still coming in."

She was right. There was a line all the way to the main road.

Her next customer was a '72 Dodge Challenger, filled to the brim with drunk twenty-somethings, all grinning like fools. George kept his eyes on them. He had seen stunts from chooches like this at the gate once or twice. The driver, smoothing back his long hair, began the opening exchange of hellos, but suddenly the car engine died. Right there. He kept turning the key over, hoping to restart it, but with no success. Cars behind started to honk. This was not looking good.

"What's going on?" Kathy said. "What's wrong?"

"Damn thing won't start," said the driver. "This has happened before. Gotta get this thing to the shop. Shit, the timing." His cohorts were all looking shameful.

"Kathy, what's that beeping out there?" Lee-Willie's voice cracked over the radio.

"A car won't start, Mr. Stuckerson," she said into hers. "It's blocking the other traffic from

getting in."

"Well take care of it, we're swamped over here. And get George back this way."

Now the blocked crowd was getting vocal. "C'mon, get that hunka junk outta the way!" "We want in, clear the path!"

Driver said, "Can we just push it through and pay when we get it out of the way? We really wanna see these movies, just let us do it so we're not holding other people up." Kathy looked at George. *I don't know about this.* They had unblocked the gate. "Please? We're holding people up. We'll pay when we move off to the shoulder."

Kathy sighed. "Okay but hurry up. George, can you help them?"

"Sure."

The driver stayed behind the wheel, his three buddies clambering out, getting behind the vehicle to start pushing, George, himself, piling in on it, ready to show off his strength. He flexed his biceps for Kathy. The friends gave the signal and the driver slipped the ignition into neutral. George and the three loopy dudes rolled it through, pulled up behind Kathy's Malibu, off to the shoulder. Satisfied with a job well-done, George began to mosey back to the box office, believing the fellows were behind him. Instead they jumped back in the Challenger, started the engine up, and with howling eruptions of laughter, shot off into the drive-in, turning their lights off, screeching with elation at the prank they had just pulled.

"Shit! They suckered us!" said George, freezing on the spot. "They're in! Kathy: radio the Crusaders, tell 'em what's going on, tell 'em I'm running after 'em—right now!"

George put his athletic prowess into gear, sprinted off after the Challenger already deep inside the joint, making rounds through the rear rows, trying to avoid capture, speeding then slowing, speeding then slowing.

"Alex! John! Steve!" Kathy was sputtering into the radio back in the booth, "George is running after a Dodge Challenger that just snuck in. They pretended they could not get their engine to start. We had them push it through the gate and then they took off! It was all a fake-out!"

"What the fuck?" interrupting Lee-Willie, jumping in on the call.

"We got it, Kathy!" said Steve. "We see it now!"

With car's lights off, it did not matter. The boisterous muscle was obvious. Lots of patrons were out, watching the fiasco. Dust was being kicked up from beneath its tires, drifting like low-hanging clouds. Steve and John joined George, Alex directing from the rooftop.

"Guys! It's headed towards the back! That's it, Steve, go between those vans! George, they're gonna turn left again! Pour it on, John!"

John was the fastest in a foot race. He easily ran the van down when it slowed to turn a corner, avoiding a man who had stepped out to pee behind his truck. He got in front of it while Steve and George roared up from behind, forcing the driver to slam on the brakes. As the idiots laughed and hooted it up, having brilliantly entertained themselves, George reached in the open window, threw the transmission into park, grabbed the keys and turned the engine off. Steve and John were going to pull the fools from the doors and throttle them, but Lee-Willie jogged in huffing-and-puffing, angry as a hornet, telling the occupants he was going to call the police and have them arrested. The driver threw his hands in the air— "Honesty, I didn't think it would start!" he appealed.

"Bullshit!" said Lee-Willie. "You knew exactly what you were doing, I've seen it before. John—go in the stand, call Sergeant Leo, get him over here right away."

"Again, Mr. Stuckerson?" said the quiet one. "Do we really wanna do that? He just said he doesn't want to hear from us again tonight."

"We're leaving, we're leaving," the driver and his buddies were saying, talking over them.

Lee-Willie considered John's point. "Okay, get outta here," he said. "Now! Don't dilly-dally, get the hell out right now but you're gonna push yourselves out. Ya got yourselves in by being wise asses, that's how you're leaving. Crusaders: follow 'em out. George: don't give 'em their keys 'til they're on Sing—and watch 'em drive off. You dumb-shits come back and I'll make sure you *do* get arrested."

"All right, man—mellow out, mellow out," the driver whined.

And that's exactly what happened—the Crusaders accompanied the chooches as they pushed the Challenger out, the driver sitting behind the wheel, transmission in neutral, forced to endure the humiliation of cheers and jeers from the crowd, giving them a proper send-off. It was not until they were on Sing Road, like Lee-Willie wanted, that George threw them back their keys, watched them go until they were just disappearing taillights in the dark.

Kathy was embarrassed. The Stuckersons had a talk with her as "H.O.T.S." began, schooling her on how she shouldn't have let morons like that pull a fast one on her. "You told me to take care of it, Mr. Stuckerson," she said, on the verge of tears. "How was I supposed to know they were faking it? I've never seen that stunt before."

Gail-Lill stepped in, comforting her. "Kathy, it's all right, they're gone now, we're just going to have to be more careful. These clowns are getting bolder and bolder."

Kathy sulked for the rest of the night. Alex watched from the roof, desperate to console her and teach her the warning signs they had learned from last summer. He coiled the power-hose and went to put it away in the junkyard that had become the back-storage room, looking around at the mess that had grown beyond imagination. There was only one small window on each side of the bunker that let in the smallest amount of light during the day, and there was virtually no space for anything else. He figured the Stuckersons must have stored much of their personal items here since last year. The still taped up moving boxes were almost tipping.

Steve, George and John came booming in, sweaty as pigs from their stint with the Challenger. "We fucking did it, Alex!" crowed Steve.

"We're the fucking champion of The Winking Moon!" said George.

They were as flighty as kites when Stanley Mason shuffled in, telling them to "clean the fuck up" and "get the fuck back in the stand to present to customers." This was Stanley in serious mode. They'd seen him like this before this and knew not to mess with him. Alex finished up his duty as the other three washed up in the utility sink, wiping off and grabbing hairnets, finally getting the breather they needed.

"You okay, Stan?" Alex asked, dragging the garbage bag over to where he was standing.

Stanley spoke low. "This place. The back-storage room. This is where Franco and I used to come in early and make our birdhouses. We'd bring 'em home for our wives to paint. They sold 'em in the church bazaars. We made a few bucks."

"Look at it now," said Alex. "Gotten a little denser since last year, it seems."

"Lee and Gail dumped a bunch of shit in here when they moved into their new apartment in October, said their place was too small. They move around more than a nomad in the desert. Ruined the space. Lookit Franco's workbench there, there's boxes of toilet paper stacked on top of it. That's no way to honor a man's memory. Thank God they didn't touch his tools."

"You really miss him, don't you?" said Alex. "I wish we could have met him."

"You woulda liked to have worked for him. Best damn manager this joint ever saw. There'd be none of this yelling and puttin'-down with the insults. I'm not gonna take it from the guy. He shows me no respect, I show him none."

"I think he's just a little stressed out."

"I think he's just a little bit of an asshole," said Stanley. "Lets the job go to his head."

I'm sorry about your loss. I really am."

"Franco's heart was too big, that was his problem. He was my best friend. If his ticker hadn't given out on him, he'd still be here. We worked together a long time. Fifteen years."

"There're customers out there. C'mon, let's go serve 'em."

Before that could happen, Lee-Willie barged onto the ramp in the doorway that fed down into the storage area, blocking them. 'What the hell have you two been doing?" he spat.

"Lee," said Stanley, staying calm, "when you gonna clean this room up? It's dangerous and someday somebody's gonna get hurt with everything stacked around. Don't touch the planks of wood or the tools, though, those're Franco's."

"Don't tell me what to do or don't do, Stanley," said Lee-Willie. "I do what needs to be done. I know those are Franco's, I haven't touched 'em yet, have I?"

Stanley turned to Alex just before squeezing past. "See?"

"'See' what?" Lee-Willie said, watching the small man move by him into the stand, then turned to the youngster. "What'd that mean? Alex, what did he say to you?"

"Nothing, sir," answered Alex, tying the bag. "Roof's all clean. I'll throw this out in the dumpster and wash up and get back to work with everyone."

"Find anything interesting up there this time?" asked Lee-Willie.

Stanley popped his head in under Lee-Willie's arm. "Certainly not your brains, Lee, those are gone forever."

The staff made it unexpectedly smoothly through their first Saturday night back. The encore presentation of "Up In Smoke," was playing on the big screen. But the second film had created discussion. As the Crusaders strolled the outer perimeters, checking on vehicles here-and-there, they mused over what the hell the title meant. "What the fork-knife-and-spoon was that?" Steve said. "Is it an acronym: 'H.O.T.S.'?"

George did not know. "Did we miss something?" he said. "I didn't catch it, either. What do the letters stand for?"

John shrugged his shoulders. "I dunno, I was busy chasing that stray cat outta the girls' bathroom."

"It's an 'Animal House' rip-off, that's for sure," Alex said. "*That* movie was awesome. Think we're gonna be seein' a lot of gross-out comedies now because of the success of that John Landis flick."

"We'll be starting full-time soon so we'll be seeing each movie all week long now," said Steve. "That'll be good."

"Great," said John. "More to occupy our noodles."

After the Stuckersons picked up the money from the till, the patrolmen escorted Kathy through the parking lot, so they could get at their chores. After the stint pulled earlier, they were determined to make sure she got there in one piece.

"Is this how it's going to be all summer?" she asked, a smile in her voice as she was massively amused. "You four, walking me back to the stand every night?"

"Not every night, just tonight," said George.

"We feel really bad about that Dodge Challenger," Steve said. "Could've happened to anybody."

John agreed. "I haven't even seen a stunt like that," he said.

Kathy shook her head. "I'm trying to forget about it."

"Pretty cool how that worked out though, huh, Alex?" said George. "You as look-out on the roof, us below, taking care of it like a team. Alex?"

"Yeah, I'm here. It was cool grooves." Alex could not keep his eyes off Kathy. He wanted to throw his arms around her, squeeze her tight, tell her that it was no big deal letting that car through.

They made their way over to the rest of the staff beyond the drive-in gate.

"Tomorrow's Sunday," Gail-Lill said, locking up behind them. "We're sometimes just as busy on Sunday nights."

"We remember," said Vicki, throwing a knowing look around.

Jim came in with his own set of keys. "You kids are almost out for summer vacation, right?"

"Right," Steve answered.

"Good, then I thought I'd christen the evening by having an after-hours party."

"When?" said Kathy.

"Tonight," said Jim, and waited.

One could feel the air leave the room. Then, the kids erupted in celebration. The girls jumped up-and-down, hugged one another. The boys punched each other in the shoulders and chest. Vicki bounced all the way over to the big guy, grabbed him by both arms— "Really?" she said. "Is it okay?"

Jim told the teenagers to settle down. "Ya sound like baby squirrels fallin' out of a nest."

"Will Jeannie be alright with it?"

"Jeannie's the one who suggested it," he said, lighting a cigarette. "She got the finger-food this afternoon in anticipation this was gonna happen. First: the rules. No waking the fuckin' neighbors. Be respectful at all times. Two: don't eat the fuckin' food in the house. There'll be plenty outside on the picnic table. Jeannie's generous and she remembers what you jamokes and jebeebs like. Catch you tadpoles sniffin' around for anything else… my gun's comin' out. Third: no grab-ass on the property. If you wanna molest each other… do it your cars. Capiche? Anybody not following the rules gets tossed. Just because I live out where Christ lost his sandals doesn't mean ya can make noise and wake the dead. I got neighbors, too, even though the tract isn't completely developed."

"We'll obey, Jim, we'll be good," said Vicki, still jumping around.

Jim took a long drag, blew out the smoke. "Good, you learned something over the course of the year."

Lee-Willie looked uneasy. Pulled away from his wife, sidling up to the big guy, kept his voice down. "Jim, can I speak to you?"

"Sure."

The two drifted off to the side, by the arcade games. "I'm not tryin' to tell you your business, but… remember… the drinking age in New York State is eighteen. These kids are seventeen, except for Kathy."

"Who says I'm supplying them with alcohol?" Jim replied.

"I just remember… last year…they told me about a few pops."

"I don't know what you're talking about."

"I just thought…"

"You thought wrong. I didn't mention anything about alcohol."

"Oh." Lee-Willie felt stupid.

Then Jim asked him directly, "You coming? I'm inviting everybody."

"Uh, um…" He looked at his wife. "Gail? Jim's invitin' us to the party. Are we going?"

This caused a stir. There was a look of horror on the youngsters' faces. ***They are not coming, are they?*** But they tried to be discreet.

Gail-Lill felt put on the spot, felt her face flushing. "Um, no. Lee, we got that thing tonight, remember?"

"Remember what?" he said.

"We uh… have to start cleaning the attic in the screen."

Jim scrunched his face. "You guys are gonna clean the screen attic at 1:30 in the morning?"

Lee-Willie turned back to him. "Um, yeah, I think so. It's bad up there."

"It's bad in the back-storage room," mentioned Stanley, all eyes turning to him. He had been choosing to ignore the conversation, instead cleaning the glass cases housing the vintage movie posters that'd been up for a thousand years.

The Stuckersons ignored the remark, Lee-Willie sticking by his conviction. "Thanks, Jim. Maybe some other time."

Jim pointed. "Don't you start doing that again this year. I invited you time-and-time again last summer. You two never came."

"Sorry."

Jim gave up, eyed the cook. "Emilio? You coming? You like late-night swimming, don't ya?"

Emilio had his crocheted hairnet off. Fluffed it up into shape. "With eight children at home, Jim? And a wife *and* mother-in-law? I don't think so. My job is to come straight home from work when I'm off my shift."

The Crusaders chuckled. "You're whipped, Emilio," Steve said.

Emilio shot back, "Wait'll you get married someday, Steve, and have a family. We'll see how much joyriding you'll be doing at that point in your Charger."

"Suit yourself, Varentez," Jim said, went for the soda machine. There was one more person he had to approach. "Stan-the-Man? How about it?"

"No thanks, Jim."

"Come on, buddy, us veterans have to stick together. Come on over for a cold one. And I mean *soda-pop*."

"I don't think so. I wanna do some deep-space observing."

Crusaders chuckled again, George the loudest. "That sounds dirty," he japed. "Whose window are you gonna be a Peeping-Tom into?"

Stanley wheeled around— "Jocavelli, shut your mouth before I put a boot up your ass."

"Ha-ha, only kidding, sir."

Jim threw up his hands, gave up on the older crowd. "Okay, well that settles it. Vicki, Kathy, Steve, George, John, Alex: you're it. You're welcome."

"Can I call Jody?" Steve asked.

"Jody McBrennan! Of course!" acknowledged Jim. "Almost forgot about her. How could I, with that mouth? You two still together?"

"Yes, sir," said Steve. "Going strong, over two years now."

"It's a marriage," joked Vicki.

"Don't say that," said Jim, kiddingly giving the redhead the evil eye. He started walk out, saluting everyone with his mug. "I'll call Jeannie before I leave, let her know who's comin'."

"We earned this, Jim," said Alex. "Look at all we did tonight."

Stopping at the double-doors, he turned around. "Look at all that was *required* of you. You were doin' your jobs. And you all better get your asses up for church tomorrow morning." He let himself out.

CHAPTER 10:

THE PARTY

Jim and Jeannie's colonial house were off the beaten trail, but the gathering sounded like a small sports arena that could be heard from miles around, despite Jim's warning. Nothing but laughing, hooting, hollering, water-splashing. Jim and Jeannie sat in their backyard, paused from their food-and-drink preparations, staring at the young jamokes in the above-ground pool in disbelief. "I… thought you talked to them, honey," said Jeannie.

Jim answered, "I did. I'll murder 'em later."

Under the night sky with the stars overhead, John was trying to slam-dunk Vicki underwater, George and Steve were pulling Jody's arms apart, making her shriek, and Alex and Kathy were engaged in a face-splashing contest. They'd gone home after work, changed into swimwear, resurfaced at Jim's, ready to have the time of their lives.

Jim and Jeannie checked their next-door neighbor's house. Nothing, so far. No reaction. That was good. To their left was just an open field, and the night was pitch-black, save the candles burning on the picnic table and the one spotlight above the sliding-glass entry into the house. Behind them, the yard ended in a cornfield. Very few lights were seen from the houses out that way.

Steve won the arm-yanking battle, hoisting his girlfriend up over his head and dropping her. She grabbed a hold of his head and sent him plunging below the surface. As he tried kicking and thrashing to get up, she stood on him, holding him under. "Take that, suck-wad! Try to rip me apart, will ya?"

Jim ordered them to stop immediately. Jody's good-natured cursing was becoming all-prevailing. And there *was* alcohol. The blondie had hijacked beer from Lapping Waves. When Jeannie had asked how the sixteen-year old had pulled that stunt off, she'd answered, "Simple. There's a couple of dumpsters in the back of the mart, one for cardboard and paper-recycling, the other for the gross garbage. When I take the trash out, I slip a couple twelve-packs into the paper-recycling one. I come back later and fish it out."

Jeannie had stared at her. "Oh… the younger generation thinks. That's good."

Jeannie Monocco was Jim's girlfriend of four years. Another fine-looking specimen. Brunette. Years younger than the veteran. The two were a great match: her upbeat optimism to his quiet intensity. With her constant tan, impeccably feathered hair, and legs extending from her Daisy Dukes down to China, the boys had to keep their peepers constantly in-check. "Rochester," George often cited, "was stocked with foxes."

When they got out of the pool the first time, the three girls staked their ground at the picnic table, wrapping towels around themselves, getting the water out of their hair, and launching into a deep conversation with Jim and Jeannie about life, family, and other philosophical matters as they helped them set out the plastic silverware, plates, cups and napkins. Vicki had known Jeannie a year, but Kathy had known her for much longer. Always, the girls asked Jeannie how she could keep hosting bashes with her crazy trick-work at Kodak. Jeannie always gave the same answer: "You do it for the people you love."

John, George, Alex and Steve would not stop making noise, shouting about the macho details of the "saves" they had pulled off tonight, openly relishing the physical intimidation they'd dealt. "Did you see the look on the face of that guy in the Challenger?" Steve said. "He was shittin' bricks when you ripped the keys out, George."

Alex joked that their toughest opponents could be the old geezers from the retirement home behind them. "They got the sticks and canes," he said. "Edgewater could prove to be our worst enemy."

"Yeah, that's what we need—" said Kathy, "a physical sparring-match with the elderly. Good idea, Alex."

Jim fired up the grill, flames shooting into the sky, and shortly after, burgers and Italian sausage sizzled on the hot coals. When Jeannie returned from the house with taste-tempting sides (potato salad, fruit Jell-O), she laid them on the table, put Jerry Rafferty's *Baker Street* album on the LP, low enough to cast a mellow mood over the scene. The Crusaders could not wait until tomorrow night, even though they had school the next day. For the next forty-five minutes, the eight shared food, drink, laughs, rude jokes and excitement. "To adventures ahead," George toasted.

"To adventures ahead," was the chorus.

The big guy promised he was going to kill the patrolmen separately and bury their bodies in the cornfield if they did not keep their voices down.

It was all "feeling good" and "gettin' back to normal," when Alex—buzzed on two beers—mentioned his balls tingling when things got good, drawing scrutiny from the crowd. He certainly did not want to get into it, especially in front of Kathy. "But now you have to," said Vicki. "You can't just stop at that dumb comment."

George filled in the blanks for everybody. "Ever since sixth grade, Alex has been tellin' us that when he gets excited—and not in the humping-kind-of-way—his balls tingle. That's when he knows something mint is about to happen—like cracking skulls at The Winking Moon."

"I didn't exactly say it was *that*," rejoined Alex. "But that's guy-talk. Sorry, ladies."

They were laughing. Jeannie, Jody and Kathy were practically falling off their chairs. Jim was just staring at the boys, flipping the meats. Despite the frivolity, it was a rather sad affair without crusty Stanley, or feisty Emilio, or even the Stuckersons. But that's how it was, they agreed. People had varying priorities in their personal lives. Jim drank several beers, smoked more than his share of cigarettes—Jeannie lobbing dirty looks of disapproval, wishing he'd stop—for her *and* for their future. They'd talked about this many times and the dispute sometimes came to his co-workers' ears. "This is why I work at the drive-in," he told the group. "To escape her."

Kathy got around to sharing what she had heard the Stuckersons talking about through the office door before the high schoolers started. "Heard them trying to get a hold of Kurt Bannabock. I don't know if you kids remember, but he's our regional manager at Bluestone."

"We remember," said Vicki. "But what were they wanting to talk about?"

"They tried several times but couldn't reach him. Mr. Stuckerson was saying to Mrs. Stuckerson that he believes something's going on with the company. Something they are keeping secret from us. We've all heard the rumors. Might be about keeping us open."

None of this sat well with anybody. Jody said, "They're gonna fucking close the drive-in?"

"I don't know," answered Kathy. "I didn't want to eavesdrop too much."

"Wait, what's going on?" asked Jeannie, setting her lemonade down.

Jim enlightened her. "Rumors have been flyin' around that The Winking Moon and The Smirking Star might be in danger of closing. Who knows if this is the truth or not? God knows how much the regular community hates us. Anyway, there's also something called the 'home video market' that's comin' in, and that could be impacting drive-ins across the country. All this has been swirling around, making us think."

"You didn't tell me about this?" said Jeannie.

"It's all rumor and excuses. It's like buttholes: everybody's got one and they all stink."

"Jim, don't be gross."

Alex said to Jeannie, "They're sayin' we're too much of a nuisance. People who don't come to The Moon only hear of the problems. And Jim's right, they're talking about the next big thing being stores where you go to rent Hollywood movies. Like a library or something. I dunno how successful that would be."

"I don't think that would ever take off," mumbled Steve. "I said that at the Mastersons."

"Regardless," Jim added, "Entities like Edgewater really have it out for us. They're callin' the police, they're callin' our answering service. Edgewater's a powerful political component in Rochester, nobody wants to upset old folks. But… enough shoptalk, didn't we say this was an after-hours party?"

"Fuckin-A," Jody said, enjoying her stolen beer.

"The Moon will never die," offered George, finishing his, then erupting with the loudest belch heard to mankind, the echo slapping off the house next to them. Then the light in the upper window next door came on. A silhouette appeared behind the curtains, but never parted them.

"Thanks, Jocavelli," said Jim. "Well done. That's 'Sam,' our neighbor, he's a nice guy. Some people work in the morning."

"I apologize," said George.

They wrapped up the get-together at three-thirty a.m. They cleaned up, just like at the theater, helped Jeannie take the leftovers back inside the house, and wrapped the garbage in plastic trash-bags. As they got set to leave, Vicki decided to revisit her request from the previous summer.

"You guys promised to take me out on 'foot-patrol' this year. You better not flake."

"Oh, not that again, Vicki," Steve said. "I thought we put that to rest."

"No, we didn't. Jody, tell your man he—*they*—promised me last year. They have to carry through with their oath or their crap in my eyes."

George assured her they had not forgotten. "We gotta go, Jim and Jeannie, thanks for everything."

"Remember: church in the morning," Jim reminded.

Jeannie said, "We want everyone to get home safely."

But Vicki was insistent. "You guys also told Emilio you'd take *him* out."

Alex said, "We're not taking Emilio out, Vick."

"So, you lied to him, too?"

"Plus, you're a girl," said John. "You couldn't handle it."

That stopped the party dead. Vicki was shocked John could say this. Her crush. She thanked her hosts and stormed up the hill, the others following her. Jody chugged the last of her beer, said at random, "I'll fuckin' kick somebody's ass."

Jim and Jeannie waved to all the vehicles as they pulled away from the curb. They could finally get some rest.

At the same time the party was going on, Lee-Willie and Gail-Lill were nowhere near the screen attic. They were at home in bed, fretting about their landlord, the drive-in, and their lives in general. The Stuckersons felt "stuck." *Stuck* in their cramped, one-bedroom, low-rent apartment, watching their black-and-white Zenith set upon a corkboard stand, supported by cement cinder blocks.

Tonight, the film they had tuned into on television—although "watching" would be too strong a word—was "Desire Under the Elms," from 1958. Was hard to get a fix on the specifics as the picture kept rolling. The tube was going out.

Lee-Willie broke the silence. "Maybe we shoulda gone to Jim's party. He's right: we did blow off all the ones he invited us to last summer."

Gail-Lill has smeared so much facial cream on herself in bed that she appeared to be glowing in the TV light "Oh Lee, he knows the nights catch up with us."

"Does he? The night catches up with him, too, but he still throws parties."

"You're in competition with him. Stop. You just don't like seeing him receiving more attention from the kids than you. Always measuring yourself up to him."

"What kinda psychological mumbo-jumbo is that Gail?"

"It's so obvious. You work tirelessly to earn their respect and you see how they adore Jim so

effortlessly."

"Enough, already. You're just getting into this 'cause I said I don't want you reading your

poetry at work."

"No, that's not true. It's the same with me. They listen to him more than they do me, too. Going to their parties and seeing them fawning all over Jim and Jeannie will just reinforce everything."

"Gail…"

"I'm just saying…"

"You got everything covered, don't ya?"

"Lee, just drop it, it's been a hard night."

"I can't see shit on this TV."

"But I'm telling you, you can't go around insulting our employees all the time like you do, that doesn't help."

"I don't 'insult our employees all the time.'"

"Yes, you do."

"No, I don't. I'm just motivating them. Jim throws these big, gala blowouts with alcohol for underage children and *I'm* the bad guy. He's trying to get them in his corner, undermine me."

"See? That's what I'm talking about."

"We should go one of these nights."

"Whatever you want, dear."

He could not get his head comfortable. He began beating his pillow to a pulp with the back of his head, several times. "This pillow and mattress sucks, too, we need a new one."

"This mattress was given to us by my mother. We're not getting rid of it."

"Feels like she's in it."

She rolled on her side, away from him. "Okay, honey… shut your mind off and go to sleep. The night's over."

"We gotta succeed."

"Huh?" she said.

"You and me. Our lives, what we're doin' here, as a vocation."

"We can't do it all at once, Lee. I mean, I'd like all new furniture, but do you think that's going to happen anytime soon? Especially the way we are with finances?"

"You want new furniture?"

"Of course, I want new furniture, but I'll save that fantasy for when my unicorns blow pots of gold out their ass in our direction. Now go to sleep, you're putting too much on *my* mind."

"You get a chance to connect with Bannabock yet?"

"Are you kidding? He's so busy he never responds to us. You said so yourself."

"He's playin' us, Gail, I can feel it in my gut. Something's wrong here, there's something to these rumors. No communication after he knows we've been reaching out to him forever? He thinks we're losers."

"Whatever the hell's going on, don't spout off about it to the kids, you'll scare them."

"Think Kathy hears us talkin' in the office? I mean, she's right within earshot."

"Nah, she plays her radio and gets so deep into her painting she's not paying attention to us. And speaking of 'earshot,' would you please turn the TV off? We can't see anything on it, anyway, with that rolling picture. One more thing that doesn't work."

"Providing my wife with nice things is essential."

"That's nice, dear, now shush."

"I love you, honey," he said.

"I love you, too, dear," she responded.

He had to get up to turn the set off. Stumbling to it, he turned the volume down first, tried to fix the picture by adjusting the knobs and dials. When that did not work, he pounded a fist down on the top of it, blowing the tube out permanently, plunging them into total darkness.

Both Alex and Randy missed church the following morning. They woke up to find a hand-written note from their mother on the fridge: *"As your mother, I just want to thank the two of you for getting yourselves up out of bed this morning and attending church with me. I appreciate the respect. Signed - the one whose house you're living in."*

Yikes. Randy felt as guilty as original sin. He'd seen it first. Both he and his brother had cavorted about so late the night before, neither woke until 11:30 a.m.—just as their mom arrived at Mass. To make up for it in her absence, he cleaned the dishes in the kitchen sink, straightened the living room, vacuumed and went out and got the Sunday newspaper, which had arrived late this morning. When he saw the headlines in the Local section, he barged into Alex's bedroom again, pulled the shade up with a giant snap, spilling the bright sunshine directly into the room and practically blinding Alex. "Randy, what the fuck?" Alex yelled.

The older brother tossed the section onto his brother's chest, leaving the room with a bang, hollering through the door— "Read it and weep. I told ya, little brother: your pride-and-joy's going down like Becky did to me last night."

Alex thrashed sitting up, still squinting from the flood of daylight. He checked the time. *Shit, almost noon!* Church. He would have to make it up to Mom. Jim Barenta's words rung out in his skull: *You better get your asses to church in the morning.* His head swirled as he looked at the page, trying to focus. He finally spotted the headline.

CHAPTER 11:

GRIM REALITY

"Local Retirement Home Eyeing Drive-In Property For Expansion"

His heart sank. He jolted straight out of bed, grabbing the paper with both hands. "What the hell?" he said, reading it over and over again as he stood. Indeed, the Edgewater Retirement Home was advertising that it was in conversation with Bluestone Incorporated to potentially buy the land the Winking Moon sat on, perhaps for development purposes. The article went on, but Alex was too sick with dread to continue.

By the time he was dressed and pacing around the house, he desperately wanted his mother to return so he could borrow the Chevette. Randy was camped out on the sofa, gearing up to watch baseball, he was anxiously awaiting his mother's return, as well, but more so out of nervousness for her reaction to them skipping church. "I told you this was gonna happen," he said to Alex, not turning to face him.

"Don't rub it in, Randy," said Alex. "It's all just speculation now."

"Yeah right: 'speculation.' Read Mom's note?"

"No, where is it?"

At that moment Mrs. Carver walked in, both sons springing up to meet her in the foyer. Both were full of excuses and apologies as to why they did not get up earlier—neither disclosing the full truth. Angela was clearly upset but did not want to talk about it. She wanted to get out of her best church clothes and start dinner for the night. "You could've at least *told* me you were not going with me," she said to both.

Before Alex got the keys from her and was granted permission to drive over to Vicki's—where the gang was meeting up, considering the newspaper story—he and Randy surrounded her and hugged her tightly. They held on for a while to make sure she knew that they were deeply and sincerely sorry. Angela was near tears.

"I want company at church," she whispered. "My two sons. The family I still have with me. It's vital now."

They understood.

Before they made it to Vicki's, Alex and Steve had to fill up their automobiles. They were stuck, unable to move, Steve with George, Alex behind them with John in his passenger seat, lodged in a line stretching a quarter mile from the filling station. Most drivers were not even idling their engines. They had them off. This was how it was, as of late. The look on the Crusaders' faces said it as best: pure annoyance. Not even Aerosmith could wipe away the irritation.

George griped from passenger side. "Damn you, Jimmy Carter, when's this energy crisis gonna end? That's who my Dad blames."

"Right when we don't have to get somewhere fast," answered Steve.

The Plymouth Road Runner behind Alex tooted the horn. Alex stuck his head out— "Beeping ain't gonna help any of us out, so cool it!" he shouted.

Honk! Even louder.

John asked, "What'd Vicki say she was gonna make us to eat?"

"Fondue," Alex answered, staring straight ahead.

"What's that?"

"Molten cheese in a crock pot. Supposedly ya dip bread into it. Supposed to be fashionable."

"Are we 'fashionable'? We're warriors." Then he laughed.

"She said if we're goin' out with a bang, might as well do it right. It's the latest thing, you know her."

Honk! Honk! The Road Runner had the balls to lay on the horn again. George got tired of it, got out, strode past Alex and John in the Chevette, walked up to the sixty-something man behind the wheel of the car, simply said to him, "Why?"

"I'm not beeping at you, son," answered the man, looking beyond George to the ghastly line before them, "I'm beepin' at the cars ahead of us, holding us up. How long's it take to fill up?"

"We're all in this together, sir. If there was some way to assist you, I would."

"Who are you?"

"Someone who knows about honking."

By the time Steve and Alex filled up their tanks, the attendant posted a sign saying **OUT OF GASOLINE**. The honking then became so loud, the boys could not even hear their music any longer. The older man in the Plymouth Road Runner got out, looked like he was going to cry. The Crusaders came to his rescue, offered the man Steve's five-gallon spare he had filled for his jerry can, helped him fill his tank in private, away from the fuming onlookers.

"Thank you," the man said to him, tried to give the kids money."

"We won't accept that," said Steve.

"Why not?"

"Karma. Give out to get back."

The man looked confused. "What?"

"Never mind, sir, have a nice day."

The four got back in their cars, drove away, feeling bad for the poor saps behind them who were out of luck. "They'll go on to the next station," said Alex. "Another sign of the times."

"Well let's hope this 'Karma-thing' Kathy's always talking about is a sign of the times for us and they won't close The Moon," said George, with shaky hope in his voice.

They all sat around a round table. Vicki's parents weren't home, and she was playing the role of "ever-gracious hostess." But even in the most stressful of times, Vicki needed to be in control. "No square tables for this," she said, a presentation of delicious-looking fondue arranged neatly in the middle of the round table. "I pulled this up from the basement."

"Why does the table have to be round?" asked Steve.

"Because this is the way the adults do it," she answered, handing out napkins, paper plates, more toothpicks. "I read about this in magazines. John, you're not doin' it right, let me show you." She showed her crush how to eat fondue properly, dipping the bread delicately into the cheese. "Now you all follow that."

The Crusaders stabbed the chunks of marbled rye with fancy toothpicks like savages, dunking them into the bowl, blowing on the melted cheese like pufferfish before popping them in their mouths. Vicki rolled her eyes.

"Vick! This is super-hot!" exclaimed Alex. "Ya tryin' to kill us?"

"Just relax, Alex. All of you—relax."

"Vicki, we don't give a crap, c'mon, let's talk about why we're here," said Steve. "We care about The Moon. You read the article, you're just as worried."

"I've always been worried," she said. "All winter I've been worried.

But that doesn't mean we can't enjoy ourselves when we're together. At the end of last year, when we rolled-out for the last time, I was worried. This was bound to come."

"So, you're just giving up?" said Alex. "You think this thing's for real?"

"It's in the paper, it's gotta be something," she said. "I'm not givin' up. You should know me by now: I don't give up."

"Well I wanted to get everybody together so we can prepare for it," said Alex. "I'm glad everybody was home today."

"How can we prepare?" Vicki asked.

Alex elaborated. "Well tonight's Sunday night. We still got school left, we're not gonna see the Stuckersons after tonight 'til Friday. Just know they're gonna be bigger knobs than they already are. Well, *Mr.* Stuckerson. Things are gonna get nuttier, and when they do, they're gonna be blowin' their stack twice as loud. I just think it's important for us to talk about it before it happens—either way."

"Do ya think they know?" asked John. "Think they get the Sunday paper? They're always complaining about money. You ever seen the complex they live? It's not that nice, I drove by it once last year."

"I have no idea if the know now but they're sure gonna," said Alex. "Kathy says she hears 'em trying to contact Bluestone all the time. The shit's gonna hit the fan."

"This is so upsetting," said Vicki. "Can't even think of Rochester without the Winking Moon. It's like peanut butter without jelly."

"Boobs without butts," George chimed in.

"George!"

"I'm just kidding, Vicki."

"Sure, ya are."

"Well this isn't happening for sure yet," said Alex. "I just don't want it to get everybody down. We're in for a helluva fight. If they actually end up doing something to The Moon, they'd better do it to the Smirking Star, too."

"Those guys are a buncha wimps. That drive-in would close before us due to boredom," George chimed in.

"Well they're the sane ones," said John. "I wouldn't say that."

George spouted off. "They got five patrolmen to our four, and they got nothing goin' on. They play G-rated movies, they're chooches. Kyle Daten and his Melvins think they're so cool. We kicked their asses in football and they still think they're better than us. Took our names from us. 'The Avengers'? Not too original."

"They're another enemy," admitted Alex. "Mr. Stuckerson and Mr. Saxon hate each other."

"We're owned by the same company and we still can't get along," said Steve.

"Rich bastards," George bemoaned. "Thinkin' they're better than us 'cause they have more money on the east side."

"It's because they don't have problems like we do at The Moon that they might stay open if we close," said John. "Like it or not, we're their competition. That's not good."

"Kyle, Seth, Gary, Newton, Pauly and Mr. Saxon," said George. "They can all kiss my ass. Vick, you shoulda invited them over, we coulda poured this fondue on 'em."

Vicki was not laughing. She was thinking. "Wonder if they know about this yet, too?"

CHAPTER 12:

THE SMIRKING STAR AVENGERS

"We got The Winking Moon by the balls," said Kyle Daten. "George Jocavelli and his band of do-gooding Neanderthals can kiss our asses, they're going down."

His current opponent was Seth Byrd. Seth did not quite share his friend's viewpoint. "Kyle, what about us? We're owned by the same company. If the Moon goes down, don't you think our drive-in will?"

"Seth's right," said Pauly Cicco. "I've been reading about that home-video market in magazines. If that thing takes off, it could impact theaters all over the country."

"Bullshit, never happen," said Kyle. "Plus, most of Rochester despises The Winking Moon, that article this morning practically said so. People love the Smirking Star."

The Avengers were spending their Sunday afternoon trash-talking—a favorite pastime. The five boys were the east side equivalents to The Crusaders, patrolmen of The Smirking Star, *sister* drive-in of The Moon. The players were Kyle Daten, Pauly Cicco, Seth Byrd, Newton Tallis and Gary Halinsky, all seventeen, heading into the summer before their senior year. They had gathered where they usually did on days like today, in Kyle's parents' basement, engaging in contested games of foosball.

Kyle was playing no-holds-barred against Seth Byrd, banging the game's hard, white ball about the cabinet as hard as he could with the flicking of his wrist, activating his soccer player's plastic foot. One caromed so viciously off the side wall, the ball flew off the table and torpedoed his dad's empty beer can collection adjacent to them, knocking the whole set-up down and making a hell of a noise. His mother immediately appeared at the foot of the stairs.

"Kyle, what are you doing down there?"

"Sorry, Mom," he said. "Just got a little carried away, we'll keep the noise down."

"You're not starting that silly rivalry again this year with those boys at the Winking Moon, are you? Why be concerned with kids you don't even attend school with?"

"You don't understand, Mom. It's a man's thing."

"Oh, please."

The guys laughed. That was a stupid response.

"Mrs. Daten," Pauly answered for her son, "our box office girl, Stephanie Mason, talks about them too much. She has a granduncle who works at The Winking Moon. She wants to meet them."

"So, what's wrong with that?" Mom asked.

"Kyle's jealous," said Gary Halinsky.

"I am not, Mom," said Kyle. "They're just jerking your chain."

"'Jerking my chain,'" Mrs. Daten repeated. "Nice."

"That drive-in's crazy, Mrs. Daten," said Newton Tallis. "Ours isn't like that at all."

"Well, thank God you don't work there," she said. "Wasn't there something in the paper about it this morning?"

"Look at the wall down here, Mom."

"You have it taped up?" she said.

"Yup. With joy."

It was. The newspaper article was right there, in plain sight.

"What's *that* supposed to mean?" Mom asked.

"Nothing," said Kyle. "We're just very serious about our jobs, as are they."

"Do all of your parents know about this?" she asked.

"Yes," they said at once.

"Can the guys stay for leftovers, Mom? We're going to work tonight and we're hungry."

Mrs. Daten was at first unsure. "You're going to work tonight? On a Sunday? Gary, Seth, Newton, Pauly—don't your parents feed you at home?"

They all chortled, answering with various affirmatives. "We're proud patrolmen, Mrs. Daten," said Pauly. "We're in constant need of fueling up."

"No, you're teenagers. You all eat like horses," said Mrs. Daten.

Seth Byrd said, "We spend most of our time there like we do here: playing video games and eating popcorn. It's the easiest job in the world."

"No, it's not, Seth," said Kyle. "Whose side are you on?"

"The most dangerous thing we got going on there is tripping in the dark."

Kyle glared at Seth. Mrs. Daten said, "Break that table and you're not getting another one. Your father got that with his Christmas bonus. And pick up his collection before he gets home."

"We're on it, Mom, right after this."

"Be up in five," she said, turning to ascend.

"Yes, Mrs. Daten," the boys answered.

Pauly Cicco gave Kyle the business again. "You're so jealous."

"Of who? George Jocavelli? We've known each other forever. He was a douche bag way

back in Pop Warner football."

"Hey," Mom snapped before she got to the top of the landing. "Language."

"Sorry."

As they picked up the beer cans and put them back in order, Newton Tallis admitted candidly, "You know, we've got to face it, we did sort of steal their idea of calling themselves 'The Crusaders' when we deemed ourselves 'The Avengers.' I don't even know what we're avenging."

"We might see them at Hamlin Beach on 'last day,'" said Gary. "There's going to be a shitload of schools there."

"Well la-dee-dah," Kyle said. "We'll see who has the better drive-in, regardless if we're going away for good. Mr. Saxon will tell us."

Pauly said, "And Saxon can't stand Mr. Stuckerson the same way you can't stand the Crusaders, Kyle. How'd that whole thing come about?"

"I don't know," said Kyle. "Something about an argument at a company picnic three summers ago, when Stuckerson first moved to town. Long before us."

"Freakin' ridiculous," said Gary. "Whole crew is nuts. They're all crazy over there. Who in their right mind would go to the Winking Moon when they can come to the Smirking Star and actually enjoy the movies?"

"Everybody," Seth, Newton and Pauly said.

"Your five minutes is up," Mrs. Daten called from the top of the stairs. "I guess you're not that hungry."

That was it. A stampede broke out to see who could get up the stairs first. Kyle swiped up a dirty sock from the washing machine, pelted Seth

Byrd in the back of the head with it.

CHAPTER 13:

THE FIRST SUNDAY NIGHT BACK

Vicki and the Crusaders fired off the question to the Stuckersons about the newspaper article, Alex leading the charge. Lee-Willie—with his wife subserviently behind him—lined all five of the teenagers up against the wall of the concessions, patrons peering in through the glass, knocking, wanting to know why they were not being let in. Stanley, Emilio and Jim were in the room, also, but escaped being the focal point of Lee-Willie's wrath.

"Do you actually think I'd keep something like the drive-in being bought-up by Edgewater from my employees?" sizzled Lee-Willie, despite being secretly unsure of the future of the Winking Moon himself. He marched up and down the line like a drill instructor. "Thanks, guys and gals, I hire ya back for the summer and you repay me by accusing me of skullduggery."

"Lee…" said his wife, "they weren't exactly doing that." She cut in uncomfortably. He kept on going.

"Who do ya think I am, Baron von Frankenstein, cooking something up in the castle to unleash on people when they least suspect it? I thought you had more faith in me than that."

"Mr. Stuckerson," said Alex, "we didn't even know if you'd seen the paper this morning. We were just askin'."

"Of course, I saw the paper this morning, do ya think I'm ignorant?

I keep up with the news, I'm always looking and listening to see if there's anything to these goddam rumors. Hell, Gail and I are here every day, listening to the grievances coming in over and over again on the answering machine—when people are supposed to be calling to get information about the movies. We field complaints night-after-night about what we could be doin' better, what's going wrong. Bet ya didn't know this but we've been calling Kurt Bannabock from Bluestone, trying to get through with him, ask if there's something we should know about. Do ya think I'd unleash hell on *him* immediately, accusing *him* of hiding shit? That's not in my book."

"But it's probably true," said Stanley, unable to keep his yap shut.

Lee-Willie whipped his head around to face him— "Stanley, I'm talking to the young people."

"Well excuse me, master commander."

"John, George, Steve, Alex, Vicki..." he continued. "Next time put a little faith in me that I—*we*—know a thing or two and aren't keeping secrets from anybody. We've been doin' this a long time. When we know somethin', you'll know somethin'."

"But watcha think of the article, Mr. Stuckerson?" asked Vicki. "Ya haven't told us one way or the other if you feel it's true, deep down."

"I don't have a freakin' idea, Miss Richards!"

That took the wind out of everyone's sails. Gail-Lill led her husband out of the stand, apologizing to everyone for his blow-up, and opened the doors for the flooding patrons. Lee-Willie reached for the Mallo Cups in his pocket and stuffed them in his face, one after the other. They walked all the way to the office as more and more vehicles rolled in. In the stand, Jim pushed off the wall, drinking his carbonated soda. "Okay, everybody, that was fun. Now get to work."

Operations began. Emilio, Vicki and Stanley put their hairnets on, greeted customers with smiles and pleasantries. The Crusaders sprayed-up with *Off* Mosquito Repellent, blasting a rising cloud of choking fumes out from behind the dumpsters, people coughing and looking as they walked in. They then rolled out into the crowd when they were ready.,.

Right off the bat, the three in the concession stand had to deal with two sparrows that had flown in, dive-bombing people's heads. Stanley figured it was the insane honking in the lot that had spooked the critters. "Probably flew in to escape that infernal noise," he said, hustling for the back room. I'll get my broom."

"Don't you dare, Stanley," Vicki said, alarmed. "I think we can get 'em out without your loving approach. For the love of God don't you hit them with that thing."

Instead, Emilio ran out from behind the counter, chasing the birds with the oven-rasp, goofball patrons thinking it funny, some getting in on the act, taking off their shirts, snapping them at the creatures, cutting loose, acting like jackasses, jumping up on the stools and benches, pretending to be male strippers, showing off for girls they didn't know.

The sound of the arcade games mixed with the manic screeching of the birds made a racket.

Although it was still too light, the obnoxious audience continued with their horn-orgy. Remarks began to fly: "C'mon, start the show!" "Whattya waiting for, an invitation?!" "Let's get the show on the road!"

"People, ya do this almost every night," Jim stated calmly into the P.A. system from his booth. "It's too bright out. Let's hold off on the horns and the shouts until it gets darker, okay? If I started now, you wouldn't be able to see it. Let's show some maturity and understanding, okay? Whattya say?"

BLARE! BLEEP! BLAAAA! The horns got even louder; the insults saltier. Gail-Lill appeared at his door, asked Jim if he could start a little earlier tonight so they would give it a rest.

"Gail, I'm tellin' ya, you know as well as I do, they're not gonna be able to see it, and they're gonna get even-more pissed."

"Yeah but… it's been so tense, already. Maybe we could get some good vibes flowing?"

"Darlin, I don't control the sunlight."

"We paid our money now we want our movie!" someone shouted.

"Winkin' Moon, you're dicking with us!" shouted another.

"Yeah, we're gonna pull out our home movies and show 'em if you don't get going!"

Jim tossed his *Popular Science* magazine aside, went back to the mike. "You want your movie? I'll give ya your movie. Hope ya enjoy it."

Jim flipped the projector switch, reel one and two already loaded, threaded within from top to bottom, film-head to take-up. Inside the lamp-house, the light source was generated by carbon rods, powered by electricity—equal to that of a welder's arc. 120 amps of DC current raced through the monster, generating its power to display the cinematic magic.

"Up In Smoke" was completely washed out. Barely discernible blobs of movement shifted about the screen as the soundtrack could be heard, crystal clear. The horns—and shouting—became unfathomable. "We can't see shit!" people yelled. "Stop the movie, it's too light out!" bellowed others. Still one crowed, "We can't see the shit! Turn it off, you jack-wads!"

Jim ignored the pleas, smiled to Gail-Lill, and sat back down on his sofa, picking up his magazine again. "Hope ya enjoy it, suckers," he said to no one.

Lee-Willie hounded the Crusaders all night, catching them sneaking into the stand to cool off and screw off. Despite a more-serious mood cast over the drive-in, the Crusaders still managed to "Boof the pooch," as they called it. Stanley caught George pretending to roast his donager on the grill to make his friends laugh when no patron was looking. He did not do it, of course, just pretended to. But nonetheless, John stood by on the side with an open bun, faking like he was ready to accept it. Stanley called them all "sick children," told them all to get the hell back outside when Lee-Willie was preoccupied with other matters.

All Cheech & Chong-movie long, there were patrons entering the stand, mentioning the newspaper article and trying to seek answers from the employees. It was growing oh-so-weary. The constant din of the arcade games combined with the loud soundtrack and ever-present sound of the popcorn popping was slowly driving Vicki insane. Defending the drive-in against the allegations and innuendo once again, she became distracted, accidentally drenched a little kid's popcorn with melted butter. She handed it to him, anyway, prompting him to scream at the top of his lungs and bring his Dad over to assess the damage. His chest puffed as he accused Vicki of drenching his son's popcorn on purpose so that she could charge double.

"What?" said Vicki. "How in the world does that work, sir?"

"Well, the newspaper story. Those old folks say you do anything over here for a buck. For sensationalism. Use it up so you have to charge higher prices for more."

"That's… crazy, sir, we do not do that here and we never would."

"Are you calling me a liar?"

Emilio stepped in. "Sir, we'll take the popcorn back. We'll get you a new one, it's as simple as that. Vicki, get the nice man and his son a new popcorn."

"*Less* butter," the man gurgled.

"I was gonna do that, Emilio," Vicki said, already moving toward the old-fashioned maker.

She filled it up carefully and handed it back. Satisfied, the man and he moved off to the register, his son already face-deep in the popcorn.

Vicki was livid. "The customer's always right, Vicki, just relax," Emilio said.

"He'll 'relax' when I give him five to the teeth," she replied.

Two seven-year old boys strolled in next, no parent in sight. Vicki was already appalled. They were both playing with their individual Click-Clack toys: two spheres of hard plastic about the size of golf balls, linked together by a finger-ring at the end to get them swinging back-and-forth in a vicious pendulum-motion, cracking off each other to make the "click-clack" sound.

"Hey, you kids," said Stanley, "I've seen those things on TV and they're really dangerous. Stop doing that in here."

Immediately, one of the boys said, "Up yours, old man, we can do what we want."

"What?" Stanley was outraged. He marched over to the brats, yanked the toys out their hands, and told them they could have their mommies and daddies pick them up after the movies. "We don't play with dangerous toys in here and we always listen to adults. These things shatter. I read Consumer Reports." The second boy's eyes went wide.

"Hey, we're gonna tell our daddy you took 'em."

"Go ahead." Sure enough, minutes later, Big Daddy Tough-Guy was looking for the "old guy who took his sons' Click-Clacks."

"Right here, what of it?" said Stanley. "They were being obnoxious and fresh. You ought to teach your kids manners."

There was an audible gasp from the crowd. All eyes turned. Vicki and Emilio froze up, instantly thought of calling Big Jim. But Stanley was tough, they knew this. They watched as the jamoke got up in Stanley's face, much taller than the worker. Stanley stood his ground and was not afraid. The man told him he had better give the toys back or there was going to be trouble.

"And I told them there was no playing with dangerous toys in here," said Stanley. "We have enough trouble already without dealing with potentially lethal play items. You can get them back after the show."

"Stanley…" warned Vicki.

"I got this, Miss Richards," the senior said.

The jamoke said, "Trouble to add to your already-pathetic stories I read about in the paper? I see how you people are now. Maybe if you were a little more polite to your customers you wouldn't have the issues you do." Stanley reached behind him, grabbed his stool at the register, stood up on it so he was level with his opponent's mug. "Maybe if you didn't bring your kids in to R-rated movies your sons wouldn't act up. It all starts at home, dad, and unless you have something further to add, I suggest you get the fork-knife-and-spoon outta here and pick your Click-Clacks up at the end of the show."

Dad stood there for a moment, stunned, his children behind him, waiting to see what was going to happen. Everybody was waiting. The father backed off, told his kids to be quiet, clarified with Stanley that they could pick up the items after the show, then walked out. No treats, no candy.

"But Dad," whine of the boys, "we want pizza!"

"You want a couple of fine bruises, is what you want," said the father. "Now move!"

When they were gone, the crowd erupted in appreciative applause, surrounding Stanley and clapping him on the back, exalting him like a hero. "You tell 'em, Winking Moon," said one dude. "Way to go, Daddy-O," said another.

Emilio and Vicki breathed a sigh of relief.

Stanley grinned. Sort of. "Hey…" he said, "ya mess with the bull, ya get the horns."

At intermission, fireworks flew from Lee-Willie Stuckerson. And not the Independence Day kind. Everything blew up as the Crusaders entered the concession stand obediently, donning their ludicrous hairnets, reminding Mr. Stuckerson that they had to leave after "H.O.T.S." They couldn't stick around for the encore, "Up In Smoke."

They had to split early because they had to get up for school the next morning. It was their last Sunday night before school ended. Starting next week, however, they would be around for all the Sunday nights.

"Vicki, you too?!" he said. "You can't stay tonight, either? When the hell didya tell me that?"

"I did tell you that. On the day we picked up our smocks, sir," said Vicki.

Lee-Willie stomped his feet, threw his hands in the air— "This is bullshit!"

"Lee—" said Gail-Lill, swooping in, placating him again, "they did tell us, I remember."

"Damn it, Gail, why don't you just tell me what I need to know."

"'What you need to know'? 'What you need to know'?! All right, I'll be straight-forward then: I want those 'Three's Company' posters taken down in the back-storage room."

"What?"

"Those two posters from that TV show. All I see when I go back there is those two girls' boobs from that show flashing me all over the place. It's sexist and I've been meaning to say something to you about it anyway."

"Gail, you never said anything about that before."

"Well I'm saying it now. You know—to be 'straight-forward.'"

The look on Lee-Willie's face was that of someone who had been struck by a blunt object. "You're serious. You want me to take down the posters of Janet and Chrissy?"

"Yes."

"The same two posters that have been up there since the dawn of time." Pointing at Stanley— "*Franco* put those up."

"Don't blame him, Lee," said Gail-Lill. "How do you think they make me feel?"

The whole staff was watching.

"It's a 'guy-thing,'" Lee-Willie said as an excuse. "You want me to take them down?"

"Yes, Lee," Gail-Lill said. "I do."

"Oh no, you're not going back there messing with Franco's stuff," Stanley cut in, visibly upset. He broke into a jostle for the back-storage room, leaving the register with patrons waiting to cash out. Gail-Lill was right behind him. Everyone could hear the senior as he went, "This was *his* space back here, those were *his* posters. This a shrine! A memorial to him! Don't start rippin' stuff down, he's got personal belongings back here. Lee, Gail, most of this shit is yours from your move here, right? Why don't you chuck that first? It's a fucking fire hazard back here." Lee-Willie followed in next, their voices rising above the clamor in the concession stand, customers shouting orders, getting loud at the arcade games. The Crusaders—who just happened to be coming in—had to take over along with Vicki and Emilio, doing their best to placate the avalanche of business. Steve, John, Alex and George helped take orders, flip the extra hamburgers, roll out the cotton candy. One of the pizzas started to burn. Emilio had been distracted by the ongoing argument and had forgotten that it was in the oven. He yanked the oven door open, slid it out with the pizza peel, and threw the black, charred pie it into the sink, dousing it with cold water. The whole room filled with the smell of burnt pizza. Some guy asked what he was putting in his sauce to make it taste so good and Emilio clammed up. "Not saying," he said.

"What?" said the patron. "You can't not tell us what the ingredients are."

"Wanna bet? Family secret. It's my future, I ain't telling." Emilio was swatting away the smoke with a hand towel.

This got the customer peeved but Emilio did not care. He was too busy. Others listened in on the controversy, also wanted to know what was in the pizza sauce. Emilio would not budge. Jim was nowhere to be found.

He was in his booth, working on his Revell WW 2 Spitfire model.

Just before the end of their shift, the Crusaders had to deal with a couple more familiar headaches. First, a jamoke and his overly amorous girlfriend drove in late, leaving their brights on as they slowly cruised up-and-down the rows, looking for their ideal spot. They were taking their sweet time, blinding everyone, forgetting (or ignoring) the PARKING

LIGHTS ONLY rule once they entered the darkened theater. It took shouting, cursing and more honking from the general crowd for them to realize their mistake, and turn them off once they finally settled on a spot in the back. Pulling himself from sucking face with his date, John and Steve had to kindly remind the driver to pay attention.

"Next time," Steve said, "study the humungous sign hanging in front of your face as you pay for your ticket."

As that was going on, Alex and George dealt with a few spirited games of "Whoops, Wrong Car." Drunken clucks had gotten bored with the movie, stalking the lot in search of random vehicles to jump into, pretending not to know they were not theirs.

"Oh! I'm sorry, wrong car," they'd cry, jumping back out and laughing, leaving the occupants startled and shaken.

Twice they interrupted a hot-and-heavy scene getting all steamy with the kissing and the groping.

"Oops!" they said, faking to be embarrassed. "Thought this was our ride in the dark. Say, your girlfriend's much better looking than ours. Wanna trade?"

Had the patrolmen not put an end to it, things would have gotten ugly. They averted two fistfights as a result.

Finally, Vicki and Crusaders made their rounds to say goodbye, a pretty active evening for a Sunday night. Kathy was sorry to see them leave early but completely understood. She asked if Mr. Stuckerson had remembered they had to cut out early.

"We won't mention that," Alex said. "Let's just say we put him into an even-worse mood."

When they came across the Stuckersons to punch-out and say goodbye, George tried to make good with them and lighten their spirits a bit. "Hey Mr. Stuckerson, found out what 'H.O.T.S.' stands for. 'Hold-On-To-Sex.' The dean in the movie says it."

Lee-Willie slapped his thigh, looked at his wife and said to the kid, "Thank you, Mr. Jocavelli, I've been waiting all night to learn what the title meant. I wouldn't have slept a wink without your confirmation. Get the hell outta here."

CHAPTER 14:

JEANNIE

"Jimmy" liked waking Jeannie in the middle of the night. She liked it, too. Loved it, for that matter. Just the two of them in their quiet, darkened house. It was a great way to end these nutty nights. When she was home at this hour, finally off her shift—when *he* got home—everything was magical, so tranquil, so… sane.

Like he'd done many nights, the projectionist roused her as she lay on the waterbed, liquid sloshing beneath her like a disturbed ocean current, crescent-moon nightlight at the base of the nightstand the only source of illumination on her face. She rolled over, smiled without opening her eyes, wrapped her arms around him, pulled him close and kissed him. Then she was repulsed. "Ugh!" she spat. "Your breath! What the hell? You been licking a chimney?"

He laughed, pulled his face away. "Too much buttered popcorn and two different kinds of cigarettes… if ya know what I mean. Sorry."

"Go brush!"

Embarrassed but making a joke of it, he entered the master bathroom— "Ya know, baby, your breath ain't exactly a bouquet of lilacs, either, at this hour. Been sleeping how long tonight, a decade?" He caught a pillow to the left side of his face. Motoring the toothbrush up-and-down on his teeth, he replayed the highlights of the evening in his head. "Only shittin' ya, love, I'd cherish you even if you reeked like a dead walrus—which ain't too far off."

She sat up, removed the hair from her eyes, saw the time of night. "You're smoking both pot *and* cigarettes again? Do you ever think of me?"

"All the time."

"And you're just getting home now? It's extra late."

"Had to counsel Stanley a little. Poor guy got upset, they're messin' with Franco's belongings. He and Emilio had to pull double-duty; the kids had to leave early 'cause of school tomorrow."

"Bet Lee wasn't happy."

"He wasn't, at all. Neither was Gail but she knew it was coming."

Jeannie was wearing one of his oversized tee-shirts. When he peeked around the corner from the bathroom, he liked what he saw. "Can't brush fast enough," he teased.

"Kids have a good first-weekend back, though?" she asked.

"They did, and they thanked you for last night."

"Last week of school, right?"

"Right, then they'll be around all the freakin' time."

Jeannie chuckled. "I remember the last week of school before summer vacation."

"How was your night?" he asked.

"Manny Rodrogo called."

This caused Jim to stop. He came fully around the corner. "Manny? What'd he want?"

"To talk to you, like always. He needs you, Jim, he's finally coming out of hiding. He called here about nine, he's got that sound in his voice again."

"Really? Well, a door-gunner does that, they have a tone."

"Look Jim, I love Manny, too, but that 'tone' is worrisome."

"Manny's nothing to worry about, he's got people to watch him. He's got us."

"Nothing to worry about? Remember last year? He was so desperate to help at the drive-in that he stationed his Jeep in the middle of the entrance, hitting every car coming in with that spotlight of his, telling people to 'Behave or be tomahawked.'"

Jim came back into the bedroom, stood there. "Leo and I talked to him. He knows he can't be doing that again this year."

"He means well, baby, we all know that, but I think he wants to get involved again. It's a drive-in theater not a military operation. I think he read that article in the paper."

"He saved my life, Jeannie, I'm gonna be there for him no matter what."

"I'm not saying not to, just keep him at a safe distance from your work, I don't want new stories."

"I'll talk to him."

"You're *seeing* him. He told me he'd be stopping by soon."

"Figured that, too. Better get ready for him."

"Changing topics…" She went stretched out on the bed again, tapping the mattress with her hand. "Snuggle me, I feel like being your pet cat."

He shut off the bathroom light. "Pretty pussy."

As they spooned, she purred. "Since everyone turns to you when they need something… I need to be made an honest woman. My parents are asking about the lack of a ring on my finger again."

"Traditionalists."

"*I'm* a 'traditionalist,' sugar-bear."

"We have to discuss this now? It's Monday morning, you're on afternoons, right?"

"You never want to discuss it. You don't want to lose me, Guido-Man."

"No, I don't wanna lose you. Whatcha have for dinner?"

"Nothing, I was beat." That surprised him and he sat up. "Oh no—" she moaned, "we're not doing this now."

"Yes, we are." He pulled her out of bed, picked her up in his arms, carried her to the kitchen. "No woman of mine's goin' to bed hungry."

He rustled up two mushroom-and-cheese omelets, with toast and fresh-squeezed orange juice. They ate, laughed, spent another half hour on the back porch listening to the night breeze play through the cornfields and crickets singing to the stars, just the two of them, alone in the dark, cuddled together on the couch. This couch was better than the one he had in the booth. "It's moments like this that make the universe right," he said.

She responded, "Be even 'righter' if you got your big toe outta my ass."

CHAPTER 15:

FLYERS

Vicki and Jody McBrennan spent whatever free time they had putting up flyers around school to advertise the upcoming season at the Winking Moon. They were enthusiastic and trying to do their part by luring-in the "good kids" instead of knobs, losers and cretins of Galileo High. "The more 'normal kids' we get, the less room there'll be for the rowdies and yahoos," Vicki explained. "We're trying to be proactive, stock the joint with winners."

One halfwit went to rip one of their flyers off the wall, but Jody stopped him. "If ya think for a second, you're gonna take that down and throw it away, think again. I'll give ya an uppercut so hard you'll be the first human on Mars."

All school day long, Vicki and the Crusaders were besieged by questions from peers who were excited to hear about their first weekend went back at the notorious nuthouse. "It went great," John defended, trying to downplay the lowlights. "We did our jobs, we kept ticking like clockwork."

One kid was practically on the edge of his seat in the cafeteria. "'Ticking' as in a time-bomb? Everybody's read that story in the newspaper. Do you think it's gonna close down?"

George shrugged. "We dunno, but why don't you come anyway before it does—one way or the other."

A lot of the males gathered round the lunch table wanted to go and do what they did best: get rowdy and have the time of their lives. They wanted to take dates and score (or at least get to third base), run around and get as crazy as they possible could while the going was good.

"Guys, I'm tellin' ya—" said Alex, not liking what he was hearing, "you gotta respect the joint. You know we work there. If we catch ya messin' around—no-mercy, take no prisoners—we're gonna have to take care of it. I don't care if you are our friends, you start fuckin' with the joint, there'll be hell to pay. We want the drive-in to stay open."

Then the meatball at the end of the table said, "Nice lecture, now tell us how many naked broads you've seen already, getting knocked to the stratosphere."

Alex waited, then, "Plenty," he admitted.

Oh yeah! Handshakes, guffaws and high-fives ensued.

There was an after-school meeting with Coach Iacona, the head football coach. He brought the team together to discuss the upcoming double sessions. "Come August 20th, gentlemen," he said to all, hands as large as catcher's mitts on his hips, you're going to be here at school twice a day, sweating your asses off, preparing for a fantastic football season. I want all of you to take care this summer, work hard at your summer jobs, have fun but not too much, stay in shape, lift weights and do your damn running. Be an asset to the community. Set an example. Be upstanding citizens and take care of your families as well as your local businesses." Alex raised his hand. "Like the Winking Moon, coach? You comin' to visit this year?"

There was an outburst of laughs and hand-slaps. The players thought it was a grand idea. Coach did not think it was as much. He stymied the excitement, calmed everyone down, looked Alex square in the eye.

"Are you kidding, Carver? You think I'm coming to the Winking Moon? I have a wife and children. That place is a den of iniquity."

More laughter. Coach put an end to it a second time.

Alex said, "Coach, I promise ya, they'll bring back 'Snow White and the Seven Dwarves' one of these nights."

Coach Iacona smirked. "'Lawrence of Arabia.' When they bring back 'Lawrence of Arabia' I might think of going. Good luck at that place, guys."

"'Joint,' sir," Steve Laneske said. "We call it a 'joint.'"

Coach asked the Crusaders, "Didn't they play a movie last summer about a plumber who had sex with every woman whose apartment he worked in?"

Hilarity ensued. The laughter could not be contained. They were having fun, everyone knew it, and good-natured energy was in the air.

"Yes, sir," said Alex. "That was called 'Adventures of a Plumber's Mate.' Dumb title, delivered the goods."

Coach shook his head. "See? That's what I'm talking about. You expect me to bring the missus to that? I don't think so."

Most of the kids had gigs lined up. Some did not. The Crusaders promised a good time at the movies for anybody who showed up. They wanted them all to come. The team promised to be there, at least once or twice. Coach Iacona stayed out of the discussion, steering the young men back to football-talk when he had to.

On the way out of school, Vicki, Jody, Steve, John, George and Alex all caught Mr. Fantuzzi and Mrs. Brady—teachers at Galileo High and infamous flirts, equally obsessed with one another—playing around down the hallway, unaware that anyone was watching them. The halls had pretty much emptied since the bell had rung five minutes prior, but the gang had been taping-up the last of the flyers.

"Look at Mr. Fantuzzi and Mrs. Brady," said Vicki, all of them snickering, ducking around the corner. "Why don't they just get married? They're both single, both can't keep their paws off one another. They're carrying on like a bunch of teenagers."

"Like us?" said Jody. They burst out in brays of laughter.

Mr. Fantuzzi got a full hand—all five fingers—right on Mrs. Brady's bottom, goosed her good, making her squeal and giggle. Both escaped into an empty science lab then, lights out. Vicki turned to the gang. "It's just like The Winking Moon, only it's daytime."

"They'd fit in perfectly with our clientele," Alex said as they walked away.

CHAPTER 16:

MANNY RODROGO

Lee-Willie's Monday morning was consumed with the bother of being out Vicki and the Crusaders through Thursday. He had been stewing about it all night. Now that they were up, readying to go into work even though they did not have to be there for hours, he was particularly snarly.

Both were in dingy tee-shirts, shorts, flip-flops, attempting to make their sloppy apartment into as much of a passable living environment as possible. And now they were hungry. Gail-Lill had the radio set to country-western. To avoid listening to music he thought was grating, Lee-Willie set out to grill, grabbing the plate of raw hamburgers in the refrigerator and made a move for the door. Instantly, Gail-Lill stopped him. "Lee, don't go out there 'til more cars are gone from the parking lot."

"What? Why?"

"We don't want onlookers."

"For what? What the hell does that mean?"

Summoning the strength to risk another argument, she said, "It's Monday morning. Let everyone go to work first. If they see us out there, they'll think we're unemployed."

Lee-Willie could not believe what he was hearing. "What? That's ridiculous. Who cares what people think? I certainly don't."

"Have you even cleaned the grills out there?" she asked.

"You mean the ones that everyone in the complex can use but never does? Hell no."

"Well you should."

"Why?"

"Lee, they're filthy. God knows when they last had a good cleaning."

He shook the notion away. "Have you paid the rent yet?"

"Yes. Drove it to the office before you got up." He continued outdoors, disregarding her wishes to remain out of sight. She got flustered and followed him out to the two barbecue grills sunk into the uncut lawns by the sidewalk, just out of reach of the vehicles parked there in the parking lot. The grills did not look that appetizing. They were funky looking, a little crusty, a dilapidated picnic table aside it for lone company. Gail-Lill looked repulsed, and Lee-Willie was not exactly pleased, either.

"Son-of-a-bitch," he said. "Look at the shape these are in. Is our useless landlord ever going to fix them?"

Gail-Lill looked around. "Lee, shh, someone will hear you."

"So?"

He set the burgers down on the rusty shelf of the first grill, dug into one pocket for a wire brush, pulled it out to see that implement was worn. He cursed, used the brush anyway, did his best to rid the surface of charred remains of meat and God-knew-what-else. Sweat flew from his brow. After a couple minutes he stopped and looked up at his wife. "You just gonna watch me?" "Lee, let's put the burgers in the oven."

"The hell we will. I like mine flame-broiled."

When his eyes shifted to the apartment complex's windows around him, he caught sight of nosy eyes peeking out from behind frilly curtains and venetian blinds.

Raising his voice, he said, "Like what ya see, people? Why don't ya come out here and help me clean these grills for once in your lives?"

"Lee," Gail-Lill said. "Stop!"

He went back to scrubbing, went at it furiously. When it still was not working, he reached into another pocket, pulled out a small container of lighter fluid and began dousing the apparatus.

"Lee! What are you doing?"

"Screw this scrubbing. Cleansing by fire is what this infernal thing needs."

"Lee, don't!"

"I'm just in that kind of a mood, Gail. How dare those kids slip out early last night. Stand

back woman."

"Lee!"

He had matches with him, too. He pulled those out, struck one, held it up before throwing it aboard. "These botulism-bays are gonna end now. This'll kill all the germs."

PHOOOM! He tossed it and the whole thing went up—not just the one grill but the second! The lighter fluid jumped grills to the other in splatters and the flames followed with it.

"Jesus!" Gail-Lill exclaimed.

"Keep back and stay calm," he instructed. "That thing's had gunk on it since the dinosaurs walked the Earth."

"Lee, you're drawing attention."

"So what? This is the most exciting thing they've seen in months. If they want a show, we'll give 'em a show."

The few businesspeople that were in their vehicles, backing out, were unable to believe what the maniac was doing. Booth grills were ablaze. Lee-Willie stared at his wife and said, "Would you go back in and grab the spatula or something I can turn the burgers with?"

Gail-Lill was hesitant, looking around, mortified. "Lee, you don't know who could be watching us. I mean what if our landlord saw us?"

"Who cares? He's a putz."

Right on cue, a copper-colored Dodge van made its appearance, pulling in from the street into the parking lot, immediately heading toward them.

Lee-Willie cursed. "Well-well-well, speak of the Devil. Recognize his van? It's 'What-A-Chump.' Think he's comin' to thank ya for delivering the check? More likely to give us another hard time. Suck on this fire and your crappy equipment, oh mighty landlord and property manager." "Lee, pronounce his name properly: 'Winnechum.'"

"No, it's 'chump' to me."

The vehicle zeroed in but kept its distance, tinted windows making it impossible to see the driver. Lee-Willie jutted his jaw— "He ain't gettin' closer. Chicken-shit."

"Lee, this is his place of business. I'm sure this isn't making him happy. Are you going to put this out?"

"In a while."

"Show respect. We were really late, he's shown restraint."

"Screw him, he's kept us at bay with repairs around here," Lee-Willie said, then called out to the anonymous driver. "Yeah, it's ten in the morning! Yeah, we're barbecuing on your crappy grills. Yeah, I'm dousing it with flames! It'll finally be nice and clean!" Then, to Gail-Lill, "Lookit him just sittin' there, all mysterious-like. Who does he think he is, the 'Phantom of the Opera'?"

Winnechum drove off, not saying one word. Lee-Willie shouted after the van— "You do that, What-A-Chump! Just leave without addressing anything! Elitist!"

He turned, noticed she had not fetched the utensil he needed. "Where's the spatula? Gotta flip these puppies once the flames die down. Whattya expect me to use, my hand?"

At that she turned and walked back in the apartment. "You'll be using your hand for a lot of things at this rate. Call me when lunch is ready, I'm cleaning the bathroom."

He watched her slam the door. "Hmm," he said, waving the smoke away with his hand. "An attitude now…"

Jim and Jeannie did not have to wait long before Jim's army-chum, Manny Rodrogo, showed up. Tuesday afternoon, as the couple were enjoying their favorite spot in the backyard—swaying on the hammock between the maples, watching the corn frolic like Hula dancers—he pulled up in front of the house on a motorcycle, obliterating the tranquility. Jeannie sat up and swung her legs off, sending Jim toppling off the other side with its misbalance. "Sorry, honey," she said. "That must be him. It's a Harley all the way."

As Jim got up, brushing himself off, he said, "No shit."

"Did you talk to him? Did you ask him to come over?"

"I haven't spoken with him. Like you said, we just knew it was comin'."

"So much for a relaxing afternoon, this was our one full day off together."

"When Manny Rodrogo needs ya, he needs ya."

Both assembled themselves as they heard the good-natured "Yoo-hooing" coming around to the side of the house, then saw the legend as he ambled down the steep grade, wearing the darkest pair of sunglasses ever made, full can of beer in-hand, ten-gallon cowboy hat, mustache rivaling Dennis Hopper in "Easy Rider," and a wide smile upon laying eyes on his buddy and best girl. Jim got right to the heart of the matters— "Manny, what's going on, pal?"

It took a while for him to stroll to his friends, but when finally arrived, the two embraced like they had not seen each other in decades. "Jimbo, how are ya? Jeannie, a big hello. Look at you two, pretty as a picture, as usual. Made an honest woman of this girl yet?" He had a low, potent voice, like a watered-logged rolling stream.

"You, too, Manny?" Jim replied. "That's the first thing you got?"

Manny stood back from Jim, continuing to enthusiastically clap his hands on the projectionist's shoulders. "Figured I'd take a chance and come on a Monday," he said. "I remembered the Winking Moon's not opened on Mondays, right, Jimbo?"

"Right."

"Jeannie, forgive me for just dropping by like this," he said.

"Nothing to forgive. Our house is your house." She meant it—even though reservations percolated inside her.

"And a home is where the heart is. Jim, can I, uh… talk to ya for a second?"

"I was waiting," Jim said.

Manny was part of Jimmy's soul. Jimmy was part of Manny's. Jeannie understood this and was ready to give them their space. "I'll be indoors," she said, giving her man a kiss. Jim thanked her, and she walked inside.

The two brothers-in-arms then beheld each other, processing a common past no one else was privy to but them. Jim guided his anxious friend to the edge of the cornfield, where Manny stared into its expanse. "Jeannie told ya I called, right?"

"Of course."

"Do you mind I showed up so soon?"

"Not at all."

Warily, Manny asked Jim how he was doing. *Really* doing. Jim was fine. Manny asked how Jeannie was doing. *Really* doing. Ditto. Manny offered his assistantship in their wedding if they'd plan to go that way. "I could be Best Man. We'd go to Vegas or something, get Elvis to perform the ceremony. It would be spectacular."

"I'll take that into notice."

"How's the gig at the drive-in?"

"Still loving it."

"Still loving the nighttime hours? Working with the kids? Being your own boss?"

"You know it."

Then Manny looked around the neighborhood: the house next door, what he could see of the ones across the street (tips of rooftops), the tract over the cornfield. "Gosh Almighty, still got this great country getaway. Let's hope progress doesn't creep out too far too fast." Then he pulled out a joint, paused at lighting it up. "May I?"

Jim didn't see Jeannie's face in the kitchen window, so he said, "Keep it discreet, I don't even do that here. She's riding me for cigarettes again."

Manny chuckled, gestured at the massive crop before them. "How am I gonna keep it discreet, go in there?"

"Not a bad idea."

"Manny why are you here?" he asked.

"I need more to do, Jim," the man answered. "I'm going crazy at the VA and at work. They shaved my hours at the dock, and I need more… accomplishments. Went to Sturgis last week on my hog, don't know anybody in Sturgis. Boring, but felt like I needed excitement. That didn't cut it."

"I have all the excitement I need."

"Know ya do, I read that article, in the paper, that's one thing we can agree on."

"Manny, in no way, shape or form do I want ya tryin' to help out again this year with the punks, hooligans, yahoos and rowdies."

"C'mon, Jim, I was pretty good at it last summer."

"You scared that one kid so bad he skateboarded straight into the box office, scared the shit out of Kathy. Thank God he wasn't hurt. Lee had to make sure that stayed off Kurt Bannabock's clipboard."

Manny snickered at the mention of the manager's name. "Lee-Willie. Incompetent twerp. He ain't gonna rid your joint of the problems, he's half of 'em. You should be running the joint."

"Well I'm not, we're in civilian life now and we gotta do things a certain way."

"I told that artist-girl I was sorry for messin' up her painting in the box office when I did that. I thought it made it look like a lightning bolt was streakin' across her canvas."

"A bright green one? That was a landscape she was painting. Stuckerson hasn't forgotten you, Manny, he doesn't want you back this year, he's already told me that."

"I got new tactics; I'll stay outta the lot. Lemme show ya one or two in the next few weeks. Your problems are even worse this year."

"No."

"Jim, ya got more hijinks ruining things for people tryin' to watch the show than you need. I can help, I want people to have their entertainment, God knows I need some. The Winking Moon used to be a place of solace. Now it's just a wild zone. Got good memories of the joint. Remember Anne-Elizabeth Cattacho from high school? She kept me entertained all the way through 'Fantasia,' if ya know what I mean. Best French-kisser I've ever had."

"Been taking your meds?"

"Yup."

"On the straight-and-narrow?"

"Except for this—" Meaning the doobie. "Yes."

"You always were a hard worker, Rodrogo, but I'm afraid I just can't let ya tear loose on The Moon. Leo doesn't want you interfering, either. He got mad at you last year."

"Leo's one of us, Jim, he'll watch our backs."

"To a certain degree but he has the law to uphold."

"I'm talkin' under-the-table shit, Barenta. Stuckerson can flip me a few bucks when he sees what I can do. Hell, you told me he's throwin' his own bread at the joint all the time."

"And he's going broke doing it, his wife tells me he's gotta stop."

"Still no changes in The Crusaders? No new faces?"

"Nope, it's still John, George, Steve and Alex."

"Still get a kick outta that— 'The Crusaders'—they're a good crew, Jim, they're loyal and unafraid. They'll grow up to be fine men."

"That is true, and they got it handled, I taught 'em well."

"Everybody can always use a helpin' hand. You were my mine over in the shit, Jim."

"As you were mine, you saved my life. I'll do anything for ya, Manny—Leo will, too—ya just can't turn The Moon into your hunting-zone, we'll work something out."

"Really?"

Jeannie slid the window open— "Jim, can you come in and put some rub on the meat? We're eating early. Manny: you're staying for dinner."

"Thanks, darlin'," said Manny, then to Jim, "She wants you to put 'rub on the meat.' Ha-ha."

Jim took the doobie from his friend. "Now you sound just like The Crusaders, maybe you *should* work there." He snuffed it out on the bottom of his sandals, handed it back. "Here's what's happening now: you're gonna come in, eat with us, then you're gonna mellow-out here for the evening and stay with us for the night. We'll assess in the morning."

"Well now, Jimbo, I wouldn't want to impose."

"Course not, that's why you stopped over unannounced in the

middle of the fucking day."

Manny appreciated the offer, but first had to justify himself. "Remembered how to get to your house, even though I was here only once."

"You are a man of many talents—*with* initiative."

"'With initiative.' Love that."

Jim put his arm around the man's shoulder, led him to the house. "Love the hat, by the way. Do ya like 'Green Acres'? While I'm rubbing my meat, you can laugh at 'Wilbur the pig.'"

"'Wilbur the Pig'? Ain't he one of your regular trouble-makers at the drive-in?"

"Yo-ho, could be. C'mon, ace, you'll shower up, too."

Jeannie watched them and made a personal credo to herself: *Love the people your man loves. That is the way it is.*

CHAPTER 17:

STRANGE RUMBLINGS

The Crusaders and Vicki ending up filling in at The Moon on Thursday night. Lee-Willie could not take it anymore. He had phoned the parents, pleaded with them to let their daughter and sons come in one day early. Mrs. Carver never took the call. Randy had answered. Upon begging his big brother not to say anything, Randy had let it go, Alex informing her on his way out. "What? Wait! You can't wait one more day until you're officially out of school?" she said, calling after him as Steve picked him up in the driveway, John and George already in the Charger.

The night was dramatic right off the bat. With 'Ole Stuckerson already worked-up like a cornered badger, as soon as operations got underway, the manager got on the warpath, scolding patrons for playing their radios unrelated to the drive-in's music system, and criticized questionable drivers for taking up too much room between speaker-poles. "You're not leaving proper distance between you and the other vehicles. There's such a thing called 'drive-in etiquette,' you know."

"Yeah—" said one rummy, "like leaving your customers in peace and quiet."

Minutes into "Up In Smoke," Kathy looked up to spot a 1970 Cadillac Sedan Deville sneaking into the exit with its lights off. She radioed the boys as they were laughing at Cheech & Chong's license plate— "MUF DVR"—helping females in the back row trying to hook up their speakers. Unfortunately, Lee-Willie got to the offenders first, pissing them off enough that they spouted off to him.

"Continue to disrespect me and face severe consequences," Lee-Willie said back, shaking a fist at them.

All four men got out from the car, each over six-feet-two, one was even six-foot-five. Lee-Willie stood his ground, trying to be intimidating.

"You better take your tone down a notch," he said. "I'm the manager here," he responded. "And I shouldn't have to even be addressing you guys with these stupid stunts."

"Who are you calling 'stupid'?"

"I was calling your *actions* stupid, but if the shoes fits…"

The men stepped closer, looked like they were going to deck him. Suddenly, the Crusaders stepped in. A crowd gathered in anticipation of a fight.

The Crusaders were skilled scrappers. They maneuvered quickly, got in between the factions, Lee-Willie willing to go at anyone, flashlights gleaning in all directions— "C'mon, you wanna come at me? Huh? Think you're gonna try something?"

Stanley, Vicki and Emilio were watching from the double-doors of the concession stand.

"Everybody take it easy," Alex broadcasted.

"This guy's an asshole," the driver said. "We were gonna leave but this jerk starts acting all tough and shit."

Lee-Willie went baritone. "Hey Lurch, I'll tell 'The Addams Family' cast you're missing from the set."

Then things got physical. The tall guys moved in. George had no problem pushing his challenger back, away from the fray. They were the same height. Steve did not have the same luck. His match was taller than him, but Steve was a skilled fighter, effectively taking his opponent down. Alex had one of the chooches by the arm before he was able to take a swing at Stuckerson. He wheeled around and Alex put his hands up— "Let's not do this," deflating the jamoke for a moment.

John had the toughest opponent—the driver—attempting to put the patrolman in a headlock to get at their boss. John wrenched himself free, got behind him, held him against his own Jeep, arm twisted behind his back, forcing him to drop his keys. The one Steve was guarding swept in, snatching them up at the same time Steve did. A tug-of-war ensued, Lee-Willie getting in on the act, all three wrestling for custody. Someone from the crowd yelled, "What are you clods doing?" and taken aback— Steve released his grip, sending their rival's hand inadvertently recoiling into the manager's face, striking Lee-Willie's upper lip. Lee-Willie dropped to his knees. At the sight of their boss holding his mouth, the Crusaders were ready to unleash hell, but before that happened, Big Jim was there to end it all— "Who wants to go to jail?!"

The tall guys froze. Jim had such a commanding voice in moments like this. Gail-Lill arrived next, flailing her flubby arms, lighting her husband up with her flashlight, freaking out when she saw the state of him, blood trickling from his mouth onto the dark pavement.

"Lee!" she shouted, getting him to his feet, practically dragging him to the office to get medical assistance, flying open the door, running at the First Aid kit, throwing gauze wrappings at his injury. Kathy was in the doorway having left her post, stunned.

"Kathy, we have everything under control, just make sure Mr. Stuckerson's okay. He just took an elbow to the lip. If he can't stand it, we'll have to run him to the hospital." Big Jim was enduring the litany of excuses from the aggressors, all blaming Lee-Willie for the incident.

Jim told the crowd around them to get back in their vehicles, gave the knuckleheads two options: either get out now or get locked up. They chose the former, jumping back in the Cadillac, barreling out and vowing to never return. "Kiss my ass!" they shouted on their way out.

The whole movie-experience had been disrupted, and it look a while to calm the audience down after the altercation. Jim got on the P.A. system, apologized to the crowd, and assured everyone that things were under control.

Lee-Willie held his ice and gauze to his swollen mouth, blood droplets on the dingy carpeting.

"You just had to do it, didn't you, Lee? You just had to stir up the trouble when there didn't have to be any. This is what you get… I've told you a million times…" Gail scolded.

"Oh, Gail…" was all he could utter back, sounding like "Ohff,

Ghh…ail."

In the aftermath of the fight, the Crusaders spread apart and patrolled the lot like industrious beavers, searching everywhere. As it was, they knew they were going to be blamed for the incident. "First casualty of the season," Alex informed Kathy. "And it's gonna be our fault."

Jim always had the youngsters' backs. He set the pace, instructing the soldiers to get back to duty and not get too wrapped-up in the negativity from earlier in the evening. He believed they had done a fine job. "I'll talk to your bosses," he said.

In the meantime, there was more activity at the brush. Alex and John heard it, converged at the spot where they believed a kid was sneaking over the fence. They were right. In the distance they could see a kid's portly silhouette struggling to hoist himself up, hovering at the top on the pointy top section of the barricade, one arm and one leg over, determining whether or not to go for it. They could hear him breathing heavily. John and Alex did not say a word, but waited for the meatball to drop over, assuming he got away with it. The kid fell flat on his face, clumsily, unable to support the weight of his descent into the boulevard. When he got up, the duo pounced, grabbing the child by his arms— "A-ha! Think you're sneakin'-in, eh?" quipped Alex.

"Hey! Let me go! Who are you?"

"Your worst nightmare," John replied.

The kid was in a panic. “What’s happening? I was only seeing what was going on.”

“Sure, you were, kid,” said John. “You snuck over from Roller Town; thought you were gonna be watching the movie for free.”

“Well that ain’t happenin’, bucko,” followed Alex, “and you’re gonna tell all your friends about it.”

“Up yours! Shove it up your ass like you’re packing your lunch! Let go!”

The Crusaders didn’t like his insolence and began dragging the boy— “You’re coming with us,” Alex said. “You’re gonna walk out the exit, go back to Roller Town, go back inside where you belong and tell your freakin’ friends: no more sneakin’-in the Winking Moon.”

“What would your parents say?” said John.

“Same thing: pack it up your ass!” He stomped on John’s foot, nearly escaping. The Crusaders only grabbed him tighter.

Alex blew his top. “Okay, he ain’t doing this the right way, let’s show him what comes down must go up.”

The hooligan panicked again. “What?”

John said, “We’re throwin’ ya back over, kid, you asked for it.”

“No!”

“You’ll land softly, there’s scrub-brush there,” said Alex. Now they were right under the point-of-entry, re-grabbing an arm, a leg, lifting the thrashing chub in the air, getting the momentum going, getting the kid higher. When they had reached maximum height, Alex said, "Ready, Crusader?" and the countdown began— "One-two—"

"Hold it!" an adult male's voice came. "What are you kids doing?"

They stopped and set the kid down, but kept a tight grip. A man was standing there, medium height. Even in the dark light they could see he was dressed inappropriately for a drive-in. Tie, dress shirt, dress pants, good shoes.

"Who are you?" Alex demanded.

"A patron," the man answered. "What are you doing?"

What the Crusaders did not know was that this was Kurt Bannabock, regional manager for Bluestone Corporation. Alex asked, "Do you have a *tie* on?"

"Were you about to throw that child over the fence?"

"Yes, they were, mister," said the child. "Help me! I was just screwin' around, I didn't mean no harm."

"Shut-up, kid," John said.

"Isn't this the kind of behavior that initiates problems here, rather than ending problems?"

This made Alex even more suspicious. "Who *are* you?"

"Why don't you put the child down?" the stranger suggested.

"Why don't you mind your business?" said Alex, issuing John to help him start moving the little shit again— "C'mon, kid, we're escorting you out the exit. You're goin' this time."

"Mister, they're brutes!" the kid decried.

Alex told the stranger to forget what he had seen, his outline fading into the darkness as they began their walk. Alex and John were left speechless. They "accompanied" the perpetrator out of the exit, feeling his waves of blubber undulating under in their grip, and released him to the wild with shooing gestures, the kid throwing the finger back and running away. Par for the course.

Kathy had been staring, aghast. "What's going on now?" she asked.

"Typical hooligan trying to sneak-in," answered Alex. "Hey, did you see a lone dude driving in by himself, wearing business clothes and a tie?"

"Not that I remember. They moved in pretty quickly tonight."

"Are you sure?"

"You know I don't engage my customers. Most of them bug me."

"Weirdest thing," Alex said, more to himself.

John agreed. "Yeah, c'mon, now we have to tell George and Steve."

As if the night hadn't been stressful enough for a Thursday (not even regular season yet for the high-schoolers), suddenly, out-of-the-blue during "H.O.T.S.," Stanley burst into a tantrum having learned someone had thrown out his deceased buddy Franco's old toolkit from the back storage room. A patron had tipped him off having stumbled drinking a beer, rusty old box in hand, claiming he had found it in the dumpster while fishing out his keys that his friend had tossed in it as a joke. "It was just sittin' there on top. Pretty heavy som' bitch, too."

Stanley was swinging his arms and swearing at the heavens, swearing and blaming Lee-Willie as the culprit drawing confusion from the patrons inside the stand. Vicki got Jim, did not want to use the radio. Jim calmed the man as best he could, reluctantly had Vicki radio Lee-Willie anyway, tell him to come over. The manager arrived looking like death-warmed-over, ice pack to his lips, eyes bleary, wife by his side, wondering what on Earth had transpired now.

Stanley was virtually upon him, asking about the toolkit. Jim had to hold the senior back and take the crew in the back. Lee-Willie was not going to have an employee cause a display in front of customers. The two shouted at each other, Stanley demanding Lee-Willie never touch another item of Franco's again, Lee-Willie ruling (with great facial pain) that the old man had better settle down and cool his jets before he was ordered home.

"Go ahead, send me home," Stanley seethed. "I don't wanna work in a joint like this, anyway, if you're gonna lay your petty hands on the sacred belongings of my buddy. I've told ya a million times to leave everything of his alone!"

"That was *his* toolbox?" Lee-Willie replied. "I didn't know. Half the tools in it were rusted-out. We need room in here to store present stuff."

"You had no right touching anything without consulting me. I've been here longer than you, remember, I was plannin' on taking his stuff home one day. You're a disgrace to his memory!"

Gail-Lill stepped in. "Stanley, we were only trying to do what was right, it's a fire-hazard in here. We had no idea his toolbox meant so much to you."

"Yeah, you just want your crap in here! Gail, how many times have you heard me asking to leave Franco's stuff alone? Tell your husband to stop actin' like king around here and ask first before throwing anything out. Look at that busted lip! Probably deserved it."

Jim took the poor man to the side, spoke to him gently—as a brother-in-arms, vet-to-vet. Got Stanley to at least stop firing vitriol.

The Crusaders came in having been told of the disturbance, wanting to know what was going on. Vicki and Emilio explained. The boys wanted to help but did not want to make the situation worse. Stanley was excused for the rest of operations to sit in Jim's booth and dry his tears. Jim conversed with the Stuckersons about the need to leave their predecessor's belongings alone. Gail-Lill felt awful. Lee-Willie felt bad, too, but mainly because his throbbing lip was killing him.

"He's off to Mars, Jim," Lee-Willie said to Jim. "He's going Looney

Tunes. He just continues blowing up over the littlest things."

"It's not 'little' to him, Lee," Jim said. "You've got to relax, brother, you're gonna cause something real bad to happen one day."

"Oh, I dunno about that…"

Gail-Lill said, "Lee… for now… put yourself in Stanley's shoes. He's a senior, he should be in that retirement home behind us."

"Thanks, snookums," Lee-Willie snarled. "If I need a lecture from you, too, I'll ask for it."

Up on the screen, boobs were jiggling and bouncing aplenty, entertaining the crowd. Some guy shouted that there was a little kid in the lot, riding around on a bicycle making honking noises with his mouth every time a girl showed off her "major-league bazoombas" in the film. That needed investigating, lickety-split.

The Crusaders crept into the dark lot together, looking around for signs of a kid on a bike. They thought they spotted him. Sure enough, there he was in the middle of the crowd near the south side of the stand. He rode a Stingray bicycle with a sissy bar up back, sticking high with an American flag on it. His eyes were glued to the screen. From what the Crusaders could gather, he looked about nine years old. He was wearing a leather jacket with the collar turned up, pompadour for a haircut, jeans, battered sneakers. "Oooh, look at them watermelons," the child was saying to himself, infatuated with the female parts. "Baby, I'll shake your pom-poms any night of the week."

"C'mere." Alex gathered his chums, doled out the plan. "The 'old round-up.' John: you're over there. George: you come from that direction. Steve: that's your spot. I'll stay here. We'll close in, trap the little bastard. He'll never know what hit him."

Slowly, surely, they each spread out, forming a quadrangle about their intended target, hiding in the shadows of vans, inching in, getting nearer, closing in until the child would have no way out. Someone dumped a soda out the window and the kid snapped his head, thought he saw Steve, panicked— "Huh? Wait! No way!" Jumped on his seat and went to take off.

"C'mere you little punk!" hissed Steve and they all rushed in, running after him.

The chase was just as concentrated as the Cadillac, running this way and that, trying to catch up. Again, John was the fastest. He caught him by the boulevard, nabbing the sissy bar, holding it tight. The others caught up and grabbed the bike, Alex getting in front, latching onto the handlebars— "Gotcha, ya little beetle-grub. Who do ya think you are, Arthur Fonzarelli from 'Happy Days'?"

"Lemme go!" he squawked, voice far from maturing. "Whattya doing? Don't touch my bike! Who are you clowns?"

"We're the Crusaders," George answered. "The Winking Moon Crusaders."

"You the bouncers?" the kid asked.

Steve rolled his eyes. "Not 'bouncers,' we're the patrolmen."

"Sure, ya are," said the boy. "And I'm Cardinal Richelieu, foreign secretary to France."

"What the hell?" John said, surprised at the comeback.

"Lemme go!"

"We *are* the patrolmen," said John. "And we got reports of you pedaling around here, buggin' people trying to watch the movie."

"So? I like girls in sorority uniforms," the kid said. "Is there a law against it?"

"Actually, there is—" said Alex, "when it's called 'trespassing.' And you're doing it. Did you come here in a car?"

"No, I pedaled in by myself."

"That's what we thought. From where?"

"From home. What point you tryin' to make, 'cept clarifying the shape of your guys' heads?"

At once all four started dragging the punk forward, toward the exit— "We're throwin' ya out," said Steve. "Not tonight, you're pulling this shit."

The kid dug heels into the gravel— "Wait! Wait! I've actually come here to talk to ya."

They stopped as John said, "What?"

"I've come to talk to the bouncers. Seriously. Everybody's heard of you guys, I came to meet with you."

"About what?" said George.

"Givin' you puds a heads-up. Although you don't deserve it, the way you treat a little kid."

"A 'heads-up' about what?" Alex said, putting a little force into it.

The little kid looked around, uncomfortably. Lowered his voice. "It's too public out here. Can we go somewhere to do this?"

Crusaders looked at each other. *Is this for real?* Alex said, "You ain't bullshittin' us, are ya? If this is a ploy to stay in, it's not happening."

"It's not," said the kid. "I think you guys are cool. You took care of my older cousin last summer when she had some asshole press his naked ass up against her car window."

"That's gross," said Steve, then, to his mates, "Masked Mooner. Had to be him."

"Who's that?"

"Never mind, boy," said Alex. "We get a lot of characters in here."

"If I disclose information you jamokes will find critical, can I finish watching this movie? I like the special effects. Each girl has very realistic ones jutting outta her chest."

Ignoring the pun, Alex thought, huddled in closer to Steve, George, John. "Stanley's in Jim's office. Stuckersons are in theirs." Meaning…

The lightbulb went off over their heads. "Back storage room," said George. "Let's go."

The four teenage studs walked their prey back to the stand, two on one side, two on the other, making sure their catch was not going to flee. They had him off the bike, George and Steve ready to grab on should the intruder try to run. When they entered the bright stand, they squinted their eyes as normal, Emilio and Vicki tending to customers, looking over with wonder.

"What's going on here?" Vicki said.

Alex did the talking, leading them all to the back— "Somebody we caught out there, has something to tell us. We're taking him to where we can talk for a minute. Don't tip anyone off while we're back here, we won't be long."

Okay, was Vicki and Emilio's expression. *Mum's the word.*

Alex started the briefing. "What's your name, kid?" The back-storage room was perfect for this, away from sight of the patrons. Amazing as many could fit in here at once, given the clutter, especially with the miniature greaser's Stingray still in their possession.

"Frankie," the kid said. "Little Frankie. Little Frankie DiPonzio."

George turned to the guys. "Good name. He *is* Arthur Fonzarelli.'"

Little Frankie did not like that, decided to get wise. "And lemme guess," he aimed back at George, "you're Richie Cunningham—" and to John, "you're Potsy—" to Alex, "you're Ralph Malph—" and finally, to Steve, "and you're Joanie."

"Joanie?" Steve exclaimed. "You wanna pop in the mouth?"

"No," said Little Frankie, "but I'll take a real pop."

"Later," said Alex. "Talk."

They found out the kid's name was "Little Frankie DiPonzio." Small surprise there. They found out Big Frankie DiPonzio did not know his son had snuck out of the house. Little Frankie did this frequently in the good weather, when the drive-in was open.

"And being cool means almost getting your ass punted outta here?" said Steve. "What's the reason for the visit?"

In the better light they could see his bike was rife with *Odd Rod* stickers. *Odd Rod* stickers were a favorite of Alex's from years ago: bubble-gum trading cards in packages, depicting wild-looking monsters behind the wheel of muscle cars, trucks and motorcycles. Alex reached out to touch one— "Speaking of 'cool,' lookit these stickers. I love *Odd Rod* stickers. I used to collect—"

"Lay one finger and you're gettin' a fist to the temple."

Little Frankie pulled up the stool from Franco's old workbench, sat on it, looked at the staring faces, blew out a breath. "Okay, here's the deal: watch your backs, Winkin' Moon, they're coming for ya."

"Who?" asked Alex.

"Everybody," answered Little Frankie. "All the kids. Sooner or later."

"What are ya talking about?" said George.

"All the schools, once summer's out. They're all comin' to get ya. All those kids."

"What does that mean?" John asked.

Frankie turned serious, enunciated each word through his teeth. "The worst of the worst. Hijinks galore. Pranks and stunts like you've never seen. Shenanigans so profound, it'll make your kids cry who aren't even born yet."

The Crusaders became worried. "Jesus… how do you know this?" asked Alex.

"The little I do attend school… I hear things. I ain't a snitch—so you're not getting names—but I am here to tell ya they're gearing up, ready to stage an all-out war on your drive-in."

"A war?" said George. "That sounds violent."

"Well, maybe not violent," Frankie said, "but much worse—tomfoolery up the ass."

Steve furrowed his brow. "Holy shit. Why? Why's it happening? What do you know about it? Why's the Winking Moon the target for so much insanity?"

"Because you're here… like Mount Everest. You need to be conquered."

"Why isn't this happening on the east side?" asked John. "At the Smirking Star? Don't kids know about that drive-in, too?"

"That's the east side. Nothing fun and deviant happens there. The west side is where the bad-boy action happens."

Alex gulped. "When's all this gonna happen?"

"That I don't know," said Frankie. "I catch pieces here-and-there. In the cafeteria, on the playground, over at Roller Rink—*when* I go."

George was growing dubious. "And you came here to tell us this why? Why aren't you part of this?"

"As I said: I like you guys, you helped my cousin. And family helpin' family is big where I come from. And I like the movies, especially the big-breasted one you got playin' now. Can I go watch it?"

Jim walked in— "Who's this? This the twinkle-toed little snot riding his bike around out there, disturbing my customers? A Stingray, huh? Better not scratch any vehicles with that thing, son, you'll pay dearly at the hands of the customers."

Frankie was confused. "Who's this bush-head?"

Jim mouth twitched. Immediately, he was about to move in. Alex stepped in front, lifted a hand— "We got this, Jim, we got vital information to tell ya."

Jim checked his watch. "Well the movie's almost over. Better hurry up in here, your bosses are on their way."

Then Kathy appeared in the doorway, wide-eyed and curious.

"Kathy?" Alex said, all turning. "What're you doing in here? Thought we'd see you earlier."

"I was helping the Stuckersons clean the attic," she answered. "It's a mess up there. Who's this?"

Vicki stuck her head in, right over Kathy's shoulder. "When the Gentlemen's Club is through with the party back here, think you could come out and help a little? That *is* our job."

Little Frankie gawked at Vicki and Kathy. "Man, you cats really stock the joint with babes, don't ya? Did either of you girls come off the screen just now?"

"Who's this?" Vicki inquired.

"Little Frankie DiPonzio," said George. "His father's Big Frankie DiPonzio."

"Nice to meet ya," said Vicki. "Watch your mouth."

"Stanley and I need some help in here," said Emilio, the next to crowd the doorway. "Some guy is trying to sit on the pinball machine while eating his pizza. He's wearing short-shorts, so God knows what kind of a print he's going to leave."

"Who's this with the ponytail and gay hairnet?" Frankie asked next.

"That's Emilio," said Steve. "The cook, be nice to him, he makes your pizza."

Frankie nodded affirmatively— "I've heard about him. Whattya put in your sauce to make it taste so good?"

"Not tellin'," said Emilio. "Family secret."

Frankie looked at The Crusaders. "Tight-ass, ain't he?"

"What the hell's going on back here?" It was Lee-Willie, Gail-Lill. Both on the warpath again. Well, Lee-Willie was. He moved Emilio and Vicki aside so he could storm into the center of the room.

"Mr. Stuckerson, Mrs. Stuckerson," said Alex, playing emcee, "this is Little Frankie DiPonzio. Yes, he rode his bike in illegally, but he had important information for us. He told us the schools are gearin' up to attack us this summer."

"'Attack us?'" said Lee-Willie. "With what?"

"The worst thing imaginable—" said Frankie. "Hijinks on steroids."

Lee-Willie brushed all that away, focused on his employees. "I need all of you to do your jobs. Me, Kathy and Gail were just cleanin' up the attic. I can't have you peabrains hangin' back here, having social hour with a child."

Frankie instantly did not like the guy. "Who's the prick with the swollen lip?" he asked.

"He's the manager," said John. "*Co*-manager. His wife here is also a manager."

Frankie turned back to Lee-Willie. "Mister looks like you been through a meat grinder. If my dog was as ugly as yours, I'd shave its ass and make it walk backwards."

Lee-Willie's temper shot up. He stowed it, broadly sweeping at the patrolmen— "Get him outta here."

"He lives a long way from here, Mr. Stuckerson," said Alex. "He really did help us. We'll fill you in more later."

Lee-Willie looked at Kathy. "Kathy, can you drive him home? We don't want him pedaling around this late at night, God knows what idiotic fools are out there, with this night."

Kathy was stunned. "You want me to drive him home?"

"Put the bike in your trunk, drive him home," Lee-Willie said. "I'll pay for the gas."

"But my paintings," Kathy complained.

"Take 'em out, put the bike in," said Lee-Willie.

"I'll go with her, sir," blurted out Alex, stepping up. "Ya know, all those 'idiotic fools' and all. This kid primarily being one."

"Go," said Lee-Willie, granting his permission.

Everyone else was staring at Alex, corners of their mouths turned up, winks in their eyes. *Nicely played, Alex, well done.*

Kathy and Alex drove Little Frankie home. A *long* way home, practically in the city of Rochester. Part of town that Alex and Kathy did not know well. Alex rode shotgun and turned to face the kid in the backseat. "Just how long did it take you to pedal to The Moon?"

"Who cares?" he shot back, then to Kathy, "Hey Angel-face, mind telling me who the tag-along is again? I thought you and I could have some quality time together."

"Behave, Little Frankie," Kathy replied, keeping her eyes on the road. "His name is 'Alex' and because of him you weren't tossed out on your head."

"Whatever," he said.

Old maples, elms and oaks, hung over the neighborhood avenues and boulevards, like a picture book from Rochester of yesteryear. Some branches were so low, surely a box truck or bus would scrape its roof on them. Alex had all kinds of thoughts crossing his mind. Here he was, sitting in the Goddess of Galileo's car, driving a little shit home, the FM radio playing *You Can't Change That*, by Ray Parker Jr. and Raydio. It was very surreal, and they were not sure where they were going.

"Little Frankie," Kathy said, looking at their guest in her rearview mirror, "you're going to have to tell us where to turn. Pretend I'm a taxicab."

"I'll pretend you're more than just a 'taxicab, honey,'" Little Frankie fired back.

Alex grimaced. Held up a fist to show the kid. Little Frankie got the point.

They finally found the house, pretty dark and quiet, the only light on being the one on the front stoop, illuminating "Big Frankie" with his big, hulking body, sitting there, waiting, smoking a cigarette, drinking what was probably a beer. He saw the vehicle approaching at the same time they saw him. Even in the dim lighting Alex and Kathy noticed him checking the time on his watch. "Shit," spat Little Frankie, sitting up. "Didn't expect that—damn—how long's he been out here? Musta discovered the mannequin I'd made in my bed."

Alex and Kathy did not bother commenting. They were scared, too. This did not look good. As she slowed the Malibu, pulling up curbside to stop, turning the radio off, the bulky body got up from the stoop, paused and lumbered across the lawn toward them.

"And that's my Dad. Holy shit."

"We figured," she said.

"Damn, don't shut the engine off, just lemme escape."

"'Escape'?" said Alex. "We gotta get your bike out first. We'll explain what happened. He's probably worried sick about you."

"*He's* worried sick? You should see his belt."

With the car at an idle, Mr. DiPonzio lowered his large head, trying to get a better angle on who was in the thing. "Little Frankie, that you in there?" His voice was like a bass drum reverberating from the bottom of a barrel.

"Y-yeah, Dad, I-I'm in here, I'm alright, I'm not kidnapped or nothin'. These nice people gave me a ride home. I was at the Winking Moon."

"Again? You took your bike to The Winking Moon *again*? Christ Almighty, how many times have I told ya not to do that? Figured you did that—get out here!" Big Frankie had no shoes on, sported a bulbous gut bulging under a Dago-tee, bald as a bowling ball, and what they could see of his puss… he resembled a bulldog that hadn't been fed in a week.

Alex stepped out passenger side, purposefully keeping distance as to not inflame— "Mr. DiPonzio, my name's Alex Carver and this is Kathy Berenger. We work at the Winking Moon. Your son's safe, we were just driving him home, he rode his bike all the way there to tell us some important stuff. Our boss asked that we have him delivered back home safe-and-sound."

"I did, Dad, I did. I wouldn't have slipped out unless it was important."

"It's 'important' not to scare me half to death, I'm gonna whip your behind."

"Sir, it's okay," Kathy said, remaining in the car. "He didn't do anything bad, no need to get upset anymore, he's safe."

"Don't tell me what to do or not do, young lady, you don't know me or my son."

Kathy swallowed hard. "Um… you're right, sir. Sorry."

To Little Frankie— "Where's your bike?"

"In the trunk, sir," said Alex. "We're about to get it out."

Big Frankie huffed but let them proceed. Little Frankie scrambled out but stayed a safe distance from his dad. Kathy popped the trunk from under her seat. Alex took the Stingray out, set it gently on the surface of the street. Little Frankie ran to it, swept it up from under Alex, jumped onboard, began pedaling it up the driveway into the dark maw of the open garage. Big Frankie watched him go, turned back to his guests but still called out to him— "Pull that dummy-trick in your bed again, son, and you're dead meat."

Little Frankie scurried into the house using the front door where his dad had been sitting, shutting it behind him, not appearing again until poking his head out a front window to the far end of the house, probably his bedroom. They could all see him.

"Honestly, sir," tried Alex, "he's not in trouble with us. He gave us useful information."

"He coulda gone after school."

"We're not open 'til night, sir."

"Oh."

"He actually wanted to help us, sir, said we helped his cousin last year."

"With that naked guy?"

"Yeah, I guess, sir."

Big Frankie just glowered at them, did not say a word. Then he grumbled, "Your Winking Moon's nothing but trouble."

"We know, sir."

"But my kid loves it."

"We know that, too, sir," said Kathy.

Big Frankie had a wallet stuffed into his Bermuda shorts. Grabbed it, began thumbing out a few bills— "What do I owe ya?"

Alex stopped him. "Sir, no, we're not doing that, we just wanted to get him home safely. We just met him, and he was very honest with us. We're just tryin' to keep the joint open, ya know."

"I know," said Big Frankie. "Thanks."

"You're welcome," said Alex.

"He's done this before, but he didn't talk to no one. He just wanted to watch the movies."

"That's what he told us, sir."

"He lost his mother."

Both Alex and Kathy felt their hearts lock up. "Sir—" Kathy said, "we're so very sorry." Alex was, too.

"It's his aunt who lives with us. I'll try to have ya not be bothered by him anymore."

"He wasn't bothering us, sir," said Alex. "He's a funny kid. Sorta."

Little Frankie impishly called out from the window— "Long live the Winking Moon."

Big Frankie whipped around— "Shut-up, boy, it's the middle of the night, people are sleepin.'" Back to his guests, "I'm goin' in."

Big Frankie ended the conversation, walked in through the front door, shut the light off, leaving Alex and Kathy in the dark, save the lamppost the next house over. All the stars in the night sky were out. They could be seen through the thick canopy of trees. Alex turned to Kathy, "That was… something. Ready to go?"

"I am," she said. "I like the kid."

Alex gave her a look—*You do?* —and climbed back in the Malibu. "Remember how to get back?"

"I do. I'm good at navigating. She turned the radio back on. *Baby Come Back*, by Player was on. Awesome.

Kathy was so amazed at how Alex conducted himself with Big Frankie—AKA Mr. DiPonzio—that she offered him a ride home when the evening was done-done. She even volunteered it in front of the others, making Alex blush.

Alex asked the Crusaders, "You guys meetin' out somewhere? I can see if I can borrow my mother's Chevette when I get home, meet you guys at Durand Eastman Park or something."

"Go, little one," said Vicki. "Spread your wings."

And that sealed it. He was going.

Mrs. Stuckerson walked up to the youngsters, had a kind smile on her face despite the way the evening had gone. "Well, good luck with school tomorrow," she said. "Last day, I bet that's exciting."

"It is, Mrs. Stuckerson," said George. "And we'll be back tomorrow night—full-time."

"Oh, joy of joys," Lee-Willie mumbled, nursing his swollen lip through an ice pack. "I get to see your faces every night."

"Lee, be nice."

"Before we leave," Alex said, "did any of you see a man in here tonight in business clothes? Shirt and tie, looking way out-of-place?"

"No, why?" said Lee-Willie. No one had.

"I never did see that guy, Alex, after you told me," offered Kathy.

Alex answered. "He caught John and I getting ready to toss a hooligan over the fence. He was acting really self-righteous."

Gail-Lill eyed her husband. He was thinking. Then he spoke up. "Kurt Bannabock from Bluestone sneaks around at the drive-ins every so often. He's been known to do that: drop in unannounced. Sure hope that wasn't him. What'd he look like?"

"It was too dark to tell," said John. "We just know he was in business clothes."

This bewildered everyone. No one said a word. They were thinking, too. Then, Lee-Willie waved it away, wanting to get on with the departure, pointed a nerdy finger at Alex and John again, said— "Watch what you're doing."

Jim clapped Stanley on the shoulder, jolting him out of deep thought. He looked resigned through his bifocals when the big guy asked him, "Stanley, you good to go home? You can do your late-night, deep-space observing now."

Stanley sighed. "I… might just go to bed. Been a long week so far."

The crew felt sorry for their crabby colleague. He had run out of energy, and that was obvious and probably for the best.

"And next time I send ya on a mission, Carver—" Lee-Willie said, shooing everybody away, "don't take so long." Naturally, he did not say anything to Kathy.

They all said good night to one another while the background played to the usual gallery of drunken and high stooges and morons, ripping out through the exit, hurling insults and nondescript noises at them. As Emilio got into his '76 Volkswagen Kombi, his parting-shot was, "If what that little shit on the Stingray says is true, God help us. Look at what simple exiting gives us."

Everybody split. Kathy and Alex drove off to Yvonne Elliman's "If I Can't Have You." During the surreal ride, she asked him about his home situation. He did not know she even knew.

"Your brother," she said. "He's still bugging you to work for him? And your poor mother, picking up after you father left. I've never had to go through anything like that, Alex. You're awfully strong for being such a young age. You're magnificent."

Alex beamed with pride after Kathy's compliment. He liked her even more than he thought he did.

CHAPTER 18:

THE OFFICIAL START OF SUMMER

Friday, June 15th, 1979

When the bell sounded at 1:50 p.m., it felt like the walls were going to collapse from the force of Galileo's student body charging the doors. Summer had officially arrived, and teens ran unhinged through the corridors, convoys of vehicles blasted out of the parking lots, performing doughnuts and spinouts, heading for Hamlin Beach: seventeen miles from school. The make-up mostly consisted of parents' wheels, but some owned their own rides. Once everyone arrived at the beachfront, they went bonkers, celebrating the end to another school year. The Crusaders… sat in the cafeteria at the same lunch table, biding time, considering the athletic fields and Lake Ontario beyond them. Memories made, memories to come.

A classmate ran in hollering about finally being free and whipped a raw egg clear across the open room, meaning to hit the wall a hundred feet away. Instead, it skimmed the stucco ceiling, pulverizing the shell, sending a thin layer of yolk over everything. The patrolmen did not even bother to get up. They been there, done that, already.

Mr. Fantuzzi and Mrs. Brady—the notorious flirting teachers—walked in thinking they were alone, saw the boys, and told them it was perfectly okay to go home. The Crusaders said hello, but the educators were insistent they leave.

"Gentlemen, you're free," Mr. Fantuzzi said. "Get out of here. You don't want to waste one minute of your summer vacation, do you?"

Mrs. Brady joined in, trying to be funny. "Yeah, Steve, John, George, Alex. Go. Go play in traffic or something. Have a great time. See you in September."

The Crusaders got up, said goodbye to both of them, wished them a great summer themselves, and George said, "If you're gonna hang on each other ya might as well come to the drive-in and do it, it's the natural place for it," leaving them gobsmacked.

In the vacant hallway, they ran into one of the most notorious pranksters in the school, all geeky-looking and spry, looking like he was up to something holding a box in his hands and drinking furiously water from a fountain, and drinking water from a fountain, box of something in his hand.

"Chucky Bark?" Alex said. "What the fork-knife-and-spoon are you still doing here?"

"Getting my stuff ready to take to Hamlin Beach," the kid said. "You guys coming? Everyone's gonna be there, including other schools. We're free, puds, time to fly."

"Yeah, we know," said Steve, "we're just taking our time, absorbing the fact we're now seniors."

"Screw that, time to party," Chucky said.

Chucky, like so many class clowns, had a habit of smiling like the

Cheshire Cat when he was up to something. Mostly he was liked, even when he did stupid things. The Crusaders braced themselves, eyeballing the box. Chucky saw them staring at it, set it on the fountain, opened it up.

"Lookit this, chumps," he said. "And this is where the party begins."

There was an enormous cache of bottle-rockets, air-bombs, ball-rockets, crackling-comets, peonies, chrysanthemums and Roman candles. The Crusaders gave him a dirty look and Chucky slammed the lids shut.

"Chucky…" Steve said, "where'd ya get all that?"

"And what are ya doing with it in school?" John followed.

Chucky said, "Best hiding place of all: right under everyone's noses. Been waiting months to get this stuff outta here. If my brothers woulda come across it, they woulda blown 'em off already. My uncle in Indiana gets tons of this shit every year, gives it to me at Christmas. Imagine how much fun we can have at the Winking Moon with this?"

"You're doing nothing of the kind, Chucky," Alex said. "We're not having any of this at the Moon this year. None of it. Heed to our words: Ya bring it in, we're gonna beat you severely."

Chucky giggled. "Relax, Carver, I'm not gonna get you guys in trouble."

"No, but you're gonna get yourself in trouble," said George.

"With us picking up the remains," said John.

Steve was thinking into the future. "You're not bringing 'em in, Bark. We're not getting in trouble because of you. You did enough damage last year."

"Oh, come on," said Chucky. "Leading the family cow into the drive-in and terrorizing only a couple people with it before you kicked us out wasn't so bad, was it?"

"We still don't know how you got that animal into the Moon," said John.

"With great, mastermind plans," Chucky replied.

The Crusaders had enough. It was time to go. George nudged the others, pointed a final warning-finger at Chucky, and urged his friends to move. "Let's make like an amoeba and split," he said. "Chucky, if we go to Hamlin, I'm sure we'll see ya there."

"You mean you'll *hear* me there," Chucky said. "With these." He tapped the box with his fingers."

As they departed from the building, they caught sight of Mrs. Brady and Mr. Fantuzzi, again slipping-off into an empty classroom, Mr. Fantuzzi with a large bong in his hand.

"Cheech & Chong don't have one that big in the movie," John muttered.

Hamlin had a massive turnout, over half a dozen high schools represented. Across the numerous pavilions about the park, hand-painted banners stretched from cedar beam to cedar beam, delineating who was who and who was from where, to celebrate the end of another school year. Galileo was one of the largest represented. From the sprawling, grassy fields to the lakefront, volleyballs, Frisbees, Nerf footballs, soccer balls, and one boomerang (plastic, thankfully) soared across the sky. Some were from the other side of town, including, ironically, Copernicus: home of The Avengers. Kyle and his four comrades arrived in his '75 Audi Fox Wagon, parking near Steve and his Charger. George and Kyle had a long history of competition in the sporting sector. "We meet now, we meet on the football field," Kyle said. "Next time as seniors."

"You know it, Kyle."

"Good luck at the Winking Moon this year, you got your work cut out for you. It *is* a penal colony, after all."

"Good luck at the Smirking Star, Kyle—I hope you'll *have* work to do."

"Funny."

The Crusaders partied with numerous classmates up in a bluff at the far end of one of the campsites, at the peak of the crowds, celebrating, laughing, rejoicing. Throughout the late afternoon, the area was endemic with grilling, drinking, smoking, smooching, horseplay and more. Jody McBrennan joined Steve with some of her junior-to-be classmates, putting her tongue down Steve's throat immediately upon getting together. As before, she had "borrowed" beer from her job at Lapping Waves, doling it out now. "It was gonna be thrown out anyway," the blonde, potty-mouth touted. "That Fort beer-brand doesn't go fast."

With such a great location and an audience like he had, George did not have a problem busting his best friend John's balls in front of everybody, making a spectacle of the kid's shyness.

"The reason you don't speak much is because you have blue balls," the big kid said. "If you released some of your testicular tension every now and then, ya might be making public speeches." Then he snatched John's Cincinnati Reds baseball cap off his head, attempting to toss it a few feet away to make John retrieve it, but instead got it caught up in a crosswind—lifting high into the sky, helicoptering off over the water—eventually landing in a tiny, white splashdown, never to be seen again. John then connected a solid kick to George's chest, sending the muscular teenager ass-over-tea-kettles down the sandy crag to the lower grounds, their audience laughing twice as hard, some capturing the event on their Super-8mm Kodak motion picture cameras.

The festivities had to end early for the patrolmen. They had to work. So did The Avengers, on their side of the park. Just before splitting, the Avengers and Crusaders met once again, in the parking lot, both factions balking at the coincidence. *Of all the luck.* Adding to the ultimate irony was the sudden appearance of Stanley Mason's grandniece: box office chick from the Smirking Star. She stepped out of an Econoline van with a handful of girlfriends. "Stephanie!" Kyle said, Gary, Pauly, Newton and

Seth all turning as well. "What are you doing here? We have to work tonight."

"Not 'til seven, Kyle," Stephanie said, instantly turned off by Kyle's approach. "Relax, I can have fun, too. We're officially done with school."

Kyle disagreed. "You're sixteen. You're not supposed to be here."

She glared at him. "What are you, my father? You try to tell me what to do at work, you're not doing it here. Nobody wants to miss these annual bashes at Hamlin Beach."

The Crusaders were stunned, George really liking what he was seeing. He spoke up, at once pouring on the charm. "Who's this? Kyle, is this Stephanie Mason, *our* Stanley's grandniece?" To Stephanie, "You work at the Smirking Star, right?"

"Right," Stephanie said, smiling back. Instant chemistry.

"We've heard about you, seen your pictures," George went on to announce. "Stanley's told us all about you, we never met last year. He's very proud of you—and protective."

Stephanie giggled. "Yeah, well, he doesn't like you kids very much."

Crusaders laughed. "We know that much."

Steve Laneske was next to speak. "Who are all these other nice ladies? Girls, you all from Copernicus? We're from Galileo."

Greetings, introductions, flirtations. One of the Copernicus cuties asked, "Are you kids the infamous 'Crusaders' we've heard so much about?"

"Defenders of the Winking Moon? Protectors of the night?" added Stephanie, smiling.

"In the flesh," George replied. "And at your service."

Kyle was growing disgusted. "Please…" he said, then, "Stephanie, can't you and your friends go find the Copernicus Pavilion? It's right over there—*far away*."

"Stop by the Winking Moon some night so we can talk to ya," George said to her. "We'd love to get to know you. All you girls." Kyle was seething. George was smitten. The rest of The Avengers were not liking this very much either.

"Right," said Stephanie, enjoying toying with George. "And you and I can disco-dance together, maybe right at the box office."

"Good a place as any," George said.

Kyle turned to his men, tried to make his nemesis look bad. "George thinks he's cool. Can't do much disco-dancing when the drive-in is as crazy as an insane asylum."

"And you could do plenty at yours, Kyle," George rejoined, "since there's nothing else goin' on. What, it takes five of you to watch a kid messin' with the soda dispenser?"

Pauly Cicco let loose. "You're a riot, Jocavelli, our drive-in doesn't require bullet-proof vests and helmets to work there."

"Just dunce caps, Cicco," fired-off George, drawing filthy looks from all five Avengers.

"Stephanie, get going."

"Don't tell me what to do, Kyle, I can do what I want." She and George continued to smile at each other as the pack was ready to go. The two *definitely* liked each other, the twinkles were obvious. There was an embankment before them. The girls were going to walk down it. Was time for the Crusaders to go, too.

Alex nudged his friends, "Come on, let's go, we don't wanna be late."

"Listen to Carver, Jock," said Kyle. "You don't want to be late. Got to get that electric fence up around your place before first show."

George looked at his buddies. "That's a good idea, actually."

"Ready?" Steve asked.

"As a ripe banana," answered George.

Kyle made a face. "What the fuck? You guys are weird."

"Wouldn't have it any other way, right Stephanie?" said George. "That's what your grand-uncle says."

"He says a lot," said Stephanie.

"Nice to meet you."

"Nice to meet you, too."

Just then a bottle rocket zipped between all of them, flying up from below and exploding at a car, ten feet away. The group reacted, ducking, flinching, not knowing what was going on. A few moments later an explosion erupted down below, where the bulk of the activities were taking place. There were loud screams of surprise, followed by a stunned silence as everyone looked around.

"What the hell was that?!" Alex said, speaking for all.

They found out. The whole damn crowd found out after a guttural laughter broke out from an individual emerging from the bushes. It was the Crusaders' buddy, Chucky Bark, holding a handmade fireworks launcher. His Air Bomb Skyrocket had found its way into Tamley High's pavilion, banked against a wooden support beam, and blown up under a picnic table. The smell of gunpowder was already overtaking the crowd, a large cloud of grey smoke covering them in obscuring greyness.

Chucky was guffawing his head off, proud of his accomplishment but apologizing at the top of his lungs to everyone who could hear him. He spotted the Crusaders up high and waved at them, pointing to his contraption which he was quite proud of.

"See, guys?" he hollered. "Lots of fun for the summer!"

The Avengers were horrified.

"Is he one of yours?" Newton Tallis asked the Crusaders.

"Unfortunately, yes," answered John.

"But we don't like to admit it," followed George.

The Avengers just shook their heads. "Figures," mumbled Gary Halinsky.

Alex cupped his hands to shout down to their friend. "Bark, you maniac, have you lost your mind?"

"Yes!" Chucky shouted back. "And if ya find it, don't bother giving it back!"

Then he laughed again, preparing the launcher with the next firework.

CHAPTER 19:

STANLEY

Stanley was trying to set up his Celestron telescope before work. He was out in the backyard of his house. Private space, extremely high fence to hide himself from neighbors. Few trees, wide-open vista. Already, his new smock from The Moon had UFO and space buttons clipped all over it. It had been tightly pressed-and-ironed by his adoring wife, sauntering out now, dressed in her bathrobe and slippers, plate of chocolate chip cookies in-hand. He tried ignoring her as she moved around, purposefully trying to get in his line of vision. "Tonight's the night, Stanley-dear. All those sweet kids back, full-time. Aren't you excited?" Her voice was as song, her white-white hair like cotton.

"Doris, I'd be excited if you stayed out of my way while I'm tryin' to calibrate this thing. It's hard to do in the dark when I get home late. Would you excuse me?"

"But, Stanley, they're such nice children. You should be eager to see them."

"Yeah, and I'm eager seeing bunions appear on my feet."

"Tonight, when you get home from work—before you observe the heavens—why don't you observe me?" She set the cookies on their own picnic table, coquettishly showed off her bathrobe.

He ignored her again. "Doris, I'll take the cookies, forget the nookie. C'mon now, only a few more minutes before I have to head off here."

"But I just got my hair done. You should at least look at me."

"I've looked at you for fifty years, is there somethin' I've been missing?"

Sliding past to check the legs of the telescope, he found them sturdy. Next, he straightened, cracked his back, looked to the sky shielding his eyes, checking for cloud formations. Doris grew annoyed. "For crying out loud, Stanley, you've looked through that thing four times this week before coming to bed. Can't you give me a little attention?"

"We're back in-season, Doris. I must find my aliens"

"Yes, I know, Stanley: they're coming any day now, the warmer weather is back, and you have to do this now while you can. Those of us tuned into this silly nonsense will be rewarded."

"It's not 'nonsense,' woman, they're gonna provide me with things you can't."

"Like what, an anal probe?"

That stopped him. Grimly, he looked at her. "You're my wife and this'll be worth invaluable treasures meeting my galactic brotherhood. You could benefit from this, too."

"How, they going to do the laundry?"

"Doris, please don't trivialize my efforts, ya know I've been at this for a long time."

"A little too long, honey-bunny. You're *my* ambassador, you don't have to be anyone else's. And what are you going to do, abandon me to go off traipsing around the universe like The Flying Dutchman? You weren't this bad when we were newlyweds."

"Exactly. When we were 'newlyweds.' You should know me by now: I'm more focused in my old age. It's called 'wisdom.'"

"Well I don't want you to lose 'focus' on me, Stanley, we have many more years to come. And you can't be doing this drive-in thing forever. The Winking Moon *is* getting hurly-burly."

"Doris, I love ya with all my heart, but you're driving me crazy. Just lemme adjust this in peace before I go to work. I've given you my life, lemme get these thirty-five minutes."

"When are you going to quit the drive-in, honey? You've been there a long time. It will go on without you."

"I've told you as I've told staff: it keeps me outdoors at night where I'll have a better chance at first contact. I've told you this a million times, Doris."

She then took a gander at him in his uniform. "I'll say this, Stanley, you sure are handsome in that new gussy-up. I'd say Lee-Willie and Gail-Lill picked out good ones this time. You got my engine running."

"And you'd get mine runnin' if ya didn't have face cream plastered all over your face when I get home all the time."

"Oh! I… don't have it on *all the time*."

"You kiddin'? Last night it looked like ya got into a fight in a toothpaste factory and lost."

"Stanley, be nice."

He checked his watch. "Okay, all set, I do have to run. Thanks for the treats, dear." He wolfed down three cookies, crumbs dropping to the grass, kissed her on the cheek and sailed by, Doris staring back in horror. "Oh my God, Stanley, you're acting like a possessed loon."

"'Oh my God' is right. God made lots of folks in the universe and it's my job to be welcoming to 'em so they don't think we're a buncha idiots and buffoons like I deal with at work."

She stopped him at the back stoop. "Our grandniece is starting up again, too, tonight. Did you call her? She's certainly not an 'idiot' or a 'buffoon.'"

"No, Stephanie's not, but the boys she works with certainly are. 'Avengers'… 'Crusaders.' All of 'em are morons. Better keep their teenage mitts off her, too. My guys, as well. I'll tear anybody's heads off tryin' to mess with our Stephanie."

"She'll be fine, go call her," Doris replied.

"I will."

At this, the saintly woman grabbed the plate of cookies, headed toward the house with Stanley waiting for her, holding the door open. "Let me know when you're out the door, would you please, Stanley?"

"Hope there's something good for you on television tonight," he said.

"Gee, thanks. Glad you're concerned."

He had a final word for her. "And I hope ya didn't make another batch of cookies for my coworkers. Don't show up, passing 'em out. You've done that way too many times and it causes a great disruption."

"They love me, and they loved my baked goods. And you're a great disruption."

The insult went nowhere. Stanley looked hopefully at the sky once more, whispered under his breath— "C'mon, make it soon, make it soon, people. I'm ready for an adventure beyond stupid teenagers with their stupid, teenage antics. Dumb clucks, God help us."

CHAPTER 20:

WINKING MOON, FULL THROTTLE

As the Crusaders and Vicki (in her father's work truck) ripped into the parking lot of the drive-in an hour before the show, they landed eyeballs immediately on the large, hand-made banner strung across the double-doors of the entrance to the concession stand on its north side, facing them: ***WELCOME BACK CLASS OF 80***. It was a friendly—and appreciated—gesture.

"Wow look at this," said Steve. "A welcoming committee."

"No doubt the work of Mrs. Stuckerson," said Alex. "Very nice."

The two vehicles parked behind Jim's Fleetside, and were careful not to scatter stones as Steve was fond of doing as a joke.

As all five got out and were talking about the sign—how friendly it was and how much they appreciated the gesture—Mr. Stuckerson came out from behind the building and said, "Like the sign? My wife did it. I have a better one when you go in the back and punch in." There was still dried blood caked on his split lip and he still looked like hell.

NOW YOUR ASSES BELONG TO US was Lee-Willie's effort, just as large, just as hand-made, and tacked-up right above the time clock, impossible to miss.

The five each clocked-in, looking over their shoulder at their boss, standing there snickering sardonically until he had enough, moving off to get on with other matters.

When they were in the clear, Vicki was the first to speak. "Not quite as heart-warming but what should we suspect?"

George said, "Wrong choice of wording given we're kids and he's an adult."

Nevertheless, they brushed off the insult and got on with matters themselves, straightening their smocks ahead of the first official Friday night shift of the summer, Stanley walked in, checking in on them. He appeared to be in a better mood from the previous night. "Why are you dunderheads all sunburned?" he said. "I thought all of you were Italian."

"Only two of us are full-blooded," George responded. "Alex is half and Steve is Scandinavian or some such shit. Vicki? We dunno what she is."

"Watch it, fool," she told the big kid.

Alex answered. "We were at Hamlin Beach this afternoon. All the schools celebrate the last day of school goin' out there. It was a riot."

Stanley said, "I just called my grandniece Stephanie before I got here. She said she was there. Did ya meet her?"

"Unfortunately, we did," said George, pretending he was disappointed.

Stanley looked at him. "Whattya mean 'unfortunately'? She's a great kid."

George had been holding back. He erupted with over-the-top with energy— "And super fine, too! Holy shit, Stanley, she's mint. Ya never told us how sexy she was." The others were laughing, holding their sides.

Stanley's face crunched up, irritated. "Oh, just busting my balls, eh? Touch her and you die!"

"Relax, Mason, she's a good kid," said George. "Though I would like to talk to her sometime."

"I mean it, Jocavelli!"

They were all enjoying major frivolity at the coot's expense.

The noise had attracted Emilio. He came in smiling— "Well, welcome back—full-time. Even though you worked last week, here you all are: one big happy family, all set for the big summer every night except for Mondays."

"We're ready," said Steve, and they all walked out with Stanley slapping them each on the back, on purpose, to make their sunburns sting.

Jim was there in the stand to surprise them again, holding up a carton of smokes in one hand (one already in his mouth), six-pack in the other— "And you jamokes and jebeebs ready for this? Beer and cigarettes!"

Lee-Willie and Gail-Lill had been standing by the door, watching—and allowing. "Jim, put that away," said Gail-Lill.

"Kidding," said Jim. To the teenagers, "Last night for 'Up in Smoke' and 'H.O.T.S.' We got two slice 'em-and-dice-'em's tomorrow night: 'The Hills Have Eyes' and 'Texas Chainsaw Massacre.'"

"Awesome!" yelped Alex. "Can't wait to see 'em. 'The Hills Have Eyes' is Wes Craven's latest film, director of that ultra-creepy last one he did: 'Last House on The Left.'"

"I saw that," said Vicki. "I never want to see that film again as long as I live. Gave me nightmares for a month."

"Well tomorrow night should keep you up then," said Jim.

To which Vicki said, mockingly, "We're *already* up."

To John, Steve, George and Alex, Jim smirked, "That's my slogan for you gentlemen now that you're here again: work hard, play hard, stay hard."

"Jim…"

"Sorry, Vick, a little man-humor," he said.

She gave him a fake-smile. "And it's only 'little.'"

"Get to work," Lee-Willie yawped.

In the parking lot, the spaces were filling. Already, a hippie-chick with a great body, wearing a tight tube-top and a Flower Power headband was standing atop a bumper of a '69 TransAm, dancing to the pre-show music, obviously inebriated. The boyfriend was behind the wheel, fiddling with the speaker, yelling at her to get down. When she ignored his instructions, flashing her breasts to the howling and honking crowd, he got out and physically pulled her inside with him. She was laughing away and even he had to chuckle after a few moments. They were the first to be spoken to by the patrolmen.

Over at the Smirking Star, their Friday night crowd was filling up the lot, too. This venue, however, was lightyears more mellow. Their lot was the same layout as The Moon—rural setting, away from the city lights, fresh air up the wazoo—but there was no Roller Rink or Edgewater Retirement Home to entice the punks or hooligans into attempting to sneak into the drive-in. Even the clientele was boring. Mostly families. Good, clean, law-abiding, going-home-when-the-show-was-over families. Pauly and Gary shook their heads at a family already asleep in their station wagon, dad's noggin hanging out the window, drool pooling from his open mouth to the ground below. Mom had smeared her lipstick dozing off, smeared it halfway down her face, still strapped into her seatbelt. Grandparents were even here!

The two movies playing were in big red letters on the small marquee located at their entrance: G-rated "Muppet Movie" and "Apple Dumpling Gang Rides Again." The Avengers were already sick of it. "Two more, lame-o cinematic treats down the drain," Newton Tallis said.

"Thank God tomorrow night starts new ones," said Seth Byrd.

"I was beginning to want to blow my brains out," said Gary

Halinsky.

"Speaking of 'blowing-brains-out,'" said Pauly. "Just once I'd like to get an R-rated movie in here, see somebody get theirs cleared clean off their shoulders from a shotgun blast."

Kyle did not say anything, just looked at the marquee, rolled his eyes at it.

Walking back up the road, they saw Stephanie in the box office booth, dealing with customers. She had been at it awhile already, just didn't want to spend time in the concession stand, where she'd run into The Avengers.

"Hey Steph," Newton called out, waving to her.

Stephanie saw the whole bunch. "Hello," she said, in-between vehicles.

"Did you stick around to hang out with the Crusaders?" Kyle said, making his voice loud.

This made her wince. She knew it. "Kyle…" she said, "please drop it."

"Aren't we good enough for you? That name on your smock should read 'Benedict Arnold.' Or the female equivalent."

Stephanie braced, keeping her mouth shut. She didn't have to respond as Mr. Brent Saxon, manager of the Smirking Star, came out of his office. "They bugging you, Stephanie?" he inquired as he approached, evil-eyeing his patrolmen, banking into the exit upon seeing him. Saxon was about the same age as the Stuckersons and wore a similar attire as Lee-Willie: shirt, extra-wide tie, dress pants with a belt, very wide belt-buckle. He was lanky, mustached and had a chin with a perfect dimple.

"No, Mr. Saxon," answered Stephanie. "They're just being them."

"Guys, get over here." He waved the motley crew to him.

"What is it, Mr. Saxon?" said Seth, all five obeying.

"Don't be hanging around here all night, bothering Stephanie. She's got enough to do without you kids distracting her from work. Go out and patrol—you're out of school now—make yourselves useful."

"There's nothing to patrol yet, sir," commented Gary.

"That's not what I pay you for. Patrol!"

"Yes, sir," they said, booking.

When the five were gone, Saxon stood around doing exactly what he told his patrolmen not to do: bother the young girl while she was trying to do her work. Stephanie rolled her eyes when he was not looking. She had heard this all before, a thousand times. before. The manager bragged of his new Cadillac and the steal he got it for from his brother-in-law who owned two dealerships and wanted him to take over ownership of one of them.

On their pre-show rounds, all was fine. The Avengers saw a van with airbrushed mountains, rocking back and forth, a sure sign something lewd was taking place. They knocked on the back door. It opened, revealing a vanilla-looking mom and dad playing with their twin daughters, tugging roughly on the cord of a Chatty Kathy doll, trying to get it to work, thus creating the disturbance.

"Darn-tootin' thing won't talk," said the father.

"We've been trying for minutes," said the mother. "Do you boys have a battery?

Disappointed, they continued on. The Avengers shuffled for an hour and found nothing but peace. Pure, innocent, peace. Some tots had coloring-books, others played on the swings, giggling with their parents. Still others had board games, engaged in a friendly game of Monopoly waiting for the show to start. There were young people here, too—young men and women, on dates—but no hanky-panky. The patrolmen only saw one kiss and there was no tongue. Certainly, there was no contraband alcohol or drugs to confiscate.

"You know," Seth observed, "the Crusaders *do* have us whipped in the action-department, we can't deny that. Last weekend the biggest excitement we had was scraping those Wacky Ad decals off the bathroom doors. Took us fifteen minutes, with razor blades."

Kyle tried beating Pauly Cicco at a game of *Space Invaders* in the concession stand during the opening moments of the first film. He was going at it all psycho-like, like he was doing at his house with foosball. Kyle was the overly competitive type, and currently he was making the biggest whoops, hollers and "Oh yeahs!" of the inside population. Folks were quietly standing in line, looking at him like he was uncouth, obeying the guidelines one could, never getting out-of-line. The Star's register man (not quite as old as Stanley) had to kick them out and tell them to get to work.

They came across girls they knew from Copernicus. They had been at Hamlin Beach that afternoon, too. "Did you meet your competitors from The Winking Moon?" they asked.

"'Competitors'?" said Kyle. "Why do you say that?"

"Well, aren't they? They do what you guys do, only there."

"We don't see them as 'competitors' but, yeah, we saw them."

"They beat people up at their drive-in," said another chick, swooning. "So sexy."

Gary Halinsky said, "Beating people up is sexy?"

"It's caveman-like, so yeah, kind of. I don't think you kids do that here."

Seth Byrd stepped in, showed a scar. "I got this from tripping over a tire left in the lot."

"Oooh," the girl said, mockingly.

The driver turned their attention— "Oops, that little kid over there just dropped his rubber ducky from that car. Can you pick it up for him? His parents didn't see."

Humiliated, they walked round and round, not nearly as charismatic and friendly to their customers as the Crusaders were. One man even asked Newton Tallis for assistance in placing the speaker correctly in the window.

"Um, maybe when I get back," Newton replied. "I have to check on the popcorn."

But, over at The Moon, tomfoolery was already alive and well. As Cheech & Chong smoked their gigantic doobies, clouding up their car, belting out "I'm Just A Love Machine," by The Miracles, an all-encompassing cacophony broke out in the lot, the result of two eleven-year olds pelting the screen with tennis balls. Half the lot's vehicles laid on the horn in objection, making the Crusaders—and others—cover their ears. "Have to get used to this joy all over again!" John shouted to George, taking care of the problem. The patrolmen escorted the perpetrators back to their parents, threatening to throw them out if they did not get a handle on their children.

Steve and Alex ran into skylarking themselves. Steve dealt with another escapee of parents' supervision. A brat, about twelve-years of age, ran into the playground alone, grabbed the swings by their seats, began whirling them around so they would get coiled up high on the cross bar, no longer able to be accessed. Alex had to grab the eight-foot ladder from the back-storage room and unwind the seats just to get them back down to earth again. He was told by the kid to lick his testicles.

George and Alex had a fun one next. Two wasted-but-mint foxes, dressed in bell-bottoms and tight blouses, went to step out of their '76 Ford Mustang to make a visit to the ladies' room, miscalculated the task, and both went down, one catching the cuff of her pants in the shut door. Both started laughing and drew unwanted attention. The one with her leg stuck brayed so loud she sounded like a mule, her noises fitting with the movie's soundtrack perfectly. Thankfully, she was not hurt. The heroes had to clear the crowd gathered to save her, get the one unstuck, and accompany them both to the bathroom, making sure they were safe. The boys waited for them to be through, asked if they both had washed their hands, and accompanied them back to their Mustang. "Can't be helping you all night," said George, joshing. "So maybe ya wanna keep the car doors open."

And finally, just before intermission, they got into another snafu when they had debated long enough out in the parking lot about who had the bigger knockers, Janet or Chrissy. God knew what was to become of the "Three's Company" posters in the back storage room given the current ambiguity with The Moon, so when they needed a drink anyway, they snuck into the back storage room, making sure the Stuckersons weren't around to yell at them. Downing water from the utility sink, they cast their vote. Chrissy was the winner.

While there, they took note of the stuffed room, jammed to near capacity with junk and boxes of memories representing Franco Esposito: the manager they had never met.

"Look at all the wood, nails and hammers he had in here," said Alex.

"What was he makin' besides birdhouses with Stanley? Looks like Gepetto's workshop in here."

It was all a mystery. So much "shit" had been stored here, they often joked that it was a miracle they could find their way out.

George had placed the eight-foot ladder back against Franco's old workbench. "Better put this somewhere else," said John, moving it. "Ya never know what Stanley would say if he saw that leaning against his buddy's table."

They found an old smock from last year's stash and rolled it into a weapon, snapping each with it like towels in a locker room, and throwing hairnets around. Lee-Willie burst in again, angrier than before. "Look, I dunno how many fucking times I can say this to you nitwits but we ain't startin' off the year with this kind of bullshit."

"We're cleanin' up for intermission, sir," said Steve. "Movie's almost over, nothing bad's happening out there."

"Yet. I wanna make this clear, this is gonna be one, difficult season, goddam it. You schlubs better do your part to keep it in-check. *This* is the spotlight of your summer now. Make sure you behave professionally at all times. Just 'cause school's out doesn't give ya the excuse to screw-off and prance around in here like little fairies."

"Fear not, sir," said George. "What's 'weird' is that John wants to cut holes in your posters and have a little fun with 'em… in his bedroom… *alone*."

George got a solid punch to the gut, nearly doubling-over.

Lee-Willie pounded out, saying, “Now let’s keep this place afloat. If someone so much as pops an erection in the wrong direction, kick ’em out!”

Steve was dispatched right after intermission and drove his Charger to the corner of Sing and Hewey, seeing the vehicles in the parking lot at Lapping Waves. Through the window he could see the line of customers, talking with Jody behind the counter as she laughed and smiled while overseeing the purchases of beer, cigarettes and junk food for the night. Some asked if the current movies playing were any good.

“Would we play anything else?” Steve responded.

He proceeded with his usual routine: flirting with his girl from his unique vantage point up high, exchanging waves and sweeping, theatrical blow-kisses. When nobody was looking, Jody flashed her bra and then covered up, making Steve quite enticed. He turned back to the job at hand to avoid either of them to get in trouble.

Mr. Smith was now visible, also chatting with folks in the mart, keeping extended eyes on Jody, unaware that he, himself, was being watched. Steve saw what he thought was a check of her hindquarters when she turned to reach high for a carton of cigarettes. This shot a spur of alarm through his body, but he had to dismiss it. He finished, came down, examined his handiwork, making sure he had spelled everything correctly.

THE HILLS HAVE EYES

TEXAS CHAINSAW MASSACRE

RATED R

Yep, looked good. He turned to present his masterpiece to Jody, but instead was met by Mr. Smith outside on the sidewalk, waiting for the youngster to turn and notice him. "That's what passes for movies these days, Mr. Laneske?"

Steve scratched his head, holding back a bristle of fury. "Not my decision what plays, Mr. Smith. But it seems to do the trick, the joint's packed tonight, and it'll be just as busy tomorrow night."

"I see. My 'joint's' also packed."

"With customers coming down to see us, sir."

"They're not supposed to bring in their own food and drink."

"We can't stop everybody, Mr. Smith."

"Nice attitude. I'd like you to work for me with that outlook." Steve directly looked at him, told himself to bite his tongue. Then he was shocked when the man next said, "Stop bothering her."

"What? Who?"

"Jody. I've told you to stop bothering her. Just do your work and get back down the street."

"I'm not 'bothering her,' sir, she is my girlfriend, after all, it's completely innocent."

"Nothing's 'innocent' when she's on my clock."

This guy really is a dick, Steve thought. Again, he suppressed his feelings, thought of Mr. Stuckerson's words. "I'm putting everything away, Mr. Smith," he said, folding up the ladder, gathering the plastic crates. "I'm done here tonight."

"Good. I'm sure your bosses—Mr. and Mrs. Stuckerson, I think?—wouldn't be too happy knowing you spent half your time down here making googly eyes. Probably take you half the time if you put your mind to your job only."

Steve re-emerged from the shed, had the padlock in-hand. "Probably… sir. Right. Have a nice night."

"Jody's a good employee," he said. "I'd like to keep it that way."

"Of course, sir."

"I keep an eye on her."

"I know you do, sir. *Too* long of an eye."

"What? What's that supposed to mean? Come here, tell me what you meant."

"Gotta return to work, sir, you said so yourself."

Steve locked up the shed, brushed his clothes. Dead bugs, cobwebs, sometimes collected on his smock. The tubby manager stared as he got in his car. When the door to Lapping Waves briefly opened for the man to go back inside, Steve shouted— "See ya later, babe!"

"See ya, honey!" Jody hollered back, meeting the immediate, disapproving burn of her boss. Customers turned, laughed. If it was not for them, who knows what Mr. Smith would've said.

Just before he drove off, a carload of jamokes drove by in a Camaro, the driver startling Steve. "Can we get up there and have sex with our girlfriends?"

"Be my guest," said Steve, and drove away.

As Steve came back from the grand marquee, George and John were helping a couple clean up an entire pizza they had accidentally dumped in their Ford Pinto. At this very same time, Alex got his nose fractured. He got caught on the wrong side of bad attitude, alone, confronting a group of young men in two cherry Chevy Bel Airs from the '50s who'd been behaving really badly. Every time a cheerleader in "H.O.T.S." showed her endowments, the jerks would first wolf-whistle, then take a swig of illegal beer. It was a game, and they thought they were hilarious. Alex took it upon himself to deal with the Melvins directly, leaving the rest of the Crusaders to their current duties.

He had approached the assembly, polite at first, asking them to kindly keep down the noise. They did not like being told what to do. Alcohol had a way of bringing out "the beer muscles," as the Crusaders were fond of saying. They told Alex to mind his own business. Alex asked them again to cool it. "I know this is a comedy," he said, "but you're bothering people."

"The hell kind of a smock is that? You supposed to be important or something?" one of the assailants asked.

His friend followed. "I heard of these bozos; they're supposed to be tough. They're high school kids with nothin' to back up their mouths with."

"Nobody's trying to be tough," said Alex. "We just need ya to stop the whistling, please, and keep your voices down."

One took a step closer. Alex could smell the alcohol on his breath. "This is a drive-in theater, man" the goon said. "You gonna tell us what we can and can't do out in the open here?"

"It's not exactly 'out in the open,' sir, everybody around still can hear ya. I'm asking you to be cool, everybody else paid their money to get in, just like you did."

"Yeah, but you know the reputation of this place as well as anyone. Anything goes, man, it's a free country. Go back to the popcorn stand or something."

Unfortunately, the guy reminded Alex of Randy. They were about the same age, nearly the same build. Randy had, many times, confronted Alex in this fashion. He was sick of his older brother's tactics, was not going to take it from this asshole. Without bothering with his radio, he said to the fellow, "Now you're being a wad."

"'A wad'? Really, man?"

They all stepped closer, surrounding Alex. He felt his body begin to quake. "All of you step back."

"*You* take a step back." The main antagonist poked Alex.

"Don't do that," said Alex.

"Or what? You're what, fifteen?"

"I said take a step back."

"We're not 'stepping back,' you're bothering us. We have a right to defend ourselves."

"There's nothing to defend."

"Ain't there more of ya round here?"

"There are, but I'm telling ya to quiet down."

"That stupid uniform give ya special powers?"

Alex grabbed his flashlight to turn it on and got it snatched away by one of them behind him, turning it on, shining it in Alex's face. People were starting to get out of their cars. "Give that back," Alex commanded, then had his radio messed with, clipped on the other side of his belt. They were trying to take that, too. Feeling the cold shiver of power shooting up his spine, he turned and shoved the yahoo, holding tight to his communication device. That got *them* pissed-off. He heard someone saying, "D'you just shove me, pee-wee?"

The one trying for his radio—like Randy was fond of doing—rushed in and attempted a chest-shove. Alex countered, using his considerable agility to stave off the most of it. He got off a "Guys, I need ya—" into the walkie before there were more on him, pinning him to the rear of the Mercury Monarch in front of them. Alex had his feet set, kept his head down, pushed his assailants back as far as he could, one falling to the pavement. Alex launched on him, holding him down, hissing in his face— "Don't you fucking touch me!"

Alex sensed he was vulnerable. Many were around him, the circle was closing in. One of the idiots got something from the trunk. Alex saw it but had his head mostly down. Was it a club? Fishing pole? As the guy came up behind him, he turned anticipating the attack. He caught the blunt end of a closed umbrella on the bridge of his nose, cracking it. There was a pop and blood shot out from both nostrils, stars filling his vision, dropping him like a chopped tree. Then the lights went out.

John, George-and Jim—pounded as many of the knuckleheads as they could, coming to Alex's rescue. They had heard enough over the movie, anyway, and when the clipped call came in: it was over. They landed punches. They landed kicks. Because of the chaos that filled the space like water into a vacuum, the situation quickly became a melee. Other good patrons helped, restraining the assailants and breaking up the fight. John was a wrestler. He took his foe down, locking his neck in an unmovable hold. George picked up one of the offenders over his head, slammed him on the hood of one of the Bel Airs. And Jim… well,

Jim… had two empty film canisters with him. Big, solid, metal things. Clapped them together against the sides of the biggest opponent's head, toppling that chump like a blown tire, ending the free-for-all.

The Stuckersons ran in. Vicki hustled from out of the stand. So did Emilio. Stan-the-Man went for The Moon Tower, blooming it to life.

With shouts to call the police rippling around, Jim picked the unconscious Alex up in his arms, told everyone where he was going, ran him to his Chevy Fleetside—instructing George and John to get license plate numbers, turn off the projector and lock-up his booth, getting blood all over himself—raced Alex to the hospital himself. Kathy was hysterical finding out, seeing the blue pickup blasting out the exit, "H.O.T.S." playing to its bawdy end, last reel flapping in the gate, giant screen going blinding-white in the lot.

The Stuckersons informed the crowd over the P.A. that there had been a medical emergency and that "Up In Smoke" would not be played for an encore, leaving the grounds themselves, tearing out in their Lincoln following Jim. "Kathy, mind the shop!" Lee-Willie bellowed. "Have everybody lock the place up, make sure everyone's out!"

When Stanley came to his senses, he knew to quickly dole out what was referred to as "redemption tickets" in compensation, guaranteeing any audience member who wanted one could come back any night of the week and get in for free. The gang had *that* to deal with—and lock up the money bags in the back-storage room—before they, themselves, went to the hospital. The end of the night could not come fast enough.

Sergeant Leo had arrested the chooches—the first arrest of the season. Jim had that news. The emergency room doctor confirmed Alex's nose was fractured, not broken. "Hairline," he told The Mooners in the waiting room, an hour after they'd been there. "Six weeks to heal, looks worse than it is." Then, when they were told they could visit him in his room, two and a time, they all went at once, clogging the halls, freaking out the nurses. There was no more space in the double with everyone represented, even Stanley. "Hey Mr. Stuckerson," Emilio said, trying to ease the tension, "it's as crowded in here as it is in your back-storage room."

"Shut-up, Varentez," the manager said, eating his *Oh Henry* bars.

Alex's puss was bandaged, eyes already blackening. Nobody had alerted his mother. Yet.

A male nurse came in. George, Steve and John snickered at that job title behind his back, straightened up when the well-read fellow, no stranger to westside venue himself, said, "What kind of a loony bin are you guys running over there? The Winking Moon was wacky when I was going there. Now? Why don't they just build a hospital *inside* it?"

Sergeant Leo popped in, checked on everyone, shook his head in dismay as he informed the cluster that the chuckleheads responsible were currently being held overnight. It was up to Alex if he wanted to press charges.

"Naw," said the teenager, sounding like a nasally sea lion. "Let's just move on, another night at The Moon, right? What's throwin' the book at 'em gonna do, fix the joint?"

Kathy began crying… again. She had lost it twice already since being here. She hugged Alex, rested her head on his chest. The first "F-F-F" (First-Full-Time-Friday) had drawn to a close. Jim said it best: "Welcome back, people. Ready for the First Full-Time Saturday?"

When Alex finally returned home, Angela Carver blew into the house like a chariot on fire, flying to her son's side past his coworkers (which she did not acknowledge), lying supine on the sofa in the living room. She dropped her purse, keys, collapsed, and burst into tears, hugging him frantically, emotion so intense, one could almost feel the floorboards shaking with her sobs. She had arrived, finally, after the alarm-call on her night shift. Randy had let everyone in. It was the middle of the night, but with all the lights on and everyone present, the energy was that of four o'clock in the afternoon.

Mrs. Carver could not contain herself. Her son with his feet up, head back on a pillow, marbly eyes glazed under a bandaged nose, dried blood having seeped to the sides, flecks of it on his cheeks, ice pack pressed to his forehead. Alex watched his protective mother simultaneously cry while trying to contain a volcanic temper. Lee-Willie, holding his wife by his side, was the first to speak, setting the woman off— "Mrs. Carver… um… your son… it's not as bad as it looks."

Angela shot up and turned to him— "'Not as bad as it looks'?

You're Mr. Stuckerson, right? Manager, correct?"

He cleared his throat. "*Co*-manager."

"Who's this next to you? I'm guessing you're his wife, Mrs. Stuckerson?"

"Co-manager," she squeaked, barely audible, avoiding eye contact.

She let loose. "I know all about you people and what goes on there at the Winking Moon. It's my business, too, as Alex's mother! He's told me. My son, Randy, has *certainly* told me—" Randy was hanging back, taking the whole thing in stride, one elbow on the mantle over the faux fireplace. It was electric. "It's come to this already? Again? What kind of an insane breeding ground of madness are you people running over there? I get a call from my oldest at work, saying my youngest—who was injured last year at about this time—is at the hospital on his first night back, full-time. On his 'fun, little summer gig.' Haven't you bozos learned anything from last year?"

Alex tried to interrupt. "Mom…" he croaked.

"Alex, quiet! I demand answers from all of you. You're here, in my house, at two o'clock in the fucking morning. Now I appreciate you looking over Alex, but since you're here, I think I deserve those answers, directly. What the hell happened, Mr. and Mrs. Stuckerson—co-managers of The Winking Moon?"

Steve Laneske was closest. "Mrs. Carver, it was an accident."

"Steve—" she said, turning to the boy. "This is no accident. This is the way you 'professionals' go about running your business. This isn't the Wild West, none of you are Wyatt Earp. Someone swung a weapon at my boy, and I'm supposed to be okay with that? This is a freakin' summer job, for the love of God!"

"But the most *noble* kind of a summer job," said Lee-Willie, now drawing the looks from all the employees, not just Mrs. Carver. He hung his head in silence.

Everyone felt like shit. That was a given. They were all doing their best not to stare the woman in the eyes. They knew she was right.

"They were arrested, Mrs. Carver," said George. "We got 'em all."

She turned to George, incredulous. Did not know what to say, was shaking her head back-and forth-in disbelief. Then she locked in on the full-grown man in the corner, also keeping distance, stared deep into his dark, brown eyes. "You must be Jim Barenta… projectionist… the hero. I've heard about you."

Jim drew a breath. "Certainly no 'hero,' ma'am."

"You carried Alex to your truck? Drove him to the hospital?"

"Yes, ma'am."

"What are you doing, allowing people to swing objects at my son's head, defending whatever he was defending, keeping the peace, I guess."

"Mom," Alex tried again, "it wasn't Jim's fault, it was no one's fault. They were just a buncha morons, acting up. No one's to be blamed, that's part of the job."

"That shouldn't be part of anyone's job, dammit! That's what I hate about this fucking job! You all think it's so glamorous but it's not! It's fucking ridiculous!" She turned back to Jim. Everyone felt the heat of the moment. "Where were you? You're the protector I've heard so much about."

"Ma'am," said Jim, "we weren't with your son at the time it happened. We got there right afterwards. As George said: we got the ones who did it."

Angela Carver closed her eyes, opened them. "John… George… Steve… Vicki… I've known you since you were in elementary school. I know you're all defending your drive-in and you all love it, but somebody help me understand something: how does this continue to happen time and time again?"

Before the kids could answer, Jim chimed in for the group. "Mrs. Carver, there's no

gettin' around it: this sucks Royal Canadian. This happens at The Winking Moon. Patrons know it, employees know it. Things get outta hand. Your boy responded to a situation he knew could get dicey, and it did. We all do. We're sorry this happened, but everyone was spread thin. It's a matter of chance."

Her eyes were unflinching, surveying every face in the room. "My boy's face looks like it did last year. I'm absolutely going nuts with all of this craziness. He insisted on working with you all again and he gets this.

Is this some kind of macho rite-of-passage, to see who's toughest? Can you answer that, Mr. Stuckerson? Looks like you're in that same camp with that lip."

Lee-Willie dabbed his face, could barely make eye contact. "Mrs. Carver, technically Jim is right. Everybody knew the risks they were taking signing up again. Nobody can sue, they all signed a waiver." Angela nearly blew her top again, shooting up to face the man.

Alex sat up as best he could to prevent bloodshed— "Mom! It's okay! Would you all just calm the shit down? I'm okay, it's just a fracture, I'm gonna be fine in six weeks and I'm goin' into work tomorrow night."

"What? No, you're not! I want you quitting right now!"

"Mom, no! I'm not quitting The Winking Moon, that's just ridiculous!"

"Alex, tell everyone you're done with all this," she said.

"No!"

"I want you to take that job with Randy."

"I'm not takin' that job with Randy."

This alarmed everybody. "'Job'? What job?" Steve asked. "Al, what're ya talkin' about?"

"Nothing!" Alex snapped. "Forget it. Mom, no deal."

Angela wheeled back to the managers.

"Mr. and Mrs. Stuckerson," Angela said, "you're going to have a full-out war on your hands if you don't change things real quick. I'm not the expert but the whole town's talking about this."

"We know, Mrs. Carver," said Gail-Lill.

Vicki's turn. "Mrs. Carver, it's not gonna get that bad. Things peak, then level-out. It's the natural course of things."

"Really, Vicki, you know this? You're a sweet girl, I love you like a daughter, but don't be naïve—this is only going to get worse. You'd all better understand this." To Alex, "Are you going to press charges against the maniacs who did this to you?"

"No," said Alex.

"Why not?"

"Because… it's all part of the job." Angela Carver simply did not know what to say. She was shell-shocked. Kathy and Emilio had been together in the background, remaining silent. The pressure had just become too much.

Suddenly, Kathy let loose. "Mrs. Carver I know you don't know me and this is the first time meeting you but my name is Kathy Berenger and I work in the box office at The Winking Moon and I just want you to know your son is very, very brave and he would've never done something like this if he thought it was going to turn out this way but it didn't matter to him because he's so great—I even heard him put the call out on the radio."

Angela was speechless. Then Kathy added, "They're all brave. Every one of them."

"And I'm Emilio Varentez, ma'am," said the lean culinary artist, smiling, stepping right in front of Kathy, hand out to shake. Angela did not shake. "Nice to finally meet you. I'm the cook at the Winking Moon and I've seen a lot of things in my days, but I've never seen the courage and dedication Alex and these boys displayed tonight. We all feel so much better having them there with us and I know he would never, ever, want to disappoint you, ma'am. Not his mother. And Alex and the Crusaders never disappoint *us*, they are numero uno."

Angela continued to stare, batting her eyes. She then dropped to the sofa where Alex was, buried her face in her hands, put one, loving hand on her son's foot and began to decompress. Then she spoke, softly, more to herself than anyone. "All right, Dear Lord, Sweet Jesus, you have sent your Angels to watch over my son. And they're right here in my living room. Got all of them here. Kathy: the one who Alex always talks about… Emilio, the one who cooks all the food… and the rest of them. I've met them all…" Then she looked up. "Where's the UFO man?"

"It's a little past his bedtime, Mrs. Carver," said Jim.

Angela's face returned into her palm— "Sweet Jesus, please look down on all of us."

Gail-Lill practically shoved Lee-Willie into movement— "Now it's really time to go."

"Okay," he said, heading toward the door. Everyone went to file out, following their lead. Mrs. Carver abruptly shot a hand up, stopping the crowd cold— "Wait!"

"Mrs. Carver?" said Vicki. *What was going on?*

She fed them all lasagna. And rolls. And salad. All sitting at the dining room table. Even Randy joined in. By the time they were finished the sun was nearly up.

"THE HILLS HAVE EYES"

&

"TEXAS CHAINSAW MASSACRE"

CHAPTER 21:

SATURDAY NIGHT ENERGY

The Stuckersons had invested last season in something called an Automatic Voice-Recording Machine and it was the latest in technology. When someone called the theater for showtimes and ticket prices, the outgoing message was there to greet them. And because of the fiasco the night before, this week's recording had never been completed. Everyone had been so shot leaving the Carvers in the wee hours of the morning that it had slipped the Stuckerson's minds completely. Gail-Lill reminded Lee-Willie as they drove home and barely an hour after Steve Laneske's head hit the pillow his boss was phoning, asking a favor.

"Can you do it, Steve?" Mr. Stuckerson asked. "Can you record the message? We can't even form a sentence. You have a good voice; you can do it."

Steve said, "How will I get in your office? I don't have keys."

"Stop by the apartment. We'll leave it under the rock by the door."

Yeah, Steve knew where their complex was. He did not like going to his boss's home, though. It was bad enough spending all that time with the Stuckersons at work. But he had agreed to it anyway.

A few hours later he picked Jody up, begrudgingly, and told her about the incident with Alex the night before.

"Omigod!" she said. "Is he gonna be okay?"

"Yes, he's gonna be okay. Just do this for him. Accompany me and make his day." He had a big grin on his face. A seductive grin. Jody knew what it meant, smiled herself, liked it.

"Okay, I'll 'do it' for Alex, but you'd better be careful. I'm an impressionable girl."

They'd stopped by the apartment complex, marveled at what appeared to them to be two completely charred barbecue grills in front of the Stuckerson's unit, wondered what that was about, and got the key from under the rock. Steve still felt uncomfortable, so he knocked on the door and got Mr. Stuckerson to come to the door. The man looked like something out of one of their horror films, and Steve asked what he was supposed to do with the key afterward.

"Just hold onto it," Lee-Willie replied, "Like you do everything else."

"What's that supposed to mean?" Steve demanded.

Lee-Willie ignored the question, said hello to Jody, and shut the door.

When they got to the Moon, Steve and Jody could not stop commenting on the state of this new, unfamiliar space.

"I never come in here, but damn, is it a mess," Steve said. "Just like the back-storage room. Holy shit, they can't keep a place neat. No wonder their such mental wrecks."

Jody asked what the winding staircase was in the back of the room, leading to a trap door in the ceiling.

"That's the staircase going up into the screen, the attic's in there," Steve answered. "Here's the desk they sit at to add up the tallies every night. He probably does the missus right here on the top of it to relieve stress."

Jody laughed, told him not to be "fucking gross," but said it would be fun to try it themselves.

Steve propped Jody up on his lap and began recording the outgoing message on the cool, fancy new piece of technology. "So mint," he put it first before pressing the button. "'Welcome to The Winking Moon Drive-In, owned and operated by Bluestone Incorporated, located at 394 Sing Road, just three miles east of Hewey Avenue. Today is Saturday, June 16th. We offer under-the-stars entertainment every night except Mondays. Ticket prices are two-fifty for adults, fifty cents for kids under twelve. Honestly, no one under twelve should be here. This week's features are 'The Hills Have Eyes' and 'Texas Chainsaw Massacre,' both rated R. *Real* R. Box office opens one hour prior to sunset, all shows begin at sundown. No need to lay on the horn before it gets dark, that's really annoying. Tasty snacks and refreshing drinks await you at our clean-and-friendly concession stand. Be checked-out by our legendary curmudgeon, Stanley Mason. Concessions stay open twenty minutes after the last show, so don't tell us ya didn't have time to stuff your pie-holes. We play an encore presentation of the first film on Friday, Saturdays and Sundays, if you're smart enough to know what that means.

We offer crystal-clear clarity from our state-of-the-art speakers. Don't leave 'em in your window as you're driving away—your window ain't gonna win. So come in, have fun, and we'll see ya under the smilin' Man-In-The-Moon, all night long.'""

Jody loved it. She laughed, cooed, kissed. Steve loved it just as much, if not more. As they were getting hot-and-heavy, enjoying the freedom of finally being alone in private with no one to bust their balls, Jody asked again about Alex. "Did you guys kick the shit out of the assholes who did it?"

"We did. Jim used film canisters on one guy."

"Really? Awesome. I woulda loved to have been there. I woulda kicked some ass. You taught me well."

"'Taught you well' what?"

"To beat people up for the cause."

"What 'cause,'" he asked.

The 'just 'cause' cause," she answered.

"I see."

They both told each other they loved one another and by the time they were finished, they had to remember what mess they had contributed to the papers and books all over the room. When the dropped the keys back off with Mr. Stuckerson, he asked if there were any problems.

"No sir," said Steve. "I could record like that again-and-again-and-again…"

Lee-Willie eyeballed him. *What the hell?* "Have you heard from Alex?"

"Nope, we only saw him just a few short hours ago."

"Don't be wise. See you tonight."

"See you tonight."

"Is someone in your car?"

"No, sir," Steve answered. "Just early morning shadows."

It was a Saturday night with two new horror films (always crowd-pleasers), and practically every living soul who had been asked to leave the night before with redemption tickets came back to mix in with the packed crowd. They were honking horns like crazy people, taunting those without the free entries, and some didn't even bother to wait for Kathy to validate them, zipping right by in their automobiles, waving their tickets like prize money, racing around the screen to hog the best spots in the house. Kathy, already, was getting a headache. The lot was filling with dozens of these jamokes and jebeebs, whooping it up, acting like they had won the lottery, having the time of their lives joyriding while they still had the chance.

But Steve, John and George were there. They had arrived early, in

Steve's Charger, parked against the building in the usual spot. Alex was not with them. He had been ordered to stay home and nurse his face. The three patrolmen sprinted after the jackasses, chasing them down, halting them, telling them what they were doing was wrong and that they still had to be accounted for at the box office.

A Turk's Auto Service & Towing pickup truck—with a flatbed for towing—pulled in, did the same things the scofflaws initially did upon entering: floor it past the good people waiting in line. Just when Kathy thought she was going to see the monstrosity bulldoze its way in, it laid on the brakes, coming to a screeching halt right beside her in the box office. It was Randy Carver, dropping his brother off. Alex had been stubborn, decided that the best place for him *was* at work, not home, feeling sorry for himself. "Mom doesn't know but I'm here," he said to Kathy—Steve, George and John spotting him, running in, pulling him out, hugging him.

Randy just watched, shaking his head. Kathy gave him a big peck on the cheek, checking his bandaged nose, telling him it looked bad. "You look like you're in a lot of pain," she said. The horn-blasting at this point was awful. Mr. Stuckerson sprang on the radio, asked what was going on.

"Alex is here, Mr. Stuckerson!" Steve said animatedly. "He decided to come to work!"

"What?"

Mrs. Stuckerson heard to, jumped on her radio. "He's here? We told him to stay home. He's hurt, he didn't have to do that!"

"And look how he looks!" Lee-Willie added on the radio, of the youngster's aesthetics. "What kind of an impression is he gonna put out there with that way his face looks?"

Off the radio, George said, "Look who's talking," eliciting laughs.

Some customers, upon hearing that Alex had gotten beat-up in a fight the night before, thought it was cool, called out to him. "That's tough, man!" said one dude. "In a good way."

"It's a badge of honor, dude," another said. "Wear it with pride."

Some wanted pictures with him, pulling out their flash-cube cameras and Kodamatic instants, posing with Alex and pointing to his facial injury.

"That's what I like from *my* drive-in," said one tough guy. "An ass-kicker who can take it."

"Alex…" Kathy sighed. "We better get these people in."

Jim came racing up the entrance in his Chevy, setting to bomb into the exit. Seeing his young friend, he paused at the commotion. "Alex! The fuck you doin' here? You're supposed to be home, resting."

"Not gonna do it, Jim," said Alex. "Can't miss a night, you know me. You're late."

"Dealing with an old buddy of mine."

"Manny Rodrogo?" Steve queried. They all knew.

Jim did not answer the question, he just drove in.

The group dispersed and Randy remained in his truck to speak with Kathy. "That Alex has shit for brains. Could not keep him away, Kathy. Got a better job waitin' but he hasn't taken me up on it yet."

"Your towing job, Randy?" she said, continuing to work the line of cars. "I don't know why he would, he was talking about that last year, sounds even scarier than this job. I mean, that's the streets."

"Kathy, comes a time for little boys to grow up and become men. He sure as shit won't grow up here. By the way, how are you? Haven't seen you in forever, do you remember me when you were a freshman?"

"Oh, I remember you, Randy. We all do. How are you?"

"Good. The usual, hangin' in there, making lots of money, makin' it work."

"That's good. Please look out for Alex."

Before Randy said goodbye to Kathy, telling her he'd someday be back to "save all their butts," an angry Jeep, blocked by him, tooted the horn at the bruiser.

"Beep your horn at me again, mister," Randy warned, "and I'll hook your hunk-o-junk up on my flatbed and haul ya off into freakin' Lake Ontario."

The Crusaders brought Alex to his coworkers at the concession stand, Emilio and Vicki elated to see him, Gail-Lill shocked, Stanley and Lee-Willie staring at him like he was a complete fool. In fact, Stanley called Alex an idiot.

"First, you're stupid for getting sucker-punched anyways, then ya show up for work when ya don't hafta. What a boob."

Alex was smiling. "Sorry to disappoint ya, Stanley," he said, lightly tapping his bandages, "but around here it's one for all and all for one."

"Spare me the moronic quotes, Carver," he said.

Lee-Willie was still staring at Alex, hands on hips, subconsciously tapping his own injury. "Alex," he said, "I told you to stay home. What are you doing here?"

"Can't sit around, sir, my brothers need me."

Lee-Willie scoffed and turned around, disappearing into the back-storage room for food supplies. Things were getting nutzoid in here, too.

Patrons were streaming in early to get their refreshments. They noisily played the video and pinball games, laughed like jackasses and ran untamed about the room when they scored high points. Stanley excused himself to yell at them, then returned to the register to say the place "already stunk of the devil's weed."

"Like your armpits, Stanley," mocked George.

Gail-Lill was complaining that all day long their answering service was playing back crazy calls from the residents at Edgewater. "They're griping about the light pollution from the screen. They say it keeps them up at night. They're demanding something be done."

George said, "Ya mean, something on 'em 'keeps-up'?"

"I don't know how these old bitties are getting our number," she said. "Do they all have access to the Yellow Pages?"

"Or don't they have curtains?" Vicki added.

Steve piped in, "Speaking of your answering service, like my recorded message, Mr. and Mrs. Stuckerson?"

"It's over-the-top, Laneske," said Lee-Willie. "We'll let it go for now, we're too busy."

"Think I got a shot at doin' professional voice-overs?" Steve asked. "Like in those movie trailers?"

"You have a better shot at cleaning the bathrooms tonight if you don't get your ass outta here," said Lee-Willie, barking again at all of them, sending them off to work, bitching at Alex again for even showing up.

"Can't keep a good man down, Mr. Stuckerson," Alex said as he jogged away with George, John and George.

An hour into the first show, Alex and Kathy were called into the Stuckerson's office. They had rarely been in there, which made them nervous, both being called in at the same time. Lee-Willie and Gail-Lill looked gravely serious, had them stand as they also stood—but behind their desk—a mess of papers dividing them. This seemed way too official.

"The reason we called you to in here," began Mr. Stuckerson, taking the lead, "is because we need you to do a mission for us."

"'A mission?'" Alex said.

"Remember how earlier tonight Mrs. Stuckerson told you about the calls we keep gettin' from Edgewater?"

"Yes."

"They've multiplied, ten-fold, just in the last hour. We need to do something. We need the two of you to go over there—regardless of how ridiculous this sounds—and just address the few residents who are expecting to see you. We've been on the phone with the Director of Operations, Roberto Quizzy—he's with 'em. He called on their behalf, says his clientele feels one-hundred-percent slighted that we've never bothered to personally go over and address any of the residents with the problems they have with us. They said a little face-to-face respect is in order."

"So why don't you do it?" Alex said, then, "Sir…"

Mrs. Stuckerson jumped in. "We've never met Mr. Quizzy, just had a couple phone calls with him. He seems reasonable enough, like he's on our side. He says us—meaning Mr. Stuckerson and I: management—might not work as well speaking to his people. He said maybe 'ambassadors'—younger people—might be better."

"Because old fogies respond better to youth?" said Alex.

"Yes, quite frankly," said Mr. Stuckerson. "And rule-number-one of ambassadorship: don't call them 'old fogies.'"

Alex and Kathy stood for a moment, stunned. Then Alex said, "You've gotta be kidding. You're sending us into the line of fire?"

"Mr. Quizzy said you're just going to be meeting with a few people," Mrs. Stuckerson explained. "He said for you to just come into the commissary—they're expecting you. There, you'll chat for a few minutes, take their grumbling, explain that we're doing everything possible to address their issues. And their complaints are valid. The most recent one is the light pollution from our screen, says it keeps them up at night—the ones facing the screen."

"Don't they have curtains?" Kathy said.

Mrs. Stuckerson continued. "We don't want them thinking we're dismissing everything, that their words are falling on deaf ears. Lee and I thought you'd be the perfect candidates, you're both natural-born leaders."

Again, Alex and Kathy were taken aback. Alex pointed to his nose. "Look at my face! It's got bandages on it."

"Exactly," said Mr. Stuckerson. "Let's use it to our advantage. Shows how dedicated we are. Since you decided to report to work when we told ya to stay home, this is a good way to make up for it. It'll keep ya safe and outta the lot for a few, so it's a win-win situation."

"You'd be doin' us good," said Mrs. Stuckerson. "And we know that means a lot to you."

Yet another long cessation. "I wouldn't know what to say to 'em," said Alex. "I don't think either one of us would."

Lee-Willie approached, unfurling a sheet of note paper, writing on it. "Basically, you're there to listen. We've written a few things down, Gail worked on it." Kathy took the paper. "It's not poetry, thank God, it's bullet-points to cover should they come up: we're workin' with the police, not allowing anybody to linger—we have you Crusaders. I mean '*patrol-men*.' Stress 'patrol-*men*.'"

"You're just going to be popping in and popping out," said Gail-Lill. "This is a public relations maneuver, we're appeasing them. It's a new approach, we just want to see if this'll help. We have to start somewhere."

Alex looked at the messy floor. "I've never been comfortable in front of crowds."

"Kathy's in front of 'em every night, have her do the talking, I don't give a hoot," said Mr. Stuckerson. "Just sit there, listen, say a few words maybe, get out. Report back when you've returned. Vicki's taking over for Kathy while you're gone. Now go."

"This is a lot to ask, Mr. Stuckerson," said Alex. "This is bold."

"You wanna save the drive-in, don't you?"

"Is it closing?" Kathy asked.

"We don't know," said Mrs. Stuckerson. "But this may be a way to help deter that."

The knock-out turned to her co-worker. "Let's just do it, Alex, we'll take my car."

A way to be alone in Kathy's Malibu with her again? Even if it was for just a short time? "I'll do it," said Alex. "But do we get a raise for this?"

"Move," Mr. Stuckerson ordered.

On their way out, Alex paused, turned. "There's gonna be just a few people? That's all there's gonna be with this 'Mr. Dizzy-guy'?"

"'Mr. *Quizzy*,'" emphasized Mrs. Stuckerson. "He's the Director of Operations, we want to establish a good rapport with him. And yes, there's only going to be a few of you."

CHAPTER 22:

A VISIT WITH EDGEWATER

The commissary was packed. Standing room only. It looked like every senior citizen in the building was jammed into the large room used for food service and entertainment. The old goats were united in their passion, shouting and snarling over the God-awful Muzak that pumped into the room from corner speakers. If they did not know better, Alex and Kathy would have sworn the residents looked like they wanted to kill somebody, shaking their fists, rattling their walkers and waving their canes. One octogenarian was thumping his oxygen tank against a table so hard he was told to stop before it blew up.

Kathy was cowering behind Alex on the raised platform—used for announcements, guest speakers and a frequenting kazoo band—Alex beside Roberto Quizzy, the big-wig front-and-center, trying to tamp down the audience's wrath, flapping his hands up-and-down in a shushing movements. *Let's have a little quiet! Let's have a little quiet.*

Quizzy was a tall, thin man, who was clearly overwhelmed as he checked the orderlies at the corners. They were standing by in case things got out-of-hand. The residents shouted and complained of all sorts of shenanigans: hellions running amok on the property, wits being scared out of the residents at night, pre-teeners peering in windows on the ground floor. Sweat dimpled on Quizzy's upper lip. He finally had to instruct staff to pull a foldout picnic table from an antechamber, essentially creating a barricade in front of his guests for extra protection.

A cookie sailed across the room, hitting him in head.

"People, please!" Quizzy shouted. "Let's get this underway! How are we going to get anything accomplished if you're just going to scream all night? Please, let our guests talk! Their bosses were kind enough to let them come here tonight. They want you to know they're aware of our problems and are doing their best to address matters!"

"Bullshit!" someone hollered, voice old, cranky. "Blow it out your ass, Winkin' Moon, you're just giving us lip-service!"

"Our guests' names are Alex Carver and Kathy Berenger. Why don't we show them some respect and give them our full attention?"

"We should give 'em barium enemas!" another male crowed.

Kathy was terrified. "Hold my hand, Alex," she squirmed.

The belligerence was getting under Alex's skin. They had been kind enough to follow their boss's wishes, come here to show the coots their own respect, but they could not get any in return. This whole operation was in danger of going south—even as he devised an escape-plan, surveying the room for quick ways to dodge out. He finally got up the will and the power to fill his lungs with air to bellow-out at the top of his lungs— "SHUT-UUUUP!!!"

That worked. That stopped the crowd. All voices hushed-up, all wrinkled grimaces went still. Stunned faces. Stunned staff. "Thank-you," Alex followed. "Mr. Quizzy: thank-*you* for inviting us here. Good evening, ladies and gentlemen, nice to be here, thanks for giving us your time. As mentioned, my name is 'Alex Carver' and this here is 'Kathy Berenger.'"

"Who cares?" fired off a voice. "We just wanna know if you're going away!"

Alex and Kathy looked at each other. In no way, shape or form were they to get into that: the possibility of "going away." They were not to discuss Bluestone or leading on that they were aware of Edgewater's involvement with them.

"No, we are not 'going away,'" said Alex. "We're here to let ya know we're sensitive of the problems you're having with us."

"Problems *we're* having with you?" stoked someone else. "How 'bout the problems *you're* having with you! Lookit your face! All ya gotta do is look in the mirror to know your drive-in ain't safe! It's not safe for any of us! The nightly hijinks and folderol prove that!"

"Now-now, let's be nice. Let the young people speak."

"What happened to you, boy?" someone shouted at Alex. "Didn't ya put enough ice in somebody's Coca-Cola?"

This drew a vicious round of derisive laughter.

"I'm sorry about this," Quizzy whispered to his guests. "Let's just get through this."

Alex moved on. "We are Winking Moon employees, that is correct. I'm a patrolman and Kathy here is our box office girl."

"'Woman,'" Kathy corrected.

"As you know, this meeting was arranged between our managers and Mr. Quizzy: your Director of Operations. This all came together in a matter of minutes so you're gonna have to forgive us if this doesn't go perfect."

"It ain't 'perfect' alright! Far from it! You've been the bane of our existence for years now!"

"It's true, we know things have gotten out-of-hand. I promise we don't like it either. We're here to let you know we're trying our best to fix these issues and develop *positive* solutions, so we won't be buggin' ya anymore."

"You're buggin' us by being here and patronizing us! Get outta here!"

Kathy's turn. "We're here to listen to your grievances, *one* at a time, take them back to our bosses, let them know—the answering-service is such a bad way of communicating—and solve our differences. Your problems truly are our problems. We're being honorable, can we ask for a little of that back?"

"We did! We told ya to blow it out your asses!" More nasty laughter. A frail man in the front raised his hand, got called on by Quizzy.

"We don't care about your fancy introductions, fancy uniforms and polite facade," the man said. "Words are just words. We know you're here to just shut us up so let me get straight to the point. We've paid our lives' dues and now we want to live out the rest of our years in peace. Once and for all, get serious about the crap and get your heads screwed on right. It's bad enough we have to listen to the filth coming from your screen each night, it's another to have your pesky, little troublemakers coming right into our backyard, pulling pranks with their monkeyshines and skylarking. Enough is enough! We want an end to it!"

"Yes, and we think you should play movies like 'The Ten Commandments,'" spouted a feeble old lady, not far away. "Maybe it could teach you heathens some manners."

Quizzy raised his hands again. "Now-now, I'm sure if the Winking Moon wants, it could deliver on something like that."

"Unlike you, Quizzy," a bald geezer said. "You couldn't deliver a rectal thermometer."

Quizzy swallowed his pride and deflected his gaze. His clientele—his obstinate, uncooperative, rude and short-wicked clientele—were gaining traction. The faces out there were locked in scowls, grinding bridges, popping dentures. Sagging bosoms hung from ghastly bathrobes. Wispy wild-hairs and bald noggins were not showing any interest in making the meeting productive. Quizzy apologized again.

Before losing his temper, Alex brushed the comment off, said to Quizzy, "We deal with conflict every night," then turned and raised his voice above the crowd, wanting to be clear. "Look, folks, we really do care! I mean, this face tells it all—" he was pointing to his bandages. "This is the face of seriousness. Stop with the freakin' insults and listen to what we're tellin' ya. We're trying to work with ya, solve your problems. Stop your bitchin' and moanin', realize that we're trying to help, listen to what we have to say and put that in your dentures and smoke it!"

Kathy noticed one old fella in the very back, nudged Alex—*Hey, look*—sticking out like a sore thumb. The senior was small, unassuming, Italian-looking, had an air of calmness about him. Even from here they could see his kind, non-judgmental eyes. He was a stand-out. Alone and smiling. He nodded at his visitors. *Everything's fine… they don't get it.* he seemed to convey, then it was back to business, dealing with the rebellion.

"How do we know that's not make-up on your face, kid?" an old muck-a-luck hollered. "You could be made-up that way to distract us, get sympathy from us."

"It's not," Alex said.

"If ya want real bruises, we'll give 'em to ya."

Quizzy spread his arms again, tried to look as important as possible. "Now quit that, we won't have you talking that way—any of you. We'll end this dialogue here and now. We have no right accusing them of lying."

One man shook a bladder-control diaper at him. "Put a sock in it, Quizzy, you lie, too! We said we wanted fruit in our oatmeal, and you can't even arrange for that!"

"I'm the Director of Operations, not of Food Services."

Kathy tried herself to speak up over them. "People, we're here to take suggestions. If anyone has any ideas for us to take back to our bosses about the problem—please—let's hear them."

"We know your company, Bluestone Incorporated," cried out another angry resident. "We've been having discussions with them already. What do we need you for?"

That caused pause for Alex and Kathy, sent chills down their spines. *So, it was true, the newspaper article.* They looked at Quizzy. "There have been phone calls," he mentioned, as an aside. "That's all I know. Don't know what any of it means."

Suddenly the teenagers wanted out of there. As Quizzy moved them along, more orderlies were coming in to aid. Alex and Kathy were upset. The Stuckerson's faith a reaching-out gesture had been flushed down the proverbial toilet.

"Good to be ambassadors of goodwill, huh?" he said to her. "These people are worse than our goons."

Kathy was not listening. She was too busy ducking a handful of rubber medical gloves and a dill pickle that sailed over her head.

At the Moon, chuckleheads had switched signs on the restroom doors—while there were people inside, using them! **LADIES** got posted to the men's-room door, **MENS** went to the ladies. Steve, John and

George had to deal with that chaos. The shrieks, screams and hollering that ensued from having men accidentally walk into the latrine while ladies were on the can—and vice versa—was substantial. Some people thought it was funny and just rolled with it. Others were not quite as amiable. One fellow blasted out of the ladies' room (which he, of course, thought was the men's room), bellowed, "This establishment's so screwed up they can't even get the shitters right!"

Lee-Willie cornered the Crusaders in front of Jim's Forbidden Zone—the fenced-in area surrounding the projection window, in front of the booth. They assumed they were going to get reamed-out for the bathroom-stunt, but…

"No, I don't give a rat's ass about that," Lee-Willie said, brushing off their concerns. "I just got another goddam call from the retirement home, saying there were punks and hooligans over there, runnin' around the backyard, getting close to the building, running around like maniacs. Let's go take a look."

"But Mr. Stuckerson," said John. "Remember last time? Why don't you let us handle it?"

"Think I'm losin' it or something, Tambone? Why don't you kids shut the hell up and just accompany me over there? These are just hiccups, boys, it's time to get serious."

"Kathy and Alex are over there," said Steve. "Why don't we just radio 'em, ask if seeing anything? Might be effective: seeing stuff from the inside-perspective."

"Lemme check if they have 'em on." Lee-Willie pulled out his walkie, radioed for the two. No answer. (Alex and Kathy had their radios with them, just left them in Kathy's Malibu.) "Nope, they're not answering. Let's take a look."

The four trudged through the lot, hearing the screaming and hysterics from the horror film echoing over the entire lot, messing with the ability to hone-in on real sounds. Patrons were shouting, also screaming. Made for highly off-putting concentration. They jumped up on the fence, like last time, peered over into the woods—through the woods—saw the backside of the Edgewater facility, could not really see any figures running around the lawn.

"I don't see anything," said George. "And we can see a lot with that backlighting. Look—there's Kathy and Alex inside. Holy shit, look how many people are in there."

Lee-Willie felt guilty. *Just a few folks,* he had told them. Sure enough, there was a clear angle on the commissary in there, past the back patio, ground floor. The place was packed.

"Looks like they have their hands full," said George. "Want us to go over there, Mr. Stuckerson?"

"Hell no," he answered. "You stay here, I can't have you leaving the grounds, too."

"Wait a minute—!" John pointed. "Look. There's graffiti on the wall. Over there—to the left—above the fountains. Hooligans and punks *have* been here."

Sure enough, written in big spray-painted letters, in black: the mark of obnoxious and immature minds…

LAWRENCE WELK BEATS HIS MEAT

"Gotta give 'em credit, they got balls," George said.

Lee-Willie called out— "Ya out there, you little bastards? Show yourselves."

Patrons shushed them. They jumped down, Lee-Willie planning. When he whispered, they heard a noise on the other side, where they had just been looking. Lee-Willie held up a hand. *Shh.* "Someone's there now, be still."

All three peered through the slats, saw a silhouette. Small, adolescent-size, backlit by the porch lights they had just referred to, activity in the commissary still going on. The figure stopped short of the fence, feet away, his skinny frame apparent against the trees. He lit a cigarette — a cigarette? — and began smoking it, curls of gray smoke rising above the barricade. Lee-Willie became mad as hell. "They're smoking now?" Was all he could do to keep it at a whisper. "Little fucks'll start a forest fire." The red glow came-and-went, came-and-went.

"Easy, Mr. Stuckerson…" Steve hushed. "Easy…"

"I can't take this—" With surprising nimbleness, fueled by

adrenaline, the twerp jumped up, bent on destruction— "Got you now, you little toad!" John tried grabbing him. Did not work.

Instead, it was an adult male who was smoking the cigarette. He let out a terrified scream as the body came flying down on him— "Aggghhh!!" Lee-Willie landed on top of the poor chump, smashing him flat, crushing the smoke right against his face, petaling the paper, tobacco, out in different directions.

John, George and Steve went up and over, yanking their boss off his quarry, hitting the flashlights, seeing it was an old man—a resident! —one of the select *not* in the meeting. Lee-Willie also stared into the face of his victim. "Who are *you*?" he said.

The furious, weathered mug spit out tobacco, growled back, "Who am I? Who the fuck are *you*? Can't a man go out for a little night air? Ya stupid son-of-a-bitch, get off me!"

"Franklin? Franklin?" came a voice. More residents—old men—hurrying, hustling, through the woods to rescue their friend. "Are ya there? You alright? We heard ya yelling!"

"It's the assholes from the Winking Moon!" their sufferer responded. "They almost killed me jumpin' over the fence while I was having a smoke."

"For the love of… Stay where you are, Winkin' Moon! We're gonna murder ya!"

John and George attempted to pull the old man from the muck and leaves. He did not like it and slapped their hands away, attempting to pull himself up on his own. Lee-Willie grabbed what was left of the cigarette, began stomping it out, the onrush of octogenarians closing in.

To his attackers, Franklin said, "My war-buddies, they'll kick your ass."

"Mr. Stuckerson, let's go!" John said, pulling their boss to the fence, Steve and George shoving him up, throwing him over, the four landing back in friendly territory, Stuckerson's pant leg was caught and tore off. The aged marauders caught up to their friend, helped him up and went at the fence, banging and kicking— "We'll get ya, Winkin' Moon, if it's the last thing we do!"

"We'll teach ya to jump on Franklin! Come back here!"

John, Steve and George dragged their boss to safety, pulling off the getaway just in time, and made it into the back-storage room. They ran inside, closed it and locked the door. Stanley, Vicki and Emilio watched with confusion.

The mob in the commissary became aware that something was going on, which only made things worse for Alex and Kathy, already amid an impossibly cantankerous crowd. The hollering and braying were the most exercise the residents had gotten in a month. "I hate to admit this…" Quizzy told them, "but this was one bad idea."

Kathy was at her breaking point, Alex trying on his thinking cap.

"That telephone back there," he said, seeing the public device on the wall, not far from where the serene Italian man was standing. "Can it be hooked-up to the intercom in this room?"

Quizzy looked confused. "Huh? What do you mean?"

"Can we patch an outside call into the phone system in this room? Have everybody hear a conversation taking place between us and the drive-in?"

"I don't know. Maybe."

"I'm thinkin' they'll listen to our bosses since they don't wanna hear from us. We gotta do something, we can try calling Mr. and Mrs. Stuckerson, get 'em to explain in their own words what we're doing. I'm convinced it would be better coming from them. Whattya think, Kathy?"

"Yeah, try it," she said. She was desperate.

Quizzy beckoned another orderly and deferred the inquiry to him. Alex explained in further detail, the aide nodding in understanding. "I guess it can work," he said. "Got the system in place for emergencies. Front desk has the switchboard."

"Then do it—fast," said Quizzy. "We're about to have 'Mutiny on the Bounty' here."

Kathy ran around the building to obtain their walkie talkies from the Malibu. When she returned, Alex radioed the Stuckersons, got Mrs. Stuckerson and told her what his plans were. "This ain't workin' this way, Mrs. Stuckerson," he said. "You gotta do something, Kathy and I are gonna get shish-ka-bobbed here."

Set-up took a few tense minutes, but the orderly came back in and noted that all systems were set-to-go, Quizzy throwing up his arms one more time to make himself well. "Ladies and gentlemen, ladies and gentlemen, we've patched into The Winking Moon. We're going to be hearing from one of the managers herself, Mrs. Stuckerson. Alex?"

"Yes, Mrs. Stuckerson, do you hear us?" he said into his device.

Gail-Lill's monotone voice could be heard throughout the room. And hallways. "Yes, I hear you. My this is strange." She was in the office, looking garish under the harsh fluorescent lights.

Alex explained what to expect. "She'll now tell all of you what we've gotten underway to start making your lives happier. Mrs. Stuckerson?"

"I'm here. What?"

"Mrs. Stuckerson, we need you to explain that we're doin' stuff to assure these good people of Edgewater that we're doing everything in our power to ease their stress about the punks and hooligans invading their property."

"I thought you and Kathy did that."

Alex closed his eyes, opened them. "Mrs. Stuckerson, we did but it wasn't convincing."

"Sure as shit wasn't!" someone interrupted.

"We think it would be nice hearing from one of the top dogs: you,

Mrs. Stuckerson."

Kathy grabbed the radio from Alex's hands. "Mrs. Stuckerson, we got a rabid crowd here. They won't listen to us, they're not taking us seriously. Alex came up with this idea to have you speak to them through the phone system here. There's a lot of people gathered, all residents. They're more than eager to speak their mind. They need yours."

Taking the radio back, Alex said, "You can do it, Mrs. Stuckerson. We gotchya patched into the intercom, just like at the drive-in. We need you to give the residents a good pep-talk, tell 'em everything's gonna be okay and that we got their backs. They need to hear it from an adult. Tell your new friends that things are gonna be okay."

Gail-Lill did not know what to do or say, just processed the data. "You… want me to speak to the crowd? Where you are? At Edgewater? In the commissary?"

"Yes, stop asking questions and just do it."

"Everybody can hear me? Right now? They have *their* intercom they can hear me on?"

"Yes, Mrs. Stuckerson, they do. And yes, everybody is hearing you, right now. Right, folks?"

The crowd sent up a loud roar.

"See, Mrs. Stuckerson? Everyone can hear you. Go ahead. We need you. Go!"

Gail-Lill thought further, churned the possibilities, then said, "I… guess I can do this. Thought you kids could handle this but guess we have to chip in."

"Please, Mrs. Stuckerson," pleaded Alex, "don't get into that now—we need you to do this, they're ready to murder us."

Gail-Lill cleared her throat and said, "Okay."

The crowd quieted, anticipating that the healing was about to begin. They stared at the speakers like they were about to hear the voice of God. Mrs. Stuckerson cleared her throat. Multiple times. When they thought it was over, she did it again. Coughing, hocking, clearing the phlegm loudly. Her disembodied voice introduced herself, said hello, wished everyone well. Kathy squeezed Alex's arm, pleased by her companion's cunning. "This is it Carver," she said. "Good job."

"Thank you." He wasn't altogether humble.

"What's that reverb I hear?" Gail-Lill said.

The director took the radio. "Mrs. Stuckerson, Roberto Quizzy here. That's just the simple static cross-over you're hearing, it's not reverb, we're all ready for you. You're coming in as clear as a bell."

Her detractors were spitting fire. "What is she waitin' for? C'mon, before we die!"

On her end, alone in the booth, the woman swelled at the power she now held, metaphorically. An entire audience. "The whole facility can hear me? Every room?"

"Every room!" Quizzy said.

"Every floor? Every staff member?"

"Yes!"

"And they're all hearing me right this second?"

"Yes! Now Mrs. Stuckerson, we want to hear about restoring law-and-civility! Now, please!"

The residents heard paper crinkling, an unfolding of note paper or something. Alex and Kathy looked at each other, recognized the cadence, texture, a terrible notion dawning over them. "She's not…?" Kathy whispered.

Alex's eyes flew open. "She wouldn't…"

Mrs. Stuckerson began her reading. "A poem, by Gail-Lill Stuckerson. 'Strife is the salt-and-pepper of life. To benign the sight is not right. We must all go through challenges in this world...'"

There seemed to be a loss of oxygen in the room.

"'I view the whirl of turmoil, something to unfurl. We hurl the churl at the girl—the girl being me, of course, myself and I, not a horse…'"

The room erupted in chaos. "What the hell?!" a woman shrieked. "Is she reading poetry?!"

"Is this a joke? What kinda trick is this?!"

"Is this to make us look like fools?! The nerve of you Winkin' Moon animals!"

Pandemonium broke out. Food started to be hurled all over the commissary, straight at the guests and Quizzy. Gail-Lill kept on going, completely unaware of the firestorm she had started. *"For I am a challenged femme. I hear you, my kindred spirit, I feel your pain. No gain is too insane. I reach out to your hearts, dear children, appeal to your aches, your breaks. For they are mine, I yearn for my rightful stakes. To fake the sake of hate is to contribute to the slate…'"*

Seat cushions began to sail. Chairs were overturned. Alex, Kathy and Quizzy ran for their lives, the orderlies making unsuccessful attempts to hold back the surging seniors, intent on ripping them apart. "Inconsiderate brats! Let's teach 'em a lesson!"

"Get the tricksters, we'll show 'em what's funny!"

Quizzy took a side turn down a hallway and hid in a closet. Alex and Kathy ran out the front entrance through the main lobby, the receptionist looking at them like they had three heads, Gail-Lill's voice still droning on overheard. They ran into the parking circle, Kathy throwing Alex the keys. Jumped into the Malibu, Alex fumbling the ignition, dropping the keys to the floor. Kathy screamed at him as he finally fished them up, got the engine started, dropped the transmission into drive and peeled-out, rutting the manicured lawn, blasting shrubs along the way, cans of Metamucil bouncing off the trunk as the old monsters came out throwing them.

Back in the commissary, the small, kindly Italian man stood alone, processing the scene that had just unfolded. He had much on his mind.

Alex and Kathy came back hollering and shouting, outside the box office, Vicki in the booth, wide-eyed and silent, looking at the bunch before her with no clue as to what had happened. "The bunch" included the two escapees from behind them, both Stuckersons, Steve, John and George, and Jim, who had emerged from his lair to arbitrate. No one had ever seen Kathy like this before. She was on-fire, worked-up like a raving badger. "Look at my car!" she had already bellowed several times. "Look at the dents they put in it with laxative products. Laxative products!"

Lee-Willie was just getting the scoop on what had transpired with his wife's poetry. He was as livid, shouting at her so loud, Jim corralled everybody inside the office, getting them out of the open. "You cats have got to calm down," he told all of them. "*You* don't hold it together *they* don't hold it together."

Lee-Willie was snapping to his spouse— "Gail, how could you? You used this opportunity to make peace with Edgewater to exploit it for a poetry slam?"

"I… I… had a huge audience," the woman responded, head down, quiet.

"Gail!"

Alex spoke over them. "Do we get hazard pay for this? We barely escaped with our lives! Mr. Quizzy ran and hid somewhere, even he was scared shitless."

Steve, John and George were talking about their "near-death experience," too. "With the murderous fogies!"

"Mr. Stuckerson nearly killed the guy," John said. "Flattened him like a pancake."

Gail-Lill did not know about that. "What?"

Lee-Willie was dismissing all that, grabbing Snickers bars out of the desk drawer, shoving one after the other in his mouth, sweat breaking out on his face.

Emilio cut in on the radio, "There's something called 'a concession stand' in here that needs your assistance." He and Stanley were again holding down the fort, dealing with all manners of "horseplay and horseshit," as Emilio was describing it. "While we've been listening to nothing but screams from the movie," he accounted, "caused by the gene-damaged mutants on-screen massacring everybody in the family, we also had yahoos and rowdies running around, having an Indian-burn contest, had an idiot walk in with a rubber balloon sticking out his pants like a penis, and someone put fake dog-crap on the floor."

"We'll be right there, Emilio," Lee-Willie said into his radio, muffling his words. "Start making your pizzas."

"Start making my pizzas? What the heck do you think I've been doing since we opened?"

Jim was the calm, steady rock. Presiding over his co-workers, he warned, "We got a long summer to go, folks. Better get your shit together."

They were a mopey bunch at closing, sitting by the office, leaning on the white picket fence, barely waving their hands to vehicles as they drove out, patrons beeping at them, most openly satisfied they'd had a good outing. "I think my girlfriend out-screamed the movie!" said one happy jamoke. "And we weren't even watching, if ya know what I mean."

This had been a lot for the first week. The gang tried to not get overwhelmed. Jim had been right: there *was* a lot of summer left to go, this being the first, true test.

Emilio was off by Kathy's Malibu with her, examining the trunk, trying to determine if he or his outside friends could buff the dents out. "I dunno, Kathy," he told the girl. "These are pretty deep. Most of 'em would also need a paint job. Amazing the damage old people's poop-products can cause."

Alex was off to the other side, thinking about the zaniness of their experience, but also thinking of the closeness he felt toward her, the bond he hoped had been forged between them. They had gone through nearly being torn apart together. He had assisted in saving her. She had said such nice things about him. She had brought him *home*. He took the view that things were beginning to look up, for he was, secretly, an eternal optimist. All this encouraged him, helped him push aside the pangs of abandonment that still hung in his gut with his dad leaving his family. He would have preferred telling Dad about these adventures in person, but that wasn't going to happen.

Jim and Mr. Stuckerson had gone to the bank, leaving the staff to wait by the fence until closing. Gail-Lill stayed with them, sulking. Stanley, in an unusual gesture of compassion, walked up to her. "Gail…" he said, as if talking to a child, "artistic devotion does not necessarily mean endangering the lives of others. We all heard about how your poetry affected the old coots at Edgewater. I mean, don't get me wrong, I believe in following your bliss. Lookit, one of these days I wanna board my spacecraft and rise to the stars, showin' my alien brethren all the creative stuff I can do."

"Stanley," she said. "Shut-up."

When Jim's light-blue Chevy Fleetside pulled back into the entrance, the horn tooting success, they all started toward their cars. It had been a long night, an exhausting night. Tomorrow was Sunday. As George said, he hoped a church would go in Edgewater's place should they ever decide to pack up and leave. "At least the chooches and Melvins staying here all night could just wake up and walk over in the morning, get in their Sunday service for all the sins they committed."

Instead of going home, Kathy drove to Durand Eastman beach, a Rochester public park popular during the summer months, by herself to think. The beach stretched five-thousand feet along Lake Ontario. This time of night, it was lawfully closed. No one was to hang here at these hours, but Kathy and the Crusaders had made a habit of it last year when things got thick.

The lake itself looked like an ocean. A half-moon hung in the sky, waves undulating like soft shag carpeting, inviting her to dump all concerns into the starlit horizon. Kathy was a deep thinker. Like her art, she studied the scene before her, thinking of it as a painting. How would she best capture it? At this nocturnal hour, this panorama was a respite from the craze and mania of the drive-in. She turned on the radio, keeping it low. One of her favorites was on, *Heart Hotels*, by Dan Fogelberg. Her mind soaked so far into it she was almost dreaming while awake.

A male voice called out, a Charger ripping in— "Hey good-looking, is this beach taken?"

Thankfully, it was Steve, with the whole gang: Jody, John, Vicki, George and Alex, cranking the first Boston album, pulling up next to her. Jody straddled Steve behind the wheel, battery-operated toy-microphone in one hand. Everybody was smiling as wide as could be.

"What are you guys doing here?" Kathy asked, shaking the cobwebs away.

"Looking for you," said Steve.

"Why?"

"'Cause we knew you'd be here."

"How'd you know that?"

"'Cause we all go here when we've had a really rough night."

She giggled, turned the radio off. "True enough."

"Cops been around yet?"

"Nope, nobody but 'lil 'ole me. Park closes at midnight; we shouldn't even be here."

"But who cares?" said George from the backseat. "Let's go out for a walk like we did last year."

"Okay," Kathy said, pulled the keys from her ignition.

Alex stuck his head out the window. He had been in the back as well. "Kathy, you mind?"

She looked at him and softened. "No."

They went for a stroll along the shoreline. All seven of them. Along the moonlit lakeshore. "'Watching submarine races,'" Steve joked.

"What's that?" asked Jody.

"That's what they used to call it when everyone parked here late at night, gettin' it on. My older brothers did it all the time."

The sound of the waves was intoxicating: a gentle breathing in-and-out. The rummies encircled Kathy, squeezed her until she could not stand it. She yelled at everyone to get off, all laughing.

"What was that thing you had in your hand when you pulled in, Steve?" Kathy asked.

"'Mr. Microphone,'" he replied. "Ever see the commercial? That dipshit says: 'Hey, good-looking we'll come back to pick ya up later.'"

She chuckled. "Yeah, I've seen it. Hate that commercial."

"It's gay," said George.

Jody asked Kathy how she was feeling.

"Good," Kathy answered. "I'm not physically hurt, only my pride."

"Then you won't mind if I play 'Big Sis.'"

"'Big Sis'?"

Jody jumped on Kathy's back. "Big Sis!" she squealed, yukking it up. "I'm Little Sis, let's go for a ride."

Steve told her to get down.

"Suppose you heard about tonight, huh?" Kathy asked the blondie.

"Fuckin-A, I did," Jody answered. "Totally royal. Stuckerson flattens an old guy, you kids almost get flattened by the old folks. A conundrum, isn't it?"

"Don't use big words," said Steve. "If you're gonna use your mouth, kiss me."

She did. There went Jody and Steve, passionately. They drifted off. Took their shoes off, went splashing down at water's edge. George said,

"Why don't you and Vick do that, John? Now's your chance to be together."

"Shut-up, George," both John and Vicki sounded in unison.

But Vicki was sneaking clandestine glances at John, swooning over being with him under the stars. John didn't mind so much, either, but he wasn't going to say that. There was a large chunk of driftwood where the water met the beach. They went to it to sit and talk. Totally innocent, but George could not help but be the smart-ass. "There they go, folks, finally doin' what comes naturally. Go get her, Johnny-Boy." They ignored him.

Kathy said, "George, why do you always bug John about Vicki? If they want to go out, they'll go out."

"I'm just bustin' their balls, Kath. I love those two."

George split off to do push-ups along a sandy dune. Alex said to Kathy, "Speaking of 'ends,' how far we walking?"

"I don't know," Kathy said.

"Do ya mind that I'm with you?"

"No, of course not. You were with me all night, why should it stop now?"

"That was pretty wild, wasn't it?" he said.

"It was. Thanks for saving me."

“I didn’t save you.”

“You kind of did.”

“Well, you’re welcome. Anything for you, Kathy.”

She looked at him, laughed. In a good way.

“Herbal Essence?” he said, shaking off the embarrassment.

“What?”

“Your hair. ‘Herbal Essence’? The shampoo, I can smell it.”

“Yeah, Herbal Essence. You’ve got quite the senses, Alex. What are you, a super-hero with super-powers?”

“Nope, my Mom has that in the bathroom.”

She then asked, “How’s all that going, at home?”

“It’s goin’,” he answered. “I’m gonna keep this night from her.”

“I don’t blame you. You’d tell your Dad, though, right? You told me that last year when you told me about things.”

“Yeah, yeah, I would, Kathy. This is gonna be a summer to remember, huh?”

“Yup, a summer to remember.”

Jody made Steve chase her, caught her forty feet into the shallow water and the two had a mini boxing match. Steve had coached her well in the art of pugilism. Jody’s leg movements became encumbered when she went out too far. She lost her balance and face-planted in the water, dragging Steve down with her. When she surfaced, she was full of piss-and-vinegar. "Ohmigod!" she shouted. "It's fucking freezing! It's summer already and the lake's as cold as ice!"

"Hey, you kids, get up here." It was the police, up high on the bluff. Two of them, one with a bullhorn to his mouth. When the seven returned to parking lot-level, they had flashlights on them, lighting up their faces. "You're the kids who work at the Winking Moon, right?"

"Right," George conceded. "That retirement home behind you is quite the pain-in-the-ass."

"Tell us about it," said Vicki.

"Be careful," said the second officer. "We're getting' a lot of calls from them. From

everybody. Now get outta here: you weren't supposed to be here in the first place."

Vicki smiled. "Okay, officers, thanks, we're leaving. Tell Sergeant Leo we said 'hi.'"

And they did. Alex was hoping Kathy would offer him a ride home again, but she didn't this time and he didn't want to get pushy.

CHAPTER 23:

DEBAUCHERY & RIBALDRY

As George and the Crusaders were putting in a pretty grueling workout in the basement of his family's house on their Sunday afternoon—Alex, not so much, taking it easy—Steve's girlfriend Jody McBrennan was already at work, at Lapping Waves, pulling the garbage out the back, throwing bags into the dumpsters she used to hide her smuggled beer.

There was a mighty roar from an engine, a screeching of tires. She looked up, saw a

daunting sight in the road: a jet-black, four-door sedan, the words **DEBAUCHERY & RIBALDRY** spray-painted on the sides of it in blood-red, executing a sharp left turn onto Sing Road from Hewey, heading in the direction of the Winking Moon. It was a beast that struck alarm immediately into her heart. There was laughter inside, cackling laughter like jackals, or hyenas. She watched it until it faded out of sight. Two words slipped from her lips. "Holy shit."

She ran back inside. Smith was not around. Customers were few. She had the time. She jumped on the phone, dialed George's house and got his mom on the line, asked to speak to her boyfriend quickly. Mrs. Jocavelli opened the basement door, handed Steve the phone, he stretched it all the way down to their workout area, the cord quaking at maximum extent.

"Steve, I just saw it," she said.

"Just saw 'what'?" he asked, wiping sweat from his brow.

"The Delta 88. *The* Delta 88. From last summer. The one you kids tried running down all summer and never got. It's fucking back. I was taking the garbage out and there it was: bombin' toward The Winking Moon. It's back, baby."

Steve's face drained of color. The others noticed. John racked the bench-press bar. Steve held the phone away. "It's Jode. She's at Lapping Waves. She saw The Delta 88. *The* Delta 88."

George, John and Alex's jaws went limp. "What?" Alex said.

"From last summer," said Steve. "*The* Delta 88, Ribaldry and Debauchery written on the sides of it. It's back."

"God have mercy," George said.

"Jody, you sure?" Steve asked, speaking into the phone again.

"I'm sure," the youngster said, looking out into the store from the back room. "I know what I'm talkin' about, had those two funky words that-I-still-don't-know-what-they-mean painted on the sides of it. It had those tinted windows that you also told me about, everything. Black as the devil, whitewall tires. I heard laughing inside—like freakin' devils—just like you said. Baby, I think you're gonna have your hands even more-full this year."

The words haunted Steve. Took him a moment to respond.

"Thanks, honey. Damn. We'll uh… see ya tonight. Everything else cool? Smith shown up yet?"

"No, he's not around, he put me in the charge. The first customers are startin' to pull in, gotta go, honey—watch your asses—I didn't like the looks of it."

"Nor me. We don't want that beast coming back."

"Just thought I'd warn ya."

"I'll talk it over with the boys."

"Fucking-A," Jody said, and they hung up.

There was a vacuum where the positive energy had been. Steve waited for George to walk the phone back up to the kitchen. He returned to his friends, feeling the icy, cold chill of the prospect creeping in his veins. "Well this strikes terror in me," he said. "The Delta 88."

Steve, John, Alex, agreed. Pondered it, remembered the horror the vehicle inflicted on them last season, when it appeared. "Never caught the damn thing," said John.

"It kept sneakin' in, never us seeing it 'til it was torquin' around, acting lunatic," said Alex. "Kathy never saw it. It was a ghost, a specter, terrorizing every living soul in the drive-in."

"Terrorizing Mr. Stuckerson," George accentuated. "It was *his* Moby Dick."

"And he's no Captain Ahab," said Steve.

"Ever read 'Moby Dick,' George?" John asked.

"No," George replied, "but I heard about it."

"All summer long, we never got it when it snuck-in," said Steve. "Mr. Stuckerson almost went to the loony-bin because of it."

"Evil thing showed up, what, three times?" said George.

"Like it teleported in," said Alex. "And that laughter… that disturbing laughter. Musta been seven or eight jamokes jammed into that thing, all hellions. Never saw 'em, either. Damn tinted windows, took us on a helluva ride."

"Yeah, can't have *that* thing entering our grounds again," said John. "Stuckerson'll kill us."

"And how about those headlights?" said Steve. "Brightest fuckin' things I've ever seen. Rivals the Moon Tower."

John was concerned. "If Mr. and Mrs. Stuckerson hear about this, they'll flip."

"Let's just see if it shows up first," said Alex.

"Ball-sacks," said Steve. "Public Enemy Number One from our Rogue Gallery."

"Fuck me," said George.

From upstairs, Mrs. Jocavelli called down from behind the closed door. "I hear a lot of bad language down there."

"Sorry, Mom," George said.

"Sorry, Mrs. Jocavelli," said the others.

All four remained inert, halted in their exercise… mulling… anticipating…dreading…

Just then, one of George's little sisters came popping out the pile of dirty laundry beside the washer, startling the hell out of the Crusaders. "Surprise!" she beamed. "See if you clucks can lift me!"

She broke into laughter and George chased her up the stairs.

CHAPTER 24:

BROKEN BULBS

"Hills Have Eyes" and "Texas Chainsaw Massacre" were electrifying the audiences. They'd had violently graphic horror movies many times before in the past, just not this extreme. The thing about horror films at a drive-in, it seemed, was that it made the crowd hornier. "Release of fright leads to release of other things," Jim had once told them.

The Crusaders were out in the field, discussing this theory. Alex, being the movie-expert, was being referred to by John, George, Steve. "One of the phenomena about horror films," he was suggesting, "is that they cause teenagers and young folk to become extra-horny. There's always sex in horror films. Adrenaline flow livens-up the metabolism, causes it to pour-out the hormones. These films bring wholesale slaughter to an all-time high, I've never seen any like 'em. Nothin' but screams, torture, buzzing implements. Patrons have to take breaks."

John said, "Vicki, Stanley and Emilio asked Jim to turn the volume on the speakers in the stand to save their nerves."

"Yeah, even we're pushed to our limits with these gems."

"Jim says 'Texas' is based on a true story," said George.

"I've heard that," said Alex, citing Edgewater, behind them. "It was probably about one of those residents, the psychos." He touched his bandaged noise, winced in pain.

Intermission was drawing near, and the Crusaders were hanging around the stand, making sure things there were functioning properly. The area smelled of whiskey and God-knew-what-else, drawing attention, practical jokes on the rise. People were walking on their hands in the stand.

"Get up!" Stanley scolded. "You cretins know how many dirty feet and sandals have been walkin' on this floor? And you're puttin' your hands on it?"

Some jokester had Fun Snaps: mini explosive-caps that made a loud "snap" when they were thrown against something. That caused enough screaming. Still other fools imitated the mutants in the film and began lumbering around, terrorizing their girlfriends, pinching them in the sides and other, more private, place. One chowderhead asked Vicki and Stanley if they were serving up body parts tonight, frying 'em up good—making other customers nauseated.

"Stop saying that, will ya?" Stanley said to the moron. "You're killing their appetites." He turned to Vicki. "I'm getting' a little tired of these patrons just doin' whatever the fuck they want. We need to shed a little light on the subject. I'll go turn the Moon Tower on."

"Stanley, don't!" Alex snapped. "You'll ruin the movie, it's still too early."

"I don't care."

Before Vicki could stop him, Stanley practically ran into the back-storage room, flicked the light switch to the power structure off-and-on as fast as he could, flashing the multi-bulbed, metal pillar like a strobe. It was too much for the grid, and three of the lightbulbs in the uppermost row, way up high, blew out—Pop! Pop! Pop! —scaring the crowd with its jarring sounds, glass tinkling to the ground, severely dimming the overall lighting used to see, sending them into obnoxious and riotous reactions. Emilio had been in the middle of tossing pizza dough into the air. The sound scared him so much he had launched it too high, got the whole thing stuck on the ceiling.

Stuckersons had been in the office, Kathy had been in her booth. Both heard the crowd reacting, wondered what was going on. Alex fielded the walkie-talkie and explained to the managers what had happened.

"Stanley blew out bulbs on the Moon Tower, flickin' it off-and-on.".

Lee-Willie entered the concession stand, swearing up a storm and blaming Stanley for the incompetence, asking him what the hell he was thinking. Stanley got mad right back, gave it straight to the man.

"Don't you yell at me, Stuckerson. I'm tryin' to save this drive-in. All this rampant disrespect for the general operations we do here on a nightly basis is driving me insane."

Through the chaos, Jim strolled in, blowing a big ring of smoke out of his mouth, asking who the genius was who knocked out The Moon Tower. All fingers pointed to Stanley. Jim walked up and put a thoughtful hand on his shoulder. "Nice going, champ. We don't have any bulbs."

"We couldn't have replaced 'em anyway!" Stanley retorted.

"Yes, we could. I know how. I'm the only one qualified to do that. But my union doesn't know that, nor could they be made to know. Being a Ranger in the Army taught me to climb many things."

"Well where could we get replacement bulbs anyway?"

"The Smirking Star," Jim answered. "Zeke has 'em, they always have surplus supplies. They don't have anything go wrong over there. He's their projectionist, I know him. Would only be a matter of drivin' over there, borrowin' a few. They'd cough 'em up."

"Driving over to The Smirking Star?" Lee-Willie said, clearly not keen on the idea. "That's all the way over on the east side."

Jim looked at him. "So, you want people sittin' here in faulty lighting all night long? Think of what closing's gonna be like."

That struck. Lee-Willie whipped to his staff. "Who wants to go for a late-night drive?"

Alex turned it down, instantly. "Not me. Don't think Kathy's gonna volunteer either."

The Stuckersons surveyed the face. George was next to John. George was grinning, wanting the detail.

Mr. and Mrs. Stuckerson timidly handed the keys to their Lincoln Versailles over to John Tambone. George was beside him, anxious to get underway. He was riding shotgun. Kathy was in the booth, staring, amazed this was even being allowed to happen. "Now don't go boofin' the pooch," Mr. Stuckerson was telling them. "We're trusting ya with our car."

"We wouldn't do anything to your car, sir," said George, twinkle in his eye. "We'll take the best care of it as we would our own."

"And just remind me again: you two imbeciles *do* have your licenses, right?

"License? What license?" George said. "Ah, just kiddin', of course we do."

Lee-Willie and Gail-Lill looked like they'd had the wits suddenly scared out of them. Then, the nerd said, "Hated callin' over to The Smirking Star. Saxon gave me grief, asked how we even blew out the bulbs."

"Did ya tell him?" George asked.

"Are you kidding? That's all we'd need."

Jim was there, also. Stepped up to the Lincoln, mug in his hand. "Make sure they're still in the packages. Those bulbs are special, factory-made ones, good for a long time but only for these Moon Towers. Can't take a chance on faulty ones. No hardware store's gonna be open this time on a Sunday night."

"We'll hurry back," George promised, practically shoving John in the car.

The shy kid started the engine up, George trying hard to tamp down his excitement. Kathy leaned out the booth, "If you see Stephanie Mason, say 'hi' to her for us. She works there in their box office."

"We know," George said, earning surprised, guarded looks.

"Hey, that's not why you two volunteered, was it?" Lee-Willie asked.

"No, sir, 'course not," George fired off. "Just don't tell Stanley."

"Be careful. And take it easy."

"Yes, sir," John said, then shot out of there like they were blown from a cannon, kicking up gravel, leaving the crew coughing, waving the dust-cloud from their faces, Jim already having stepped back. He knew what they were going to do.

Lee-Willie was left simmering like a teapot, questioning the wisdom of what they had just allowed.

On the road, George messed with every dial, button and instrumentation he could find, particularly the FM stations, blasting Jefferson Starship's *Jane*: a great one. He turned the windshield-wipers on high, even though it was not raining. He hit the high-beams, blinding people coming the other way. Twice, he grabbed the wheel in jest, jerking them off-course, pretending he wanted to run off the road.

The Stuckersons must have eaten at every fast food joint in Rochester, judging from the state of the interior. There were paper bags everywhere, crumpled paper cups, discarded straws, empty Styrofoam containers from takeout, all over the backseat. "What were they doing?"

he said. "Eating like a nuclear war was imminent?" Empty Tupperware bowls bounced, bopped and bounced along with every turn and swish of the streets. George found a six-pack of Mello Yello between his legs. "If we drank 'em, we could belch in the Avengers' faces."

John cranked the song louder. "Let's try to refrain from doin' that."

It seemed to take forever getting to the other side of town, but John and George sure enjoyed the ride. They shouted at the top of their lungs just to shout, reveled at being away from Chooch-Man, loved the free reign of being behind the wheel of an automobile. When they finally pulled into The Star's entrance, they saw Stephanie Mason immediately—alone in the booth, petite as petite could be, cute as a button—reading a magazine in the ticket booth. As they approached, she put down the magazine down.

"Stephanie," George hailed. "Remember us? George Jocavelli and John Tambone from Galileo. Hamlin Beach."

She had to crane down, bend. When she recognized them, a full-out smile bloomed on her face, like a dozen roses. "George, John—hi! Of course, I remember you. How are you doing? We were expecting you."

Ducking himself, so he could see across John, he said, "We're far from home, like 'The Wizard of Oz.'"

"And there are *two* 'Dorothys'," she said.

George felt his heart thump. "You work the box office like our

Kathy does."

"I know," Stephanie said. "I've heard about her. She paints, huh? Pretty cool."

"Yeah, she's great. Does it get scary out here by yourself? Kinda freaks Kathy out."

Stephanie playfully frowned. "Only when goons like you two show up. Hi, John."

"Hi Stephanie," John said, trying to stay out of it.

George laughed. Stephanie laughed. There was chemistry here. Hamlin Beach had not been a fluke. John sat there like an awkward toad on a toadstool, feeling silly. He may have been the quiet one, but he wasn't stupid. When the googly-eyes became too much, he sighed, turned the music off— "Wait a minute…" then backed the Versailles up, turned the vehicle around, backed-in so George was on her side. There, much better clearance. The two guffawed at that gesture, too.

"Good one, buddy," George said. "Thanks."

Before either boy could say another word, Stephanie turned her radio down, reached down between her legs at the floor, came back up with a cardboard box of the tower-bulbs they had come for. "Looking for these? Personally, delivered by Mr. Saxon himself."

George was impressed. Took them, said thanks, opened the box and looked in. A half dozen of the suckers stared him in the face. Big things. Way more than he expected. "We're gettin' all these?" he asked.

"That's what the boss-man said. We heard you blew out The Moon Tower. Fantastic. How'd you do that?"

George offered a playful smirk and inspected them, making sure each was still individually boxed, just like Jim requested. "They're good," he said to John.

"What is this, a drug deal? Of course, they are, who do you think we are: the Winking Moon?"

"That was a cheap shot," said George. "Our projectionist just wanted us to make sure."

"'Jim? He's awesome. Stanley tells us about him all the time."

"We don't know how we're actually gonna replace 'em but we're gonna try."

"Well good luck, I'm sure you'll figure it out. Whose wheels are these?" She was referring to the car.

"Our bosses. That's how cool we are. It's good to see ya again… Stephanie… and so soon."

She smiled at the big kid. "John, you playing disco in there? I know George likes disco."

"We're not," said John.

"How is my granduncle, by the way?"

"Crazy as ever," George answered. "But we love him."

Stephanie smiled again. "But he doesn't love you kids, I told you that."

"We know."

She moved a blondish curl from her face. "Don't call him 'crazy.' He's a bit eccentric but he's a fantastic guy."

"We know that, sorry. We didn't mean he was *crazy*-crazy."

"You know about his interest in UFOs?"

"Oh yeah, big-time. We've known that about him since we met him at the beginning of last year. Heard he's always been like that, way before we got involved with The Moon."

"Way back when he worked with Franco Esposito. You kids heard about him?"

"Many times."

"I never knew him, personally, either."

"We give Stanley flack about his UFOs, Stephanie," said George. "We're just kidding."

"We do, too," flirted Stephanie, and their eyes met again.

Just then the Avengers emerged from the shadows. All five of them—Kyle, Seth, Gary, Newton, Pauly—entering the light, chests puffed out, sauntering up to the invaders. Kyle was leading the pack. "Well-well-well, George Jocavelli and John Tambone. The prodigal sons have returned to the better drive-in, this time asking for help with the stupid lightbulbs they blew out."

George and John rolled their eyes. Figured this would happen. "'Prodigal son,' Kyle?" said George. "Pretty sophisticated dialogue for this time of night."

"That's about the only thing 'sophisticated' you kids have heard all night."

George looked at John. *Dick*. John agreed, decided to take the higher road, say hello. "Pauly Cicco, Newton Tallis, Gary Halinsky, Seth Byrd, Kyle Daten—the Avengers. How you kids doin'?"

"We're doing fine, *Crusaders*," said Seth. "Now did you get what you were looking for?"

"Guys be nice," said Stephanie.

"Yes, we did, Seth," said George. "Thank-you very much."

"Good," said Kyle. "Then you can go."

"Guys show some hospitality," said Stephanie.

"Stephanie," said Pauly. "We'll show them 'some hospitality' if they get off our property."

"To show them more on the scoreboard in the fall," said Gary.

Newton laughed. "Yeah, and that's going to be way lopsided."

George laughed. "Well… we'll see about that, fellas."

Kyle was his usual curt self. "You morons blew out your bulbs? How wonderfully idiotic of you. How'd you do that, killing someone in a shoot-out?"

George ignored the question, instead counted off each one of them, using his finger to count. "Let's see: one-two-three-four-five of you. All five patrolmen at once, walkin' around together, not in the lot. Takes all five to come here and check us out, huh?"

"We wanted to make sure you didn't linger," said Pauly.

Stephanie could not take it any longer. "Oh, this is fucking absurd. Can't we all just grow up for a minute?"

"This is men's business, Steph," said Kyle.

""Where's Mr. Saxon?"

"Right here," came a voice of reason. Sort of. Brent Saxon, manager of The Smirking Star, emerged.

"Mr. Saxon!" said Gary, all five patrolmen surprised.

He did not like what he was seeing. There were too many people gathered round the box office. No traffic, though, things were slow. George held up the box. "Hello, Mr. Saxon, we just came for these, Stephanie got 'em for us. Thank-you. We greatly appreciate the help. We didn't have any."

"Of course, you didn't, George," the man said. "I don't expect the Winking Moon to carry any back-up supplies. Things are always getting broken there."

Another cheap shot.

"We'll be headin' back now," said George. "Thanks for having 'em for us ahead of time."

"So, you don't bug our staff with drawn-out chit-chat," Kyle threw in.

Saxon turned to him. "Kyle…" That was all he needed to say. Then, to his guests, "You're welcome. Tell Mr. and Mrs. Stuckerson they can return the favor when Bluestone sends them a box. I don't know how long that will take, though, they seemed to be drag on certain things these days."

His patrolmen spread out, appearing like they were at least going to move away, letting him move in. "John Tambone and George Jocavelli, right?"

"Right, sir," said John.

Mr. Saxon studied the situation, looked at Stephanie, looked at George. Kyle was growing impatient. "Glad to be of assistance," Brent said. "Tell Lee and Gail his employees park weird. Well, if you'd excuse us, we all have to get back to work—*don't* we, fellas?"

"We do," said Pauly. "Keeping our drive-in sane."

At this, George could not help himself. "Well, Pauly, I'm also sure you're keeping busy playing video games, probably not much to defend around here."

"And you've got too much to defend," said Kyle. "Wild cuckoos."

Saxon told everybody to cool it, go their separate ways. "We won't play into this rivalry here." But George ignored the instruction, said to his opponents, "And what movies are ya playing here tonight, Avengers, G-rated material, no doubt? We got 'Hills Have Eyes' and 'Texas Chainsaw Massacre.' There's still people comin' in at this hour. I don't see anybody here."

"Didn't you read the marquee on your way in?" Gary said. "We got 'Escape From Alcatraz' and 'Moonraker.' Total action." George scoffed. "We got more action in our bathrooms on any given night."

Stephanie giggled, drew dirty looks from the Avengers. Once more Saxon told everyone to settle down and for the Crusaders to be on their way. "I'll call Lee-Willie," he said. "Tell him your business is through here."

"You don't have to, sir," said George. "Mission accomplished, thank-you. Sorry for getting a little out-of-sorts. Stephanie, nice seeing ya again."

"Nice seeing you again, too, George," Stephanie responded. "John, nice seeing you."

"Stephanie," John said.

George wished the Avengers a good night. "If there's anything to these rumors about our drive-ins we're all hearin' about, let us know.

We'll return the favor."

John inched the car back and pulled out of the lot as Saxon swept the Avengers away with one mighty swing of the arm. When they were gone, the man turned to the box office girl, an expression of consternation gripping his face.

"Show-offs," he said.

CHAPTER 25:

THE MOON TOWER

In John and George's absence, the Stuckersons had been besieged all during intermission by complaints of poor lighting due to the blown-out bulbs. Now they were all together again and the fresh lightbulbs were taken out of the box. With his military background, Jim Barenta was the only one qualified to even think about climbing The Moon Tower. Certainly didn't want to call in Firechief Pete for a favor. By now the tower was completely shut off, and "Texas Chainsaw Massacre" was grossing out patrons everywhere, watching a masked psychopath rip his victims apart with a chainsaw, and the tower was completely off. It was time to get the job done.

"And keep the damn power off," was the number-one imperative issued to Stanley as the big guy strapped the harness from his skydiving gear around his torso and waist in the back storage room, the sling fitting snugly to his midsection, clips secure. Lee-Willie and Gail-Lill stood by, shaking life a leaf, terrified about the operation about to kick off.

Jim commanded the patrolmen— "I need you rummies to stay under me at all times, flashlights kept on me the entire time. Got it? If I circle like this with my hand, it means gimme more light. Keep the goddam noise down. If we're careful, we can get this done with nobody noticin'."

Within the next ten minutes, up went Jim, climbing the metal edifice into the night sky, hooking one bungee cord safety-clip after the other over each rung, ascending, replacement bulbs clinking quietly in the cargo-pouch on his utility belt. He'd told them earlier it was something new, something called "a fanny pack that Jeannie had given me as a gift. Fuckin' thing's cute, ain't it?" In the pack he also had his tools: pocket light, tweezers, screwdriver, everything.

Vicki and Emilio were an edgy wreck in the concession stand, trying not to talk about what they knew was going on. The horrid screaming and mutilating sounds coming from the movie did not help matters much.

At the site, the Crusaders and Lee-Willie were keeping an eye out, shining their flashlights up, like prison guards at a watchtower, keeping their beloved comrade sharp at all times. Lee-Willie was masticating on rock candy and Charleston Chews— "Jim, be careful. Jim! I said be careful."

The obviousness was not lost to the soldier. "Thanks for the tip, Lee," he responded, "I'll try that."

Kathy was in the booth, awaiting updates. Alex had given her the scoop. Everybody was to throw off any inquisitive pest asking what was going on. Stanley remained at the till, pouting. He did not like to be kept from the center of the action. "If Franco was here," he mumbled to Emilio, "none of this bullshit would be happening."

"What, you blowing up The Moon Tower?" said the cook.

"Shut-up, Varentez."

The chainsaw and shrill music indeed helped mask the sound but made concentration difficult. Jim rested a quarter way up, wiping his face before proceeding.

Halfway there, he slipped. Lee-Willie and the Crusaders caught their breath. The rung he had put his foot on had seagull droppings on it, which made for a slimy surface. The harness had done the trick, held him fast. With a thumbs-up confirmation, the warrior continued to the top, to the seven-foot-wide platform where he could stand, replace the bulbs with sure footing. Sure, it was precarious and way the hell up there, but the hero knew what he was doing. The corrugated steel plane under his boots felt sturdy. He got set on it, steadied his balance, allowed for a moment of re-centering, then began the delicate procedure of removing the blown-out bulbs at the furthest-out casings (of course they were the furthest-out), changing them out with the fresh ones. He did not look down.

Jim needed more light and did the circle-thing with his hands. The boys provided him with what was needed, but it still was not enough. Alex snatched the mega-flashlight from Mr. Stuckerson's holster, pissing him off.

"Hey, Carver, what the hell?" he barked.

"Shh, Mr. Stuckerson," Alex whispered. "He needs more light. This'll do."

"If you ever grab something off me agai—"

"Lee, hush," said his wife. "They have to concentrate."

Lee-Willie ate more candy, tried to be patient, but just could not keep his mouth shut. "Hey, Jim," he hissed out. "How's it going up there? Gimme a status report."

Jim balked, got annoyed, looking down at the man and answered him just as Leatherface onscreen bifurcated another victim to massive screams. "Lee… keep your voice down. I got a couple in. A *couple*."

Lee-Willie did not quite hear. "What? I didn't hear that. Are they in? How long before we can test it and turn it on?"

"When I say so, Lee, now shut-up."

"Movie's almost over, hurry."

"Lee, don't tell me to hurry."

Jim told himself not to erupt. Lee-Willie's stupidity had drawn some curious onlookers, noticing something was happening in the rear of the lot.

"What are you guys doing?" one asked.

Lee-Willie grumbled, nastily told them to go back to their car. John quietly reminded his boss that Jim told them all to be quiet. "Don't tell me what to do, Tambone," he replied.

Jim got the next bulb secured in its casing, but the Lee-Willie kept needing the affirmation. "Answer me, Jim! Can we turn it on? Can we *turn it on*?!"

The two 'turn-it-ons' were loud. There had come a sudden—and rare—lull in the movie. The victim was dead. The screaming had stopped. The words came in loud-and-clear, all the way to the concession stand, where Stanley heard at the register, Gail-Lill still at the switchbox.

"Where're you going?" Emilio said as the cashier started for the storage room.

"Didn't you bozos hear that? Lee said to 'turn it on!' He was yellin' it, we gotta get Jim down off that thing now."

"Stanley!" said Vicki. "That's not what they said."

Stanley practically pushed Gail-Lill out of the way. "Don't touch that!" she said.

"We've been told to, woman, I'm thinking of Jim."

With the bugle call sounding in his mind, he reached for the switch—FLOOM!—he snapped it on, sending full electricity to the monstrosity, instantly lighting the lot up like a Monday Night Football, blinding Jim, hands shooting to his eyes, accidentally releasing his grip on the handrail, sending him stepping backward, toppling off toward the ground.

"Jim!" the crew down below shouted, others in the audience disobeying the orders to get back to their cars gasped, also screamed. Was quite a combination: the screaming of the audience and the screaming of the movie, starting back up again.

Jim feel twenty feet, the harness catching him, jerking him, saving his life but slamming him against the support-girders, knocking him hard, wrenching the shit out of his back, neck.

"Omigod!" Lee-Willie said.

Everything was lit now, drama reaching a crescendo as tons of patrons poured from their vehicles, Vicki, Emilio and Gail-Lill all running out, screaming at the sight of Jim hanging from the tower, Kathy in the booth, shouting into the radio to find out what the hell was going on and why the lights were on. She could see the glow from the exit.

Everyone on the planet was now witness to the hapless soul dangling from the massive spire, swaying in mid-air, trying to get a grip so he could steady himself, the crowd shouting for the fire department to be called. The projectionist was twirling from side-to-side, caught in a dangle. Lee-Willie and the patrolmen were scrambling skyward to assist.

"Don't come up! Don't come up! I'm alright!" Jim responded. "Goddamn safety cords caught me. Who turned on the fucking power? Gimme a minute to get my bearings, I can't feel my back. Who turned the power on?"

Stanley was now staring at the scene, the light from the new bulbs reflecting in his bifocals. His mouth was open, he was not moving. *Jesus-Lord-Mercy, what have I done?*

Vicki, Emilio, Gail-Lill were in hysterics, yelling their heads off and freaking out like they'd never freaked out before Jim remained hanging upside-down, keeping calm, a little freaked-out himself, but unable to right himself from his predicament.

Firechief Pete ended up being called in anyway. With his entire engine and ladder company. Firechief Pete's was Jim's friend—and war buddy—just like Sergeant Leo. They looked out for each other.

The big guy was brought down and loaded into an ambulance, taken away to the same hospital Alex had been in just a few nights ago. Everyone showed up, except Stanley. That nutter drove himself home as soon as he knew what he'd done, and that Jim was safe. He had never felt worse in his life. Doris checked on him. He told her he was a little queasy, wanted to stay in the cellar where it was cool, recover for a while.

"Well do you want me to bring you some lemonade?" she asked him.

"Your lemonade's ten-times sourer than I feel right now. No thank-you."

Jim was treated for abrasions where the cords rasped his skin, along the ribs. And there were bruises already forming where his torso met the girders. All replacement bulbs had been taken care of. Once the firemen found out what the nonsense had been about to kick off the problem, they had done it themselves, the firechief asking the managers why the fuck they didn't call them in the first place.

"We gotta business to run here, Pete," Lee-Willie had told them. "You should see this joint after midnight."

They had cancelled the encore presentation of "Hills," doled-out more redemption tickets, bracing for the negative inflow they knew this would surely produce in the near future. They also prayed Bluestone would not find out about this.

"Whatever you nincompoops do," Lee-Willie said to the Crusaders, "don't let the Smirking Star find out about this. That's all we need, this gettin' to Bannabock."

They were all feeling awful, frozen. "This is just the start," Kathy sniffled. "We haven't even gotten to the bulk of the summer yet. I'm so sorry, Jim."

"Don't worry your little pretty heads about it," Jim said to the two girls, sucking on ice water. "The tough will make ya strong and the strong will make ya tough."

"Want us to call Jeannie?" Vicki asked. "There's a payphone right down the hall."

"I ain't that strong or I ain't that tough, Vick. I'll save the explosion for later."

And the explosion did happen. Jeannie Monocco was a wreck watching her man sleeping for the last hour on this dour Monday afternoon, mourning over how close she had come to losing him. The way he was now—gone-to-the-world, slosh-style on the waterbed—he appeared more dead than alive. With his shirt off, torso on full display, she easily counted the contusions and grazes his midsection displayed: a horrific accompaniment to the ghastly newspaper headline in this late edition of the daily paper, unfolded on the dresser:

Projectionist Hangs From Tower After Drive-In Fall

Unable to keep away from him, she sat on the corner of the bed, staring at his form, consequently sending waves undulating beneath the vinyl lining. He awoke, flailed his arms, snapping eyelids about the room in distressed search— "Wha—? Huh? What's goin' on? Jeannie? The fuck's happening?"

"Shhh, everything's fine…" she whispered. "I'll tell you 'what the fuck's happening.' You're a shithead, that's what."

"What? Whattya mean?"

She recognized the ironic juxtaposition of the scene before her. There was the love of her life, lying in bed, struggling for consciousness after a very serious night that could've killed him, their Smiley-Face poster with "Have A Nice Day" written on it hung on the wall behind his body.

She tossed the Local Section at him, let him take it off his chest, read it, grimace in pain and revelation as he sat up, first asking how the fuck "they'd" gotten the story so fast, then asked how he looked as a superstar in print, and finally asked how long she'd been there. She did not answer the questions, simply said, "I don't want to lose you."

Their eyes met for a moment, then he pointed at the headline. "This should've been in the funnies section," he japed.

"Don't test me, James," Jeannie said this when she was madly serious. She stood. "It was on the local news at noon, too."

"Am I getting royalties?"

"I'm going to my parents' in an hour. You have some very serious thinking to do this afternoon."

"About what?"

"About what's going on here—with your job *and* everything."

"Jeannie, come on, that's too much brain-work on my day off."

She sent the bed undulating again, rocking it purposefully with her knees and hands— "Think you'll have a job much longer with the way things have been going? Falling from The Moon Tower? Having to be rescued by your chums at the fire department, tempting fate? This shit goes on almost nightly. How many times do you think I want to be come home from work and read these real-life horror stories?"

"Look at it this way, hon, we're providing entertainment for the masses, on-screen and off."

That was the first time she bonked him with a pillow. "Really? This is how you're going to play this? Make a joke of it? How hurt are you? You look awful."

"Only my pride's hurt. Should've seen the boys last night, Jeannie, they jumped right in, no hesitation, started up that tower. Have to admit, Stuckerson did, too."

"I'm glad everybody surrounding you is so courageous; they've been raised right. But who are they going to save if you end up dead?"

"Manny Rodrogo?"

There came the second blow. "I mean it, better start thinking of the big picture, and you better have me on top— *'cretino.'*"

"I would love to have you 'on top.' And our Italian lessons are paying off, you remembered the word for 'bozo.'"

She tried to leave the room but he didn't let her, leapt at her as best he could—wincing as he did it—pulling her on top of him, both falling back onto the bed, sending the whole mattress sloshing like the Irish sea. At first, she protested, but quickly gave into him.

How could she not? She thought. They made love and Jim made her a fantastic breakfast-for-dinner. Eggs Benedict, with tomatoes, fresh-squeezed orange juice, then sent her off to her parents. He spent the rest of the day perusing cookbooks and drinking wine, nursing the aches, pains, thinking of how serious he knew his darling was.

CHAPTER 26: MONDAY

Lee-Willie and Gail-Lill spent most of their off-day vacuuming their residency, dusting, spackling the walls ('cause "What-A-Chump" hadn't gotten around to fixing the damn fissures), erecting a slapdash bookshelf of cinder blocks and boards in the living room, setting their black-and-white RCA television atop it since they'd blown out the one in the bedroom… and feeling like garbage about what had happened to Jim.

It was a welcomed fact that the crew had Mondays off. Typically, on their Mondays off, Kathy and Vicki volunteered together for the Parks & Recreation Department, where they went to various parks and forest preserves in the area and cleaned up. Usually they melded well with the rest of the volunteers, but after this morning's newspaper headlines, it was a different story. Their cohorts had read the paper and now everyone knew of the Moon Tower mishap. All day long the sarcastic snide flew.

One jamoke said, "Hey girls, how's it hanging? I mean… literally." He busted up, walking away with his trash bag and gloves, thinking he was quite clever.

Another Melvin said, "Got anymore projectionists swinging from a light-tower out your way? That place is gonna get ya sooner or later. Stay here: the woodchucks won't kill ya but it sure looks like your drive-in will."

The last straw came when the next chooch said, "Sure you chicks ain't special forces? You sure you ain't actually undercover commandos, moonlighting at the Winking Moon to quell the nuttiness, volunteering here to keep a low profile?"

Vicki threatened to do some ass-punting.

At the end of the afternoon when the group of volunteers was wrapping up for the day, a state trooper said to the girls, "Afternoon, ladies. I see your shirts read 'Monroe County Helping Hands: Chip-In with Your Chin-Up.' Maybe it should say 'Chip-In and *Get* Hung-Up'—like your projectionist."

"Not funny," Vicki said, and they both walked away, fed up.

They had Jeannie Monocco's number. Found themselves near a public payphone. Before they left in Kathy's Malibu, they called, wanted to see how she was holding up. They got Jim on the blower instead.

"Don't worry about me, I'm made of Teflon: nothing sticks," he said, breaking into a good-natured laugh. "Jeannie's not here, she went to her parents' to get a divorce from me and we're not even married."

Kathy and Vicki chided Jim for always "underplaying shit," asking him how he felt.

"Like shit," he answered. "How do you think I feel?"

They hung up.

Their program-leader gave them one more jab. "Hey, you two, I wasn't eavesdropping, but the next time you guys need a hero at The Winking Moon, try Batman."

The program-leader's name "Bartholomew." Vicki told Bartholomew to pack pinecones up his butt.

At the Varentez household (top floor of a rented Colonial-style house, next county over) the emotional weight of Jim's nearly grave accident weighed heavily on Emilio's mind. The cook had not slept since arriving home from the hospital early that morning. Good thing it was Monday. What he'd said to the Stuckersons in the wee hours, just before driving home was absolutely true: between the anxiety the drive-in gave him and trying to provide for his super-sized family, it was amazing he wasn't hanging himself from The Moon Tower.

He was dealing with them now: the "familia grande." Since he was "Papi Chef," he typically insisted on cooking for them. Today was no different. But all eight of the children (including two sets of twins) chose today to fight and yell, tearing the house apart over who-wanted-what to eat, impatiently anticipating the jaunt to the beach they were promised that afternoon.

Several times Emilio raised his voice to tell everyone to stop the nonsense. "All night long I deal with chaos," he said. "I don't need to have that in my own home. Where's Mama?"

He made pancakes. His middle children did not want pancakes. They screamed for the Quaker Oats cereal, *Quisp*, instead. "You know,

Papa, the one with the funny Martian on the box and the beanie on his head."

Emilio lost it. "No kids of mine are eating cereal for brunch. I'm a culinary specialist, damn it, I see enough junk food going into children's faces to fill a continent. You're getting wheat pancakes; you're getting them right now and I'm putting bananas on 'em! Try to stop me."

Emilio's wife and live-in mother-in-law were wanting Emilio to drive them to the mall so they could shop for shoes. Emilio could not believe it.

"What, another shopping spree? I've driven you two to the mall twice already this week."

"Suegra wants shoes, baby," said his wife, Marisol. "More of them, many more of them. And I want a new make-up kit."

"And who's going to pay for all this?" Emilio asked.

At once, everybody in the household shouted— "YOU ARE!"— pointing at him.

Emilio served his food. Scrambled a carton of eggs, hacked-up fruit like he blazing a path through the Amazon jungle with a machete, told his monsters to cease pulling the shower curtains down in the bathroom and to not slap any further Topp's "Wacky-Packages" decals on the furniture. "You've been collecting them all year. I've been peeling them off the walls and chairs for a year. Stop it!" He told them to sit down, shut-up, fill their pie-holes with his cuisine. "Eat and be quiet! I want you so filled with my food you'll sink to the bottom of the lake."

A bowl dropped and smashed on the rug, staining it with ketchup. Marisol reminded the children to be careful, that they all were merely tenants in the house. "The casa doesn't belong to us," she said. "We have to take care of it, our landlord lives below us." Naturally, the very landlord came knocking, wanted to know what all the noise was about. Emilio stepped and tried to explain. "Sorry, we're just on our way to the beach and the kids are excited."

It was hard to communicate as the youngest son was blasting the volume of the TV. The child had turned it up, recognizing the news story about a local projectionist having to be rescued the night before at a local drive-in. Marisol flew in, changed the channel before the landlord got involved.

"Madre De Dios," she said. "Let's not get into that while we have a guest."

As the kids ate breakfast, Marisol and mother-in-law were determined to find out more about the mishap at the movies. "Is that your novio, Emilio? Your 'Jimbo,' as you say? This happened last night?"

"Jimbo's fine, Marisol," Emilio answered. "No problemo, the story's just sensationalized by the media for ratings."

After the landlord was gone and they were collecting beach balls and towels, he told the kids to switch over to "Sesame Street" with the remaining minutes they had left. He did not want any more news. The oldest daughter took notice of the current commercial, advertising some type of home computer that was supposed to be the next best thing.

"Look, Papa," she said. "A frutas computer. What is it?"

"I've seen that," he answered, just glancing at it and dismissing it. "It's called an 'Apple Computer.' Something else that'll never get off the ground, just like the stupid idea of renting movies from a store and watching them at home."

Stanley had barricaded himself again in the basement. He'd done this three times prior in his life. He sat there for hours, feeling guilty and helpless about what had happened to Jim. His wife, Doris, had been knocking for the past five minutes, trying to coax him out. As always, she was upbeat, perky, inspiring. And, as always, she knew what had happened. "Stanley," she said, putting her sweet head to the door, "Jimmy-Wimmy told the crew he'd be fine. Stephanie called this morning; said she knew the story from some firemen who know both drive-in managers. It was all an honest mistake, you don't have to beat yourself up about it, you were just doing what you thought was right. He'll be back tomorrow, I called him."

From the depths, an irate voice shot back. "You 'called him'? Why the hell ya do that?"

"Because I care about Jim, too. We all do. It's no big deal, snookums. After you told me what happened and then I read the paper, it was all I could think of. Poor James."

"Well I still don't feel like comin' up."

"Why not, Stanley?"

"Doris, do I hafta answer every question? I'm staying down here 'til I'm good-and-ready to come up. Now go knit a sock or something."

"What are you doing down there?"

"Gathering my thoughts."

"Stanley, you've been gathering too much of your thoughts lately. Come up and spend the afternoon with me. I'll cheer you up, I'll put on some music… we can dance…""Dance'? No way."

"The boys at the Winking Moon told me they like to dance. *We* should, Stanley."

"Only that overgrown baboon Jocavelli dances. He thinks he can woo girls with it."

"I bet it works. We were young once, too."

"And speakin' of that kid, he damn-well better stay away from out grandniece. I heard he's talked to Stephanie a couple of times already."

"So?"

"So, he's a caveman. They all are. Damn kids, full of hormones and stupidity."

"Oh, for Heaven's sake, Stanley, let them be teenagers. We should take lessons from them. Come on, dance with me."

"I'm not even gonna grace that ridiculous statement with a response."

"Stanley, get up here. I'll make you your favorite sandwich."

"No."

"When *are* you coming up?"

"I told you when I feel like it. I deserve to be in darkness, sittin' on the washing machine."

"Get off that, you'll dimple it with your weight," she said.

"Haven't you already done that with your girdle and undergarments you lay on it?"

"Stanley, be nice."

"I'm tellin' ya, Doris, coulda sworn Lee was shoutin' to turn that power back on."

"Stop rehashing the accident last night, Stanley, you'll only drive yourself mad. And our Jimmy's okay. He was not injured badly. I'm going to put on 'The Blue Danube' waltz from your favorite movie, '2001: A Space Odyssey,' and you can waltz with me to it."

"I can also shoot myself in the head," Stanley said, "but I'm not doing that, either."

Doris got fed up. "Suit yourself," she said. "I'm going to the store to do shopping."

"Go ahead."

Instead of leaving the house, Doris tricked him. She put on the soundtrack from the film on the hi-fi system they had in the living room, turned the volume up, and the famous strains of Johann Strauss's classical waltz began to fill the house. She pretended to leave, jangling her keys, opened and closed the front door, and waited. Stanley called out, thinking his spouse had pulled a fast one.

"Doris?" he shouted. "Did you leave? Woman, ya left the music on, ya crazy ninny! Ya trying to make me come up? Well it ain't gonna work!"

But it did. He ascended the staircase after several minutes, slowly emerging from the self-induced exile, peeking around the corner to see if the coast was clear. Doris jumped out at him, having been hiding in the pantry, scared the bejeezus out of the grouch, sweeping him up in her arms, forcing him to waltz with her, around-and-around-and-around—in various rooms throughout the house. There was nothing he could do. He was her dancing captive.

"This ain't fair, Doris," he complained. "That was a dirty, rotten trick. Ya Shanghai-ed me."

"Oh, Stanley, just indulge me, ya lovable killjoy."

"We may not be Viennese royalty," he said, "but ya sure are Baroness Von Break-My-Balls."

Stanley was pretty good, actually. Graceful. But the scowl on his face still resembled a slow-moving mudslide.

Angela Carver got to enjoy her Monday evening off with a rare treat: dinner with both of her sons. Having both boys present over a home-cooked meal that all three prepared meant the world to her. Before sitting at the table, Angela made her sons promise not to have one cross word flung at each other during dinner. Between Alex's hammered nose and Jim Barenta's "hanging-story," she did not want the treasured affair to be tainted. For now, she'd agreed to let Alex keep his patrol-job. She asked when the last time was he'd changed his bandage.

"This morning," Alex answered.

"Do it again," she said. "Before we eat, it's grotesque."

When that was taken care of, and all three sat down like civilized folks—Randy, taking the chair across from Alex—asked his younger brother to pass the potatoes. "Please," he added. "And don't leave me hangin' like ya did Jim."

The fork dropped in Angela's plate. "You're eating in the garage if you start."

Randy laughed. Alex said Jim would be fine. He was one tough son-of-a-bitch.

"Language…" Mom said.

As they dug into their chicken casserole and delicious sides, the front doorbell rang. It was Vicki Richards, in need of company, not wanting to intrude on the trio but finding herself unexpectedly solo for the evening. "Y'know, after last night," she said, remaining on the doorstep until invited in, "I just don't feel like being alone. My family's at my siblings' soccer tournament—that's gonna last a long time—and with Kathy and I listening to smart-ass comments all day at the parks, I need to be around sane people. Hope ya don't mind."

Angela loved Vicki and her son's friends. As long as they didn't dwell on drive-in talk all dinner and weren't bringing up the horrible accident that'd happened last night, she was okay with it.

"Sure, no problem," Vicki said.

"Then I'll get a plate for you, dear. Come on in, you're always welcome, honey. You're like a daughter to me. How long we've known each other?"

"Since I was in third grade, Mrs. Carver: spot-high to a ladybug."

"My how time flies."

Vicki said hello to Randy, Alex, who said hello back, both giving hugs. Randy cracked a dumb joke about "two peanuts walking down the street and one was a-salted," and asked why Vicki always had her father's truck.

"He lets me drive it," Vicki said. "It looks good to have something official in the parking lot at the drive-in."

"Yeah—paddy wagons," Randy quipped.

They talked about many things: her family, her family's business, how they had not gotten The Moon's account yet because Bluestone wasn't paying for anything, that's why Mr. and Mrs. Stuckerson had to do all the work.

Randy said, "With that kinda damage being done to the lawns night-after-night, I think Bluestone would be more than happy to pay for a good manicure. That playground area? Whew, looks like it hasn't been touched since the '50s."

"How do you know?" Alex asked him.

"I drive in on occasions, during the day. I look at the lay-out. Just wanna see what you kids deal with and you're dealing with a lot."

"It's a work-in-progress," said Alex.

"Probably not," said Vicki, eating fast herself. "More likely it's on its way out and Bluestone just doesn't care anymore."

"What?" said Mrs. Carver, pausing. "Do you know something we don't? I read the papers and know about that retirement home behind the drive-in, but is it the same thing on the other end, the drive-in's end?"

"No, Mrs. Carver, just speculation," said Vicki, Alex giving her a *Be-Careful-What-You-Say* look. "You just start putting two-and-two together, the joint's getting crazier..."

"Better the reason Alex is gonna come work for me," said Randy.

Vicki looked at her chum. "You are?"

"No," Alex said. "I'm not."

But they had opened the topic. Angela said, "That would make my year if 'the joint'—as you kids call it—came down. Now I know I'm not popular saying it, but I just don't care anymore. I mean, look at my son."

"I see him," said Vicki, then, knowing Alex wanted to change the subject, said, "I see Johnny-Boy, too."

Alex furrowed his brow. "Whattya mean?"

Vicki looked around, put her silverware down. "Um… this might be a little embarrassing, Alex… but… another reason I came here… Kathy and I talk all the time… and excuse me for bringing this up, Mr. Carver, Randy…"

"Just spit it out, girl," said Angela, "you have us in suspense."

Vicki was now staring at Alex. "Is John… interested in me?"

Alex almost spit out his green beans. "What?"

"You know… does he like me? As in, to date?"

Alex was embarrassed. "Vicki…" Vicki bit her lip. "Now I know this is sensitive subject, but what isn't these days? I've tried everything I could to get his interest. I think he's responding—slowly, to me. He doesn't say much."

"If John puts five words together in a sentence it's a miracle," Alex said.

Randy was holding back laughter. He was loving this. "Now her *real* motives come out," he said about their guest. "You sure your family's even at a soccer tournament tonight, Vick?"

"Randy…" said Mom.

Vicki nodded. "They are, I swear."

"Vicki—" Angela interjected, "do you want us to leave so you and Alex can have a private discussion?"

Alex was already shaking his head no before his mother had even completed the sentence. "No, Mom, that's alright."

"Yes—*please*—Mrs. Carver," said Vicki. "We're through here, right?"

"We're through eating," said Angela.

But Randy said, "I'm not."

Angela was already standing, clearing the table— "Yes you are, Randy, and you're cleaning up while I put the leftovers in containers. And don't use the dishwasher, I want to save on water. You two take showers like you're under Niagara Falls."

"Mom—" Alex said, trying to stop her, "we really don't need to do this. Vicki, I dunno John's feelings, there's nothing to discuss."

Wryly—and cleverly—Vicki said, "But I know about Kathy's feelings toward *you*."

That stopped him. Alex said, "Mom, you can take my plate, too—now."

They spent the after meal in front of the TV, getting into "The Love Boat." All four of them. They were full and the conversation had gotten heavy. Mrs. Carver, Randy and Alex were trying to concentrate. Vicki couldn't keep her yap shut, kept "speculating" about John, talking about his shyness, the fact the Crusaders had promised to take her out on patrol this year, the way she should approach things, should John show any interest in going out on an actual date. "I mean, we all work together," she said, interrupting the television dialogue. "Is it cool to date a co-worker?"

Growing tired of it, Randy said back, "Who knows, Vick? Ask Alex if he thinks it's cool trying to date Kathy. Speakin' of 'miracles,' it'd be a big one if that girl stooped that low."

Angela slapped the throw-pillow under her arm— "Is this how it's going to be all night?"

Alex stood up, sick of it all. "Vicki, wanna go for a drive?"

"Sure," she said, surprised.

Alex turned to his mother. "Mom, can I borrow the Chevette?"

"No bother," Vicki said. "Let's take my truck."

Vicki and Alex went for that ride, to Lake Ontario, in her dad's work-truck. At this hour, as they parked at the same beachfront as they had a few weeks back, but now it was loaded with summer-farers: much different from the mega-late hours they were used to. She had backed-in, like the big vehicles did at The Moon. They sat in the bed, wind blowing through their hair. Had a gorgeous sunset to watch and they enjoyed it. There were children down the embankment, running after seagulls along the shore, their parents keeping watch over them. The crowd was dense. What a different vibe it was from the other night.

Vicki spoke up as they were both lost, deep in thought. "Hope I didn't embarrass you too bad about Kathy."

Alex brushed it away. "That's alright. So, she does talk about me?"

"She does, quite a bit."

"Really?"

Vicki smiled. "Proceed slowly, Carver, she's more sensitive that you might think."

"I don't think anything. And John has talked about you."

"He HAS?!" She practically jumped on him, coming alive like a child on Christmas morning. "Tell me: what's he said?"

"That you're buggin' him to take her out on-patrol one night."

"You did it with Emilio last year."

"That was not sending him out on-patrol," he said. "That was sending him out to take the garbage out. We had him walk to the playground to see for himself how accurate the graffiti was of the penis drawn under the screen."

"You didn't let me see it." She sounded almost disappointed.

"Well, some things are better left… unseen."

She looked back out to the magnificent sky. "I really like your new house."

"Ya do?"

"Yeah, it's a lot better than your old one. I mean, who wants a pool in their backyard, basketball hoop in the driveway, two floors and a basement with how many bedrooms?"

"You're being sarcastic."

"That's my job. I can see why your mother wanted to downsize. I mean, who wants the memory of a husband who takes off on his family lingerin' around?" She caught herself, looked at him— "Sorry, didn't mean to bring that up. Ohmigod, sometimes I'm an ass."

"No, you think?" Alex said.

"Now *you're* being sarcastic."

"It's okay, Vicki, your heart's in the right place."

Her hair got tangled in her eyes. She moved it away. "It was good to see your family tonight."

"Thanks."

"You're really not working for Randy?"

"No."

"Your Mom looks great. She should start dating."

"Don't even say that."

"You have to take initiative where it's needed, right?"

"I guess."

"*You* take the initiative and get John to ask me out," Vicki said, as if a joke-command. "I'll see what I can do about Kathy. You've always been a good kid, Al, any girl would be lucky to have you."

"Thanks, Vick, you too."

"Any *girl* would be lucky to have me?"

"Any *guy*," he emphasized.

"We got each other's backs, don't we?" Vicki asked.

"We do," said Alex.

She turned and exposed a surprise-cooler that had been hidden under a throw-rug, got out two beers from it, gave one to Alex. He opened the bottle, opened hers, they clinked them, saluted, drank. "To friends, right Vick?" he said.

"To friends," she responded. Vicki looked down the bluff. A couple now was sitting on the same petrified log the gang had sat on. "Look at those chooches down there—same piece of driftwood we were sittin' on just the other night."

"Let's stake our claim, Vick, throw a rock at 'em."

She looked at her buddy, doubted his sanity. "You been workin' at The Winking Moon too long."

CHAPTER 27:

THE BIG MAN RETURNS

Jim returned the following night to chaos, in the midst of Lee-Willie ranting and raving about the Delta 88, having just found out about it. Big mouth Vicki had spilled the beans. She had heard from the boys who'd heard from Jody, at Lapping Waves, who'd seen the thing bombing down Sing Road in the direction of The Moon. Lee-Willie was nearly absurd in his anger, already having erupted at his wife.

"But Mr. Stuckerson," said Alex. "We only found out Sunday. We were closed yesterday."

"But you weren't gonna tell me, were ya?"

He had everyone lined up outside the concession stand, Emilio watching, Vicki watching (feeling awful), Kathy already in the booth on other side of the screen, getting set to open.

"I mean, what can we do about it, Mr. Stuckerson?" said Steve, posing the question.

"Pray it doesn't show up here," Lee-Willie answered. "We're all goin' to the hospital, it seems, that thing nearly did me in last year. I don't wanna end up there."

Stanley was in the back-storage room, not wanting to face his coworkers. He had been monkey-fiddling around with Franco's old tools since he got here, putting things away that did not need it, sweeping up where there was no dust. He was still feeling terrible about the incident with Jim and was reluctant about coming in at all.

There was supposed to be a substitute projectionist from the union coming but that did not happen. The big guy drove in right on time—Vicki, Emilio and the Crusaders surprised to see him, breaking off from their boss, running to him as he stepped out of his truck, surrounding him and hugging him (as he winced). The boys shook his hand, asked how he was doing. "I'll be doin' better once you monkeys back the hell off," Jim replied.

"Where's the fill-in projectionist?" George asked.

"I called the union, told 'em not to send him. I'm here."

Lee-Willed, irked his team abruptly left him, walked up. "Jim, you were supposed to stay home, too."

"Well, I didn't, Lee."

"You and Alex were *both* supposed to stay home. What is this, total disregard for my jurisdiction? See, Gail?"

"Lee," she told him. "Calm down."

The teenagers continued flooding Jim with concern. Was he hurt? How did he feel? What did Jeannie say when she found out?

"That," he stressed, "we won't get into. Get outta my way, I gotta get ready for operations. Where's Stanley?"

"In the back-storage room," the cook said. "Hasn't said a word to us nor has he come out of there since punching-in. I think he's beyond remorse for what he did to you, Jim."

Jim corrected. "He didn't 'do it' to me, Emilio, it was nothing he did on-purpose."

"Well he's back there now. He won't talk to us. Mrs. Stuckerson even asked him if he wanted to go home."

Jim considered the comment, smiled, patted Emilio on the shoulder. "Who would we pick on all night?" he said, going into the stand to see for himself. Entering the back storeroom, Jim saw the downtrodden man, dressed in his smock, hat, pushing the broom around aimlessly. "Stanley," he said. "What's up?"

The old man was startled. "Jim? I didn't expect to see you here."

"Well I'm here. What's goin' on? Got some new buttons?"

Stanley did not answer. He went back to his business, head down, was not even making eye contact with the big guy. Jim was going to give the crank the business. No use letting an opportunity go to waste. But before that could happen, there was an explosion of excitement outside. It was too early for the crowd yet, so they knew it wasn't that. Then, they heard the name, "Mrs. Mason!"

Doris was here. Disobeyed her husband's wishes, showed up anyhow even though he had told her not to, delighted the shit out of staff.

"Oh shit, your wife's here?" said Jim, breaking from Stanley. "I have to go see her; it's been a while. Who could be married to you, Stanley?"

They were surrounding her just as avidly as they had Jim, smothering her with affection and love. Even Gail-Lill was glad to see her. Practically everyone loved Doris Mason. Not Lee-Willie, not at this moment, at least. His angry words would not reach his intended audience.

A fresh batch of cookies had already been delivered to Kathy in the box office. Kathy was told not to say anything as Doris had driven into the lot in her mint, 1960 Morris Minor convertible that she rarely took out: same blue color as Jim's Fleetside. Now the rest of the clan was enjoying the charm of her hospitalities.

When Jim walked out the double-doors, he met eyes with the 67-year old saint—who lit up with great spirits. Doris handed the giant batch of cookies and brownies to Vicki. "Jimmy-Wimmy!" she exalted, and the two came together, embracing like son and grandmother. Doris was at the point of tears, seeing her young friend so soon after his accident. "I'm so glad you're not hurt," she said. "I heard what happened to you. I wanted to see you and the others so badly."

"Did Stanley send you here, darlin'?" Jim said.

"Ha! Are you joshing? He's forbidden me to me to even step foot on the grounds."

"Nice husband," Emilio said.

"Stanley!" she hollered. "I know you're in there! I'm here! I didn't do as you asked!"

Stanley did not move. He was bristling.

"How could I stay away from my favorite drive-in trouble-makers?" Doris said. "Stephanie's one, too, but she's at The Smirking Star."

"We know," said Vicki, nudging George.

They wanted her to stick around but she could not. She had to get back for her TV shows: "Hart to Hart" and "Dukes of Hazzard." Gail-Lill thanked her for stopping by, the first vehicles now beginning to trickle in. Time to get things moving. Squeezing his cheeks, asking about the hospital beds and patting his afro, Doris said to Jim, "You should wear a different denim vest, dear, this one's getting old. And you don't want to look old before your time." She was disturbed to the core over what had happened to him.

"Doris, my darlin', I am perfectly fine. Just bruises and contusions and pulled muscles. I'll be back on The Moon Tower in no time."

"You'd better not!" Lee-Willie squawked. "And the Crusaders here say they've seen the fucking Delta 88!"

"Lee!" snapped his wife. "Language!"

Jim looked puzzled, but he remembered. "*The* Delta 88? From last summer?"

"Yes," Lee-Willie said.

"Jody saw it, Jim," said John. "When she was workin' Sunday at

Lapping Waves. She says to be on the look-out for it."

Jim thought about it and filed it away. "Well grease my wheels and leave me plenty-o-rags, we don't want that beast in here, do we?"

"Hey, can I hang from that thing?" a jerk yelled, hanging out of a brown Mustang, his buddies driving, being the first one in the lot. He was laughing like an idiot and pointing to The Moon Tower. "I got my bungee cords and harness! I'm not an Army Ranger but I sure am a daredevil."

Lee-Willie shouted back, made his point. "Ya even think about it we'll toss ya like a spoiled salad."

Many vehicles were entering now. Even more than usual, including the redemption tickets holders and thrill-seekers. Kathy told her coworkers via the walkie, "They're all talking about you guys. Everyone's read the papers."

"Well," said Doris, "I just wanted to bring my brownies and cookies and see my favorite Winky-Dinkies!" Good-night, Stanley, see ya tonight, sweetheart, I'll have toast and marmalade waiting for you! You can go out after and enjoy your telescope!"

No answer.

When she drove away, she told her friends, "Welcome back to another year of lunacy."

Staff fondly waved to her, seeing her go.

"Now that…" said Jim when she was gone. "Is a wife."

"Hope to have that someday, Jim?" said Steve.

"Jeannie would make that perfect spouse," said Vicki.

"Shut-up," Jim said.

Then the walkie sparked again. "Mr. Stuckerson, Mrs. Stuckerson. News-crews are here."

Lee-Willie was almost choking on his combination of Snickers and Three Musketeers bars, laying into the two news vans that had pulled onto the property, parked along the shoulder of the road in the entrance. A couple of reporters and cameramen were interviewing patrons waiting in line to buy a ticket. They had been asking what drives a person to come to The Winking Moon. Was it the thrill of decadence? The possibility of something going wrong, which seemed to happen all the time? Was it the movies? "Well…" one jamoke in a van expressed, "yeah… the movies… I guess. I didn't think about that." Gail-Lill was there, too, but she was trying to pull him back. She thought her husband was going to rip their faces off.

"Oh, you're gonna show me your permits and identifications!" the manager was snarling. "And you're gonna show 'em to me right now or you're gettin' off my property! Ya can't just come in here any time you want, stirring up trouble, asking my customers questions like that! Who do ya think you are, David-Fucking-Brinkley?"

One of the polished reporters with the make-up on was pushing back. "Relax, mister, you're going a little overboard, don't you think? This place has major news-stories. The whole town's asking what's going on here."

"Well I'll tell you 'what's going-on', bub! You are! You're the ones stirrin' up trouble just being here! You can't roll in and start interviewing people, thinking this is a public park!"

The other producer thought otherwise. "Sir, we know you're the manager—"

"We're *both* managers," Gail-Lill inserted.

"We know you're *both* the managers, but we thought we'd catch a few words about what happened here Sunday night. Your projectionist hanging from The Moon Tower is mighty serious."

"We got him down!'" said Lee-Willie. "He's not injured!"

"You had an entire ladder and rescue department here. With all this drama playing out, which is more dramatic: the films you played or the antics going on behind-the-scenes every night?"

"Get off the property!"

Before the intruders drove off, some of the devilish patrons voiced their own opinions— "Let 'em stick around! We'll get 'em something to show on the news!"

"Yeah, do they wanna shoot a triple-X picture? We'll be their actors!"

The Stuckersons looked as ragged as chewed goat-slop. Did not look good for customers rumbling in.

"Hello, good evening," some would say, then, "Hey, what's wrong? You people work here? Ya dressin' up for your horror films? We didn't know this was a theme-party."

"Get that lip fixed, buddy. People see that: bye-bye to any concessions sales. What happened, the screen collapse on your face?"

It was raining now and coming down pretty hard, too, enough to make Alex—taking advantage of the old, Winking Moon marketing merchandise from years back—pull out a Moon-umbrella (logo included), stand in the back of the lot, hold it over his head to watch the latest of "The Hills Have Eyes."

In this particular scene, one of the hideous, bald mutants had broken into the trapped family's trailer when they weren't there, pulled out the pet bird from its birdcage, ripped its poor little head off, and tipped the torso back to drink the blood from it, as if downing a fine glass of wine. Alex listened to the audience reacting to it, especially the females (disgusted), wondering how his three comrades were also making out.

After the Stuckersons had come back over an hour ago from reaming he reporters—who did leave but vowed to return—the couple had ordered Steve, John, George and Alex to spread apart, keep away from one another during the movies, not make the managers look like "assholes in front of the audience-world."

So, they obeyed. There was not much going on, fortunately. Rain—especially heavy rain, like this—kept the joint mellow, which gave them plenty of time to visit Kathy.

Alex started for the booth when John contacted him on the radio. "Alex, come in."

"Yeah, go ahead, John." Damn, ruined his plans.

"Me, George and Steve are in the concession stand. C'mon in, Stuckersons said we didn't have to stand out in the rain. There's not much goin' on and there isn't as many customers in here. It's pretty slow. Stop gettin' soaked and come in and join us."

Alex felt pious. "Now, John, just because the weather isn't as nice as it has been, and just because people aren't out-and-about as much as they usually are—and just because this keeps the pricks and Melvins from screwin' around, tryin' to sneak-in—doesn't mean we shouldn't be ever-vigilant, omnipresent, keeping the paying audience safe, secure, free from worry."

There was a pause. "They also said there's a shitload of hotdogs in the freezer that're gonna go bad if we have 'em one more day. They said we could come in and eat 'em all."

"Be right there." Alex ran.

So as the fearsome four stuffed one hotdog after another in their mouths, offering one to Vicki, Emilio—who turned them down—they stared at the rain from the threshold of the double-doors, peering out into the subdued conditions. There were puddles building up right at their feet, right outside the step. George got a wise idea to jump in it be funny.

"Gimme that umbrella," he said, snatching it from Alex, opening it up, leaping into the air like flying squirrel, landing smack-dab with both boots in the water, sending a mountain of splash up in all directions, John, Steve and Alex jumping back.

"George don't do that!" said Alex. "Whattya, nuts?"

"Just passin' time," he said. "C'mon! Get in while the goings good."

Vicki and Emilio just watched as the patrolmen took turns doing the deed: grabbing the umbrella, leaping into the air, landing, sending the water displacing north, south, east and west, filling again in its vacuum. Emilio got a wild hair up his butt, ran at the bunch to join in as Stanley shouted for him to stop. "Your place is behind the counter, Varentez."

"Oh, stow it, Captain Kirk," countered the cook, grabbing the umbrella, taking the mightiest dive yet into the puddle. SPA-LASH! He landed in it just as a nice young couple was entering to buy snacks. The force of the water hitting them square in the face and chests soaked then from head-to-toe, making them appear like they had stepped out of the shower with their clothes on.

"Hey what the fuck, buddy?" growled the man. "Thanks a lot! Who do you think you are?"

Emilio was mortified, could not apologize enough. Crusaders—and Vicki—had to keep from dying of laughter, moseying-off to avoid scrutiny. Stanley stood his ground, by the register, shaking his head, judging Emilio as an idiot. The cook ended up giving the couple two free slices of pizza. Vicki told the couple not to even think about asking about the sauce. "It's all good, trust me—" she said. "I'm not sayin' anything bad—just enjoy it and move on."

There was not much to do during the rainstorm. Was getting worse by the minute but the show had to go on. Cars were leaving. This happened when it got bad. Even Jim came into the stand to get away from the dullness, ridding rain from his 'fro with the pick from the back pocket of his blue jeans. He had been thinking of a way to further bust Stanley's balls since he had the poor sap over the coals with the guilt that was eating him alive. "Jim," said Emilio. "The guy really feels awful. He stays at the register, goes into the back-storage room, comes out, goes in. He's driving us mad."

"I've never seen him like this," Vicki said. "You gonna forgive him?

"What's to forgive?" Jim responded. "I told everyone it was an accident."

"Go in there—please—fix it."

Jim obliged, strolling into the packed area, saw the senior turning over Franco's old stool at the workbench, checking for loose bolts, putzing around, doing a lot of nothing. Originally, the big guy wanted to lay it on, but seeing the man this way, he felt sorry for him. He walked over to him, loomed.

"What?" Stanley said, looking up, sad anticipation all over his face.

Jim grabbed his head—Stanley's eyes going wide—took off his fishing cap, kissed the guy on top of his bald noggin, put the hat back on his head, walked away. "There," he offered, not bothering to look back, "you can come out now. All forgiven and all forgotten."

Stanley waited until the man was completely gone. "Thanks, Jim," he said, and wiped his eyes. Tears came now, matching the rain outside the bunker windows.

Jim played a round of pinball. *Star Trek*. Did not tilt it once. He was pretty good, craved some pot. Said as much but nobody encouraged him. The Crusaders were still inside, had feasted on the hotdogs, now they were going after Emilio's pizza, trying to coax the ponytailed man into giving them a slice.

"Lay off, they're going to come in," the cook was saying. "I don't want them seeing me passing out freebies."

"Come on, Emilio," tried John. "You haven't given us any yet."

"It's only the first week," he shot back. "You'll get yours, be patient for God's sake. Where're the Stuckersons? I don't want them busting me."

"Still in the office," said George. "Probably doing this—" The big kid created a screwing motion with his hands: one finger going in-and-out of the "hole" of the other.

Vicki was appalled. "Gross! George!"

"What? We're all thinkin' it."

"No," said Vicki. "You're 'thinkin' it.' I'm not."

"George," said Jim, still at his game, "go out and do some good out there. *All* you soldiers go. No use hangin' around here, getting stupid."

"But Jim—" said George, "the Stuckersons said we could hang in here."

"And I'm telling ya to get out there and do something. Share the fuckin' umbrella."

They found raincoats, put them on over their smocks, ventured out into the lot to the sounds of yet another family member being slaughtered by a hideously-deformed monster, actually ran smack-dab into a young man, bundling their way, asking for help.

He and his girlfriend had fallen asleep in their Plymouth Cricket with the windows open. Now there was "Lake Ontario in our car," as the jamoke put it.

John and Steve hustled back to the stand, grabbed two rolls of paper toweling—Stanley protesting, "Hey, where ya going with that?"—as they ran back out, toweled off the dude's car, inside. Upholstery was soaked.

His girlfriend was pretty cute, stayed in the backseat while they dried the front for them. After they were done, the fox looked at them and said, "Thanks."

"You're welcome," said Steve, smiling. "We're here to please."

The boyfriend moved in, clearing the path, saying— "Okay, that's enough, thank-you—" worried the studs were getting a little flirty.

On the way back from throwing out the paper towels, John asked Steve, "How do ya fall asleep in a car with the windows open in a rainstorm?"

"Must be out after their bedtime, said Steve.

Alex and George were watching the movie in a corner, galvanized by how twisted it was. "Wes Craven sure knows how to disturb people," Alex said, marveling at the make-up and special effects.

"Yeah, this is nuts," George said, then their attention was captured by a carload of pretty ladies in a Dodge Colt, calling for them.

They went to the rescue. The chicks had turned the key in the ignition the wrong way, completely draining the battery. "My brother told me to do this," the driver said, blaming her sibling who was not there.

"Yeah, you did it the wrong way," said George. "Should've turned it back toward ya. Didn't you see the dashboard lighting up?"

"No, whattya think I am, a car-expert?" The girls were obviously interested in teasing the boys. Three in all. "Wanna smoke?"

"No thanks," George said, smirking at Alex, also finding it amusing. They lit up doobies right in front of them, all took drags, blew out the smoke, giggled wackily.

"Can we give you our numbers?" one of them said in the back.

"Maybe not right now," said George. "They'd get all wet."

"Wimps…" the third joked.

Then, seeing Alex's radio in his holster, the driver reached out, grabbed it quickly, held it to her mouth, pressing the button. "Breaker-breaker! We got two, cute-but-dumb fellas out here, *not* wanting our numbers. They wimped out on us, they must be gay or something."

"Gimme that back—" Alex said, swiping it away.

Within seconds, Lee-Willie came on— "Who said that? What's goin' on? Crusaders, you outside? Ya better be! Can't stay in the stand all night!"

"Sir, we're out here," explained George. "Just some nice patrons, being silly."

The driver next reached out, grabbed George's package between his legs. "Whoa!" he yelped into the radio, backed-off, the girls busting-up big-time, smoking more dope, really wanting to party. Alex and George had to go back about their business. A pickup truck with two rummies in it next to them had been watching what was going on.

"We got it!' they said, started up their engine, maneuvered the truck closer, had the girls pop the trunk, jumped the battery, got the party started with them. Clouds of weed filled up all over the area. "You children can go now," the one wise ass said. "The men got this covered." Alex and George did not even bother responding. Was too loud and too rainy out here.

"That's the first time I've turned down a chick's number," George told Alex as they walked away.

Alex laughed. "Could Stephanie Mason have anything to do with it? That's playing with fire."

Back in the stand once more, George had fashioned a sled out of an old cardboard box he'd found in the back-storage room. "We're goin' surfin'," he told Alex, Steve and John, walking into the picture, seeing what was up. "Didya see the water rushin' down the entrance? C'mon, while the storm's *really* royal."

"The Stuckersons are in their office," said John.

"That's *really* playing with fire," said Alex.

George was grinning. "And which one of us is frightened by that?"

The four ambled to the entrance, via the exit. Kathy was still in the booth, painting away, not minding the weather one bit. She had been making excellent progress on her latest masterwork. When she saw them there, she stuck her head out the window. "What are you kids doing?"

George was holding up the sled. "Using this as a surfboard! We're gonna ride the waves, Beach Boys-style!"

All parties had to literally yell over the punishing rain shower now. It was coming down so loud it pummeled the pavement, creating a river of fast-moving water down the entrance to Sing Road. The neon lights, colors, of the Man-In-The-Moon reflected deeply in the drenched surfaces.

"You're crazy!" she yelled. "You kids can't do that!"

"Watch me!" George did the test run. Ran with the box in the direction of Sing, got a good running start, threw the flattened cardboard down in front of him, jumped onboard--belly-first—went for a sluicing ride halfway down. Ran out of steam on the thing, slid to a slowing float, fell off laughing, stood up, held his arms in the air in victory, jogged back up, wanting to go again.

"Lemme try it." Steve gave it a go next, attempting for a surf. Went further than George did, gave it a longer running start.

John was the next fool. He went almost all the way down to Sing Road, stopping only when a car drove by, putting on the brakes himself and toppling off to avoid sliding in front of it. He shoulder-rolled over-and-over, sopped to the bone. The guys had never seen John laugh so hard.

"Get outta my way!" Alex said next, sprinted all the way down to the road to snatch the box from John, running back up the entrance, running back down, jumping hard—enough to take the air out of his lungs—going for just as long of a ride. The water was building up so much at the mouth it was starting to impede.

Kathy was crying she was laughing so hard, losing her mind at the gang's silliness. No way she could concentrate on her art anymore. When Alex dared her to try it, she did not hesitate. She ran from the booth, no raincoat, grabbed the now-mangled box before he could offer it, shouted—"I'm lighter than you Melvins and probably more-freaking fast so I'll probably go further than you idiots!"—and got set.

"Promises, promises!" Alex yelled, and they all stood back, George, Steve and John not believing their eyes.

Kathy did go, not caring about her make-up and hair getting ruined, her clothes soaked to the bone (and clinging!), and went sailing—almost literally—all the way down the access, across Sing Road, and off the other side where the cornfield was, disappearing down behind the knoll.

The boys were alarmed. They watched in the distance for her to get up. After 30 seconds they hightailed it down the entrance, boots slapping in the patter, to rescue her. There was no one on Sing so it was easy to cross. All their flashlights came out, lit up Kathy up in the muck and darkness, lying at the bottom of the embankment at the edge of the cornfields, face-up to the heavens, laughing like she had never laughed before. They could not believe it. Kathy Berenger, Goddess of Galileo: losing it like a madman. Alex almost said as much.

They salvaged her from the muddy escapade, assisted in walking her back up to the drive-in, all sopped to the marrow, screaming into the deluge with rapture, as Lee-Willie practically kicked open the office door.

He locked eyes with them, Gail-Lill visible behind him, adjusting her blouse, Lee-Willie with his glasses off, shirt un-tucked.

"What the hell do all of you think you're doing?!" he roared.

Kathy, not thinking, high on laughter, blurted— "Having more fun that you two are in the office, that's for sure!" The Crusaders looked at her. She caught herself! *Oh shit! Did I say that?* "Ohmigod!" she said to the bosses. "I didn't mean that, Mr. and Mrs. Stuckerson, we were having some fun out there, there's nobody coming in any way!"

The Stuckersons were glaring, frowns pulling the corners of their mouths down like magnets. Gail-Lill brushed the hair out of her eyes, rubbed the rosiness off from her facial cheeks. As they got closer, Lee-Willie was not going to let them off the hook. "Crusaders, get back in there and get to work!" He was saying it with sweeping gestures with his arms. "I don't care if it is raining—do something fucking constructive!"

Kathy hurried back to the booth, shut the door quickly.

"Kathy, do you want a towel?" Mrs. Stuckerson asked.

"Yes! Please!" she requested, feeling mortified. "And hurry!"

Lee-Willie pounded through the rain into the stand, hoping to rip the Crusaders' heads off. What he got instead was Vicki waving him down in the center of the room, arms up in a back-and-forth motion, warning him to keep his temper down, do not swear, don't say anything stupid. The Crusaders had slipped out, anyway. There was another set of double-doors on the southside, after all. *What?* his expression read. "Mr. Stuckerson— she said, voice lilting with ultra-professionalism, "these nice people came in to talk to you—personally."

"What?" He turned.

Nearing was a nice-looking young couple: a man and a woman. Customers, from the lot. They had been waiting by the arcade games and were now approaching with the introduction, shaking off their own umbrella, folding it, extending hands to shake, congenial smiles gracing their flushed faces. "Mr. Stuckerson?" the twenty-something gentleman said. "You're the manager, right?"

"Right," Lee-Willie said.

"*Co*-manager," Vicki exacted.

Lee-Willie shot her a look. *Really?*

"We wanted to come in and personally thank-you for a wonderful evening."

The dweeb's eyes shot around. "Huh?"

"Mr. Stuckerson…" said Vicki, "as I've said: there're plenty of patrons who come here to be civil and just enjoy the show. This is 'Thomas' and 'Veronica.' They drive an Oldsmobile Toronado, they've been out there all night. They're very happy with the way things have been going tonight, they're really glad you're still playing the movies through the storm, and they wanted to personally meet you. Should I call Mrs. Stuckerson?"

"No," said Lee-Willie, wanting to absorb the credit. "Don't bother."

"Mr. Stuckerson," the man with the thick sideburns continued, "it's all true what your employee says: my wife and I want to thank-you for a most memorable evening."

Lee-Willie darted his eyes around again. "Is this a joke? Emilio? Stanley? These your friends? Did you put them up to this?"

Stanley was annoyed, at the register. "No, Lee, I wouldn't do that."

"Neither would I," said Emilio. But they were all watching. "This is legit, enjoy while you can."

"We've been coming to drive-ins for a long time. We *love* horror films. We love storms and being up late at night. Just something we like, romantically. This has been fantastic. We wanted to talk to you before the second show, also wanted to let you know we know about the troubles and strife you people are going through here, just wanted to show support, let you know not everybody wants to kick the snot out of The Winking Moon, leaving you workers face-down in the dust."

That set Lee-Willie back, as it did the others. "Uh… thank you," he said. "I hadn't heard it put quite that way…"

"We thought you just might like to hear it," said the woman. "We're completely serious. We just wanted to offer our 'thank-you,' let you know we think The Winking Moon is great."

Lee-Willie stared at them for a moment. Then, he had a thought, trying to see the clock on the wall. "Um... how much time before the second show?"

"Fifteen minutes," Emilio said, as intrigued as his coworkers.

"Do you think you could come with me for a minute?" Lee-Willie asked them. "Come into the office, let my wife hear this so we can write it down?"

"'Write it down'?" the man said.

"A testimonial. A good one. Usually we get nothing but complaints, so having what you're telling me in quotes could help our cause."

"What's your cause?"

Lee-Willie did not want to say, "*keeping the joint open*," but that's what he meant. "It just would help us out. Our bosses would love to hear this. We work so hard."

The couple looked at each other, did not mind. "Sure, we'll do it," the man said.

"Where do we have to go?" said the woman.

"The office. It's in the screen."

"Cool, we'd love to see it."

"It's not that glamorous, trust me."

They slogged through the rain, Lee-Willie with the raincoat pulled over his head, them with the umbrella, knocked on the door before they entered.

Gail-Lill opened, looking confused, and Lee-Willie enlightened, asked if they could come in and if she could dictate. "Ya know, like you do the poetry. You're such a good writer and note-taker. This would be good."

"Oh, you write poetry?" the woman said.

"Yes," said Gail-Lill, "I—"

Lee-Willie cut her off— "Please, come in and sit down."

They sat at the same desk Steve and Jody had recorded the outgoing message on the answering service. Spaces had to be cleared, the mess at least situated. Lee-Willie had Gail drag over the extra folding chairs, set them up. Their youngsters took their seats.

"Now," said Lee-Willie, "could you repeat what you told me in the stand?"

The couple were yielding, though feeling self-conscious "Um… sure," he said. "We're… having a great time… we love The Winking Moon and its movies."

Lee-Willie was avid, at the edge of his seat. "Go ahead, go ahead. Gail, you gettin' this? You writin' it down?"

"Yes Lee, I can walk and chew gum at the same time," she answered. "Go ahead, sorry for the interruption."

And so, it went. The Stuckersons got their testimonial: a kind and atypical testimonial. Charitable and favoring words they could use in print. Gail-Lill did a competent job. Got it all on paper—in her notepad, naturally—in ink, nicely printed. They would type it up later. Not as gentle as he was before, Lee-Willie thanked the couple for their time, heard the announcement that the second film was about to play, hustled them back through the parking lot to their Toronado, forcing Vicki to come into the shower, giving the couple free popcorn and sodas. When she and her boss were out of sight of the husband and wife, Mr. Stuckerson leapt in the air, a triumphant win— "Hell, yes! This'll be great PR."

"'Public rant'?" Vicki questioned.

"'Public *relations*,' smart-ass."

Once more hassling Gail-Lill, Lee-Willie re-explained just what he planned on doing with the memo. "You type this up, we make copies of it, include the date, their names—they gave us permission—we'll have it fucking notarized if we have to. It'll be super-official. We'll give it to blowhard Bannabock the next time we see him. I know they're messin' with us, Gail, Bluestone's gettin' ready to drop the hammer on us somehow, I feel it in my bones. This'll be a weapon to use against their tyranny."

"What, one letter?"

"It's a start. A way to start buildin' the political clout to keep the joint open, just in case."

The door blew open from the force of the storm beating against it, rain and wind sweeping stacks of important documents and papers right off the desk. It was a scramble to save everything.

As if on cue, the door blew open from the force of the storm, wind and rain sweeping in, clearing off the desk and just about everything that was not weighted down. It was a mad scramble to get everything back in order.

Jim knew something was wrong the instant he heard the sputtering. The girls in the film had just gotten to the old house where Leatherface lived. They were about to start meeting their demise, too. There just was not enough carnage in these two gems, he was thinking. He got up from his *Popular Mechanics* magazine, waited for the vehicle to start honking, opened his door and looked outside for signs of upheaval. He was fearful the sound would cut out altogether. It had happened before, was clear on his mind. If it occurred again, the paying crowd was not going to be happy.

And sure, as shit: "Hey, what's going?!" someone hollered. "Sound!"

Jim prepared for action. Grabbed his kit, flashlight, donned his own raincoat—camouflage-style—called for the Crusaders to try to find the source, and went on a hunt for its source. His body was still aching and panging, but he ignored it: this was just too crucial. He did not like the notions of so many technical things going wrong at the drive-in already. That did not portend well for the season. They used their flashlights to see where water was rushing in, and Lee-Willie and Gail-Lill were coming out of the office themselves, asking what was wrong.

The storm had opened the dam to a problem Jim had been warning Bluestone about for years. As a result of the corporation failing to act accordingly, upkeep the maintenance on the joint throughout the off-season, they were now seeing that problem rearing its jeopardizing head. The venue's sound system—interconnected by a network of underground cables—had begun shorting. The fissures in the pavement, creating by years of blistering heat, freezing ice, and the weight of punishing snowfall in the off-season, had allowed the water to flood in, dousing the wires, also showing their age.

The seven found the source of the trouble: a very large, caved-in "puncture" at an empty speaker-pole in the southeast corner, near the orchard, looking more like a tide pool than a parking spot. Jim had everyone train their flashlights at it, got down on his hands and knees, fished around in the water for its origin.

"Jim!" Alex said. "Aren't ya gonna get electrocuted?"

"No! It's low voltage! I'm not touching a hot lead!"

Already soaked to the gills, the boys helped remove water with their hands, spreading the tools out, John getting the electrical tape out of Jim's satchel. The Stuckersons were still trying to find them— "Jim! That's a short, right?! Jim! We can't have a short!"

"I wish that guy would shut-up!"

"For God's sake, don't climb The Moon Tower!"

"Lee! The Moon Tower's got nothin' to do with this!"

Steve told them where they were.

"We're coming!"

"Tell them they don't have to!" Jim ordered, but it did not matter—they showed up, umbrellas and raincoats in their grip, not believing the luck of the night.

"This is unbelievable!" Lee-Willie was yelling. "We have all this shit goin' wrong already, and now this!"

Gail-Lill was next. "Jim! How you feeling?! You shouldn't be doing this if you're injured!"

"Gail, I'm alright—now the two of you back off! George! John! Hold the umbrella closer! Lee, ya gotta gimme room here, don't crowd around me! I'll get this patched-up, we can't have the whole system going down!"

Rain battered their faces, sheets of rain sweeping the lot. This was a real bitch getting to the bottom of things—literally. The Crusaders and the projectionist worked in accord, pulling as much of the damaged cable out as they could, going at it with the tape, needle-nose pliers, flashlights.

"What's going on?!" a random jamoke said, having snuck up on them out of the dark.

"Sir stand back!" said George. "Please!"

"Knew this was gonna happen…" Jim was muttering, trying to keep his eyes clear. "Cheap-ass Bluestone, cable fried from all this wear-and-tear, not puttin' in a new system…"

Lee-Willie pushed past Alex, almost knocking the flashlights out of Steve and George's hands, extracting his mega-implement, shining it down, directly in the big guy's eyes.

"Lee, you're blinding me!"

Jim was growing angry, trying to mend the threadbare cable, already with loose wires sticking out of it, ancient tape flapping off.

"Don't get electrocuted again!"

"Thank-you, Gail!"

Crusaders could see more occupants looking. "We got gawkers," Alex said.

But Jim was a pro, cutting with an X-Acto knife blade, twisting, turning, clipping with the pliers, John handing him strips. "Once you've taken the bras off a dozen ladies in the dark, you'll never forget! Some of these cables are taut as hell! And brittle! If I stretch it any further, it's gonna snap—and then we'd be in a world of shit! All sound: Bye-bye! All of it!"

Lee-Willie could feel the fear creeping up his spine, did not like his security force all lumped together when there was a crowd to keep back. "Damn it, patrolmen! Keep these people away!"

"Lee, I need 'em here!"

"Laneske! Can't ya get around the other side of him?! Carver! You're blockin' the light! Step-up or step-out!"

Jim strained against the raindrops making his eyes blink a hundred times a second. "Lee, haven't ya gotten through to Bannabock at all?!"

"No! Gail and I both have been trying! They're nestled in that fancy office on the east side, chokin' their chickens! Jocavelli, you're pretty good at moving your hips, see if you can move this fuckin' crowd back! This is what you oafs shoulda been doin' earlier instead of joyriding on that stupid cardboard—"

"Lee, shut-up!" Jim bellowed. "I can't fuckin' concentrate with you flappin' your jaws all the time! Just shut the fuck up!"

Jim had never yelled at Lee-Willie like that. It threw them all off, including the Crusaders. They kept working but it had killed the spirit. Lee-Willie became sullen, embarrassed, a pupil scolded by teacher. Miraculously, 'Ole Jimbo got the snafu fixed. The sound returned, completely. Full screaming, full hacking-and-slashing. They could hear the cheers around them, even from inside the vehicles: "It's about time!" "Way to go, morons!" "Did you guys just learn your jobs?!"

"Yeah!" shouted out into the darkness. "Wouldn't want ya to miss the meaningful dialogue!"

As the precipitation continued its punishment, Jim stood, Crusaders catching their boss's face. Lee-Willie looked drained, dejected. Jim said, "This'll come back, guaranteed. Let's get outta here. Insurrection averted."

They all ran for cover in the stand. Except Lee-Willie and Gail-Lill. They had not said a word, shoulders drooped, staring at the whole where the cable had sunk back into its watery depths. The clods around them returned to their cars.

The night drew to a close on a surreal note. The storm had ended, and the sky was clearing, stars coming out, twinkling brightly, and Lee-Willie and Jim motored back in from the drop at the bank, not having said much on the run. They had dodged a bullet with the cable-short, knew that. And the news of the happy couple earlier in the evening giving a dazzling testimonial had brightened the spirits of the crew. Except the Stuckersons. They had almost forgotten about it already. Or at least temporarily. The words Jim had creamed Lee-Willie with still stung. Jim knew it, just did not want to give into it so soon after he'd let Stanley off the hook. *These people have to toughen up,* he thought, keeping the opinion to himself.

What a return for Jim. He was sore and hurting but he had to take a stand. He had to keep up appearances. Alex, on the other hand, had to change his nose-bandage completely. It had been destroyed in the storm, revealing a hideous bruising under his eyes. "You should be up on the screen with the rest of the mutants," the Crusaders joked.

He had been in the men's room for the last fifteen minutes. Kathy waited for him anxiously, taking in the parting clouds above, seeing them as spiritual signs from God, giving her hints that they should all keep fighting for what they believed in.

While folks were busy with the grand send-off to the remaining outflow of traffic, Vicki had organized friends from school who were in the choir to hang back and do their part in entertaining the audience as they drove out. There was four in, all males. And that was because they sang Barbershop Quartet-style, waving goodbye to all the good people at the picket fence by the manager's office.

"Glee Club," said Vicki to Mrs. Stuckerson, not sure what they were thinking about it.

The teenagers had been drinking beer all night and eating tons of junk food. Currently, they were performing *Sweet Adeline*, and were quite good. Gail-Lill spoke low so the quartet could not hear. "Vicki, one of them didn't look so good at the start of the encore-movie."

"I used to perform with 'em at school, Mrs. Stuckerson, don't worry," the girl replied. "They promised to make it to The Winking Moon and they did, already, so early in the season. Guess they picked quite a night, huh?"

"They're good. A little weird—and I smell a lot of booze—but good. I'll take it after tonight. What else could happen?"

So with their arms around each other in traditional performance-bluster, the quartet crescendo-ed the famous finale, swaying with their arms around each other, twiddling their fake handlebar mustaches, each note harmonious to perfection— "Sweet Ad-el-linnnnne!" A smattering of applause went up from the last van out. Suddenly, the singer not feeling good, doubled over, upchucking all over the lawn. So disgusting, no one could watch.

Stanley laughed at his coworkers as he motored out, the first to leave. “G’night, suckers. I think those were the corndogs.”

CHAPTER 28:

THE MASKED MOONER

Lee-Willie went for a stroll by himself when everyone was gone. His lip was killing him, and he had a headache. He was rethinking his life, shoving wads of Bazooka Joe bubblegum into his mouth, cheeks puffed-out like a blowfish. The night's air was sultry from the storm's aftermath, it felt like a giant washcloth was draped over the land. As he walked around the screen to where the box office was, he looked up and noticed the Winking Moon sign was still on.

"Gail? Can you turn off the sign, please?" he called out.

No answer. She was in the office herself, running cold water on her face from the stress of the recent events. The sink was filling up and she was growing annoyed.

He walked up to the screen and stared at the sign from underneath. From down here, he could hear the crackling of the neon gas running through the glass. He turned around and rested his back against it, again slipping into deep thought, wondering how they were ever going to survive the summer.

"Lee, you out here?" Gail-Lill shouted, finally coming out.

"I'm right here, Gail, you don't have to yell," Lee-Willie responded.

"Could you come in here, please? I need your help unclogging this sink."

"Alright," he said. "Gimme a minute."

"No, now, please. I want it addressed immediately."

Lee-Willie quietly got annoyed himself, pushed off against the screen, spit the gigantic wad of gum out of his mouth, kicking it with his foot, inadvertently sending it straight up. He did not see as he walked away, but the gob stuck instantly to the bottom of the neon tubing, the surface being so hot.

Wednesday afternoon, Lee-Willie decided to take matters into his own hands and do something with that testimonial from "Mr. and Mrs. Thomas and Veronica of the Toronado." He just could not wait. He got gussied up, had Gail-Lill do the same, practically threw her into the Lincoln—taking two typed copies of the statements—and motored across town to the "fancy-schmancy" Bluestone office on the east side of town.

When they got there forty minutes later, Lee-Willie sped into the lot like Steve in his Charger, plowing to a stop so violently in a lot half-flooded from the rainstorms last night, he hydro-planed a few feet, sending a tsunami of water up and over an entire row of flowering hedges demarcating the property, destroying them. The only problem was he did not leave room for them to step out. They both plunged ankle-deep into the water, pissing them off. Gail-Lill swore for the first time in a while, telling her husband he was acting as crazy as the Wild Man of Borneo.

"Don't tell me who I'm acting like," he snarled. "I'm tryin' to assure a better life for us. Who cares what I do to get us there?"

'Ole Stuck was in a frenzy, balled the directions to the joint into a ball, whipped them in the bushes. "That's littering!" said Gail-Lill.

"Let's go," he responded, ignoring her.

They had arrived just in time. Closest to the side entrance, in his reserved spot, Kurt Bannabock was stepping out of his Caddy (in far-better shape than the Stuckersons). He had had the sense to park against the building, where there were no lakes. He was immaculately groomed, with crystal-blue peepers, salt-and-pepper hair and bleached teeth. Kurt was already looking at them, wondering who the morons were who drove their car into a swamp, and recognized the couple as they approached, ties and business blouses swaying from the force of their huff. "What the heck? Lee? Gail?"

They knew who the pin-striped, three-piece King Shit was that stood frozen on the other side of the lot. Gail-Lill was behind her husband, trying to keep up. "Kurt Bannabock: we need to talk to you," the dweeb said, looking like death, despite being clad in business attire.

"What's wrong?" Kurt said. "What are you two doing?"

They came right up to him, nearly bumped face-to-face, chest-to-chest. Kurt had to step back a bit to get to a more comfortable distance. "Mr. Bannabock, we want to talk to you," said Gail-Lill, jowls a-flapping, out of breath from just the short distance.

"I… see that from your husband. Lee, could you step back, please?" Lee-Willie gave him two steps. The executive now had a great view of the state of his employee's face. "Holy God in Heaven, what happened to your lip?"

"Nothing," noted Lee-Willie. "Just walked into a door."

"Mighty violent door."

"They swing that way."

"Did you see a doctor? Gail, did you take your husband to a doctor?"

"Kurt, can we just go inside?" said Lee-Willie.

"What's going on?" he asked.

"Gail and I need to talk to you; you haven't returned any of our phone calls."

"I've… been busy."

"For weeks? This is damn serious—we don't know what the hell you've been up to."

"What *I've* been up to? What do you mean?"

"Can we go *inside*?"

"Were you at The Winking Moon not long ago? Did you tell a couple of my patrolmen they couldn't do something in the parking lot?"

"Yeah: throw a kid over the fence," Kurt answered, now a little perturbed.

"Why didn't ya come see us?"

"As I've said, Lee: I'm a busy man. I was just stopping through that night." Lee-Willie looked at his wife. *See? They're screwing with us,* turned back to the top dog. "We've had one meeting after the next, I fly to California twice a month. We have a lot of business around the states."

"We know that, we just wanna talk."

"We came all the way over to see you," said Gail-Lill.

"We have somethin' to show ya."

Kurt stared at them. They stared back. "Well…" he said, "you can't just come rushing over like this—especially the way you're driving—expecting me to take a get-together at the drop of a hat."

"It's very important to us, Mr. Bannabock," Gail-Lill said.

Kurt nodded. "Gail… I neglected to say it's nice to see you."

"And you, Mr. Bannabock," Gail-Lill replied, much warmer than her husband.

"I have meetings," he said.

"So, do we," responded Lee-Willie. "The Winking Moon *is* your business."

Bannabock considered the conundrum, knew they were right, scanned the lot for signs of other life, checked his watch, looked at his visitors again—still unable to get over Lee-Willie's horror film-like, purpled lip. "Must've been a hell of a door," he said.

"Kurt," said Gail-Lill. "Please."

As folks walked in and out of the impressive office building, The Stuckersons looked around, intimidated by the briefcases, attaché cases and power-purses. They felt out-of-place but did not say a word. In turn they were scanned, briefly. Were they being judged? People greeted all three in the parking lot and went about their business. Kurt got out his keys. "This is a bit unorthodox, this approach—wouldn't you say, my friends?"

Lee-Willie stood his ground. "All this could've been avoided if you'd just returned the phone calls you kept ignoring. We left messages."

Bannabock kicked a few loose twigs and leaves aside at their feet, leftover from the storm, unlocked the entrance after it had shut, held the door and ushered-in the two gripers, eyeballing him as they passed. He followed in behind to the opulent antechamber, sunlight breaking through a massive skylight in the atrium, raking the walls of glass and chrome with glistening brightness, amazing artwork hanging with the finest interior-design tastes. Fountains gurgled water, rising from Terrazzo floors, fat goldfish swimming in them. There was Muzak playing but the Stuckersons could not tell what was playing. *Have You Ever Been Mellow?* By Olivia-Newton John, maybe. There were massive directories, listings of every tenant in the building, nearly all corporations with an "Inc." behind their names. Some were on the upper level, some on theirs. When the couple tried handing the envelope over as they were led through the labyrinth. Kurt told them to wait. "Whatever business we have to discuss we can do it in the office."

Gail-Lill stared in wonder at the palm trees in the atrium. *Palm* trees! In the north! Lee-Willie's shoes squeaked as they walked, the din of bustle not enough to cover the noise.

"When you hired us, we met in a coffee shop," Lee-Willie said. "Why didn't we come here?"

"Can't remember that far back, Lee," said Kurt. "I was probably in-between places."

"How long ya been here?"

"Six months." Kurt looked at Lee-Willie. "We were five miles from here before then."

"Well this sure is your 'inner-sanctum' now, Mr. Bannabock," Gail-Lill said.

Lee-Willie turned around. "The 'what'?"

"Poetic for 'office,'" she said.

"Yes, about your poetry—" said Kurt, out-of-the-blue, making Lee-Willie wince. "Still

working hard at that? I know it's important to you."

"It is Mr. Bannabock. I write all the time."

"Yeah, she does," Lee-Willie conceded. "She writes *all* the time."

They arrived at the office. **BLUESTONE, INCORPORATED** was on the oak door. Kurt opened the door, ushered them in. "Here we are."

Behind a vast greeting desk was a bookish-looking receptionist, glancing up from her letter-typing and phone-answering, mouthing a friendly *Hello* to her boss and visitors, holding up a *One second* finger. Bannabock nodded, swung around the countertop behind her, scribbled something on her notepad, swung back to their side, waiting for her to get off. Seemed like he did not want his guests to see it. The split-second she did, she had a confused look—she had read the note.

"Milly—" Kurt said, voice obsequious, practiced, "delay my first meeting by a half hour, will you? These two are from The Winking Moon, we're going to my office."

"Yes, Mr. Bannabock."

"Milly" did as commanded, snagged the phone as another call rang through, spoke in friendly tones as she flipped the Rolodex, checking her schedule. Kurt grinned and led his company around the giant half-wall blocking the rest of the firm from the public, the Stuckersons catching a glimpse of what had been scribbled on the pad: ***GET ME OUT OF THIS SOON***

The couple was then guided to the end of what seemed the longest carpeted hallway known to mankind, passing plush cubicle after plush cubicle, movie posters lining the walls showcasing the finest, most expensive Hollywood blockbusters made. There was a lavish conference room three-quarters of the way down. Lee-Willie and Gail-Lill thought they were going there but that was not the case. They passed and saw the Bluestone logo presiding over the super-official meeting room there totally unoccupied. Lee-Willie grew tired of the pomp-and-circumstance and said— "Kurt, you closin' the drive-ins down or what? We gotta right to know."

Bannabock stopped, practically choked, halted advancement right before his own office, hand on door handle. "Come in. Let me shut the door."

Shut, click. The three were now in the private space. Lee-Willie could not wait to be settled, didn't bother admiring the equally impressive workroom. "Are you, Kurt? The Winking Moon? Smirking Star? *Our* drive-ins? Is Bluestone closing us down? Rumors are poppin' like popcorn all over the community and we wanna know what's goin' on."

"Nice analogy," Kurt said. "Please, sit down. Gail, can you get your husband to have a seat?"

She did a good job. Took a little doing, took a rub on the shoulder, but it worked. They fluffed into two giant chairs that could have doubled for loveseats in front of his mammoth oak-and-brass executive's desk, house plant on a stand, splitting the difference between the couple. Bannabock circled around, positioned his equally-mammoth chair on caster wheels just so (it looked more like a throne), and sat, a row of fountain pens jutting from a long paperweight-like object on the surface like Medieval pikers, protecting him from intruders.

He leaned forward, forming thoughts, resting elbows as he drummed his fingers. There was a window to the Stuckersons' left, sun at just the right angle, casting a larger-than-life gleam on the man, adding to the derision the couple was feeling being heaped their way. With hearts in throats, Gail-Lill still with the envelope, they waited for him to begin talking.

"Your projectionist…" he began, at a loss for the last name.

"'Jim Barenta,'" Gail-Lill said.

"'Jim Barenta.' He's doing well? The Moon Tower episode not sending him over the edge?"

Lee-Willie sighed. "We knew you knew about that; we just weren't gonna talk about it."

"Of course not,' Bannabock said. "Thank God it wasn't worse."

"He's doing fine," Gail-Lill said. "He's a trooper."

"To say the least. We never got an official report from the authorities."

"I don't think anything 'official' was made," said Gail-Lill.

"Of course, not to that, either. And 'of course not' to his union being contacted. I don't think there's any repercussions there, either."

"Friends in high places, sir, said Gail-Lill.

"Are you gonna tell 'em?" Lee-Willie asked.

"Why bother?" said Kurt. "Like your wife said: 'He's doing fine.'" That did not bode well. Why the nonchalance? "It's like most things at The Winking Moon: swept under the rug."

"Well we didn't do the 'sweeping,'" said Lee-Willie.

"Didn't say you did. As long as he's fine, we consider the matter closed."

"That's how we feel about it."

"We don't want you to have any more negatives."

"Meaning what?"

Milly interrupted, knocking first then poking her head in, asking if anybody wanted coffee. Lee-Willie and Gail-Lill both did, raising their hands, but Bannabock shot the idea down. "Thank you, Milly," he said. "But we're all set, thank-you."

Mysterious slight number-two. Kurt fiddled with a marble paperweight, perhaps trying to find words to ease into things. Lee-Willie and Gail-Lill lifted to their eyes to a bizarre painting behind the desk: an upside-down elephant, balancing on a tricycle. When the tension became too much, Lee-Willie lost it. "Oh, for shit's sake, Kurt, quit boofin' the pooch and come clean! Now!"

"'Boofing the what'?" Kurt reacted.

Gail-Lill took over. "Lee and I need to know if we're safe. This is our livelihood. This is *all* our livelihoods. As you know we moved here from Ohio, a small town in Ohio. We came to Rochester specifically to manage The Winking Moon and we think we deserve an answer."

"'Respect,' as I see it," Lee-Willie said. "We're doin' the best damn job possible and we like it here. We'd like to stay. We go to bed every night with these fucking rumors hanging over our heads. You jamokes aren't makin' it easy to dismiss 'em. Can't ya just tell us once-and-for-all if Bluestone's planning on killing us off?"

"'Jamokes'?"

"Yes, 'jamokes.' Fellas, ordinary folk, the average Joe."

"We started hearing things at the end of last year and it's just gotten worse," said Gail-Lill.

"We're looking into matters," Bannabock finally came out with, and Lee-Willie thumped the

table with the plant on it. Shook it, almost spilled it.

"See, Gail?" he said. "Told ya."

"Lee," said Kurt, "please don't do that."

"So, what does it mean?"

"Lee, Gail, it means we're looking into things. That's all I can tell you."

"Well that doesn't sound good," Lee-Willie said, an ice creeping through his veins. "Well we got some solutions. We could play some A-list movies, for one. The Crusaders say it works for The Smirking Star."

"'Crusaders'?"

"Our patrolmen."

"Ah, yes, your 'patrol-men.' The ones who catapult kids over the fence."

"They don't do that."

"Well what about the A-list films?"

"Lee, I don't order the films, that's California. Why do you call them 'The "Crusaders?"

"I don't, they do. That's just how serious they take their jobs, that's just how much they love The Winking Moon—and us!" Lee-Willie was fed up, snatched the envelope from his wife's hand, pulled out the letters, practically threw them at the executive. "This is what we've been callin' about. We wanna keep it open, tons of people wanna keep The Winking Moon open. Don't do this to us."

Kurt had to put on his reading glasses, took a copy. "What is this?"

"Just read it, please. It's from two, very-customers last night. It's something you and California should ponder over before ya make any hasty decisions."

"It's a 'testimonial,'" Gail-Lill added. "A lovely young couple during last night's rainstorm."

"The media just prints sensationalized bullshit," said Lee-Willie. "Consider *that*."

As Kurt read the words, Gail-Lill offered credence to the report. "We brought them to our office during the middle of it. They agreed to it, they knew we were writing it down. They told us they were having the best times of their lives. They knew about our troubles; we didn't hold back—but they didn't care—they didn't care about anything but keeping The Winking Moon open and having their fun at our drive-in. We're getting things under control, Mr. Bannabock."

Lee-Willie was frowning. "They had a wonderful, romantic time. Make a plaque of it."

His phone rang and Kurt answered it. There was a mumbling of words, but the tone of the voice sure sounded like Milly's. Kurt set the letter aside, took off his glasses. "Wow, nice. Thanks. I'll send it up the chain." It was clear the big shot did not have anything he wanted to add, nothing for the Stuckersons. "My meeting is waiting, I'm sorry but I have to get going."

"You have to go now?" said Lee-Willie.

"Yes, I'm sorry. Thanks for stopping by."

"Tell Milly she was right on-cue," Lee-Willie said. "And tell her thanks for the attempt at the coffee, that was a nice touch."

Kurt stared long and hard at the man. "I don't know what you're talking about but you're being rather rude. I took your meeting."

"Don't knock down The Winking Moon and don't knock down The Smirking Star" said Lee-Willie. "Can't believe I said that last one. And don't sell the property to Edgewater, behind us. Please."

"Look... we're *constantly* reviewing our properties—all over the country. Three years ago, after losing Franco Esposito, we hired you. As involved as the two of you are, times are changing. You've heard of BetaMax."

"Yeah, we've heard of it."

"Well that whole thing's impacted not just drive-ins but regular theaters, we don't have this all figured out. But some of the venues do seem to promote greater shenanigans that others. We don't doubt for a second you two are committed, but our interests are in the forward-progress of the company. I'm just the regional manager, I don't make the decisions."

"But you have *influence*," Lee-Willie beseeched.

Kurt came round to their side, extended his hand, for shakes. "I thank you both for coming, you have chutzpah. I'll reimburse you for the gas money, it's such in-demand these days."

"You don't have to do that, Mr. Bannabock," Gail-Lill said.

"Yes, he does," Lee-Willie said.

The handshakes were awkward, forced. The Stuckersons left the testimonials right there on the desk, envelope, too. Kurt said, "Let's not make a habit of these surprise visits, okay? I'll try to be more on-the-ball with calling you back."

"Good. We're one-hundred percent, *honest* people."

Kurt put a gentle hand on Lee-Willie's shoulder. "Lee don't read into that. And no more 'Swingin' Jim' on The Moon Tower."

"Thank-you for your time, Mr. Bannabock," said Gail-Lill.

"Milly? Would you mind writing a check for them? They'll tell you how gasoline-money they need reimbursing for."

"Yes, Mr. Bannabock," said Milly.

"And see them out of the office… into the atrium."

"Yes, sir."

Kurt shut the door behind the couple, the long walk through the hallway ahead. Milly was coming toward them wearing an over-polite grin, motioning them her way. Lee-Willie jacked-up the price up to an ungodly amount, embarrassing the hell out of Gail-Lill, who kept her mouth shut as the receptionist wrote out the check. She made a mental note: Kurt's note was laying in the trash.

Once more in the parking lot they had to wade through the giant puddles to get into their car, openly wondering whether they had done themselves any good, Lee-Willie more determined than ever. "Bastard's not gonna get the best of us, Gail," he said. "No one is. Bluestone, either, the schmucks. They're lying, all of 'em. Wanted to wipe that grin right off Milly's fake face. Thanks for dictating and making copies of that testimonial, least he had to read it in front of us."

"You're welcome, dear," she said. "And by the way, that elephant-painting behind his desk was fucked-up."

Wednesday night the Crusaders were on squeegee-detail before the show opened. So much rain had fallen the night before there were lakes of it around, some so large it would have impeded vast chunks of the audience. They would have had to avoid certain areas to park, made things utterly uncomfortable. The boys had never seen so much rain.

They had found the tools in the back-storage room. A bunch of them. They were not Franco's; they'd been around longer than that. The Stuckersons had found them in the attic when they arrived here right after their meeting with Kurt Bannabock, handed them out, had the chuckleheads squeegee the water away until it was time to gather the troops for the speech.

All afternoon-long, the Stuckersons had anticipated what they were going to tell their employees, wondering whether or not if they should conjecture about their own take on the fate of the drive-ins. It had not been good. "I dunno what to make of Bannabock's bullshit, Gail," Lee-Willie said to her in private. "It could mean he just doesn't know shit, or he just doesn't want to spill the beans, prematurely. What we for sure succeeded in doing was determining just what kind of a jack-wad he is. Still can't believe he pulled that garbage with Milly-the-Manipulator. What is she, a secretary or an accomplice to his idiocy? Did he not think we were gonna noticed how he railroaded us outta there?"

"I think we should tell them everything, Lee," said Gail-Lill. "We have to be honest. Our kids might view us as many things, but a 'liar' isn't one of them. Let's have one of your line-ups."

They called the Crusaders in from the lot. They had done a good job, gotten much the water off the main grounds. They lined everyone up by the arcade games. Much more casual this time around. The Stuckersons told them what had transpired that day in the meeting. Lee-Willie said, "We went there, first-hand, asked him point-blank: are ya closin' The Winking Moon and The Smirking Star? Kurt said they were 'talking about many things.' That did not conclude much. Concludes he's an asshole but doesn't conclude what we really wanna know."

"Lee... let's watch our language," said Gail-Lil, addressing her crew. "We intend on grilling him again."

Jim pushed off the wall. "Don't grill him too much or ya run the risk of him clamming up altogether. He probably does not know much. Just 'cause he's a King Shit here doesn't mean he's knows what California's thinking. Don't encourage him to light a fire under their asses. We want time to prove to 'em we're fixing our problems. Things have been lightening up. Think we had more raids on the drive-in before the kids got here."

"Maybe, Jim," said Gail-Lill, "but the weather also sucked and most of those hooligan and punks were neck-deep in schoolwork. They're out now."

The employees were told to go about their business, open up, start operations. Stanley was not saying much. Neither was Emilio. Kathy walked back to the box office not having a good feeling about any of it. Alex walked her there. "My gut's usually right," she said. "And it's telling me, by not answering 'no,' we're 'not closing The Winking Moon and Smirking Star,' they probably are. Hope I'm wrong. How could we let a Rochester tradition disappear? We can't let a joint like this leave Rochester."

Alex did not know what to say. He felt dejected. He did not want to get dejected at work. His asshole father who had split on his family: *that's* who got him defected. He shook the notion away and said, "I think we gotta do as Jim says, Kathy: prove we got this. The harder we work at our jobs, the more the public will know not to screw with us. Eventually, it'll just go away."

She looked at him. "Will it?"

"Who knows?"

By the shenanigans did not slow. They were on full force by the time the first intermission rolled around. Everything had gone well until it was food time, hordes of child-yahoos and rowdies banning together, racing through the concession stand, pulling practical jokes, causing mayhem, creating great stress and anxiety for the customers and staff alike. Had they planned this out in their parents' cars? Vicki and Emilio were openly questioning this, shouting for Stanley, who was in the back-storage room, taking a call from Doris, bickering with her about another late-night telescope session with a second storm supposedly on its way.

The sky was looking ominous. The patrons who were outside, not in the stand being terrorized by the little bastards were out in the open, stared into the firmament. There was a terrific display of heat lightning to the north, generating effects better than most science fiction movies. The Stuckersons were riding the Crusaders to stay on top of things. "If the sound starts sputtering again: get Jim."

"Do you want us out here, then?" Alex was saying. "There's hordes of kids inside, running around, causing issues."

"Use your brains! Where you're needed—go."

The Crusaders worked up a sweat trying to do all-of-the-above. The juvenile folderol was reaching such a frenzy, it made last year already tame in comparison. While large groups of young adult men remained outside, belting out at stage-loud voice their rendition to *Let's All Go To The Lobby*—the current commercial playing on the screen with the dancing hotdogs and drinks, stoned lunatics were also running around the lot, purposefully blowing pot smoke into cars they didn't know.

At the same time, raids of pre-teeners were scorching through the doors of the stand on skateboards, throwing them down, jumping on and screeching through, knocking people over along the way, slapping pretty chicks in the ass as they passed by—sailing out the other side to pick up their boards up and run off into the night, laughing, presumably returning to their cars.

"They probably got that idea from you kids last night in the rain with the cardboard box!" Vicki griped, aiming her disgust at John and Steve, who were the only ones in at the moment.

Took all the Crusaders to chase the chooches out, grabbing them, pushing them out the doors, shouting at the pint-sized morons performing hairpin turns under people's legs, around the pinball machine, emitting vulgar belches of seismic quality. When Stanley came out, he threw his broom at them—blunt-point out—knocking a hole through the drywall just behind the register.

"Stanley, you're gonna hafta pay for that!" shouted Lee-Willie, entering with his wife, just before getting knocked over himself by an urchin on a tricycle. A tricycle!

Even as the second film started, Vicki was finding kids hiding. Most were huddled behind the video game kiosks, giggling away, eating stolen popcorn from customers they'd "mugged." A few were ducked down behind fat customers. Some had pulled the trash receptacles around them to protect from being seen. One got up so quickly after being caught by the mother hen, he accidentally knocked the can, dumping it, sending garbage all over the floor. They had to lock the doors for a few to get the joint presentable again.

"They're getting smarter!" John said. "First the diversion-technique at the fence, now this. They must be talkin' before they come in."

"Like Little Frankie warned," George agreed.

"Geez, if they're this bad," Steve said, bold enough to pose the question, "what're they gonna do if that kid's words do come true?"

Stanley was slumped on a bench, gasping for air.

"What's your problem?" Lee-Willie asked.

"They're evolving, Lee," he wheezed. "Don't ya see it, ya dolt?" He had a Click-Clack toy with him. One of the ones they had never given back. He was prepared to use it as a weapon.

"Don't even think about using that, Mason," Lee-Willie said.

"Why? You got your flashlight, as strong as a cannon. Leave me alone, lip-man, this is war. I'll strangle one of the fuckers with it, string him up from the ceiling fan."

When some little beggar asked if he could have it, Stanley laid into the pipsqueak. "Clack your own balls together, squirrel-bait, pants around your ankles! Now get out!"

Amidst the hoopla, the theories on what was going on and why, another young twat waddled in from the southern double-doors, dressed like Charlie Chaplin from the actor's silent films, Little Tramp-style, complete with crumpled suit, ragged tie, derby, mustache, big shoes on his feet, reeking of whiskey, cigarettes, twirling a cane at his side.

"What the hell…?" Lee-Willie said. "What are you doing?"

The jamoke never answered, just twiddled his 'stache, doffed his derby, sashayed over to the line, got in it, looked up at the menu behind a diehard few, still waiting to be served. He started mimicking their movements, making fun of them to make others laugh. It worked. The entire room had stopped cold. Only the people in line did not know what was going on. Everybody but the Stuckersons and Stanley were titillated. The Crusaders, Emilio and Vicki just gawked, quietly enjoying the pantomime. When the folks would turn around, look him up-and-down, he'd stop. Was Vicki who first spoke. "Okay, why? We give up. It's horror movies out there, not comedies."

The guy simply turned to her, flirtatiously smiled, batted his eyelashes at her, went back to pretending he was going to steal popcorn from his unsuspecting new mark.

"No, he's not gonna do that, is he?" Alex said, anticipating.

Sure enough, the clown grabbed a handful, jammed it in his mouth. When he took a second helping and shoved it down his pants, that was it. Crusaders moved in. "Okay, bub—" said George, "show's over." They carried the perverted thespian out by his arms and legs, depositing him by the dumpster, telling him to stay out and not enter again.

"If ya come in again," said Alex, "we're gonna make you eat that popcorn you've stuffed around your donager."

By the time the second feature started, John, Alex and Steve were ready to get the squeegees to use against people. George had gone into the men's room to relieve himself. The tight quarters smelled like a beer factory, the dudes in there all acting stupid, shouting at the top of their lungs, playfully pushing each other around. George could not wait to get out of there.

When he pulled paper towels down from the dispenser, a bat flew out, flying around and altering the mood on a dime. The damn thing had somehow gotten up there and was now loose. It dive-bombed the group's heads, acting erratically, flapping against the walls, trying to get out.

No one could exit quickly. Everyone was crashing into each other, creating a bottleneck, hollering for the other to get out of the way. Someone would swing at it with an open hand, crack a stranger in the face, and on and on. Shirts and sandals were coming off, snapping at the terrified creature. George had to cover up he got hit so many times.

The tumult grew to a comedy of buffoonery until someone finally managed to get the door open, the bat flying out, and all the goons tripping and falling over each other, George hiding in the corner. The Crusaders were right to trounce ass, thinking a brawl was going on.

A of thunder detonated directly over the drive-in, sending more surprised screams up from the audience. Customers outside got caught in the sudden downpour and ran for cover. Vicki, Emilio, and Stanley thought they were under attack, joined the patrons inside in grabbing utensils, ready to use them in case they were under attack. George entered, pretended to be cool, brushed his thick, black hair from his eyes, one lapel flipped up.

Mrs. Stuckerson came in right behind him with The Winking Moon umbrella, watching the rainstorm pummeling the lot. The patrolmen came in to escape the brunt of it, could see the lightning flashes in her bifocals, made for a very striking visual. Stanley saw flying saucers in them. Tiny spaceships, zipping in-and-out of the rolling black clouds. "It's gonna pound again," she said, sending the boys into snicker-mode.

"She said 'pound,'" Steve whispered.

"Mrs. Stuckerson," said Vicki, "you really shouldn't be walking around with that umbrella in

your hand. Not right now."

"Oh, I don't care what happens," she replied, wistfully. "Would be a poetic end to me, wouldn't it? Would just about figure with my luck."

"Mrs. Stuckerson!" Vicki reprimanded. "Don't say that. It's not that bad, my God."

"It almost is. We're falling apart."

While Alex was talking to Kathy in the booth, checking on her, asking what she thought of another rainstorm moving in, John got on the radio, asked everyone if they could meet him in the stand.

"Sounds serious," Alex said to her. "Excuse me."

She smiled, nodded. "I'll be here."

The shy Crusader was shaken, unnerved. The whole crew was gathered, including the Stuckersons and Jim, waiting for him to speak. John never called a meeting; this was highly unusual. Must have been important. Vicki, Emilio and Stanley were listening, but they also had to deal with the few customers inside. When Jim rolled his hand over-and-over in a windmill-like motion, imploring the kid to speak, he finally did. "I think… I've seen the hobos again," John said. "In the southeast corner, over in the orchard."

There was a pause of registration, disbelief.

"*What*?" said Mr. Stuckerson.

"Just before that giant thunderclap," John continued. "I was checking that side, thought I heard noises over there, jumped up, shined my flashlight around. When the sky lit up and it sounded like a bomb was going off, I could've sworn I saw a bunch of 'em, grouped together, staring at me from the other side, real scary-like. Like they were getting ready to jump over before I spotted 'em. Freaked the hell outta me. Almost fell off the fence."

"Oh my God, John, are you okay?" Vicki asked.

Lee-Willie looked at the girl, completely rapt in the boy. "He's fine, Ms. Richards, look at him."

"Didya look again?" asked Jim.

"I did. Jumped back up. Nothing. Like ghosts."

The manager was not buying it. "Whattya mean 'hobos'? You're not startin' this again, are ya, Tambone? Last year you said you saw them over there. We never saw any. None of us ever saw any."

His customers leaving, walking back out, looking over their

shoulders at the discussion, Stanley said, "Franco thought he used to see 'em on occasions."

Lee-Willie rolled his eyes, did not want to hear it. "Stanley: you see flying saucers."

"Don't mock me, Stuckerson," Stanley shot back, joining the group. The man was finally coming out of his funk. "It's true. Hobos. Vagabonds. Bums. Transients. Hopping that freight train over there, goin' for rides, 'cross-country, lookin' to make individual stops their encampments, lookin' to take advantage of whatever's around 'em. It's still a 'think,' Lee, don't dismiss it. That orchard over there's perfect for hiding. I think the kid could be seeing the real thing."

But Lee-Willie still did not believe it. "There aren't any hobos around here. This is 1979, not 1863 with the Intercontinental Railroad. Honestly, you people make this up just to spook us more than we already get spooked. Haven't we enough drama in this damn place without you clowns adding to the folklore?"

"It's not 'folklore,' Mr. Stuckerson," John insisted. "I saw 'em. Lightning lit up their faces for a second, what I could see of 'em. Grungy as shit, dirty. But they were scary, and they looked hungry."

Vicki was certainly alarmed. "What do ya think they were gonna do?" she asked.

"Jump over," John suggested. "Steal food from people. Nobody sneaks-in on that side. Only tramps and hobos would do that shit."

"*If* they were there," Lee-Willie emphasized, then he was through with the meeting. "Get back to work, we still have plenty of movie."

As they all began dispersing, considering what they had just been told, Vicki remained, sidled up to the kid. "I believe you, John."

But Mr. Stuckerson had stopped at the door, had turned around—"Vicki, you'd believe John if he said he could sprout wings and fly over Lake Ontario to Canada."

"Let's get our act together, people, we can't let stupid stuff scare us into weakening us." As soon as the words came out of his mouth, there was a blood-curdling scream from the dark lot. "What was *that*?!"

The whole batch ran to the distress. Jim included. They came across a couple that looked distressed. She was in the 1972 Dodge Dart Swinger, him outside of it, standing, ranting and raving, shaking his fist in the direction of the back of the lot, where he was yelling after someone who'd apparently just been there—"Come back here, ya son-of-a-bitch! I'll bash your head in, ya fucking pervert!" The girlfriend was sobbing in the passenger seat, head in her hands, shaking with fear.

"What is it?" Jim said. "What happened? Who ya yellin' at?"

The young man nearly spat his response. "A naked guy! In a mask and cape! Real freak. Pressed his disgusting, naked fat-ass up against my girlfriend's window, waited for her to turn and see it. She screamed when we saw the fucking thing. Guy ran off yelling 'The Masked Mooner strikes again!" He had this laugh…"

Crusaders all turned to one another, the problem sinking in. "The Masked Mooner…" Alex said with dread. "He's back."

"Just like The Delta 88," said George.

"They're all returning," said Steve.

"*All* the Rogue's Gallery," John finalized.

"H-he l-left an ass-print on the window…" the girl cried, managing to put a sentence together, looking up from her tortured affair. "Look." She rolled the window up. Indeed, there was a greasy facsimile of two butt-cheeks pressed upon the tempered glass. Made for a clear—and anatomically identifiable—outline, as a matter of fact. Was horrible. She wailed, "I-If his cheeks were s-spread any further, I-I would've thought I was a-at a proctologist's exam." She went back to weeping.

"She's traumatized for life!" the man stated, now pointing at the Moon-folk. "You people gotta do better in keeping goons like that away! I couldn't chase him; I wasn't about to leave my girlfriend here by herself!"

"I-I'll never s-sleep again…" she sobbed.

The Stuckersons faced their patrolmen. "The Masked Mooner… He's back… We can't let him here, either… He can't terrorize our lot again… This is horrible. This is not what we need, not at a time like this."

"We'll catch him in the end, sir," said John, being resolute. "Get it? 'End'?"

Mrs. Stuckerson clucked her tongue. "Don't start with the bad puns, guys, we're not making this a joke right now." To the girl, "Do you want us to compensate you, miss?"

She yowled— "How? Take the image away? It's burned into my brain forever! It's worse than anything I've seen on the screen tonight!"

Alex turned to his friends. "That's saying a lot. Have you seen these movies?"

They carried on the discussion after they left the couple. The fiend was one of The Moon's regulars, like the Delta 88. Black cape, black leotard, black eye mask. The dude was massively out-of-shape, with a belly of blob hanging over his utility belt. Sort of dressed like Batman but obese. His modus operandi was the same last season: he'd sneak-up on unsuspecting couples, make sure the coast was clear, turn, dropped his drawers, wedge his flappy, hammy, hairy, repulsive buttocks up against the window, wait until the inevitable reaction came, then run off into the night, laughing hysterically like a villain in an old movie-serial, leaving his signature cast-off, "The Masked Mooner has struck again!"

They never did catch him, either.

The patrolmen all agreed they had serious hard-ons for these creeps. This was going to be the year to get them all. Alex's balls were tingling. This is what he said happened to him when he got really mad, *really* ready to beat the crap out of a scoundrel. Tonight, they searched all over Hell's Half Acre for The Masked Mooner, once again coming up empty. Lee-Willie was on the radio, wanting updates. Jim had returned to the projection booth, gone back to his model-making. They informed *him* they had no luck. He had little sympathy for them.

"You boys should be able to catch someone so out-of-shape, so foul, so demonstratively stupid that even a nine-year old could do it," he said. "That poor girl's gonna be seeing sphincters in her nightmares right through old age."

"Can we carry B.B. guns?" Steve suggested.

Jim got a doobie from his stash behind the faux wall. "When you do catch this walking turd, throw his body down a flight of carpeted stairs so hard he'll die of a thousand rug burns and broken limbs."

"That would do it," said Alex. They were always impressed with Jim's creative threats.

Their search for the masked assailant was, unfortunately, not fruitful. The gang decided to gather at another late-night rendezvous to the beach. All of them, sans Jody. The blondie was exhausted from working so many hours at Lapping Waves and needed to catch up on some sleep. Kathy, Vicki and the Crusaders were game to go, as they had plenty to talk about, particularly Stuckerson's visit to Bannabock. What *that* meant. There was also the Delta 88, John's hobos, and of course, The Masked Mooner: embarrassment and pest to all.

Things were building, they agreed. George had been drawing in the sand. Creations representing what was of vital importance to the health of the drive-in. By the moonlight, they gathered round, saw what he had rendered. He had drawn a crazy guy in a tie, representing Kurt Bannabock. "The chooch," as he put it. There was a primitive, long car on wheels, chicken-scratch scribbled alongside the body of it. "That's the Delta 88, with the 'DEBAUCERY & RIBARDLY' on the quarter-panels." There were stick figures, long, scraggly hair flowing off the heads: the hobos. "Let's hope John's wrong about that one," he said. "That would suck." And there was a giant, bare derriere he'd carved out, bigger than anything else. "That's the Masked Mooner. One Melvin we can't let in, no matter what. This guy's got balls."

"No—an *ass*," Steve reworded.

"That's totally gross," said Kathy, asking about, then hearing, the details of the maniac's first visit this season. "Did anybody take the poor girl to the hospital?"

George cracked wise with the answer. "What would she be treated for, ass-abuse?"

But Katy was serious. "Well we're taking everybody else to the hospital," she said.

George broke off with Steve, John and Vicki, went to toss rocks at the piece of driftwood they had often sat on. Was a good target. Alex and Kathy became alone. Again.

Despite the pressure from the week's events, Alex's interest—now—became completely fixated on Kathy. She was just so damn alluring. More and more his heart was beginning to thump for her, for real. They'd both taken to staring along the shoreline, to their right, where the bend of Durand Eastman Park hooked around a bluff, disappearing eastward, making way for the sights of the harbor lights and signs of civilization to be visible way, way out there, to that horizon. In typical fashion, Kathy became philosophical, drawing on moments from her childhood. "When I was a kid," she said, "those lights never came out that far."

The long, blowing hair was too much. Alex could not stop staring at it, watching how it moved in the night sky, the way her profile caught the light from the Moon. "Progress," is all he could say. That was all he could think of.

"We're making progress?" she said. "Seems like we're going backwards. When I was a kid, I thought by now they'd have the flying cars, like in 'The Jetsons.'"

He laughed. "I love that show."

"How far into the future does that show take place?"

"2062," Alex answered.

"You *know* that?"

"Yep, I'm a science fiction-nut, I remember the details. 'The Jetsons' took place in 2062… exactly a hundred years after I was born."

She considered the response. "I just thought they'd be hurrying up with stuff like that. Still have many years to go before that date."

The water was loud but soothing. They could barely hear the others down the shoreline. They found themselves turning to one another. The time was right, and he wanted to kiss her. Badly. For a moment, he thought she wanted him to. She smiled, held her gaze, then he hesitated, breaking her look, going back to the harbor lights and stars—killing momentum. He wondered if she had noticed him leaning-in.

"Hey you guys!" George's voice rang out. "Get over here! We found a six-pack!"

Now the moment was dead. Alex called back to them, their silhouettes, lumped in a cluster. "You're not drinking that!" he said.

"No, but we're tempted!" Vicki cried out.

Alex laughed. "Next time bring Jody! She'll have the real stuff!"

Alex had been hoping Kathy would offer him another ride home. She did not this time. He had to squelch a feeling of disappointment. What right did he have to expect one? This was getting tense. Plus, he did not want to make things so obvious in the eyes of his comrades. Maybe he was too immature for her? This drive-in with its non-stop practical jokes and monkeyshines was something he did not see for her.

"Are you sick of The Winking Moon?" he asked. He had been too gun-shy to kiss her but not to ask her about this.

"No," she replied. "But it's not going to last."

"Oh," said Alex. "You too?"

She did not want to get into it. There had been too much discussion already and it was bothering her. She drew her hair into a ponytail, tied it with a band from her slacks pocket, announced she was tired, and excused herself. "It's time for me to go home."

All of them ended up walking Kathy to her Malibu, saw her off. Vicki and the Crusaders remained for another half-hour, being free, spirited, under the Milky Way.

CHAPTER 29:

THE PAGANS

Thursday happened to be the Summer Solstice: June 21st. Employees of The Winking Moon Drive-In were not even remotely aware of the astrological significance of the date until Econoline-van-after-Econoline van—each rustier and more slap-dashed with house paint than the other—motorcaded into the lot at the very beginning of the evening, staking territory throughout the first few rows. The weirdoes who drove them wanted to assure their proximity to the screen. Why? Was not clear yet, but it would be revealed.

"Normal" patrons got crowded out of these sections, having to settle for the latter rows, the periphery, and way back. One after the other, the white-robed drivers backed the vans in, positioning them high on the humps, as was routine. The back doors seemed to open in tandem, male and female freaks and kooks coming out of them, stretching, grinning like fools, worshipping the sun still potent in the sky, and made their way—almost at once—to the playground area, taking over that.

"What the hell is this…?" Lee-Willie said to the Crusaders and employees, all staring as a group. Jim was the only one not with them. He was in the doorway of his booth, drinking coffee.

"I don't know," said Emilio, "but it looks like their getting ready for a picnic."

"Or festival," said Vicki.

Was true. The three dozen or so "celebrants" had with them tambourines and tom-tom drums! *That* worried the dickens out of The Mooners. "The fuck they gonna do with those—" questioned Alex, "bang 'em all movie?"

"We'll 'bang' their heads if they start doin' that," said George.

They had with them in their hands twig-and-leaf "tiaras" and "crowns," and baskets of flower petals and grass. They proceeded in conducting a little pow-wow by the swing sets, an old-looking man with a scraggly, long beard and mustache assuming to be their leader.

"Kathy, did you let these freaks in?" Lee-Willie said into the radio, disbelieving what he was seeing.

"Yes, I did, Mr. Stuckerson," came her answer. "I didn't know what to do. They all paid; they were very polite. Was I not supposed to? They were lined up first while you and Mrs. Stuckerson were in the office."

"No, no, we can't discriminate… I think. Let's see what they're up to before we do anything. They better have come to watch the movies in peace, I've never seen anything like this."

Gail-Lill kept her mouth shut.

As the Mooners approached, one of the younger men saw them, smiled brightly. "I know what you're thinking, 'What's going on'? It's the summer solstice, friends—June 21st—time to rejoice."

"Here? Whattya gonna do?"

"Nothing, man, just celebrate the longest day of the year. This is the perfect spot. We scouted."

"'Scouted'?"

"Yeah, man, thanks for having such an ideal place."

Lee-Willie was about to go for them, Gail-Lill pulled him back. "Honey… they're paying customers."

"They look like leftovers from a Fellini casting-call."

For the first half-hour before operations, as the regular crowd drove in and gaped at them, filled with doubt and suspicion themselves, the staff kept leery, continued to hound the managers: What *was* the summer solstice? What the hell was its significance to these Melvins, chooches and dunderheads? Should they watch 'em like a hawk? Pounce the second they acted out-of-order? Stuckersons could not answer. So far, the unique club was just gathering, swinging on the swings, rising and falling on the teeter-tawter, raising their faces to the sky, laughing.

These clowns had not come last season. In all their years managing, Gail-Lill and Lee-Willie had never seen this. They double-checked with Kathy. She had been overwhelmed with the fleet, serving as courteously and professionally as possible as they piled in, treating their remarks of needing to get inside quickly with grace and distinction. She quoted some of the lines. "'We have to get in, young lady,' they said to me. 'Can you hurry? We need to be close to the screen.' I asked them why, but they didn't say. They just paid and were very quiet. They said the sun was still high over the screen."

"Weird," Lee-Willie mused openly, suspecting something not-good was going to happen.

The crowd was all garbed in white robes, some with a symbol of the sun on it, others with the moon. Some wore glasses, all had scuffed sandals on their feet. Necklaces of dried fruit and more flowers were around their necks. The *drive-in* Mooners—Crusaders, Stanley, Emilio, Vicki—kept watching them, studying the stitched symbols that resembled ancient rune hieroglyphics on sleeves and necklines.

There was still plenty of time before the sun set and the movies were about to play. Jim had the pre-show music going: Top 40 pop hits. Was a strange juxtaposition, indeed, hearing Heart and REO Speedwagon while all this was happening? Regular patrons began entering the playground area, staying away from the goofballs, giving them space, but just as watchful, looking, pointing, giggling.

Was difficult as the robed-ones were spreading out, taking over. Things got more unpredictable when the loons formed circles, began swaying to the heavens, grinning blithely with what teeth they had left, warming up their voices, like humming. They backed completely off the equipment (finally!), opting instead to put the headgear on, noting the inclination of the sun almost to the top of the screen.

People speculated if the nutcases were on acid or something. "What're you people doing?" one ruffian crowed. Got no answer. That was not appreciated.

It was a beautiful evening and the beautiful sky was ready to swallow the bright sun and turned it into a marvelous, starlit evening. The Crusaders reassembled with the Stuckersons—no other nefarious action taking place because of the freakshow—wondering if there was going to be trouble.

"I talked with Jim, Mr. and Mrs. Stuckerson," Alex told them.

"And?" Lee-Willie said. "What did he say?"

"Not much. He's keepin' an eye on 'em, too."

"Good. I think this is uncharted territory."

John said, "He doesn't wanna be bothered unless they start doing something stupid."

The managers at each other. Lee-Willie said, "And this isn't *that*?"

"Mrs. Stuckerson," said Steve. "Do you have any idea who these people are?"

"They're pagans," she finally answered, getting their attention, especially her husband, who was all ears now. "They're a religious group."

"And you're just telling me this now?" questioned Lee-Willie.

She shrugged, had a guilty, dour look on her faced. "This is their big, summer holiday. Every year on this date, pagans all over celebrate the longest day of the year. This is a big deal to them. They're nature-worshippers, they do this out in the open. Looks like we're the lucky recipients to host it this year."

"They can't do that," said Lee-Willie.

"They're not doing anything, and they paid," she defended.

"Was this pre-arranged?" asked George.

"Hell no!" answered Lee-Willie. "I don't like the looks of it, they're stirring the pot. I swear to my God if they start shit—freedom of religion or not—they're out."

"Lee, calm down," said his wife. "We have to be inclusive; the movie hasn't started yet. It's a gorgeous evening. Did you see their license plates? Some came from Pennsylvania and Massachusetts."

"Sounds like you're sympathizing with them."

"Lee, I'm just being open."

"Well I'm surprised more of their license plates don't say they're here from one of Stanley's planets." Lee-Willie rubbed his sore lip. "Let's watch this one."

The novelty had drawn Vicki, Emilio and Stanley back to the threshold of the double-doors, even as customers were talking to them, asking what was going on. The food orders were being delayed due to the newness of the event. Emilio scratched his head through his crocheted hairnet. "Those garnishes," he said. "Bet they're crawling with bugs. Stanley, get ready to fumigate."

Stanley didn't take kindly to the remark. "Look who's talkin', Varentez. That hairnet your wife made you? What is *it* crawlin' with, rice and beans?"

Vicki snickered. "Anybody seen the boys' repellent?"

"They're like parishioners in a church," Emilio said. "Only weirder."

Vicki said, "I've seen this in my dad's National Geographic magazines. They're called 'sects.'"

"'Sex'?" said Stanley. "As in 'let's-get-it-on' sex?"

She spelled it out for the coot. "S-E-C-T-S, Stanley, sects, as in religious orders. Tonight's their Fourth of July: the longest day of the year."

"Certainly 'the longest' for us," said Stanley. "C'mon, let's get back inside. I don't like all these people piling up behind me."

Some of the patrons were holding back derogatory comments about the pagans, some pissed they'd taken all the good spaces closest to the screen, battling to get around the muckety-muck, making open comments about their decision to pick tonight, of all nights, to come to the drive-in. The concession-workers did their best to allay fears and prejudices, and asked everybody to be understanding, and cool. The Stuckersons and Crusaders overheard several comments patrolling and walking around. When someone said, "We all know The Winking Moon's a breeding-ground for 'stupid,' but seriously?" Lee-Willie had to get involved.

"Now, sir," he said. "I don't take too kindly to those kinds of remarks. We take great pride in being open to anybody who wants to come in and obey the rules and regulations."

"Yeah, but these powder-puffs look like they're about to do a human sacrifice. And the way things have been goin' here... I'm just sayin'."

Lee-Willie grimaced. "We'll keep an eye on it." Then, calling-out above the rising din to the pagans— "You'll be eatin' grass if you act up!"

"Lee!" Gail-Lill elbowed him in the ribs. When he doubled over, she pulled him off to the side, around the corner by one of the dumpsters. "Honey, listen. Our success is about numbers. Bluestone will be less likely to close us down if we keep drawing them in. We need the lot filled, no matter what. If Bluestone *is* keepin' eyes on us, then the last thing we can have happening is dips in sales. These redemption tickets we've been giving out are killing us."

"But Kathy told us, already, there was a couple asking for their money back. They didn't wanna be in here with these Looney-tunes prancing around. She was able to talk 'em out of it before I had to."

"As long as they keep to themselves," Gail-Lill said, "we should be fine. We'll figure this out."

Alex and John checked for spaces in the rear and got on the walkies.

"Mr. and Mrs. Stuckerson," Alex said. "There's two whole rows by The Moon Tower, still. Send the new people back here, let 'em know they have really good spots back here."

"And do it before the freaks decide to climb The Moon Tower," said John.

Steve, John, George and Alex were not able to focus fully on pre-show patrol. The hotspot was soaking-up the attention. Female pagans were now flitting in a circle, performing graceful, ballet-like drills around the Jungle Gym, keeping most of the "normals" away—except for the young men who came with buddies, filled with alcohol, pot and raging hormones, noticing some were foxes, checking them out, tossing lewd comments.

Crusaders made sure nothing was getting broken, nobody was getting hurt, and respect was maintained—both ways. They fielded questions, all on the same preoccupation: What were the whackos doing? Did they have to make a reservation or get permission to do this? Was this part of the show?

"That chick's boobs are poppin' out of her robe," one dude said to George and Steve. "Can I ask her out?"

When one bunch said, "Can we pound the crap out of the wimp-guys and their women?" they had to step in.

"Please, gentlemen," implored Steve. "No nonsense."

People slowly began adjusting to the presence of the pagans, setting themselves up in their own, private nestlings: laying down blankets, setting out chairs, candles, getting coolers ready (which they weren't supposed to have). There were a few Melvins who tried sneaking friends in in the trunks. They got caught, of course, and were forced to pay. Bug repellent was blasted, creating clouds of insecticides floating over the crowd, mixing with the smell of cigarette smoke and pot.

The pagans continued prancing about the playground, spreading their circle out, lifting their hands higher to the sky, beating the tom-toms (softly, promising to stop, come movie-time), draping more "necklaces of weeds" around their scrawny necks, removing what looked to be torches from the back of one of the vans…

Torches?! Now that alarming! That caught the employees' attention!

"What?!" Lee-Willie croaked. "What the fuck is *that*?! What the fuck do they think they're doin' with those?! Oh no way!" He marched over from mid-lot, waving the Crusaders with him. "Is that torches? No way in hell are they lightin' those! They promised to be good! This is gettin' totally outta hand! Hey, you people—don't even think about it! Put those back in the vans! You ain't lighting those in here, uh-uh!"

As the few who'd taken them out obeyed instruction, putting them back in, Lee-Willie ripped a giant-sized box of Good-N-Plenty's from his pocket, tore it open, slammed the candies into his mouth despite the pain from his lip, chewing the treats like a cement mixer, eyes burning a hole into the ceremony like a laser. Sure enough, the carnival of caricatures soon began upsetting the flow of things, fluttering about crazier and crazier, obtaining a Pan flute from a canvas bag, interrupting

Kool & The Gang and The Jackson 5 with twittery, grating, insipid fairytale-like music. The "percussionists" wouldn't stop thumping when asked, and many of the young females were waving straw grass in their hands, showing way too much of their naughty bits, all of them getting right up under the screen and touching the damn thing like it was a shrine. It was at this point the Crusaders told them to flat-out knock it off, lessen their circle within the enclosure, and get back to their vehicles.

Apparently, this was not going to happen. The men took on the personas of satyrs in the forest, being overtly pious, singing songs of mating with the women of the Earth. The women, in comparison, were acting like nymphs themselves, all praising Father Sun and Mother Moon, repelling guests wanting a crack at the equipment with handfuls of straw to the face. Now a few rowdies and yahoos wanted a "crack" at them. Patience was growing thin.

Alex introduced himself to the festival-makers, taking the initiative to be diplomatic. *He'd done it before, right?* he told himself. *At Edgewater?* No, those oldies nearly murdered Kathy and him. Anyhow, he asked the division to unwind, take the vigor down a notch, get back to their vans and be ready for "fun movie-time."

"Can't," said the same man who had first spoken to them, beard down to his navel. "The first star hasn't come out yet."

"Yeah but you're gettin' a little loud with your instruments and the songs. You said you wouldn't do that."

"We're letting our spirits be overtaken by the evening, young brother, we suggest you try the same."

"No, I got a job to do. Couldn't you have done this elsewhere?"

A broad with stringy hair and actual orange peels tied through it said, "Don't harsh our mellow, friend, we're relishing the alignment. This is the chosen place; the screen is essential to our celebration."

"Why?"

Just like Kathy, Alex never got an answer. She flashed him a teasing smile and a wink of the eye. There was louder nonsense with the flutes, tom-toms, inane lyrics and more straw waving. The "normal" patrons began siding with the rowdies and yahoos, telling the freaks to get off the playground.

"I've seen roadkill twitch with more grace," said one irate customer.

Steve put up his hands. "People, please, let's all move back, don't make matters worse."

The Stuckersons came around again, Lee-Willie suppressing a volcanic eruption, not at all happy with the unwillingness to cooperate, the flagrant disrespect for the code of conduct in the drive-in, the lack of concern for those not like them. Maybe it had been a mistake to let them in. Gail-Lill told him to hold off judgment, clinging to the hope that the outsiders would be good.

Stanley grabbed the radio from Vicki, who was unsure of how to handle the rising complaints coming into the stand. "Lee, Gail, you gonna do something about these scatter-brains? They're wreckin' sales.

Everybody's comin' in, griping about 'em. They wanna ring their necks. I don't think we're gonna have a very good night if those shit-for-brains carry on like this."

Six more patrons left, wanted their money back. Kathy worked them hard, trying to keep them in. "At least stay for the first movie," she said. "I think they're getting everything under control."

"There is *nothing* under control in there!" came a response.

Jim was phoning Jeannie as he threaded the first reel of trailers ahead of "Hills Have Eyes." One of the reasons he presented not much interest in the pagans was that he was preoccupied with the well-being of his war-buddy, Manny Rodrogo. The man had come around again, on his own. Jeannie had fed him! According to her report, just before Jim had come to The Moon directly from jumping out of airplanes for recreation downstate, she had said, "He's still bored, sweetie. He's still pining to feel relevant, still hoping to help you employees at The Winking Moon in any way possible. He said he wanted to flush all the dingle-berries and douchebags from the joint straight down the toilet. That's significant."

"And from the looks of what's forming out here tonight," Jim responded, "we could use him."

"Why? What's happening?"

He told Jeannie. Was not thinking about it getting back to the man. Little did he know the jest was going to register hard went it got to his friend's noodle, mashed around in Manny's mind a little bit.

The head honcho of the pagans—the dude with the longest and dirtiest grey beard of them all, addressed as "The High Priest" by his contemporaries— introduced himself to the Stuckersons and the Crusaders when he realized the extreme negativity they were inducing. "Please accept our apologies," he said to the gang. "We won't make a habit of this, but you have to understand: it's now or never. Grant us clemency for the time being, our intentions are noble. We are attempting to connect with the Higher Consciousness. We want are one with the universe and welcome you to join us. Surely our presence isn't that upsetting."

"It is," said Lee-Willie. "And we're being *very* welcoming."

"In case you didn't know it…" the High Priest felt compelled to say, "our right to celebrate our religion is protected under The United States Constitution."

"Not in a private business place, it isn't," said Lee-Willie. "We weren't born yesterday, buddy. One of your followers said it was necessary to be here and none of ya have told us what you're doin'. What the hell's the significance to the screen?"

"It's necessary for us to be here because what we're doing, we're doing before sunset. The screen holds a sacred symbolism that we couldn't find elsewhere."

"What?"

"Harmonious geometry within the universe's sensitivities."

"Huh?

"Lyrics, sir. The Poetry of Everything."

"Well you're lucky. My wife *is* a poet. And she convinced me to have a heart, show as much tolerance as I could stand."

"No need to get pernicious with things you don't understand."

"No need to get 'what'?"

"This is our second-most holy day of the year. These are esoteric studies of which you are not learned."

The Crusaders, standing by the Stuckersons' side (and lots of other folks), were ready to kick their asses, like the mob was with the Wild Man of Borneo. The managers did not like their customers looking like they were ready to start a mob, so they tried to speak calmly given how much was at stake with the Winking Moon.

"We are trying to understand," said Gail-Lill. "Once and for all: what's the symbolism the screen represents?"

The High Priest drew a conceited breath, blew it out. "Your movie-screen has the configuration of the Stonehenge megaliths, only sideways. It's pure and exact."

"'Stonehenge'?" Lee-Willie recoiled.

"The way it's shaped, post and lintel. A rectangle on its side. Stonehenge is an homage to astrological alignment, both solar and lunar. 'Tis perfect configuration." He turned to face the revelers, still dancing away, singing. "Brothers and sisters, it is in proportion to our most sacred temple. Rejoice, we've come home."

"This isn't 'your home,'" George said, having to be held back by Steve, John, Alex.

"You're one with nature here, mostly, you should be grateful, show reverence. You're under open skies year-round, trees to the sides, fresh air in your lungs, little noise, little light pollution. You're near Lake Ontario. These are natural experiences expressed in your moving pictures: love, loss, joy, terror, empathy. You show the 'we' in us. We're all interconnected."

Steve disagreed. "You're connected to 'The Hills Have Eyes' and 'The Texas Chainsaw Massacre'? That's messed-up, man."

"Silly boy, you have a lot of growing to do."

Now Steve's facial muscles were twitching. The most-macho of the rowdies and yahoos decided enough was enough. They "weren't gonna stand by and do nothing while some long-haired pile of bat guano spewed mumbo-jumbo bullshit, thinking he was superior." This was *their* drive-in, *their* Winking Moon and *their fucking playground*. Dozens of them stormed the area and took over, shoved the weaklings to the sidelines, jumped aboard the swings, swinging as high as they could, teeter-tawtering to their hearts content

This was a call-to-challenge to the younger of the pagans. They broke "script," rushed to the other equipment, commandeered the Jungle Gym, climbing and hanging like monkeys, went up the slides and down them, whooping and cheering, trying to best their opponents, giving each other a ride on the Spin-n-Puke, competing with the non-believers until they flew off, tumbling in the lawn. This was not fisticuffs but it sure was a show! People were fascinated seeing who had the biggest balls on the concourse.

The High Priest, attempting to refocus his followers, lifted his hands and shouted, "Brothers and sisters! Enough of this tomfoolery! The sun is behind the screen now! Get off the childish equipment and pay heed! Stonehenge is brought to our doorstep!"

Inside the concession stand, even though the patrons were continuing to chastise staff for not disciplining the pagans, Stanley's ears perked up like a dog at a dinner bell. "'Stonehenge'? Did someone just shout 'Stonehenge'? Why that's a UFO-landmark! I gotta see what they're talkin' about!" And he abandoned his post.

"Stanley!" Vicki shouted.

The senior ran—yes, ran! —through the lot, pushing through the patrons standing outside out of their vehicles, staring at the debacle. He reached the High Priest and the shenanigans, while the Crusaders and the Stuckersons stood near, unclear as to what was going on. He barreled his way through, spewing like an excited little boy— "Have ya made contact?! I heard ya say 'Stonehenge'! That was built by the aliens, ya know! Have any of you been there?! Are they tellin' ya someplace to meet? Huh? Are they?"

The High Priest looked at the pathetic senior with disdain, irritation.

"Be gone, old man! Do not bother us when the moment has arrived. Hail Brother Moon and Sister Sun, keep us centered, keep us virtuous in our celebration."

The Crusaders were shocked at the rudeness. Alex looked at John, George, Steve. "Ain't much of a nice priest, is he?"

Stanley became irate. "Don't ignore me, ya doddering hippy, ya! You're calling me old? Look at you, ya weedy-haired, grey-bearded hunk of wrinkled skin. You look like ya haven't had a cheeseburger or a good steak in more than a decade. Don't you disrespect me at my drive-in, ya emaciated, mangy pea-brain, I'll swab the screen with your ass! Stonehenge is for gentlemen!"

The High Priest was now in complete contempt of Stanley, looked around for support. "Who's the fool with the hat and bifocals?"

Stanley ripped the tom-tom from one of the pagan's hands, clocked the High Priest over the noggin with it, knocking him flat. The Crusaders ran in and pulled the coot back.

All hell broke loose. Everybody got in on the act. Now it was a riot, all employees, rowdies and yahoos rushing in, pushing, pulling, popping and shoving. Even Gail-Lill was getting in on the act. But she got too winded, had to stop. Lee-Willie got his glasses knocked off his face. Emilio ran out. *He* got in a few good pokes, leaving Vicki to fend for herself. Countless patrons now asked for cups of water. They wanted to throw them on the pagans. "We gotta douse 'em! They gotta be thrown out! This is our drive-in!" Scrappy Emilio defended Stanley, pushing them away from his senior buddy, elbows, knees, hands and feet all pushing and jerking and trying to break up the fray.

Even as tensions ran high, the more-lighthearted jamokes and jebeebs in the audience saw their opportunity, rushed in from the audience, filling in the vacuum on the equipment, laughing and squealing, hopping on the swings, slides, teeter-tawters, going full-out amusement park crazy, riding to their limits, swinging so high many flew off, falling to the ground, their opposite factions shouting, swearing, raising the fiasco to one incredible spectacle. Even the pagans had lost control now. They were just as mean, jumping on people's backs, thumping them with their tambourines, poking them with their thistles. Crusaders and Stuckersons had their hands full. Lee-Willie had a robe belt wrapped around his throat, as a girl tried to strangle him. Everything the pagans represented with their peaceful ceremony had backfired, and it was turning ugly. "We're gonna rip your heads off!" the more combative shouted. "If I had popcorn, I'd shove it up your noses!"

Sergeant Leo and company were certainly coming. Jim had to do something. Getting off the phone with his girlfriend, he calmly set the doobie he'd been smoking in the ashtray, sauntered out to the scene (making sure to lock his projection door) and got right into the thick of things. "My time to get involved," he told the Crusaders.

He strode to the High Priest—giving a headlock to a very fat patron, cigarettes and snacks falling out of every pocket—excusing himself politely with those around him: "Excuse me, pardon me, excuse me. Now why is everyone gettin' worked-up? All this shouting about

Stonehenge and shit. Why not a friendly discourse? We don't need a fight."

Releasing the porker from the grips of the leader, the High Priest looked up, locked eyes with Jim. "And what have you come to do, oh bushy-haired throwback? Your breath stinks of natural herb! Sunflower seeds and rose petals would be good for you. Go away. Educate yourself on anything that would get you ahead in life." He tried to thrust the projectionist away with a weak shove of his bony fingers. Bad idea. Jim grabbed them in a Hapkido hold, bent them backward, brought the dweeb to his knees, begging for mercy— "Ow-ow-ow-ow! Oh shit! Let go! Please! Okay! I get it! This wasn't the place for us!"

"You ain't kidding," said Jim, not letting go. "But I'm gonna show you where 'it' is. Come with me."

With the crowd on-hold, all watching Jim with the High Priest, the drive-in hero brought the chooch to his feet, turned him around, put him in a bear-hug and lifted him, toes dangling above the ground, and walked the rummy back to his van—first row. There, he set the man down, told him not to move, demanded the keys—which he got—opened the back doors, stuffed the loser in, shut the door on his face, turned to Steve, at the front of the crowd. "Laneske: follow me."

Jim climbed in the driver seat of the van, started it up, had Steve catch up behind him in the Charger—waiting at the exit, a good line of vision on the playground with everyone staring back—and orated a message to the sect. "Creeps and idiots in robes… you follow me, too. Your leader's momentarily kidnapped. Ya ain't pullin' anymore New Age crap while I'm around. I gave ya your chance, gave ya the benefit of the doubt. Now you're all leavin'... ya playground-pissin', panty-waisted shysters. This ain't your joint, show some respect."

He drove out, Steve not far behind. The Stuckersons, Alex, John, George, Vicki, Stanley, just stood in the back in disbelief not believing what they were seeing. Jim Barenta, ender of conflicts, stopped by Kathy—out of the booth now, arms up in a *What the fuck's happening?* mien. "We'll be back," he said, and waited a few minutes more while the rest of the cult got in their shoddy Econolines and lined up behind him, leading the entire fleet out of the drive-in like the Pied Piper: a convoy of schmucks.

Jim continued all the way down Sing, where he pulled to the shoulder around the corner on Hewey, not far from the grand marquee and put the ignition in "park." He serenely got out, re-opened the rear doors, lifted the High Priest off his feet in another emasculating bear hug, set him down on the ground and gave the keys back.

"Do not to return to The Winking Moon if you want to continue living," and watched the others pulling up behind them. "Do I make myself clear?" he concluded.

The High Priest gulped, quaking like a leaf. "As the halo around the moon, sir. I don't wanna die."

"Good. Live long and prosper."

The caravan of crazies caused quite the commotion with traffic, motoring to-and-fro, many pulling into Lapping Waves to grab food and drink. The debacle drew Jody McBrennan and Mr. Smith to the window. "That's Jim out there," she said. "And Steve. What's he doin' in his Charger? What are those fucking vans with the fucking freaks driving them?"

Steve pulled in front as Jim issued his final instructions to the flotilla, standing where his voice could be heard in both directions. "Now all of you… get the fork-knife-and-spoon outta Dodge. Do *not* return. If ya do, I'll crush you like jellybeans under a tire. Go down, go to the lake, jump in it and celebrate all you want. The stars are out. Happy Solstice."

Mr. High Priest was so traumatized, a member of his flock had to drive for him: a broad with a nice rack. Jim and Steve got a good gander at her boobs as she got her mentor in the passenger seat, driving off with the entire caravan pulling along behind them like magnet filings.

"Jim," said Steve. "Truly amazing."

"Get back to your fucking job."

"Yes, sir."

When the two returned to The Winking Moon, driving back in through the exit, they got a hero's welcome. The entire audience exploded in applause. "Hooray!" people were shouting. "A job *more* than well-done!" "Thank-you, that was obnoxious!" "We were gonna turn them into a horror movie if you hadn't gotten 'em outta here!"

In the interim, Lee-Willie had grabbed the bullhorn from the office, was trying to think of something appropriate to say, spreading the word to the whole lot. Jim snatched it away from him. "You're welcome," he said into it. "Now shut the hell up and watch the damn movies!"

The crowd erupted even louder now, laying on their horns like there was nothing funnier in the world. The Crusaders, Vicki, Stanley, Emilio, and even the Stuckersons, acknowledged their big guys actions. "Balls the size of pizza-pies," Emilio stated. "Pizza-pies."

Then the shout-up from the crowd— "Speakin' of 'pizza-pies', what's in the sauce?"

"None of your business," Emilio shouted back. "Listen to your orders."

The crowd behaved for the rest of the night. Through *both* films. Jim had made such an impression on the masses that nobody dared screwing off. Vicki joked that they should make posters with the projectionist's face on it, hang them around the joint with a warning-slogan under him: ***MESS WITH US, DEAL WITH HIM***.

Lee-Willie balked at the idea even though the girl was not serious, secretly green with envy over the attention the man was receiving. *Once again*—he brewed, *upstaged!* Gail-Lill tried to soothe her husband's nerves, rubbing his neck. Did not work. There was plenty more summer to go. All night long, patrons knocked on Jim's door, some even asking for his autograph, telling him that what he had done was one of the coolest things they had ever witnessed. He was *their* hero, especially after learning he was the same dude who had hung from The Moon Tower just days prior.

"You're a real-life action-hero, man," said one jamoke. "*You* should be on that screen."

The most unusual thing that happened after the "pagan-pummeling"—as the Crusaders called it—was Kathy being let out early from the box office. Lee-Willie stuck his wife there for punishment, upset with her for sympathizing with the sect, saying she should have known better than to cut them slack. "But you said yourself—" she grumbled, "'We can't discriminate.'"

"In that case, we shoulda."

Staff had never seen their boss be such a knob to his wife. Kathy and Vicki even questioned his motives. "I could've finished the evening," Kathy said. Lee-Willie told them to drop it.

Over the radio the couple argued and bickered about the smallest things, their tone more enraged each time. The Crusaders kept far from that ticking time-bomb. Kathy took a long break in the back-storage room, enjoying the solace from the constant grating of the horror movies. She sipped a Coke, wondering how the area became so disastrous with the piled junk, supplies, tools and old merchandise. Someday this was going to catch up with them.

The afro-ed one conferred again with his fox at home, calling again and waking Jeannie from a nap in front of late-night television. They got back on the subject of Manny Rodrogo: what they were going to do about him, how they were going to keep him away from The Winking

Moon, how could they turn his obsessive musings about the hooligans and punks into something productive. They did not come up with any good solutions at the moment, but Jim knew that he was a dear friend and needed to be kept in check.

Jim smoked severely doobies as operations wrapped up, tapping mightily into his stash behind the faux wall. Would not even come out at the *end*-end. The Crusaders, Kathy, and the rest of staff had to clean the concession stand without his presence. They had wanted to talk about his Herculean effort earlier in the evening. Lee-Willie did not want to miss the drop, had to knock on his door. "If it's one more person asking for an autograph, I broke my fingers," the big guy said through the door.

"No, uh… staff wants to thank ya for making it an easy Thursday," Lee-Willie said.

"Thank me by steppin' away from the door, I'll be out in a minute."

Lee-Willie backed up, became frustrated. No way was he going to challenge the big guy's command but how could he win over his employee's affections without showing who was boss? As the Mooners finished their duties, making the stand sparkly-fresh ("You can eat off the floor," Emilio beamed), Vicki announced she was throwing a party the next afternoon.

"What, another fondue-bash?" George said, skeptically.

"No, George—thanks for the vote of confidence, that went over like a lead balloon. An official 'We're-Back-At-The-Moon' party.

Tomorrow marks the end of our first full week. I'm having submarine sandwiches and lemonade. Making 'em myself. None of you Melvins have to put out a dime, it's on me."

"Wow," said Steve. They were all impressed, grateful. "No beer?"

"Get your girlfriend to steal some if you want."

"Where's Alex?" asked Emilio.

John said, "Helping a pair of old folks, gettin' a speaker outta the window."

"There's old folks out there?" Vicki said. "You mean, like, they're patrons?"

"Yep."

"How old are they?"

"Like, 'Edgewater Retirement Home' old."

"Are they from there?" asked Steve.

"Dunno," said John. "But they needed his help."

Kathy had been cleaning the windows with spray, turned around at the info. "Well I think that's sweet, but if they are from Edgewater, I suggest keeping a minimum distance of at least twenty feet."

Vicki said, "Just goes to show ya how unique we are. We respect people of all ages here, no matter who they are."

Stanley was mopping. He scoffed. "Somethin' like that, Richards.

Or we're so afraid of the coots we gotta try killing 'em with kindness. All you kids are dorks."

George grabbed Stanley's mop from his hand and knocked his fishing hat off. Stanley chased after him, threatening to chuck the bucket of dirty soap-water at him.

Alex actually *was* assisting an amiable, elderly couple out in the lot: one of the last to leave. They had been having trouble getting their speaker unhooked from the window, the cord was tangled. Their hands were just too feeble to accomplish the task. Alex was there for them, working his magic, admiring the cherry vehicle they'd arrived in: a '55 Cadillac, emerald green.

Both the folks were in their late seventies, the kindly old man holding the kindly old lady's hands, patiently awaiting. Alex spoke as tenderly as possible, as if he were talking with his own grandparents. "Just another minute and we'll be all set," he was saying, then, making small talk, "So, you two aren't from Edgewater behind us, are you?"

They were confused. "'Edgewater'?" the man said. "What's that?"

"Oh, never mind," Alex said. "Just the retirement home behind us."

The couple laughed. The man said, "No, a 'retirement home' isn't for us. We came a long way to get here. We're from Massachusetts, just over the New York State border."

Alex was impressed. "'Massachusetts'? Wow, that *is* a long way. Why do that? Aren't there drive-ins in Massachusetts?"

The old lady leaned forward, just as pleasant as a daffodil. "Oh yes there are, young man, we have family in Rochester we visited and now we're visiting your place. We've certainly heard of The Winking Moon."

"Oh?"

"Oh yes," she finished. "Certainly, the stories of 'recapturing youth.'"

Alex snickered. "That's one way of putting it…" he said as an aside.

The man said, "We love coming to The Winking Moon, we've done it periodically over the years. We'd drive from the ends of the earth to come here."

"To the Winking Moon?" said Alex. "Now isn't that great."

"This place is special to our hearts."

Alex grinned. "Well I certainly understand that. Wow, it's so great to hear it from people like yourselves: a former generation. It's folks like you who keep us lovin' our jobs. How'd ya like the show?"

"They were just dandy," the woman replied.

Again, Alex was impressed. "Really? Okay, didn't know if they'd work for you with, uh… all the screamin' and gory stuff. Didn't that bother you?"

The couple both dismissed it. "No," the lady said. "Not at all."

"We're not completely about the show," the man said. "It's also about atmosphere."

"It sure is," Alex said. "I mean, I'm a horror fan, too, but even I get tired of all the slicing-and-dicing now-and-again. A good comedy is what's needed from time-to-time."

The couple agreed. "That's right," the man said. "We're not all about the show."

"What're your names, by the way?" said Alex. "I'm just tryin' to be polite."

"This here's 'Mabel' and I'm 'Fred.'"

"Well, nice to meet you, Mabel and Fred, I'm Alex, Alex Carver."

"Nice to meet you, too," the lady said with a nod, then looked back at the screen. "Ah, it's so nice to re-live our youth."

Fred patted her hand. "Absolutely. Mabel here's my girl. She'll always be my girl."

"And Fred is my man," she cooed.

Now Alex was on top of the world. Screw the pagan-stuff, the former stress. This was meaningful. This was heartwarming.

"We're from Rochester, originally," the man offered up. "Met many moons ago when both of us worked for the phone company here. We came here on our first date."

"Really?" Alex said. "Here, to the Winking Moon? You had your first date right here?"

The woman nodded more avidly. "That's right. Right here at The Winking Moon."

"Well isn't that incredible," Alex said, almost done. "You two need special recognition. Had another satisfied couple in here earlier this week, used it as a testimonial to present to our parent company. There. Got it." He set the speaker back on its cradle, cord nice and tidy, brushed his hands. "No harm to your window, everything's A-okay. So nice meeting you two, hope ya come again and keep reliving your youth. Just one thing: what was it that made you folks want to do it? Was it the charm of watching a movie under the stars? Some of our delicious concession stand food? Our friendlier-than-friendly customer service?"

"No," Mabel giggled. "Fred here wanted a blowjob. And I used to give him good ones right in this lot back in the day."

Fred was grinning from ear-to-ear, waiting for Alex to look at him. "Daaaaaamn good," he said.

Alex turned bright red, too embarrassed to speak.

CHAPTER 30:

BACK AT THE JOINT

The Mooners all dragged themselves into work Friday evening, half-expecting to see the pagans back, blocking traffic, retaliating for being kicked-out the night before. Emilio Varentez suggested putting Crucifixes up, like in "The Exorcist," to repel a second approach. But luckily, business had returned to "normal." Before the box office even opened, a huge crowd waited to pile in, see the latest, blood-soaked, disgust-you films. The Crusaders and Vicki were both buzzed from the beer-drinking they had done that afternoon at her party. She had not served fondue, but she'd served some of the finest, most delicious submarine sandwiches the patrolmen had ever eaten. When she was asked by George why she had not included more Italian meats between the buns, she was careful but direct in her response. "You've got enough between your ears to fill a delicatessen, Jocavelli," she said. "Now shut your mouth and be grateful for what's in front of you."

Jim came in also particularly somber. He had been so serious as of late. They all agreed it was a miracle the High Priest was not roughed-up heavier than what he had been by the big guy. When the kids asked him if he was okay, the projectionist was unusually frank.

"You should be on Cloud Nine with what you did with your heroics last night, Jim," said Vicki. "You really saved the day."

"I'll be in my own 'Cloud Nine' in the projection booth when I smoke up a weather forecast, if ya know what I mean. Manny Rodrogo was found on somebody's lawn this morning, passed-out drunk. He didn't even know the people."

Lee-Willie was full of criticism and worry about that again, just hearing Manny's name. He was going to approach Jim with assurance that "the nut" was not going to encroach on the drive-in again, when he saw another huge cloud—of bug repellent—floating up behind the dumpster.

"What're you kids doing?" he hollered at The Crusaders, blasting the can on each other in secrecy. "That could drift into the stand. We don't want people thinkin' we got bugs here. Do it somewhere else."

"But we *do* have bugs, Mr. Stuckerson," said Alex. "We were all nailed by 'em last night: mosquitoes, the size of bald eagles."

George had nudged John, said into his ear, "Wish I was 'nailed' by somethin' last night."

"Alright, that's enough!" Lee-Willie said. "You all clocked-in?" They were. "Then get the fork-knife-and-spoon out there, start patrolling. This is the last night of these two movies and it's gonna be a packed one."

"'Pack' this," George said to the manager as they walked away, low so he could not hear.

CHAPTER 31:

THE DELTA 88

THE WANDERERS

THE DARK

BOTH RATED R

Steve moved as far back from the marquee-surface as he could, still on the catwalk, inching dangerously close to the edge, trying to view his handiwork now that he had completed the new titles. The semi-translucent, red plastic letters looked even from his limited viewpoint. Had to come down and check from afar. Before descending the ladder, he checked the Stuckerson's listings, made sure he was not missing anything, and thought about Jody. She was there, in Lapping Waves. They had already seen each other and waved but were careful not to push it further at this point. Mr. Smith was around.

But Steve was in a capricious mood. Alcohol did that to him. Thinking of what Alex had told him about the first film premiering tomorrow, the teenager began speaking aloud to himself. "'The Wanderers,' Alex? Ya say it's an 'art film'? Whatever the hell that means. Okay, buddy, let's see how 'important' of a film this is. Ya say it's an instant classic, directed by a reputable dude in Hollywood? Let's see if it brings in that 'mainstream' audience ya talk about, not the jamokes and jebeebs we're haunted by."

A passing Chevelle slowed, beeped at him— "What're those new films?"

Steve turned to them. "I haven't the foggiest. But 'The Wanderers' is directed by the same rummy who wrote 'The Empire Strikes Back.' You like 'Star Wars'?"

"I like 'Star Wars' in my pants!" the driver said.

"Get the fuck outta here."

The Chevelle took off. "Don't fall!"

When the coast was clear, Steve looked down. Yeah, he was close to the edge. Had to remind himself to be steady on his feet. And that row of spotlights aimed up at the marquee only made things brighter. *What a beast this marquee is,* he thought.

He squatted. Pulled out binoculars from he had in his smock pockets. Thought it might be a good idea to keep them in the Charger. He craned his view over to the supermarket where Jody was, seeing her through the store's window. She sure was cute in her work-apron. She caught him looking and waved obnoxiously when dickhead was not around, again squeezing her boobs to tease him.

A customer had seen her, set the six-pack down on the counter, turned to see who she was flashing. Steve put the binoculars away, pretended to be working. She rang the Melvin up—even putting his supply in a paper bag for him—and waited until he stepped out the door then threw him the bird. She was laughing now. So was Steve. When she thought *she* was in the clear, she upped the ante: stuck out her tongue, made rude gestures with it between her fingers, blew him kisses, made a muscle like she was flexing for her man. Smith came out, ending the affair right there and then.

"Jody, what the hell are you doing?"

"Nothing, Mr. Smith."

He did not believe her. Went out the door himself, glared at Steve up high on the marquee with a hand on the handle. "Just do your work, Mr. Laneske," he called out. "You don't have to bother her every Friday."

Steve stood. Put on his professional face. "Why hello, Mr. Smith. How are you tonight? Everything fine and peachy?"

The playfulness was not reciprocated. "'The Wanderers,'…" Smith read. "'The Dark.'… Combined to describe you, Mr. Laneske: wandering in the dark."

Ouch! That wasn't nice. Steve figured he was not worth his time to get angry over, though. "These are 'art films,' Mr. Smith, we're moving up in the world. Alex Carver says at least the first one is an 'A-list' film. That means a top contender in Hollywood. 'The Wanderers' was based on a novel. Can you believe it?"

Smith was not amused. "You ever read a novel, Mr. Laneske?"

"Yes, I have, sir. It was about a convenience-store owner who was attacked and killed by marauding aliens who didn't think he was very cool." In Steve's eyes, the tubby manager resembled a fat version of Mr.

Stuckerson: overly serious, bitter, and a major knob.

This guy had his hands on his hips, too. Smith just glared. Jody snuck out behind him, stifling giggles. Crouched behind his back, pointed mockingly at his fat ass. Then she stood upright, shouting at the top of her lungs, scaring the shit out of the manager— "I love you, Steve, you fucking chooch-a-maroo!"

"Get back in there!" Mr. Smith hollered, motioning like he was going to wallop the girl with the back of his hand.

Steve was cracking up, proud of his girl. When Smith glared at him again, as if to further provoke a confrontation, Steve saluted the man, said, "Ain't she great?"

"She's great all right, when she does what I tell her."

"You be careful, Mr. Smith. Keep your hands off her. Don't be pretending to hit her, that's not very nice of you."

"You don't tell me what to do, child, I run my business around here. Go to work." And with that, the bloated gasbag went back inside.

Steve, still at attention, set to come down off the catwalk, reached out to grab the ladder. Another late-night, douche bag motorist zoomed by, this time in a rusted Citation— "Hey asshole!" the driver cackled. "When ya gonna have X-rated movies?!"

Steve caught the edge of the shed to steady himself. He shouted back, "When your mother's finished acting in 'em!"

Just when they were satisfied that nothing to the same degree of the previous night's pagan incident would happen tonight, it happened. The Stuckersons were out, standing in the lot adjacent to the open double-doors of the concession stand. They had been asked, nicely, by pleasant patrons what it was like to manage the Winking Moon. Lee-Willie had not thought they were serious, at first, but they were. There *were* some nice folk in the audience. Naturally, he had stepped in front of his wife, answered for her. He was right in the middle of bloviating on the subject when "it" appeared.

"Of course, we've managed drive-ins in other states," he was saying, "but this has certainly been the most unique. We're kinda like nomads in the field, but hopefully, that'll end soon. Had many an uphill battle here in our three-year stint, but who hasn't had challenges in their line-of-business?"

"Judging from your face," one of the two guests said, "we'd say you've had *many* uphill battles."

"Ha-ha-ha, good one. This place is no different, just requires a use of extra moxie, that's all. Our patrolmen like to refer to it as 'a joint.'"

"'Moxie,'" the girl quoted. "That's a good word."

"Sure is," Lee-Willie beamed. "I'd say I was a wordsmith, but my wife here would disagree. She's the writer but I have to edit her."

Gail-Lill suddenly became unhinged. "You 'edit me'? How does *that* work?"

"Well, a-hem…" Lee-Willie coughed. "What I mean to say was—"

"What the fuck?!" It was the cry heard around the area. A young man had stopped, not far from the open doors, popcorn, soda in his hands, staring at a monstrous sedan blocking his path, revving in a devilish throttle, black-painted exterior with menacing words painted on the sides of it: **DEBAUCHERY & RIBALDRY**.

The Delta 88. *The* Delta 88. The one Jody had seen at Lapping Waves that afternoon and the one that'd plagued the beleaguered drive-in all last summer. The sight sent instant fear up the managers' spines, their eyes growing big.

John, George and Alex were on the opposite side, the south side, up along the far fence checking the apple orchard—where John had claimed to have seen the hobos. Steve was just pulling in with his Charger. The monster-length vehicle had somehow slipped in, like a ghost, idling there, waiting to be noticed. Now the customers coming-and-going were having to step around it, as it caused a blockage. Inside, one foot was on the brake, the other on the gas, ready to explode. A horde of devilish teenagers were inside, all cackling, all scheming, and ramped-up even to unleash hell upon the drive-in.

The passenger side window powered down. A lone hand came out, formed the shape of fingers holding something thick, round—like an erect donager. In rudest, most coarse fashion, the infamous, barely legal male voice shot out from the darkness: "Eat the Beef, Winking Moon!

We're back!"

The hysterics erupted from within. All the Stuckersons could do was stare in horror. Lee-Willie sucked in a breath, blew out a desperate plea from his lungs— "Holy Patty Duke Austin, it's the Delta 88!" He fumbled for his radio. Dropped it. Picked it up, spit into it— "The Delta 88's here! Crusaders! Get over here! It's in front of the concession stand—now! It's returned!"

Hells Bells, by AC/DC, snapped on in the vehicle's mega-stereo components, blowing people back, drowning out all other sound including the movie, everybody jumping out of cars, trucks, vans, Jeeps, seeing what the fuck was going on. The foot came off the brakes, just enough to jerk the car forward like it was going to mow down every soul in its way. People dove out of the way to prevent being hit. Popcorn, soda, hotdogs, burgers and candy all dropped to the ground, smoke swelling under the wheels. Finally, it cut loose, bolted in-between rows of patrons where there was space, heading toward the open lane before the front row. The Crusaders came running, connecting with Steve near the Stuckersons, all four taking off after it, giving chase. "Get it, Crusaders, get it!" Gail-Lill cried. "Don't let it get away! It's back!"

"Jody was right!" Steve shouted. "She was *right*!"

"Didn't doubt it, dude!" Alex return shouted.

The four cleared people from their path, screaming for them to get out of the way, almost knocking some over. They followed the Delta 88, which had no license plate, nothing but metal malevolence. It slammed on its brakes once out in the open, sending a wave of gravel and pebbles scattering, just before impinging into the playground area. The laughter inside was insane. Then it hooked a left, heading toward the south fences where people drove into the drive-in (thank God there was no incoming traffic, then hooked another left to speed toward the back.

"They're doin' it again!" Alex said, huffing away. "They're playin' with us, takin' us for a ride like they did last summer!"

The Crusaders were in hot pursuit. Could not believe the brightness of their beams.

"What's that thing got for headlights, solar flares?" Steve said.

By this point, nearly every audience member was watching the show like a spectator sport, some standing on their vehicles, getting a better angle, no longer interested in the movie. John and Alex were the fastest, almost caught up to the bad boys as it had to slow reaching the corner, readying for another left. More cackling. Just was out of reach from the patrolmen as it sped straight at the opposite corner—the *north* end—past The Moon Tower, making the Crusaders question chasing the maniacs on-foot.

"Which way's it gonna go?" George said, trying to outthink it.

"It's doing a tour!" Steve said. "Probably gonna race out the exit!"

Lee-Willie joined the footrace as best he could, cutting a diagonal through the audience, dodging and weaving through picnic baskets, lawn chairs, jamokes and jebeebs, car bumpers and anything in else in their path. He was manic. "Ya ain't gettin' away this year, ya bastards! Not in *my* fucking drive-in!"

He reached for his flashlight in the holster, brandished it over his head like a wild Indian ready to tomahawk, the five coming together in a stumble as, sure enough, the Delta 88 hooked one more left, aiming at the exit. They got in front of it, put their arms out, trying to corral the thing like a deranged buffalo, then had to dive out of the way as it nearly barreled *them* down, driving right past them, the dreaded hand emerging one more time to taunt them. "Eat the Beef, Winking Moon!"

The cackling never stopped, the shits experiencing the greatest joy of their lives, the five running behind, trying to catch up. Lee-Willie fell behind, winded, then was taken-out by a kid on a skateboard, scooting by to watch the action.

The Crusaders could not stop at this point, even for their boss. They had to keep going. But they couldn't catch up to the hell-car, either, as it skidded through the exit. The driver stepped on the brakes again, more gravel and pebbles going airborne, hooking right, gunning back out toward Sing Road.

"It's trying to leave!" Alex yelled. "It's going to Sing Road!"

"We can't catch it!" George shouted.

Kathy was outside her booth now, horrified. "Is that the Delta 88?! *The* Delta 88?!"

"It is, Kathy, it is!" Alex shouted, on the run. "How'd it get in?!"

"I don't know! I don't know!"

The boys pumped their arms and legs, trying to muster every ounce of athleticism in their body. But they could not catch it. The hand "Beefed 'em" once more—insult added to insult—before powering off into the night, turning right and squealing away. Some of the more athletic of the patrons ran up just behind the Crusaders, also watching the red taillights disappear off into the darkness. A hobbling and re-injured Lee-Willie—and a newly puffing-and-wheezing Gail-Lill—shuffled down the entrance, joining the crowd as they asked if it gotaway.

"Sure as shit did, Mr. Stuckerson," said George. "We just couldn't get it."

Lee-Willie was doubled-over, looking like a deranged bobcat. "W-why the hell d-didn't ya catch it? Aren't y-you supposed to be a-athletes? I thought you were f-faster than that!"

"Lee!" Gail-Lill tried to enunciate, practically impossible. Her lousy shape added to her personal ordeal. "L-leave… t-them… a-alone… They're only h-human. T-That was a *car*."

"T-that wasn't 'no car," he fumed. "T-that was the Delta 88… the f-fucking Delta 88. Not fuckin' again…"

"It's the General Motors sedan from hell," one of the strangers summarized.

"Holy shit…" exclaimed John.

"It's back…" said Alex. "Like never before…"

"First of the season…" George said.

"Better be the last…" said Steve.

"I-I… can't… breathe…" said Gail-Lill, the Crusaders flocking around her.

"Do you want us to get an ambulance?" asked Steve.

Her hand shot up. "No! N-no ambulance. No police, n-no nothing. No more of us going to the hospital…"

Alex saw Kathy running down toward them. She was about to cry.

"Ms. Berenger!" Lee-Willie blurted, turning in anger. "How… the hell did that thing get in? D-didn't you see it?"

"I didn't, Mr. Stuckerson, Mrs. Stuckerson. I'm sorry, it did just like it did last year: got in without me seeing it, I swear."

Alex wanted to comfort her, but even he was in shock. He said, "None of us did." His bandage had nearly come off his nose.

But Lee-Willie was still livid. He was holding his lip in agony. "B-but it didn't… stop at the box office?"

"No, of course it didn't," Kathy said.

"Oh, for the love of God."

"L-lee…" Gail-Lill tried, sweat beading her face, "that… thing wouldn't have stopped even it did s-stop at… t-the box office. Most likely… it drove in through the exit."

"Kathy… you're gonna have to be more on-the-b-ball. Maybe all that attention you're given your paintin' is… screwin' ya up."

"I'm sorry!" The beauty broke down in tears.

That was it. It had been too much for Gail-Lill. As she gulped, trying to regain air into her lungs, she got so pissed at her husband that she slapped him in the head, and staggered to console the sobbing Kathy. "S-same thing happened… last year," she said. "N-nobody knows how it gets in here… it just does. It's a fucking mystery…"

Everyone turned to the empty, dark road where the vehicle just, even the strangers. *Did that really just happen?* was the sentiment. All that could be heard was the sound of heaving recuperating.

"Back to torture again…" said Alex.

"And to give 'The Beef," Steve said. "Dick-size looks like it's grown from last year."

Lee-Willie lowered his brow. "If you kids m-miss it again… I'll h-have your asses."

"That doesn't sound inviting," George joked.

"I mean it… y-you m-morons b-better not… miss it…" Lee-Willie said, then as if his mind was drifting, "I'll get ya, D-Delta 88… if i-it's the l-last thing I do… I'll get ya… t-that's a promise."

His wife looked at him, cheeks sagging like flour sacks. "Lee…"

CHAPTER 32:

THE LESS-THAN-STELLAR ANTICS AT THE SMIRKING STAR

In contrast, The Smirking Star experienced a crisis of their own on Friday night. There had been a shriek that emanated from the middle of the lot. This was unusual here and got the audience up-in-arms. What could it be? The Star did not show horror films. They had PG fare, G-rated stuff. Their current film—a black horse and a child, something called "The Black Stallion"—was not scary at all.

Brent Saxon ordered his Avengers to investigate. He pulled his crack-team of security from studying a katydid that had perched on the side of the concession stand, preening its mint-green wings with its spindly legs. The five teenagers rushed to the trouble: bodies alive with adrenaline. Like their Crusader-counterparts, they were ready to boot some ass.

It had been a schlub with his girlfriend. In a Monte Carlo. He had tickled her when she least expected it, poked her in the ribs. The couple was embarrassed when the bruisers showed up to do some beating. She claimed it had hurt. The boyfriend apologized; the girl quickly got over it.

"Sorry to have brought the cavalry," the jamoke said to the team, said it would not happen again.

"Better not," Kyle glowered. "We take that kind of thing very seriously around here."

Kyle, Seth, Newton, Gary and Pauly spent the remainder of the movie comparing shoe sizes. Newton Tallis had the largest feet.

CHAPTER 33:

ALEX'S RECAP

As Alex went to sleep that night, fighting the physical exhaustion from the first few days back at the Winking Moon, he tried hard not to pass out in seconds. He wanted to revel about all that had transpired, the movies that'd played. A good number of penetrating concepts crossed his mind, one of which was the desire to penetrate Kathy Berenger, truth be told. But he had respect. Cinema. Under the night sky. As great as sex. Not that he had experienced sex yet, he just imagined…

But summer *was* here, and they were in it. There were signs—like Kathy's New Age philosophies—that things were going to get funky. Like in the movie "The Brood," with its mobs of psychotic children, bringing mayhem to the story, so the punks, hooligans, yahoos and rowdies were bringing mayhem to the joint. They had already made their presence known.

He also thought there would be "Toolbox Murders" if they were not careful. Stanley Mason would conduct them himself, growing so angry at the Stuckersons for their mishandling of Franco Esposito's belongings in the back-storage room. The undying devotion to a late, great friend—and former manager—was not to be screwed with. Even the kids needed to keep their mitts off the memorial.

Everyone's hero, Jim Barenta, was moving toward being "Up In Smoke" all the time, smoking more cigarettes and pot than before, tapping into his secret stash behind the faux wall frequently. His beloved girlfriend, Jeannie Monocco, was not to tolerate that forever. Might even cancel the Sunday-night parties. That would be a true disaster! Was Cheech & Chong themselves in the booth with the big guy, encouraging him to toke up?

Like the sorority comedy with the plentiful, bouncing bazoombas, already there had been "H.O.T.S." in the lot. Definitely a perk of the gig. Mega mint chicks, night after night—something the Crusaders would never get sick of—flocking together in silly girl-groups, making out hot-and-heavy with boyfriends, husbands, looking for what everybody sought: fun under the stars.

With the Edgewater Retirement Home bubbling over with hostility toward staff, those goats there were their own "Hills Have Eyes," with the constant keeping watch on The Moon. Seemed a sure thing they were making a play for the venue, lending credibility to the rumors that Bluestone really was thinking of closing the joint down permanently.

And finally, Alex thought about their encounter with the notorious Delta 88 had been terrible. If Lee-Willie Stuckerson *had* caught by the mysterious shits-behind-the-tinted-glass, there would have been a "Texas Chainsaw Massacre," with an audience munching popcorn and soda to watch. No teenager needed murder on his or her hands, not going into their senior year of high school.

Alex touched his fractured nose and the fresh bandage he had just applied right after brushing his teeth. He sighed. As they had driven home that night, the guy in the Camaro who had asked Steve about having sex with his girlfriend on the marquee's catwalk had taken the

Crusader up on his offer. They were up there—the jamoke and a jebeeb—grinding away, fortunately not lit. The sign had been turned off. Alex laughed to himself.

He wondered who looked worse, him or Mr. Stuckerson, with the busted lip. The last things that Alex were cognizant of before falling into deep sleep were the images of Jim, hanging from the Moon Tower; the Wild Man of Borneo falling from the tree, screaming; his Mom crying herself to sleep over Dad running out on the family; Randy barking with a perpetual insistence on him working at the garage; and the short-circuit of the sound system, spelling doom if it happened again.

They came as if scenes on a movie screen. Alex's dreams would be haunted. But not tonight, hopefully. He needed his freakin' rest.

-End of Volume 1

Made in the USA
Middletown, DE
25 October 2020

22736851R00296